FRAMED FOR MURDER

"Know anything about this, Tom?"

"About what?"

"An Indian shot over on the East fork."

"If it's the Indian who killed a cow up there maybe I do. He tried to kill me too."

Jake's frown deepened.

"You God damned fool!" he said. "You *got* the fellow."

He faced the stolid policeman.

"Now get this," he said. "Go back to the Agency and tell the Superintendent that I caught Weasel Tail killing beef and I fired and missed him. And tell him that later on he did his damnedest to kill me, and I fired back. If he got his he had it coming, and more too. And now get out. Vamoose. Good night."

But the policeman did not go at once. He took Tom's name, writing it slowly and carefully in a notebook.

Late that night Tom saddled a fresh horse and rode to the canyon, but he found things as he had suspected. The carcass of the dead cow had disappeared; not as much as a horn remained to prove his story . . .

MARY ROBERTS RINEHART

LOST ECSTASY

ZEBRA BOOKS
KENSINGTON PUBLISHING CORP.

ZEBRA BOOKS

are published by

Kensington Publishing Corp.
475 Park Avenue South
New York, NY 10016

First Zebra Books printing: March 1986

Printed in the United States of America

Chapter One

When old Lucius Dowling lay dying he sent for his will and reread it. He lay in his wide walnut bed, which Henry's wife had vainly tried to exchange for a mahogany four-poster in the best period of early American, with his spectacles firmly fixed on his hawk-like nose, and studied it with a certain grimness.

"I give and devise to my son, Henry, and my daughter Elizabeth Osborne, the L.D. ranch property, in joint and equal ownership—"

He read on through the paragraph, laid the typed sheets down on the counterpane and closed his eyes. Should he change that? Leave it in trust, insist that it be held together and carried on, as Henry and Bessie never would do? Leave it in trust to Henry's girl, and defy them to get rid of it? He smiled a little at that. They would probably try to break the will if he did so; still, there were ways.

He had lived past any illusions as regarded his children. Henry was phlegmatic, cautious; he had been a good son and a good husband. Almost too good. He had not had enough imagination to stray from the proper and correct path, nor old Lucius's own capacity for robust adventure and even occasional easy sinning. And Bessie, who had this last capacity of his in full, he disapproved of because she had it.

He had a phrase for Bessie; he called her to himself a "retarded adolescent," and chuckled over it. He had invented it the day, at forty-one, when she had shingled her hair.

But in the end he let the will ride, as he put it, and in due time—not so repentant for his sins as he should have been, but carrying over with him a sort of delicate savoring of them—he passed away. And within a week the walnut bedroom set followed him, going to some graveyard of dead sentiments and ancient dreams and, unlike old Lucius, leaving nothing behind to preserve its memory but an unfaded spot in the carpet where it had stood for twenty years.

Unlike old Lucius. He had left behind him much more than the securities in his boxes and the clothes they gave to his valet. The ranch he had left to Henry and Bessie, but those qualities of his which Henry had missed he had passed, without the sinning of course, to his grandchild; the love of adventure and the will to seek it, a craving for the open, a certain honesty and a capacity for passionate adventure, both of which latter qualities the old man had concealed in later life with rather less success than he imagined.

Kay Dowling, his grandchild, was the only person in the house who cried when the walnut bed was moved out.

She went into the room. The carpet, which was green, was much brighter where it had stood than anywhere else. It was like a patch of fresh grass, and on the mantel the faded picture of old Lucius, taken on horseback when he had lived in the West and been a cowboy, seemed to be looking at it. She knew by name all the things he wore in the picture, including a six-shooter in his belt; she knew the name of the horse he rode—which was Pronto—the details of his inlaid Mexican saddle, the purpose of the rope coiled on it. She could even see, in that young eager face, so unlike the one she had known, a certain resemblance to herself. And she wondered, young as she was then, if he had been satisfied.

Had he missed that life? What if he had never come East, and she had been born out there, free to ride a horse, to follow the trail? True, she rode now; but always with a groom following her, or the riding master. It was not the same.

It was only a mood, and like the walnut bed and old Lucius himself it passed. But once or twice in later years she was to remember it, and to wonder just what influence that heritage of hers had had in her life.

Surprisingly little was changed by the old man's death. As he had outlived his illusions so he had outlived most of his friends. Henry and Bessie dutifully erected a tall shaft, and voted down Henry's wife's suggestion that it say: "He has followed the trail into the sunset." It was odd that Katherine should have made it, really. Perhaps she had had a politely veiled sentiment for the old man, or for the more respectable portions of his past; anyhow she withdrew it at once when Bessie said that sentiments on monuments were as extinct as the dodo.

"Where'd you get that?" Henry asked her.

"I think I saw it somewhere," she said vaguely. But she lied. She had thought of it herself.

Then for several years Kay heard little of the ranch but as a hole; it was a hole one sunk money in and nothing came out. It was a liability and not an asset. Connected with this was a further fact that Bessie thought they were all made of money, and that she was a fool to want to hold on. And somewhat later further talk about Aunt Bessie, but not connected with the ranch. This time she seemed to have lost Uncle Ronald, but when she came back from Paris, having done so, she was not in mourning, and Kay learned that there were other ways than death by which one lost husbands. It was, however, not to be discussed, and if after that one wandered into Aunt Bessie's house and found a young man loudly declaiming in her boudoir while Aunt Bessie was having a marcel or a manicure through a half-opened door in her dressing room, one was not to discuss that either.

Aunt Bessie had a flair for what she called talented youth. There was another name for them, however, among her friends. They were generally called "Bessie's sympathizers."

Time went on, as it has a way of doing. The shaft was finished. It was ugly, but it was solid and dominating and uncompromising, which was rather fitting after all. Mademoiselle went back to France and Kay was sent to boarding school. She was sixteen then: a slim bit of a thing, aping her elders as well as she could, but with wide childish eyes which betrayed her essential innocence. On the night before she left Katherine summoned all her courage and went in to talk to her. She wanted, this queer reserved Katherine, to break the shocks which life would have in store for her, to pave the way a little for the woman-world she was so soon to enter.

But there was Kay beside her dainty bed on her knees, saying her prayers, and propped up on the pillow was the Princess Mary, which had been her last doll years ago. Katherine, whose own knees had been shaking anyhow, withdrew quietly and closed the door. She never found the courage to try again. When Kay came home for her first vacation she was still loving but slightly remote, and she had made her first step toward independent action. She took off her pullon hat with hands that were cold and clammy, and they saw she had cut her hair.

"Oh, Kay!" said her mother, and tears stood in her eyes. But Kay's father only looked at her and said nothing about it. Later on he told her mother that he was afraid she was going to be like Bessie. He said this in the privacy of their bedroom, however, so the servants could not hear. He always had an eye out for the servants, had Henry Dowling.

He was quite sure of this one day a year or so later, after Kay had made her début—oh, yes, she made her début; frock by Lucille, photographers and society editors, and baskets of flowers which went to the various hospitals afterwards—and had been taken to England to be presented. He came into the drawing room of the town house and found her with a half dozen other young and fluttering creatures, and she was smoking a cigarette. She put it down at once and said: "Sorry, father," but he was surer than ever.

"What we have to remember," he said that night to Katherine, sitting neat and small and subservient before her toilet table, which was covered with chaste ivory appliances, "is that there is a streak of weakness in the blood."

"Not on my side," Katherine ventured. "My people—"

"My father had it. He was a strong man in some ways, but in others—And Bessie has let her love of adventure, to call it by a polite name, run away with her common sense."

"Kay is not at all like Bessie."

"I'm not so sure of that," he said obstinately.

It was this mistaken preconception of his perhaps which made Kay's emergence into her social world only an antonym for freedom. She was always chaperoned; he himself, when Katherine had one of her weak spells—she was liable to weak spells—would remain resolutely at balls, smoking innumerable cigars in anterooms. Or he would call himself, or send Nora and the car, to bring her home after dinners. Kay herself felt rather ridiculous, but nothing in the world could make Henry Dowling ridiculous.

He was a pompous, somewhat florid man, not so tall as old Lucius and already slightly curved under his well-cut waistcoats. He liked his food; his place in the community; being a vestryman at Saint Mark's; and exclusive of Bessie, he was fond of his family. The humble origin of that family, on his side at least, he did not like and preferred to ignore, and when eligible young men called more than once or twice he would look them up furtively in the Social Register.

"Who was that boy last night, Kay?"

"Smith's his name."

"One of the Mortimer Smiths?"

"I didn't ask him. I will if you like."

"Certainly not," he would splutter, "I merely wondered."

And all that time the L. D. ranch was lying fallow, so to

speak. Not even so very fallow at that. Superintendents came, demanded more money to put in the hole, failed to get it and went away again. Only Mallory, old Lucius's range foreman, remained faithful, and his requests for farming machinery to put the bottom lands into hay and grain so he could winter the more unthrifty of his cattle met with little response.

He wrote his cramped, pathetic letters: the great ranges on the Indian Reservation and in the mountains were badly overgrazed, and homesteaders were coming in and putting up wire fences.

"We've had a dry summer, Mr. Dowling," he wrote once. "If we have a bad winter the cattle will be in poor shape. I recomend—" he was a good cow-man but a poor speller—"that we buy hay and oil cake now before the price goes up. If we don't—"

Kay went cheerfully on her way. She had almost forgotten the ranch, or those old stories about the drive up from the Mexican border to the abundant water and grass of the Northwest; the long-horned herds stampeding and scattering to the four corners of the earth, being bogged down in the quicksands of rivers they forded, being levied on by Indians as toll for their passage, going blind with thirst, falling down, dying. There had been a last eighty miles of desert, too, when men and cattle were alike exhausted; when the drive went on night and day, and grim death followed their wide dusty trail and picked up the stragglers as they lagged. But after that had come a river, and beyond it the great green valley, and rest and grass and peace.

Kay had almost forgotten, and perhaps the valley had almost forgotten too. The Mexican cattle had almost disappeared; here and there among the Indian cattle could still be seen a pair of great horns on a long-legged small-bodied animal, but white-faced pedigreed stock was the rule. Through the long valley, bounded by its mountains to East and West, now ran a thread of railroad, a string on which like beads were strung the little towns. Tourists on through trains looked out and saw, not the West of their dreams but men in straw hats like their own.

Cars were parked along the platform, muddy from the back country. Now and then a cowboy, bronzed under his Stetson, pulled up his horse and watched the train move out.

"There's a cowboy! Look, quick!"

"Probably dressed up by one of these dude ranches."

Tom McNair, top cow hand on the L. D., once had a woman call out of a car window:

"Tell me, are you a real cowboy?"

And Tom took off his hat with a great sweep and bowed to her.

"Real as hell, lady," he said, and the train moved on.

They never saw beyond the railroad and the little town, these tourists. They did not see that where the hamlets ended the back country began. There was no transition. And the back country had not changed, nor the mountains. Spring still saw its plains bringing forth grass, and August saw them burning dry and brown. Dawn still painted its dry buttes with rose, and twilight turned them mauve. In winter the whole land died and froze in rigor mortis, and men and cattle froze and died with it.

One day Kay, clearing her desk in her small orchid and blue boudoir-dressing room, came across that old photograph of her grandfather and took it out curiously and looked at it. She felt for a moment a quick wave of sympathy for that young and valiant figure which had had to grow old and die in the walnut bed, and with that some of her memories came back. She picked up the picture and went downstairs to her father's library. She knew he would be there; it was the sacred hour of whisky and soda before dressing for dinner.

"Don't you want this, father? I've just found it."

"What is it?"

He took it and looked at it. "I wondered where it had

gone," he said, and locked it in his desk. He had a drawer there which was always locked. But she did not go, as he plainly expected her to do.

"Why don't we ever go out there, father?" she asked. "I'd like to see it. The ranch, I mean."

"Well, I wouldn't," he said coldly. "If it keeps on as it's doing it will bankrupt me."

"Are there still cowboys there?"

"Crowd of lazy young devils who call themselves cowboys."

She had a bright thought.

"Couldn't you turn it into a dairy ranch?" she asked. "There must be a lot of cows."

And then and there he gave one of his rare spontaneous laughs.

"My dear child," he said, "you can't milk range cattle. They're raised to sell for beef. At least," he added more sourly, "I believe that is the idea, but the packers seem to think we're running an eleemosynary institution."

After that life seized her again. The ranch drifted out of her mind. She fell in love, foolish sentimental affairs which gave her a thrill at the time, added interest to what was the real monotony of her existence; Rutherford or James brought up boxes of flowers with small neatly engraved cards inside; Nora laid out her clothing before going to dress her mother; in the spring, while Bessie opened her cottage at Bar Harbor, they moved to the country house outside of town and the only difference was tennis or golf.

And then suddenly one day in July the valley and all the back country returned to her, never to be lost again. She learned that things at the ranch were very bad indeed, and that they were all to go out. Even Herbert was going.

There was not much time. She ordered a riding suit and boots. Her mother fluttered about, seeing that the striped linen bags were hung over the brocaded curtains, and that the needle-point chairs were covered. The Mariposa, old

Lucius's private car, was cleaned and put in order in the yards, Bessie was firmly telegraphed to remain in Bar Harbor, and then one day Kay found herself facing toward the setting sun, which was exceedingly hot, and that curious mixture of romance, grim stark tragedy and passionate love which was to be her life thereafter.

Chapter Two

On the last day of the journey she wakened at early dawn. The old Mariposa, coupled to the end of the train, rocked and careened over the single track. A fine dust had penetrated even through the double windows and settled in a gray film on her small and frivolous pumps on the floor. Later on, when the train stopped to let the eastern express pass like an explosion, she could hear the preparations for breakfast going on, the cook rattling pans in his cubicle and old William, who had been on the car since her grandfather's time, laying the table.

Once she even heard the shower bath going, and knew that either her father or Herbert was preparing for the day, taking advantage of the stop to do so. It was not easy to bathe on the train. There was a story that once old Lucius himself had been hurled in *puribus naturalibus* out of the shower into the corridor, and was only saved by his bulk from going through a window!

The water ran for a long time. That would be Herbert. He was frightfully neat and clean, was Herbert. In the new detachment that had been hers since she wakened she considered Herbert, so tidy in mind and body, so well-mannered. Neat mannered, she said to herself, and smiled over it. And of course that was something to be said for a young man who brushed his teeth every night before he went to bed.

Suppose she married him? After all she would have to marry some one. She had played around long enough. She was twenty-three. "Mrs. Forrest." "Mrs. Herbert Forrest," she said to herself, and did not dislike the sound of it.

Herbert was in love with her. She had known it for a long time, and Herbert knew she knew it. Even her father and mother knew it. She could almost have repeated their conversations about it.

"After all," her father would say, "the boy has character, and money isn't essential."

"But she could have done so much better, if she only would."

"What do you mean, better? He comes of an excellent family; he's got no bad habits, and he's a worker. I can't stand those five o'clock tea Johnnies who hang around her. Lot of idle young degenerates!"

It was only her Aunt Bessie who had objected to Herbert, and that with her usual frankness.

"Personally I think he's a stuffed shirt," she said vulgarly. "If I had my life to live over again—"

"Which thank God you haven't," said Henry.

"—I would pick a man and not a rubber stamp," persisted Aunt Bessie, valiantly mixing her metaphors and ignoring the interruption. "Of course, if Kay cares for him, that's different. Do you?"

"I don't know," said Kay. "He's rather sweet, in a way."

"Oh, good heavens! So's a stick of candy!" had been Bessie's retort to that, and she had stuck a cigarette in a long jeweled holder and lighted it, and then wandered disdainfully out of the room.

For some time the train had been climbing through a dreary desolate region. It was bleak, dry, incredibly broken and eroded. Save for the prairie dogs by the track, sitting up and yapping at the train, their small tails jerking as they squeaked, there was no life whatever. Except once when she saw a dog. It ran a short distance, looking back over its shoulder, and then sat down on a hill top and watched the passing monster. She did not know that it was a coyote. But it did begin to dawn on her that this was the eighty miles of bad land before one got to the river, and she became conscious of a certain excitement. One need not see the railroad and the water tanks; one could look beyond and watch that years-ago drama; and as if to complete her picture she caught a glimpse of a lone horseman loping over the sage brush.

It was ugly, but it was beautiful too. It was strange, grotesque and wonderful.

When Nora came in to help her dress she asked her if she liked it.

"Like it?" said Nora. "It's the worst I've ever seen, Miss Kay. Not a tree! Nothing!"

She wandered out to breakfast. Her mother was already there, and Herbert, and old William was pulling out her chair. William, who had been with her grandfather since the Mariposa had come, shiny and new, out of the railroad shops, and who had served the great men of his time when they had accompanied old Lucius west, for bear and deer hunting in the daytime and poker games at night.

"Morning, everybody," said Kay. "Well, William, we're almost there!"

"Yes, miss," said William, grinning. "I shorely am glad to get back. Grapefruit or melon, miss?"

"Grapefruit, please. Have you looked outside, you two? It's rather wonderful."

"It looks frightfully dusty," said her mother. "I've told Nora to pin some more sheets over your clothes, Kay."

"Don't *you* see anything but dust, Herbert?"

Herbert saw that something more was expected of him. Personally he regarded it as the land that God forgot, but now he stared out of a window.

"I suppose," he said vaguely, "that if one cared for that sort of thing—"

She ate her grapefruit rather sulkily. How odd they were! Her mother must know that old story, but there she sat delicately sipping her coffee and attempting to read the head lines of a paper from the Junction as it lay by her father's plate. No one ever opened the paper until her father had read it. When Henry came in she made, however, one more attempt.

"Father?"

"Yes," absently.

"Isn't this the desert they had to cross with the cattle before they got to—" She hesitated. It seemed sacrilege to offer them the valley. "—to the end of the trip?"

"What cattle?"

"Grandfather's."

He glanced out, as if for the first time perceiving that there was something outside.

"Maybe. You have to remember that I wasn't present. Better sell that C. and L., Herbert. I see they've passed their dividend again."

"All right, sir. I can wire if you like."

No answer being forthcoming, Herbert decided to wire and went on with his breakfast. Now and then he raised his head and glanced at Kay, but she was looking past him, out the window.

"Marmalade?"

"No, thanks."

He was slightly worried. He had annoyed Kay, he knew, but he could not think how. Surely what he had said about this hideous country could not matter. He had brushed himself carefully that morning, but already there was a gray film of dust on his shoulders. Alkali, probably, and his hands felt dry and rough. He dipped them in his finger bowl.

"Anything this morning, sir?"

"Nothing but what I've told you."

Herbert was Mr. Dowling's secretary. He was really much more than that, but that was his official position. He drew a nice salary and saved a part of it, and had just taken on life insurance. He had very firm ideas about life insurance, even if a man's wife should come into money and never need it. One owed it to oneself to leave an estate.

But to be fair to him, he was not considering Kay for her money. He had as firm ideas about marriage as about life insurance, and he had analyzed Kay carefully before he fell in love with her. After that, first methodically and then as nearly recklessly as he ever did anything, he found himself very much in love indeed. So much so that to his annoyance he found it interfering with his tidy daily routine, which had been, until this happened, as follows:

7:30 Rise, bathe and shave.

8:00 Breakfast.

8:30 Leave for office.

9:00 Arrive office.

And in the afternoons:

4:30 Leave office.

5:00 to 6:00 Exercise, Y. M. C. A.

(Except Saturday afternoon. Golf or squash, depending on the season.)

6:00 Home to dress.

8:00 Dine (Generally out).

11:00 Bed and sleep.

Kay had managed to shoot this schedule to pieces. Not that she had tried to; rather sweet was the nearest she came to loving him. But it is one thing to put down eleven o'clock as the hour for sleep and another to achieve it, and Herbert was already behind his schedule considerably. He had dejected moments when he wondered if he would ever catch up.

So he followed Kay out onto the platform that morning, and resigned himself to dust, cinders and a wind which made his eyes water. He even, after a time, stated that he believed that, if water were put on the ground it would grow things.

And Kay relaxed and even laughed.

"You are really a nice person, Herbert," she said.

He flushed. "Do you think that, Kay?" he asked, "or are you just saying it to please me?"

"I mean it."

He turned and looked at her. "And that's all you do mean," he said, with unexpected shrewdness. "I see. Well—"

He did not finish. Henry came out on the platform.

Kay was quite sure she recognized the river when they came to it, but it disappointed her. It flowed sluggishly between deep eroded banks, a narrow yellow stream in the center of a dried bed. There was nothing to tell her of what a river it was in the spring, when the snow on the distant mountains began to melt; how it spread incredibly and carried away bridges and what not, and how unwary cattle and even people sank then in its quicksands, and died.

"Imagine drinking that!" said Herbert as they rattled across the bridge.

"But suppose you had been eighty miles without water."

"Eighty! Why eighty?"

But she did not answer. She had somehow expected that when one crossed the river one was at once in a green valley, filled with peace and rest, but there was no appreciable difference. It was only later in the afternoon that a change became apparent, that the country ceased to be broken and began to roll, and far away mountains loomed blue against the sky.

The train was climbing slowly up the great plateau. Now and then it stopped, and milk cans, trunks, and crates of chickens were put on and off. The sun was blazing. Here and there Kay on the rear platform began to see small cultivated spots, alfalfa, grain already turning yellow. She vaguely resented them; they were trying to civilize the valley. She saw no pathos then in the shipping pens and the small red grain elevators side by side. She was conscious however of a rising exultation, a peculiar tingling of the blood, a sense of lightness and anticipation. Even of homecoming. And then the train swung out from between two tall buttes and she saw the lights of Ursula.

Always afterwards she was to remember Ursula at twilight, its streets and windows lighted, and impassive Indian with braids standing under a station lamp, the cool evening air blowing down from the mountains, and behind the town, the purple back drop of the mountains, with one peak higher than the others covered with snow and crowned with glory. And mixed with that was to be her first sight of Tom McNair.

They stood on the car platform; Nora counted the bags, her mother drew her wrap around her, her father looked about.

"Nobody here!" he said.

Then the station agent came along and peered up at them through his glasses.

"Mr. Dowling?"

"That's right."

"No hurry, Mr. Dowling. Take your time. The car's to be taken off here, I understand?"

"Yes. Who's here to get us? Mallory?"

"It's McNair, I think. At least I saw him— That you, Tom?"

A tall figure moved forward, touched its Stetson hat, stood immobile. It was an easy casual gesture, even faintly an insolent one. It was as though he said: "I'm McNair, and who the devil are you?"

That was Kay's first sight of Tom McNair. He stepped out of the shadow into the light of a lamp post and into her life with equal nonchalance. At the moment—and indeed for some time—she scarcely existed at all to him.

"What's the girl like?" they asked him that night at the bunk house.

"Like any other girl," he told them, and yawned. "She's a Dowling. That's enough."

Which it was, Henry Dowling being about as popular at that time with the outfit as a rattlesnake in a round-up bed.

But from the time she first saw him Kay was intensely conscious of Tom McNair. Perhaps it was because he typified the valley to her, and her dreams about it. Certainly he was the first embodiment of its romance that she had found. She could hardly have seen, there in the dusk, his darkly handsome face, the broad shoulders and slim waist of which he was so proud. And if, like most cowboys, his soft drawl betrayed his southern origin, he might have had bronchitis for all the use he made of it.

"I'm McNair," he said briefly. "How many are you?"

"Five," said Herbert, who did not care for his manner. "How many do we look like?"

"Plenty, for one car." He glanced at Kay, clutching her jewel case and still staring at him. "You with the party? Better give me that bag."

"It's nothing," said Kay. "I'll carry it."

Perhaps he misunderstood the tightness in her voice, the queer constraint, for he turned on his heel and plunged into the darkness, leaving them to follow as best they could.

"Stiff!" he reflected. "She's Miss Dowling, and I'm to remember it. To hell with her!"

But he was grinning to himself as he tied the luggage with ropes to the sides of the car, and gave orders for the trunks to be sent out the next day. To himself and at himself, for he had meant to be late for the train; had even, in pursuit of that amiable intention, stopped the car outside of town and had rolled and smoked three cigarettes. And the train had been late, too, after all!

When at last he got into the driving seat he found the girl beside him. He was not even faintly interested. He had had his own plans for that evening, plans which had involved a girl also; he had packed salt that day up into the mountains for the cattle there, and he had been in the saddle since five that morning. He had a night off coming to him. It was in infuriated silence that he had received his orders to meet the party, and in silence, rather less infuriated, that he drove it out to the L. D.

Only once did Kay speak during that long entranced ride.

"Do you live at the ranch?"

"Well, I kinda hit it and bounce off," he told her.

"And do you work with the cattle?"

"I play around with them some. Tame 'em, you know. They're easier to handle when they're tame."

"Really!" she said, and then caught a glimpse of his face and knew he was laughing at her.

But the enchantment continued, although she made no further effort to talk. There was a faint spicy odor in the air that she thought might be the sage, and a young moon hung in a cleft in the mountains. Above the purring of the engine an owl was calling, and a jack-rabbit ran for some time ahead of the car, long ears erect. He went incredibly fast, but the car kept up with him, and after a while her father spoke irritably from the back seat.

"What's the hurry?" he demanded. "We've been four days getting here; I don't want my neck broken *now*."

She thought, without looking, that McNair smiled again.

Then, after twenty odd miles, she saw lights again and knew they had reached the ranch. Just so must her grandfather have come back year after year, after he had gone East. First on horseback, then by coach and later on by car, he had turned the bend in the road and seen these lights and knew he was at home again. Very much the same too must have been the bustle of arrival; Mallory, the foreman, shaking hands, his wife in the background, men coming and going within the radius of the car lamps, voices, greetings, light streaming from the ranch house door. She felt strangely excited and emotional.

"We kept some supper hot, just in case you—"

"We've had dinner, thank you."

"Then, if you'll just step in—I don't know where you'd like

to put the other lady."

"My maid? I'll look around and see."

There was a narrow porch hung with creepers. The others went in slowly, as people do into strange houses. They passed Kay without seeing her, and she let them go by. Then, still breathless and constrained she went to the steps again, where Tom in the car was leaning back and rolling a cigarette.

"Thanks, very much," she said.

"What for?" he inquired, genuinely surprised.

"For bringing us out."

"And not breaking your neck, eh?"

But he smiled at her, and the smile warmed and even thrilled her.

"Good night, Mr. McNair."

"Good night."

As she turned to go into the house she heard his voice raised outside in the darkness.

"Hey! Some of you roughnecks come and get this baggage. I've been going since five this morning."

Chapter Three

When old Lucius built his ranch house of field stone at the foot of the mountains and furnished it according to the best taste of his time, there had been some who called it Dowling's Folly. He had been one of the first to put in steam heat, ordering his radiators from Chicago and hauling them from Ursula with vast expense and effort.

But when he had finished the ranch became the show place of the county. He had a vast barn, a machine shop, a wagon shed, a salt house where the great cubes of salt were stored for distribution over his ranges. His calf yard was enormous, with its feeding tables and its hay racks. Outside of the barn were his breaking corrals and paddocks, and beyond these again were the feeding yards, one after another, with shelter sheds against the winter snows and a creek for water flowing through them all. Thousands of cattle could old Lucius winter on the home ranch, and these were only the weaklings of his herds. The others, the strong steers, the dry cows, wintered themselves on the range. He had his line camps there, of course, with two or three riders, a cook and a couple of hay shovelers; the line riders rode fence and worked the unthrifty cattle in for feeding, the cook cooked, the hay shovelers shoveled. In bad winters he took a loss, in mild winters he grew rich.

During his last years, after his other interests took him East, he had come only twice a year, in spring for the cow and calf round-up, and in the early fall to ship. Then old Lucius was a happy man; he put on a pair of old Oregon trousers, he thrust his feet—beginning to be gouty—into ancient boots, stuck a battered Stetson on his head and rode out with his boys, as he called them, going like a king to survey his vast domain.

Sometimes he had not even been to bed, for he seldom came alone on these pilgrimages of his. He brought his cronies along, stuck them on horses, laughed at their groans and played poker with them at night by way of reward. Once or twice too there had been women in the party, quiet well-behaved women, but faintly dubious. Then Mrs. Mallory stayed away from the stone house and William came up from the car and took her place. When prohibition came in old Lucius had a great steel safe built in the ranch office and camouflaged it with a bookcase on hinges, and he sent the Mariposa out on a special trip with rare old whiskies and some gin. He was wasting no space on wines.

It was rather characteristic of Henry that one of the first things he did after he arrived that night was to investigate the safe.

"Better inventory that," he said to Herbert.

And he took out one bottle and gave Herbert a mild, a very mild, whisky and soda. He took one, rather stronger, himself.

Mrs. Dowling and Nora had gone upstairs, but Kay remained below. She was still excited and flushed. She moved around, looked at this, touched that. There was a large square hall, furnished in heavy old-fashioned mahogany, and with a sagging leather couch near a wide stone fireplace. Opening off it were the office, where her father and Herbert were sipping their night caps, and a dining room in heavy dark oak. There was another door, closed, and she opened it. She knew at once that old Lucius had slept here, and she slipped in and closed the door.

The window was open, and through it she could hear the cottonwood trees rustling in the night breeze and the sound of swiftly running water. Some little distance off was a separate building, lighted; now and then a door opened and figures moved in and out. She waited by the window, hoping to catch a glimpse of McNair again, but she failed. All the while she knew she was being exceedingly silly. Almost every girl she knew who had been West had developed some romantic attachment for a cowboy, and had forgotten him the moment she went home. Perhaps it was the altitude; she had heard that altitude did queer things to people.

When she went out Herbert was in the hall. He stared at her with mild astonishment.

"I thought you were safely tucked in bed."

"I've been looking around. It's lovely, isn't it?"

"If you say so, it is," said Herbert, slightly warmed by his night cap. And as she turned on the stairs he was gazing up at her, looking rather less tidy and more human than she had ever seen him.

She had quite a good room. Nora had already unpacked her traveling case and placed its gold fittings on the bureau; her dressing gown and slippers were laid out, her thin nightgown folded on the bed. In the bathroom—there were bathrooms, of course. Old Lucius was nothing if not thorough—her mother was bathing, and the delicate odor of violet bath salts had penetrated into the upper hall.

But Kay noted none of these things. She was ascertaining if her windows looked toward the bunk house. Which they did.

If, lying sleepless in her bed that night, she wondered whether she had made any impression whatever on McNair, a glance into that untidy building would have undeceived her. Tom slept the sleep of those who have been up since dawn, and slept it to the accompaniment of the snores, groans and guttural mutterings of other tired men.

He had put the car away, taken a glance around barn and corrals and then stamped in glumly. His irritation had returned. In the dining room of the bunk house, which served as a sitting room between meals, he found three or four of the men playing black-jack. They looked up, but he said nothing, hung his hat on the nail over his chaps and roping gloves, and stamped across to the door into the long, dormitory-like bedroom.

"Well?" somebody called.

"Well what?"

"Did you wrangle them?"

"I did, and if any lousy son of a gun wakes me at daylight tomorrow I'll—"

"Wait a minute, Tom! What's the girl like?"

"Like any other girl. She's a Dowling. That's enough!"

He slammed the door behind him, and they went back to their game. They were not hunting trouble, certainly not with Tom McNair. Not that they lacked courage; they lived their precarious lives cheerfully, broke bad horses, taking their occasional mischances with a grin, rode in contests and spent or gambled away the money they won, fought the winter storms, and took the usual risks of life and limb of their profession. They had drifted in, from the Powder River country or the Rosebud or Hailstone Basin, signed on and were thereafter L. D. men until chance or fortuitous circumstance sent them drifting on again.

"Ridin' the grub line, Joe?"

"Well, I'd take up squatter's rights on a job if it was offered."

But, save for their occasional visits to town, they were dependent on each other for comradeship and amusement. They preferred peace to conflict, and among the dozen of them who came and went there was an unwritten understanding that McNair was a fighting wildcat, and was better left alone. They discussed him, of course.

"Sure thinks he's God's gift to women."

"May be. But I'm here to say that boy can ride."

Perhaps that paints Tom McNair at that time as well as he can be painted. Later on life was to change him somewhat, but always he was stubborn, proud and sensitive. He was arrogant, too, of his good looks, of his ability to break horses, of his riding and roping, of the attraction he had for women.

"You keep away from my girl," Jake Mallory told him when Nellie was fourteen and began to hang around the corrals.

"You keep your girl away from *me*!" said Tom coolly, and Jake knew he was right.

Attractive to women he undoubtedly was, dark, strong featured, clean cut. Once—that was when Tom was newly come to the ranch—one of Lucius's quiet well-behaved ladies had tried to paint him. Her drawing was very bad, and she had obviated the necessity of painting the horse, which was beyond her ability, by having it stand rear-end toward her and Tom sit sideways in the saddle. She made a very good job of the creature's rump and tail, and she had somehow managed to give Tom himself a hawk-like intensity that was rather like him. Indeed, she saw it herself, and she painted the words "The Hawk" underneath it and presented it to Lucius.

"Well!" said Lucius, and got out his glasses. "The hawk, eh? And where is his prey, my dear?"

After which he sent Tom out on the Reservation and took care to leave him there until the lady had departed. He was not a man to leave anything to chance.

It is too much to say, of course, that Kay had made no impression on Tom McNair. She disturbed him not at all, but he certainly knew she was about; a slim boyish figure with a clipped head, clad in riding breeches and a soft shirt mostly, but in the evenings very feminine in her soft light frocks, with her arms bare and that string of pearls that Lucius had bought her grandmother before she died, too late because they came when she had ceased to care to call attention to her neck.

She had a way of standing—Kay, that is—with her chin up and her hands thrust in her breeches pockets, and of being about when he was.

"Good morning, Mr. McNair."

"Morning, Miss Dowling."

"It's a beautiful day, isn't it?"

"Pretty fair. Weather's what we ain't got nothing else but."

She would look after him as he passed on, leather chaps swishing, neckerchief blowing, flannel shirt stretched taut over his shoulders, his Stetson hat shading his handsome arrogant face. She always felt very small and unimportant at those times; rather, as Bessie might have put it, like something the cat had brought in. And this was the more tragic because she began to realize that the ache of his appeal to her was like a physical pain. Once Herbert caught her looking after him and had a suspicion of the truth, but she was learning guile for the first time.

"He certainly looks the part, doesn't he?" she said.

"He does," said Herbert dryly. "But take all that junk off him, the spurs and the rest, and he might be a total loss. You can't tell."

She looked at Herbert. He was dressed in riding clothes, English boots and breeches; he looked very nice and very much the gentleman, but perhaps not quite the man Tom was. It was significant that he was Tom to her already, in her thoughts.

"You will admit he can ride," she said coldly.

"That's his business. So can these other fellows. And it's about all they can do."

But after that Herbert was watchful.

"Why," he demanded of Jake, sitting pathetically in the ranch office a day or so later while Henry and Herbert went over the books, "why does the McNair fellow draw extra pay? He's down for sixty-five dollars a month."

"Well, it's like this," said Jake. "He's a top hand, for one thing, and good cow hands are scarce. Then it's not a bad thing for the ranch to have the best rider and roper in the state in the outfit. Old—your father—" he turned to Henry "—used to feel right proud when our boys carried off the money at the fair."

"What for?" said Henry, who was finding the hole even deeper than he expected. "It's my opinion we're carrying a lot of trimmings here that can be done away with. Just because this man can ride—"

"He's a good cow-man," Jake insisted obstinately. "Of course Tom's got his faults, but—"

"What sort of faults?"

"He hits it up a bit now and then," Jake explained apologetically. "About two or three times a year. Just goes to town and disappears like. But he comes back sick and sorry, and—that's all there is to it."

Henry, who had his back to the wall safe, stiffened virtuously.

"That's all, is it?"

"Well, he's likely to pick a fight if there's one handy, after he's had a drink or two. And he gambles, of course, but then where'll you find one of these fellows that won't? That's all they need money for; all the rest's found for them."

It was in Herbert's mind to pursue the subject, but Mr. Dowling turned back to the list in his hand.

"All right," he said. "McNair goes at sixty-five. Let's get on with this."

He was in a very bad humor, and not the less that he knew he was himself to blame. Some of the old cattlemen, seeing the homesteaders come in and cut up the grazing grounds with their wire, had reluctantly faced the new conditions, had turned their bottom lands into fields and themselves into farmers. They were raising wheat, sugar beets, even experimenting with flax. But these were the men who had arable land. The others, men whose wealth still lay only in their herds, were in bad condition. Their credit was exhausted. The banks were refusing to lend money on their cattle, and along with the slump which had paralyzed business the country over came the failure of the beef market. A couple of years before the winter had been long and severe and the spring late and muddy. Even when they could buy hay and oil cake they could not get the feed to the cattle.

Mallory, foreseeing the situation, had begged Henry by mail and wire to sell when he could, or to ship South for feeding. But Henry was stubborn. Shipping cost money, and he had put enought in the hole as it was. And still later on Jake had had the pleasure of knowing he had been right, and the agony of seeing his herds freezing and starving to death through a terrible winter. He bought hay and oil cake, and was close to having to pay for it himself! And when he had paid his prohibitive prices at the railroad, through a wet and muddy spring he labored to get the feed to them, only too often to be too late. The sticky gumbo caught his wagons and held them tight, his trucks went into ditches and stayed there. And in March and early April he had ridden out himself with his revolver, and shot the ones who lay dying in the fields. The rest were sold for less than the cost of wintering them.

The ranch had never recovered and now Henry was facing a calamitous loss. It would not wipe him out; unlike most of his neighbors he had other interests. He was still a rich man. And of course half the loss was Bessie's. He preferred not to think about Bessie just then.

The morning went on. Herbert made his neat figures in columns and added them. Later on they would go into ledgers, and a good many would be in red ink. But he worked automatically, glancing out of the window as often as he dared. He never saw the great sweep of the valley, treeless save where some stream wound like a green snake from the mountains; or the rolling grassy hills, or the tawny buttes, rising like vast prehistoric monsters of the plain. Or beyond it the distant misty range which bounded it far away to the East. For Herbert that morning there were no mountains rising stark and sheer behind him, no circling golden eagles, no anything.

He was watching Kay perched like a little boy on top of a corral fence while Tom McNair broke a horse.

If he had only known it he need not have worried. Not yet anyhow. Tom was extremely busy, as a man who breaks a horse must be. So far he had spoken to her only once:

"When I get on, you get off."

"What do you mean, get off?"

"Off. Down." he said impatiently. "This pot-gutted bronc's as likely as not to try to butt through or try to climb over. Then where'd you be?"

"I can jump if he tries it."

He paid no more attention to her, got his saddle on, eased into it and then taking his hat off, slapped the creature with it. It blew up immediately. Through the dust Kay, white to the lips, could see a strange mixture of man and snorting, leaping, rearing horse.

"He'll kill you," she yelled, and was astounded to have Tom glance up at her and grin broadly.

"Pretty good on his feet!" he called.

He showed his first disconcertion when, the horse having given up, weary, hard-breathing and covered with foam, he dismounted and picked up from the ground a letter in a pink envelope which had fallen from his pocket. He stroked the creature's dripping neck without glancing at Kay.

"Sure tried to shake the daylights out of me, didn't you?" he said. "Well, we can't play any more today. I've got work to do."

He led the horse out, leaving Kay alone on top of the corral, and although she waited for some time he did not come back.

It was this small drama that Herbert had watched, sitting

unheroically in the ranch office and making his neat figures on a pad.

Whatever was to come, there is no question that it was Kay who made the first overtures. They were young, delicate in a way, tentative and half timid. Perhaps she was left too much to her own devices. Henry sat most of the day in the office, smoking to keep up his courage, and Herbert had to sit with him. Katherine rose late; she was already showing symptoms of the malady which was to attack her later on, but with that painful reticence of hers she said nothing about it. And in the afternoons there were callers. Mr. Tulloss, the elderly banker from Ursula, who had helped old Lucius in that long drive from the border, and Jennie his wife, who was supposed to have had money; the kindly rector of the Episcopal church; Senator Kirkenbride, still a cattleman, and out from Washington to look after his fences, political and otherwise. Even old Doctor Dunham, crabbed, skillful and eying Katherine with a shrewd professional glance.

"Feeling pretty well, are you?"

"The altitude always bothers me a little. That's one reason we have not been out more. Cream or lemon, doctor?"

"I never spoil the appetite the good God gives me with that sort of pap. Hasn't Henry still got some of that liquor old Lucius left?"

The ranchers came, of course. They brought their wives, left them on the verandah and wandered, with or without Henry, about the place. Some of them wore breeches rather better cut than Herbert's, and English boots also. They lived like the gentlemen they were, on vast estates which no longer paid them to hold. Some of them were still solvent, but Tulloss, meeting them there, would shake his great gray head and wonder how long they would last. They were breeding and training polo ponies; some of them, like the Potters, were experimenting with sheep. They had all the cow-man's dislike of sheep, and it went against the grain, but what else could they do? It required anything from twenty five to fifty acres of land to graze a cow, and in the end they might have to give her away.

But the point is that their coming left Kay free to do what she liked. She would make her dutiful bows, shake hands and wander off; she tried, to do her justice, to make friends with Nellie Mallory, who was sixteen then, but Nellie was aloof and more than a little jealous. She would sit on the porch of the foreman's house and watch Kay interminably, but when Kay sauntered over to speak to her she had little to say.

"I never get tired of looking at the mountains."

"You would if you hadn't anything else."

"Don't you ride?"

"Not if I can help it. Give me an auto any time."

Nellie always said "auto." She considered it more elegant than car.

And Kay, rather daunted, would wander off, to watch horses being shod or vaccinated, to look at the calves, to see farm wagons being repaired. The men, apparently absorbed in their work, greeted her civilly and went on with their business, but it was quickly obvious to them where her interest lay. If they smiled among themselves it was when Tom was far enough away for safety. Not one of them saw any element of possible tragedy. Here was another girl who had fallen for Tom, and that was all there was to it.

The end of the first week, however, saw a change in the relationship with Kay and McNair. So far Kay had ridden mainly in the evenings with Herbert, and Herbert was no horseman.

"I don't want a trick horse," he had announced with great firmness, when they were selecting one for him. "I want to enjoy the scenery. How about that bay?"

"He'll show you more scenery then you ever knew there was," said Bill, the corral boss, who was doing the selecting, not too graciously.

But by the beginning of the second week Kay had got

herself in hand once more, was determined to fight her infatuation. For an entire day she stayed around the ranch house, listening to the conversations on the verandah; New York, San Francisco, Chicago. The wealthier ranchers, it appeared, had been in the habit of going East or West to escape the bitter winters. And that night she made her own effort to escape.

"Why don't we go on to Santa Barbara, mother?"

"I thought you loved it here," said Katherine, astonished.

"So I do, but—I don't think it's very good for you."

"I can't leave your father."

And, as if he had missed her the day before, the next morning Tom came to the house and asked her to ride with him.

"I've got to go up the North fork to look for some horses, and I thought maybe you'd like to come along."

She almost paled with excitement.

"If I won't be in the way."

He looked at her with his attractive smile.

"You're going to work," he told her. "You can ride, which is more than your little friend Percy can do." He glanced toward the office window. "I'm taking out an assistant wrangler, and you're it."

She ran into the house, caught up her hat and gloves and flew out again. She never heard Jake's voice from the office: "I figure if we would put that lower fifteen hundred into wheat—" The golden haze over the valley was star dust, and Tom McNair waiting at the foot of the steps was a young god, condescending to her.

"We're going into the mountains, aren't we?"

"Unless the North fork's moved down!"

It was only later that she realized how sure of her he had been. The chestnut gelding she had been riding was already saddled beside his horse in the barn. He had even provided a lunch for two, rolled in a slicker and tied to his cantle. She was too breathless, too tremulous, to notice it then.

It was a day to dream of. Tom was on his best behavior, soft-voiced, solicitous, southern.

"Comfortable?"

"Yes, indeed."

"Stirrups all right?"

"Perfectly."

"Then let's go."

Just what impulse had actuated him that morning it is hard to say. Perhaps he had genuinely missed her the day before. Perhaps it was only a matter of pride. Bill, reading a mail order catalogue the night before, had raised his head when Tom came in, said: "Haven't seen your lady friend around today. Not sick, is she?" and promptly dodged under the table.

"Not as sick as you'll look if you'll come out of there," said Tom dangerously.

Perhaps it was, like so much that he did, a gesture of pure bravado. But whatever was the reason, having made his point he was chivalrous, kindly, even tender.

"Want to kinda watch your step here. Trail's bad," or, after they had climbed to the high upland meadows and his big gray, the Miller, broke into a lope,—

"Going too fast for you?"

"I like it."

"There's no hurry. We've got all day."

She hugged that thought to her as they cantered along. All day. All day. All day.

Although the plains had already dried under the August sun, the upland meadows were still lush with grass. They passed salt licks, huge brown trampled nests in which the square white salt cakes lay like eggs, and around which the cattle stood or lay, eying them indifferently as they moved by. There was still larkspur and lupin, and here and there the paintbrush. Magpies darted back and forth, small tawny marmots watched them from the rocks, and Kay's heart kept pace with the beat of the horses' hoofs. All day. All day.

All day.

Tom too was happy, for him. As she knew him better she was to learn that he had a black streak in him, a bitter and morose side, but that day he was light hearted and cheerful. A good horse under him, a pretty girl beside him, and all about him that back country he inarticulately loved,—what more could a man want? And after awhile he threw back his head and began to sing softly:

> "I'm a poor lonesome cowboy,
> I'm a poor lonesome cowboy,
> I'm a poor lonesome cowboy,
> And a long ways from home."

He had a fair baritone voice, and when he had finished he glanced at Kay. He was astounded to see tears in her eyes.

"I never did think I could sing," he said whimsically, "but I didn't think I was as bad as all that!"

She was furious at herself, and yet she was helpless. How could she tell him that it was not his absurd song that had made her cry: that he had the strange power to stir in her emotions so profound that they shook her?

"It's the wind in my eyes," she told him. And maybe he believed her, but he sang no more that day.

They found the horses, scattered over a valley, and lunched before they wrangled them. And curiously enough the one disharmony of the day came then. After the meal she lighted a cigarette, and he reached calmly over and took it away from her.

"Don't be absurd," she said. "Everybody smokes nowadays."

"Not ladies. You leave that for the other sort."

"But nice women, ladies, do smoke nowadays, Tom."

"Not out here," he said firmly.

She thought a moment, put her case away. After all, why spoil the perfect day? And she had called him by his first name. Had he noticed it? Did he mind? Apparently not.

They had lunched by the creek, and now he rolled himself a cigarette and surveyed the panorama of mountain and valley before them.

"Pretty nice here," he said. "I stop sometimes and kinda enjoy it. I bet you haven't anything better in the East."

"Nothing so good," she said, looking at him. "Nothing so—wonderful."

"That's the way. You come out here and stay, and maybe the old L. D. will weather the storm. How about it?"

She colored; her absurd heart fluttered. But he did not see it. He was lying down, his head on his elbow, staring at the creek.

"Ought to be fish there," he reflected. "I'll bring a rod up some day and try it out. Like to fish?"

"I never have."

"You're a funny girl." He glanced at her lazily. "What do you do, anyhow?"

"Dance. Play around. Fill in time."

"My God! That's a life for you! You've got too much money."

"I haven't any money. Of course father—"

"Well, you'll marry money, I suppose. That's the game, isn't it?"

"Not necessarily. I might marry for love."

She said it painfully but bravely; not looking at him, tearing up little handfuls of grass.

"Love?" He rolled over on his elbow and stared at her. "What do *you* know about love?"

And laughed delightedly when she made no reply. "That's like a girl!" he said. "Talking about something you don't know anything about. I'll bet you've never been in love."

"But—suppose I have?"

"Who with?" he demanded. "Some movie actor? Or maybe—" he sat up and inspected her. "Maybe it's this secretary feller! Percy! How about it?"

"Certainly not."

For some reason, connected with vanity rather than sentiment, he seemed relieved at that.

"That's right," he said. "Take a *man* while you're about it." He got up. "We'd better be moving," he told her. "We've got a right smart job of work to do."

He resaddled the horses, tightening her cinch carefully, and they commenced the wrangling. It was hard exciting labor. The horses were wild after months of freedom; they ran up the mountain sides, with Tom like an avenging fury racing above to haze them down and Kay trying to hold them as they came. In the end, after the manner of their kind they accepted their fate, stood huddled together, and when the time came to start down took the trail in single file and thudded along as though no other thought had even entered their wise heads.

Even at that, now and then one of them would leave the trail and endeavor by circling around to get back again, but no such tactics answered with Tom. Spurs to his horse he would be off, up the steep hill side or breaking through the brush to head off the truant, and Kay would watch with a sort of agony of apprehension. But back he would come, cool and nonchalant, rolling a cigarette perhaps, and with the recalcitrant trotting meekly ahead of him.

It was at the bottom of the trail that he did a queer thing. The ranch buildings were in sight; the horses were moving on, subdued and resigned, when he stopped his horse, took off his hat and held out his hand.

"Good-bye, Kay."

So he had heard her!

"You're not going away, are you?" she asked in a small voice.

"As far as the bunk house. That's about a thousand miles from where you belong."

A moment later he was on the tails of the loose horses, whistling and calling, driving them at full gallop and leaving her to follow, alone. And that night in the bunk house he was in high spirits. Somewhere he had located a pair of old Lucius's broad-beamed riding breeches, and he appeared with them pinned around him, his hair gummed down with soap and a silver dollar stuck in his eye for a monocle.

"What I want in a horse," he said, in a fair imitation of Herbert's voice, "is scenery. The more scenery and the less horse the bettah."

The bunk house roared and rocked with laughter.

Chapter Four

After that, among the men, it became a settled thing that, when Kay rode during the day, Tom McNair was to be her escort. It was tacit, but now and then some reckless spirit put it into words.

"If she's playin' with Tom she'd better look out."

And once even Jake came out with a statement which may or may not have been meant for Tom's ears.

"There's nothin' goin' to happen to that girl on this ranch," he said. "If Tom's a damned fool and don't know the way these eastern girls play around, then he'd better find out quick. She doesn't mean a thing by it."

But no one had the courage to repeat that to Tom.

He himself was in a curious state of mind. He was no fool, and he knew better far than Kay herself the gulf between them. At first it is possible that his vanity was pleased, his chivalry aroused, but later on there is no doubt that she began to make a much more definite appeal.

"What about this fellow you're in love with?" he demanded once. He did not say "feller" any more. "What's he like?"

"I didn't say I was in love at all."

"Are you engaged to him?"

"No."

"Then there *is* somebody! I hope he gets lumps in his gizzard and chokes to death!"

It was when she looked at him quickly and then glanced away that he had his first inkling of the truth. It confounded him. He brooded over it, tried to laugh it off to himself, but a thousand and one little things began to bear it out. There was a button off his old leather coat one day, and she coaxed it from him and sewed it on. It was the first button she had ever sewed on in all her life, but he did not know that.

To do him justice, while the idea appealed to his vanity, even inflamed him, it gave him no particular pleasure. For the first time in his reckless life he gave serious thought to his relationship with a girl and decided to let her alone. One morning she went to the bar, to find the chestnut gelding ready and Bill saddling his own top horse. She looked around but Tom was not in sight.

"Isn't Mr. McNair coming?"

"Well, no," said Bill. "Tom's gone up to the Reservation for a few days as a rep. Saunders has started to round up."

She said nothing, rode dutifully with Bill, dutifully admired a small herd of yearlings, might have been sitting at home for all she saw, and came back with a headache which she blamed on the blazing August sun. It lasted for four days, that headache, which was the exact period of Tom's absence. And it deceived her father and her mother, but it never fooled Herbert.

"Care to ride with me tonight, Kay?"

"I think not, if you don't mind. I don't feel very well."

Or perhaps she would weary of excuses and go with him, only to be very quiet and silent, and not really brighten until they neared the ranch again.

It was a bad time for Herbert, that four days. The books were in fair order by that time, even if the results were worse than Henry Dowling had anticipated. Herbert had more time to himself, and found to his dismay that time was all he did have; that Kay had slipped away into some world of dreams and enchantment where he could not follow her. He would, if he could, have snatched her away from it, have ordered the Mariposa, sitting in the broiling heat on its sidetrack at Ursula, onto the road again. Or have sent McNair away, to drift South or to hell itself, so far as Herbert was concerned. But as the days went on, and Tom came back, and still no mention of departure was made, he began to despair.

The truth is that Henry Dowling was enjoying himself after his own heavy fashion. He had swallowed his loss, and the resulting mental dyspepsia was not as bad as he had expected; and after all he need not keep the ranch. He could sell it. The Potters had even made him a proposition. His mind, freed of the ranch books, had uncoiled like a spring. He slept late, ate hugely, even began to ride a little. There was not a saddle on the ranch big enough for him, so he sent to town for one, picked out a big quiet mare that could carry him, and with Herbert along to open gates and close them again, would amble about the fields so that he could again sleep late and eat hugely.

It was harvest time. The second crop of alfafa was in blossom and thick with purple blooms, and when the wind struck the rye it bent before it like waves of a yellow surf. Already the oats and wheat were dead ripe and golden in the sun. Jake watched these experiments of his with anxious eyes. Thank God it was not a grasshopper year, but there was still hail to be feared for the standing crops and rain after they were cut. Sometimes he even rode the mower himself, driving four horses abreast, and stopping now and then by the wagon for a drink of tepid water from the jug there.

He knew that Henry Dowling had no faith in his farming plans, and that he was thinking of selling, but he never told his wife. If the Potters bought he would have to go. Sitting there on the old reaper, his thin hard-bitten body lurching over the rough ground, he mutely prayed—for a good crop, for a decent cattle market, for no hail or rain; and cursed the horses out of pure habit as he did so.

When the old separator had lurched and jolted into the wheat fields, he watched the stream of grain as if it had been gold, and when one day Henry drew up by it and watched it, he was almost pitiable in his excitement.

"Thirty-five bushels to the acre, if there's one!" he said.

Henry however was watching the men feeding the machine. It looked like good exercise; it ought to give a man an appetite. He slid down off his horse and picked up a fork.

"Think I'll do my daily dozen," he said, almost gayly.

It was hard work, much harder than he had expected, but after that every day he came down to the fields and got in the way, and listened because he had to to Jake's hopes and boastings.

"Now look at that wheat," Jake would say, "if that doesn't grade A one, I don't know what will."

Henry would labor on, not paying any particular attention, pouring sweat and breathing in great gasps, and finally he would throw down the fork and join Herbert, who did not want an appetite—or anything else very much those days—in the shade behind the straw stack.

"Do you good, young man, to use your muscles."

"I get all I need on a horse," Herbert would say, and resume his endless questioning of a sky that offered him a sunstroke, but no answer.

Then Henry would light a cigar and perhaps drop asleep. Once or twice he almost fired the straw stack.

Yes, Henry was certainly enjoying himself. He could put a hand inside the waist-band of his trousers, a thing he had not done for fifteen years, and if any one had told him that these were indeed his golden days, never to be repeated, he would have laughed at them. He had even ceased to dress for dinner, a rite which he had maintained was a matter of self-respect, although Bessie had always said that what he meant was respect for his dinner. In the late afternoons, slightly sun-burned and more than a little stiff, he would mix a moderate highball for Herbert and a stronger one for himself, and listen for the dinner gong. And at nine-thirty he would put down his book or the Ursula paper and rise, yawning.

"Good night, Katherine."

"Good night, Henry. Don't forget to open your window."

They had not shared the same room for years.

Herbert did not dare to pierce the wall of solid contentment with which Henry had surrounded himself. Nor was Katherine more accessible. She went through her days, neat, subservient, reserved; made her shy calls, gathered a few flowers for her tea table, entertained her visitors, and looked rather yearningly, when she was alone, at the mountains. Old Dunham had advised her not to ride.

She never tired of the mountains, where little narrow trails wound up and over into the sunset, and sometimes she thought of old Lucius, who had ridden this country so long ago and now was only an unspeakable thing under the ugly shaft. She found a couplet in a book one evening, faintly marked in pencil, and as the book was poetry and was wedged between a treatise on anthrax and a report on pedigreed Hereford cattle, she rather suspected a feminine hand in it. The couplet was:

"The wide seas and the mountains called to him,
And gray dawn saw his camp fires in the rain."

On an impulse she went outside to show it to Henry, but he was asleep in his chair with his mouth open.

Herbert was quietly but politely desperate. He could not go to either of them and blurt out what he knew. "Kay is crazy about this ranch hand, McNair. For God's sake let's get the car and get away from here." He had to get up politely when Katherine came into the room, and see that Henry had a sufficient supply of cigars, and send telegrams and write well-worded letters. "Yours very truly, Henry Dowling.

Per H. F."

Henry could go to sleep, having dutifully opened his window, but Herbert only went to bed. And in the early mornings he would rouse from tormented sleep to hear Kay on her way to the corral or the barn, even to get up in his silk pajamas, monogrammed just under the pocket—branded, Tom said once, seeing them on the washing line—and from his window watch her quick nervous determined movements, the bright flash of her neckerchief, the half-defiant upturn of her head. Then he would groan and go back to his bed, to lie there sleepless until the rising bell forced him to meet another day.

And so things were the early days of September. Already some of the cattle were moving down from their summer pastures in the mountains. By twos, by eights, by twenties, they worked down the cattle trails. The green pastures up above had dried up in the summer heat, the coyote pups were growing large and hungry for young beef, and so they were coming home. Along with the threshing came the preparations for the autumn round-up. The wagons were being overhauled, a young woman from Judson, a bare little town on the Reservation, had come as cook at the bunk house, to replace Slim who was to go with the outfit. And Henry began to talk of staying on for the shipping.

Then one day, and quite by accident, Herbert overheard something which cheered him considerably, which even gave him in a small way a weapon to his hand.

Henry was asleep in the shade of the straw stack and Herbert, who had tired of asking the sky questions and getting nothing but a sunburn in reply, had closed his eyes and was apparently so. Thus he caught a bit of conversation over the roar and rattle of the thresher.

"She's sure sore on him. I seen her in town, Sunday."

"She oughta know Tom by this time."

"That's what I told her, but she seemed to feel right bad."

"How'd she hear it?"

"Nellie, I guess. That kid sure doesn't miss anything."

Herbert lay still, hat over his eyes, and pondered. So Tom had had a girl, a town girl, and even she knew about Kay. The whole gossiping town knew, probably, the county, the state. And Kay was going on in her headstrong way, not knowing or not caring, and her people were both blind and complacent. But what could he do? He had his own code, had Herbert, and this code would have permitted him to warn Henry had his own interest not been involved. But to run whining to her father that Kay was slipping away from him and into the hands of another man, never.

He looked at Henry, whose head was lolling against the straw stack. Under his unbuttoned waistcoat his figure suggested that he had swallowed one melon, whole, and between his parted lips Herbert could see gleaming a portion of the gold work which kept in place that piece of dental engineering which Henry called his "bridge." It came to Herbert with sickening force that life did these things to men, his kind anyhow. Youth and love slipped away, and after that food counted, and a soft bed and good cigars, but romance no longer lurked around the next corner, and perhaps after a time they did not care.

He hoped so, anyhow.

The point is, however, that he decided to say nothing and probably would have kept to his decision had not one or two things occurred which rather forced his hand.

One was that Kay deliberately refused to ride with him that evening, and went out with Tom instead. And the other was that Herbert, when she came in later on with her cheeks flushed and her eyes like stars, felt impelled to take a long walk before bed and thus happened on something he was not meant to see.

Had he known it, it was not such a great matter that had sen Kay home in such excitement. Her relations with Tom were still largely impersonal on those rides of theirs. He still had himself well in hand. He would stop on top of a knoll and gaze at the mountains, outlined against the setting sun.

"You ever been across? To Europe, I mean?"

"Yes. Why?"

"Well, I'll bet there's nothing prettier than that over there."

But there were times on those rides together when he seemed to forget her, to be absorbed in a nature he worshiped inarticulately, or again to be concerned with that mysterious man-life of his which he never shared with any one. She was miserably jealous then. But again he talked of his people. His father had come up from the South during the gold rush into the Black Hills, but had found no gold. And the end of free land killed him, finally.

"He'd always been used to moving," he said. "He was kind of restless, and finally there weren't any more places to go. The very sight of wire made him feel crowded. He always thought there would be a chance over the next hill, provided it lay West."

Kay nodded. She knew nothing about free land, or the sudden shutting off that took place at the beginning of the new century. But because it was Tom's father she felt vaguely sad.

"Why, say," he drawled on, "if he'd lived to have to take out a license to go hunting, he'd have had a fit. He'd shot his own meat for twenty years. He believed in free land and free silver—and he got six feet of one and none of the other."

Only once did he mention his mother. She gathered that, in his queer way, he was afraid of showing feeling.

"She was sure a good woman," he told her. "She stuck by, when her folks back home were trying to rope her back every way they knew." He hesitated. "She got her comfort out of religion," he added.

"Don't you believe in God, Tom?"

"I'll believe in Santa Claus if you say so," he said, and smiled at her. But he added, seeing that she expected him to: "When I'm in a fix I do. Once or twice it's seemed like He was the only one who could get me out. And I'm still here."

He had enlarged on that, seeing that she had rather liked it, and even blinded as she was she perceived that in the adventures he related it was he and not God who received the major portion of the credit.

But he did believe in God. He had admitted it. It somehow justified her own belief in him.

Only by the sheerest accident did she discover that he had gone to France during the war. He had volunteered "for a change," he told her, and the exploit of which he was apparently most proud had been the stealing of a mule for some nefarious purpose of his own. But like his belief in a God who got one out of tight places, this too served to solidify the pedestal on which she was placing him. He had been a soldier.

"Did you get any fighting?"

"Fired a gun now and then."

She was not fooled.

Attracted he might be. Was, indeed. She had burst on his drab life, this exotic product of a civilization he hardly knew. He was as curious about her as he was interested. But that even in a small degree he reciprocated the devouring infatuation she felt she had no reason to believe.

And then, on the night in question, she began to wonder.

They had traveled along a narrow trail over the foothills, and at last they could see down in the valley the lights of Ursula. Tom gazed at them thoughtfully, then suddenly laughed. She glanced at him.

"I was thinking about the night you folks came here. I sure was sore."

"What about?"

"I'd had some plans of my own," he said, eying her.

"What were you going to do?"

"Oh, I don't know. Play around some." And with a certain malice: "Maybe see a girl. You never can tell."

A burst of sudden and primitive jealousy sent the blood

away from her face. Her lips stiffened.

"Was it a girl you were thinking of just now?"

"You'd like to know, wouldn't you!"

But she had herself in hand by that time.

"Not necessarily. You have your own life to live, as—I have mine."

She was not prepared for his answer, however, or for the steady direct gaze which accompanied it.

"Yes," he said. "That's the hell of it."

He turned his horse abruptly and started back, and their talk thereafter was of unimportant matters. But she knew, and knew that he knew, that the relationship between them had definitely changed with that declaration of his. And later in the evening Herbert knew it too, and took his walk so that he might be too tired to lie awake and think.

Kay had gone upstairs when he started, and Henry was about to follow her, yawning.

"Good night, Katherine."

"Good night, Henry. Be sure to raise your window."

Herbert picked up a cap and went out. Was that all it came to in the end? All this agony of spirit, and then perhaps—only perhaps—a brief interval of happiness and consummation, and after that nothing but habit and association? It could not be, it must not be. He straightened his young shoulders and started down the lane.

There was a full moon. When he reached the cottonwoods he turned around, and he was certain he saw Kay at her window. Over at the bunk house someone was indolently twanging a banjo, and in one of the cattle yards a cow was calling, a persistent melancholy sound. All at once he hated the place. He wanted the cheerful lights and sounds of the city, the roar of cars, the clanging of tram-bells. He wanted his own comfortable apartment, and to dress and dine out, with Kay next to him and the orderly service of the meal going on:

"Champagne or whisky and soda, sir?"

He went a long way that evening in the moonlight, clear across the alfafa and the wheat stubble to the main road. A stray bull with a white face eyed him indifferently; a skunk watched him warily from the bank of a ditch; but he trudged on, busy with his thoughts.

Out on the road he turned back toward the main gate, to be overtaken by a ramshackle Ford, driven by a girl, a rather pretty girl, he thought. She glanced at him and glanced away without interest, and at the main gate she turned in.

He forgot her at once, until some time later he came across the Ford, parked out of sight of the ranch house, and saw the gleam of her white dress among the timber by the creek. She was not alone; a man was leaning negligently against a tree, apparently listening to her in silence.

Herbert could hear the shrill half-hysterical quality of her voice, saw the man light a match and probably a cigarette, and realized that some small emotional drama was taking place in the twilight. He went by hastily and without a second glance toward them, but he knew that the man was Tom McNair.

Chapter Five

The vast empty back country began to show signs of life as shipping time approached, and the railroad in the valley, along which the little towns were strung like beads, awakened to new activity. Locomotives pulled great lines of empty cattle cars and left them, so many here, so many there, on the various side-tracks by the shipping pens. Up in the mountains and North on the Reservation the roundups were beginning; small informal processions were starting out, the pilot on horseback leading the chuck and bed wagons, cowboys in chaps and gloves, their ropes hung to their saddles, drove ahead of them the remudas of loose horses which were to provide their extra mounts. And in the upland pastures or out on the plains, where the blues and pinks of the spring flowers had given way to the sturdier reds, yellows and purples of the early fall, the cattle stood or moved slowly about, the cows with their calves, the steers, the range bulls with their flat backs and wide heavy heads.

Already the nights were cold. At the early round-ups the night guards came in chilled to thaw their hands over the stove, and to draw their beds into the shelter of the cook-tent. The quaking aspens were bright gold; there was a thin scum of ice on the mountain pools in the mornings. And in the fields the country was threshing its grain. Trucks and wagons, their bodies built high with temporary boardings, rocked and careened along the roads on their way to the railroad or the small red grain elevators along the track. First grade wheat was bringing a dollar and twenty cents a bushel, but the profit was small. The old cow-men turned farmers figured patiently; cost of ploughing, cost of seeding, cost of harvesting and threshing. Even at a dollar twenty—

Sometimes a herd on the way to the railroad blocked the passage of a wagon of grain; the old West and the new West met and intermingled. Cowboys turned for the time into farm hands eyed the cattle appraisingly while the way was being cleared for them.

"Look pretty good this year."

"Not so bad." Or:

"Kinda poor, aren't they?"

"Shipping to the feeders. Got some better stuff coming next Thursday."

Thursday. It was always Thursday, for the Monday morning market in Chicago.

The cattle would plod on, ten miles a day, to save all the weight possible. The dust hung over them in clouds, the cowboys sagged in their saddles at ease, now that the hard riding of the round-up itself was over. But there was still much to do. In the empty fields out beyond the pens they would again work their cattle, cutting out and holding the cut, and throwing back the unwanted stock that had drifted along with the herd. Then there would be the final loading, the nervous spooky cattle balking at the gangway and milling frantically, the final triumphant start up, the prodding and slapping until the car was full, and the signal for the engine to shunt another car into its place.

But before the L. D. was ready to round-up things had come to a crisis between Tom McNair and Kay.

Fair-time was approaching. In the bunk house in the evenings the men talked of little else. "If I draw that Roman-nosed pony of Saunders's again I'll bust out cryin'. It gave a couple of crow-hops last year and then looked around for a piece of sugar!"

"The fellow that gets old Abe'll get first money."

"He'll get a doctor bill."

The Indians were already driving down their animals from the Reservation, fast running horses and buckers, and putting their money on Little Dog, their best rider. And in his spare moments Tom was going over his equipment; fastening new leathers to his spurs, looking over his chaps, examining the green silk shirt in which he meant to stand out "like a sore thumb" before the grand-stand.

Then one evening he learned from Kay that the Dowlings were not going to the Fair, and took matters into his own hands with the usual readiness for trouble. He came to the ranch house, where Henry was drowsily reading the Ursula paper.

"Mr. and Mrs. Bill Sawyer are entertaining the five-hundred club this evening."

"Dicer's Emporium reports a new importation of corsets. That's right, Sam. We still believe in 'em."

Herbert was playing solitaire, and Kay had already gone up to bed. Tom rapped outside, opened the screen and clumped in his high-heeled boots to the living room door. Henry looked up and Herbert continued to move his cards, but he had stiffened.

"Understand you're not going in to the Fair," Tom said, tall and handsome and arrogant in the doorway.

"Not this year; Mrs. Dowling—"

"How about my taking Miss Kay, then? She sure ought to see it."

Herbert put down his cards and rose.

"If Miss Dowling wants to go to the Fair I'll take her," he said.

Tom eyed him.

"She's got to decline my invitation first."

"Not necessarily!"

"How do you get that way?" Tom demanded angrily.

"Where do you come in on this anyhow? I'm talking to Mr. Dowling."

Henry, thus brought in, was puzzled and startled. He had never associated Kay's riding with this cowboy save in the way he associated Herbert with himself, as somebody to open gates. Now he was considerably outraged. He looked at the two, each so fiercely confronting the other, and put up his hand.

"That's enough," he said. "More than enough." And to Tom: "If Kay wants to go to the Fair, Tom, Mr. Forrest will take her."

"That's not—"

"That's all. I don't intend to argue the matter," said Henry, and lifted his paper once more.

Tom hesitated. A dark color rose in his face, and he twisted his hat in his hands. Then he turned on his heel and flung out again without a word.

"Insolent young rascal!" said Henry, still astonished. "Acting as if—close that door, Herbert."

Herbert closed the door, very quietly, like a conspirator.

"What do you make out of that? What about him, anyhow?"

"I don't know anything about him," said Herbert. And nobly added: "He's a good cow-man, according to Jake."

"He has had time enough, apparently, to see a good bit of Kay."

Herbert said nothing. His face was carefully non-committal.

"I don't like it, Herbert. Kay has never seen this sort of life before. God knows it's not romantic, but she may think it is. Just why a fellow who can ride a horse and look after cattle should make an appeal to women, I'm damned if I know."

"He's a handsome devil."

"Handsome is as handsome does," Henry snapped, and picked up his paper again. "Mr. and Mrs. George Pinckney are receiving congratulations today on the birth of a son and heir." Suppose Kay was really interested in this chap? Suppose she fancied herself in love with him? Kay! A man who always smelled of the stable, who earned sixty-five dollars a month and used it to gamble with! A periodic drinker, going on sprees when he disappeared for days at a time, wallowing in who knew what filth? "Lightning struck a hay stack at—" Oh, hell!

"What did you mean by saying he's a handsome devil?"

"He is, rather."

"You think she *is* interested in him, then?"

"I don't see any use in denying it. Yes, I think she is."

"What you really mean is that she's built up some sort of romantic figure out of him. Isn't that it?"

"That's a part of it."

"And what's the rest?"

Herbert hesitated.

"I hardly know, sir," he said at last. "I think it may be more than that. She's no child, and she's got a good hard brain. I think she knows exactly what he is, in the back of her mind anyhow. She mayn't know any details, but she suspects them. Only—they don't make any difference."

"You are talking as though she is in love with the fellow!"

"Don't you think she is, sir? Infatuated, anyhow?"

"I know damned well she's getting out of here if she is."

Shortly after that Henry went up to bed. He was very stiff; his back ached, and into the bargain he was more uneasy than he cared to admit. There was a little stubborn streak in Kay. She was like her grandfather in that. And Herbert was right, she had a good hard brain. Two weeks ago or three, she might have been only romantically interested. But by now she knew the fellow, or ought to; she'd had chances enough.

He grunted, and opened the door into his wife's room. She was reading by the light of a lamp on the end of the wash-stand beside her bed, and when he entered she wiped the cold cream from around her mouth with a handkerchief, preparatory to his good night kiss. But he did not kiss her at once. He sat down on the foot of her bed.

"What about Kay, Katherine? Is she making a fool of herself?"

"I don't know what you mean?"

"With Tom McNair?"

"Oh, Tom!" There was relief in her voice. "She's playing around with him, of course, but that's all. She's accustomed to attention, and he's about all that offers out here."

"There's Herbert," he said sturdily.

"She can always have Herbert, and she knows it. I wouldn't worry, she's only amusing herself. And there's nothing much else for her to do."

He got up. His back was really very troublesome; he must have twisted something in the field that day. Well—

"We'd better be getting on anyhow," he said, not entirely convinced. "I'm about through."

He kissed her perfunctorily.

"Good night."

"Good night, Henry. Be sure to open your window."

Lying sleepless in his bed that night Henry planned to leave the next day. But when he wakened in the morning he had a bad case of lumbago. He had never had anything much before, and he was convinced that he was in a serious condition. Every time he moved he groaned. It was, indeed, between groans that he had his interview with Kay.

"You mean," said Kay, staring down at him, white and angry, "that you forbid me to ride out with Tom McNair?"

"That's what I've said. I generally mean what I say."

"But—how dare you, father? How can you? You would think I'd done something wicked."

"Not necessarily." He groaned again. "Unwise, certainly."

"But what has happened? You haven't objected before. Just what is it you are afraid of, father?" she asked, more gently. "I won't disgrace you. You know that."

"He's not your kind."

"He's a *man*. And because you know he's a man and not a tailor's dummy, you're afraid. Isn't that it?" And when he said nothing to that she was suddenly frightened. "You haven't spoken to him, have you?"

"I think he understands my position."

Later on he told Katherine.

"I tell you she's infatuated with him. Infatuated! That's the only word I can think of."

"Temporarily, perhaps, that's all. Is that pillow right?"

"No, damn it. Take it out. What do you mean, temporarily? We'll look well if she walks into town while I'm laid up here and marries him."

"I don't think she has the remotest intention of marrying him."

"Oh, you don't? Well then, I wish you'd seen and heard her in here a while ago."

"I daresay you weren't very tactful."

"Tactful hell! Why should I be tactful? She's lost her mind."

When Doctor Dunham arrived he had worked himself into a frenzy.

"What have you been doing to yourself, anyhow?"

"Nothing. Pitched a little hay, that's all."

"Trying to show these cowboys you're as good a man as they are!" chuckled old Dunham, and was rather hurt later when none of old Lucius's liquor was forthcoming.

So the day wore on, Katherine applying hot water bags to Henry's back and occasionally looking at the mountains with that far-away glance of hers. Long ago she had forgotten the dreams and passions of her youth; sometimes it seemed to her that she had always been married to this heavy bodied, occasionally truculent and domineering husband of hers. But for Kay she had had a dream of her own, of love and marriage.

It was vague, like much of her dreaming. She did not care

greatly for Herbert; secretly she shared Bessie's opinion of him. But he meant safety. This cowboy— If she could only talk to Kay! But she had never overcome the feeling that as to mother and daughter, the gulf between the knowledge of the one and the ignorance of the other was somehow shameful.

She had, this queer Katherine, an odd feeling that if old Lucius had been around he would have known what to do.

Kay stayed in her room all morning. She was frightened and desperate. Never before had she resented the domestic hierarchy under which she lived, but now she did. Her face, when the lunch gong sounded, was hard and sullen, and when before descending she went to her window and once more glanced out in the hope of seeing Tom, what she saw only increased her anger and resentment.

The early midday dinner at the bunk house was over; the long table with its brown oil-cloth cover was deserted. By ones and twos the men came out, to sit on their heels or lounge about, rolling their endless cigarettes. It was the one bit of leisure in their hard-working, hard-riding days. Bill was off by himself, plaintively playing a mouth organ, and near him Tom was standing, over-cheerfully humming the words of a song. At the chorus he discreetly stopped, to the laughter of the group.

"Cowboy, oh cowboy, I hope you get rich
You're a good natured bull-dogging son of a—"

Perhaps he saw Kay at the window, and there was deliberate malice in what he did next, for the new girl from Judson appearing with a dishpan, he promptly called to her.

"Come on out here, pretty one! Come out and give the sun a treat."

She came, giggling, and he threw an arm about her and waved his free hand at the landscape.

"Ain't that pretty?" he said. "Just you and me and nature,

eh! Don't count those roughnecks over there."

The next moment, having made his effect, he released her and forgot her. But Kay recoiled into the room and held her hands to her burning face.

"He's crazy," she thought. "Crazy and wild. Maybe bad too, for all I know. I've got to get out of this somehow, or I'll go crazy too."

But it is typical of her state that within the next few minutes she was seeing it for the bravado it largely was, and that he was in his own way returning hurt for hurt. Up to that time she had not considered Herbert in the situation, but during the meal—Mrs. Dowling was lunching upstairs—she was suddenly certain that Herbert was responsible. It would be like him, she reflected, not to come to her, but to go as indirectly as possible to her father. Somebody had certainly gone to him. Well, she would soon find out.

"I suppose you think you did a good job last night," she began, resting her chin in her hands and staring across at him.

"As to what?"

"You know well enough. It was you who spoke to father. He never notices such things himself."

"Then you're wrong. It was he who brought up the subject."

"And you didn't help it any."

"Good Lord, Kay!" he said, exasperated. "What was I to say? Every one who chose could see the thing for himself—"

"Just what thing?"

"You don't really want me to say it, do you?"

"Go on. Let's hear the worst."

Her tone angered him.

"All right," he said. "That you're in love with Tom McNair. You needn't bother to deny it. I know you."

Suddenly she laughed, rather breathlessly.

"Oh, so that's it! I'm in love with him! And what about

him? Is he in love with me?"

She was not laughing now, but watching him intently.

"Is he in love with me?" she repeated, when Herbert hesitated.

"I don't know. Maybe he thinks he is. You're different from the girls he's known, of course."

"Thanks!"

But there was something subdued in her now that encouraged Herbert to go on.

"There's another thing, too, Kay. These fellows out here are all right. They're a fine lot, most of them. But they don't understand eastern girls, how they can be crazy about a fellow one minute and be all through the next. It's not their game. McNair now—I'm not saying anything against him—McNair may think you're in earnest about all this. Leaving everything else aside, you ought to be fair to him."

She had a wild desire to cry out: "But I am in earnest. It's horrible, dreadful earnest. I'm in and I can't get out!" But the sight of Herbert, taking out a cigarette and delicately tapping it on the back of his hand, killed the impulse. Herbert, with his neatly pressed trousers, his neatly brushed hair, his neatly arranged and docketed mind, how could he understand?

"It's not I who am unfair to him," she said. "It's the rest of you."

"And again," said Herbert carefully, still tapping. "I happen to know that he has a girl of his own already. *You* can't marry him. Then why spoil him for what he can have?"

"Why on earth don't you light that cigarette and stop tapping it?" she demanded in a sort of frenzy.

She got up. Herbert was too late to pull out her chair, but he did manage to open the door for her.

She went upstairs, took off her riding clothes, and lay down on the bed. She could hear across the hall the rattle of dishes on her father's tray and his voice now and then, querulously raised in protest.

"Why can't they make a decent cup of coffee? This belly-wash—"

"I'll have Nora make some, Henry."

"And get it an hour from now! No."

She was frantic with jealousy. Did Herbert really know that Tom had a girl, or had he made it up? Was it this Vera, the girl from Judson? If not, who was it? There had been an effort at casualness in Herbert's voice. "I happen to know he has a girl already." Well, suppose he had? What could it possibly mean to her? They had her; and they would hold on to her. She could never get away. She would end by marrying Herbert, and she knew what that would be:

"Good night, Kay."

"Good night, Herbert. Be sure to open your window."

She thought about her Aunt Bessie and Uncle Ronald, her husband. He had been a dapper little man with a hideous habit of posing before the servants, especially the women. No wonder Aunt Bessie had had what the younger crowd ribaldly called "sympathizers." She even thought about old Lucius and the occasional women who had come to the ranch. That was what loveless marriage was.

She was not as ignorant as Katherine believed. Much of those earnest and wide-eyed discoveries of sex by young writers to a world already sex-wise and sex-weary before they were fledged, had come her way. Even the unloading of degenerate sex complexes by older men and women who sold themselves for commercial purposes as cheaply in the market place as any prostitute.

And she knew that this love of hers was no light thing, to be dismissed by order. That it was a primitive savage thing, stronger than she was. After all, she was no child. She had had her small affairs, her light romances. This was different.

At five o'clock she dressed herself carefully and went down to the verandah. It was, in a way, a test she set herself. If Tom came to her there he cared, if he did not—

It was an hour before he came, and then he was gentler than she had expected, even rather ill at ease.

"Well," he drawled with his faint smile, "it seems like we're kinda out of luck all round, don't it?"

"You mean, about the Fair?"

"So they've told you; have they?"

When she made no reply, but sat gazing out with miserable eyes across the plains, he rolled a cigarette slowly and sat down on the step at her feet.

"Just what is the big idea? Is it the bunch-quitting they object to? Or just me?"

"It's not you," she said hastily. "It's just—anybody."

"I notice they don't mind this Percy of yours."

"It has nothing to do with Herbert. He's a member of the family."

"Like hell he is!" he said, with sudden resentment. "Oh, I get you all right. You're not telling me anything I don't know. I suppose you'll up and marry him some of these days. That's what they're saying around here, anyhow."

"Never."

"Still, you're a good little girl. You'll do what they tell you. You're doing it now, aren't you?"

"What do you mean?"

"Well, you'd like to go to the Fair tomorrow. With me," he added, glancing up at her. "But you won't."

"I don't want to worry them."

"Worry them? What are they worrying about?" he demanded. "I'm not going to kidnap you. You're safe with me—as safe as a church."

But now that the issue had come she found a certain courage with which to meet it.

"You don't really care now whether I go or not," she said. "What you really want now is to have your own way. You hate to be beaten."

He threw back his head and laughed.

"Smart, aren't you?" he scoffed. "Maybe it's partly that,"

he added honestly. "But about my not wanting you to go, Kay—God, what do you think I'm making all this fuss about?"

"I didn't know."

"Well, now that you know," he said, lightly, as if he had not been betrayed into that moment of real feeling, "what about it? Do we go, or don't we? Be yourself! Let's show them who's who in this part of the world!"

But she only shook her head. His moment of passion was gone. She knew that it was not her he really wanted, but to humiliate the rest. And although he continued to argue, cajole and bully her in turn, she persisted in her refusal. At last he leaped to his feet, jamming his hat on his head with a gesture at once dramatic and final.

"All right," he said. "All I wanted was to know where I stand. Now I know. Good night."

"Tom! Come back a minute."

But he went swinging along toward the barn, chaps rustling and spurs jingling, and as he went he whistled. Ten minutes later he was loping down the road on the Miller, in the general direction of Ursula.

She did not see him again until two days after the Fair was over.

Now and then some word of the doings in town filtered out to the ranch. Bill was brought out in a car one day, pale and sheepish, with a sprained ankle and a story of hard luck, but Tom it appeared was riding as if he wore shock absorbers and was up to the finals.

Herbert politely invited Kay to go in for the last day, and she as politely refused. Henry was able to turn over in his bed without yelping, and was planning to start East as soon as he could travel. And then on the evening of that last day the outfit came back, tired but triumphant, driving its bucking string ahead of it. And Tom McNair was not with it.

Kay could not believe her eyes. When Jake passed the house on the way to his own cottage she stopped him.

"Who won, Jake?"

"Tom McNair got first money."

"That's fine. I didn't see him with the rest."

He rested his kindly faded old eyes on her for a moment, looked away.

"Well, Tom's Tom," he said. "Maybe he's playin' poker in town. You see, ever so often Tom's got to have a little time to himself. There's no harm in him; he's just like a young colt, a bit wild and not halter broke yet."

Chapter Six

Ursula prided itself on its progressiveness. It was a pretty town, the best in the valley, perhaps in the state. It had paved streets, a park, a great stone school house, even a Zoo. (Tom McNair had roped and brought in the two bear cubs in their cage.) It had a flour mill, a beef sugar factory, and a hospital.

Its streets bustled with activity. Twenty-one, going North, disgorged traveling salesmen with sample cases, and twenty-two South picked them up again. The outlying ranches fed it and in their turn were fed by it. It even had a social life of no mean order, and in the winter twenty-one South or twenty-two North picked up the wealthier of its inhabitants and stowed them in lowers or drawing rooms and carried them away from the bitter cold.

The conductors on the railroad knew them all.

"I see it's Pasadena this year this time!"

"Yep. Tried New York last year but didn't like it much. Too crowded."

But Ursula was like the smaller towns along the track. It had no environs. Where it ended the back country began. One could leave its paved streets, its comfortable houses with their gardens, climb a hill, descend again and, as Bessie would certainly not have put it, be alone with God.

On the second day following the Fair Clare Hamel stood

behind a counter in Dicer's Emporium. She was near the door. Across the street the setting sun shone brilliantly into the one broad window of the Martin House, with its five worn leather chairs behind it and the old brass bar-rail now fastened beneath it, to keep—hopefully—the sitters' feet from the window sill. Beside it was the National Drug Store, once her father's professional stand and known then as the Last Chance saloon; and beyond that again the Zenith barber shop.

She was bored and anxious, and the outlook gave her no comfort. She knew it all; it was all she did know. Marcus the barber bending over some one in his chair; Carrie Young's baby carriage with the twins in it, parked outside of the drug store; and Indian in an old sack suit and straw hat, with red flannel twisted in his braids, driving past in a buckboard, a hungry-looking dog running along beside it; men in Stetsons rubbing shoulders with men in straw hats; the Prairie Rose café; the new bank building; a stream of cars. And over it all, for the weather had turned warm again, a haze of dust and heat.

Heat, dust and dreariness. Not even a customer to wander in, finger the dress-goods and exchange a bit of talk across the counter. Across from her—handkerchiefs, gloves, stockings and toilet goods—was Sarah Cain, likewise bored and idle. She did not like Sarah, and Sarah did not like her, but out of the heat and a certain dreariness that was in her she finally spoke across the aisle.

"Looks like a good picture tonight."

"Yeah. But it's awful hot in there. My God, ain't this weather awful again?"

"It sure is. You could fry an egg out there."

"You bet."

Silence fell again. Then Sarah, with a glance toward the rear of the store where Mr. Dicer sat at a desk, edged out into the aisle and crossed to Clare.

"Say, I seen a friend of yours yesterday."

A hand, which had seemed to be wavering over Clare's heart for a day or two, suddenly closed down on it.

"What friend? I got more than one, you know."

"Tom McNair."

"Oh, Tom!" She moistened her dry lip. "Is he still in town? Pity he wouldn't come in and say how-d'ye-do."

"He wasn't saying anything to anybody when I saw him."

There was a sort of malicious pleasure in Sarah's voice, and Clare looked at her coldly.

"If you mean he'd been drinking why don't you say it?" she asked. "It's no news to me, and it's certainly nothing in my life."

"Well, I'm glad to hear you say it," said Sarah, with assumed heartiness. "The way folks talk around here you'd think— He'd been drinking all right. *And* some."

She sauntered back, leaving Clare to stare out of the open door again. Her face was impassive, for Sarah was watching her, but she was torn within by a thousand distracting thoughts. Something had set Tom off again; he only went on these periodic drinking spells when something set him off. Was it her own visit to him? Had she had some effect after all, even this? She had seemed to make so little impression on him that night at the ranch.

"We've had some good times together, haven't we, Tom?"

"You've been mighty nice to me, Clare. I'm not forgetting that."

"Well then, what's the matter? I don't hardly sleep any more. Look here. Look how loose this belt is! I just get to worrying, thinking maybe I've done something, and I can't sleep."

"We're mighty busy just now, you know."

"I've heard that before."

"Then," he went on, unusually patient for him, "we've got the Dowlings now, and they take a lot of looking after."

"You mean she does. The girl. Oh, I'm not so far away I don't hear things. If you're fool enough to fall for that sort of thing—"

"What sort of thing?" He was ominously calm.

"Her making a joke out of you," she went on, recklessly. "What do you think you mean in her life? I'll bet she's laughing at you half the time."

"That'll do," he said roughly. "I've had all I'm taking. You haven't any claim on me and you know it. Now you get in that Lizzie of yours and go back home." Then more gently: "You better start anyhow. You've got a long ways to go."

But at this unexpected gentleness the shrew died in her, and suddenly she began to cry.

"I'm crazy about you, Tom. I never fooled you about that. And I thought you liked me too."

"So I do; fine, Clare."

"And I'm straight, Tom. You can't say that about all of them."

"Sure you are. Don't I know that? That's why I don't want anybody to see you hanging around here."

But when she was at last in the old Ford and on her way back home, she knew she had not touched him. Knew indeed that she had never touched him, that his light-hearted philandering had been just that and nothing more.

She had cried steadily all the way back.

That was almost a week ago. She had gone back home, to the one-story bungalow on the outskirts of the town. Her mother was sitting on the porch resting after her dish-washing.

"That you, Clare? I was getting worried about you."

"I was just moving around, hunting a breeze."

"Your supper's in the oven. It's pretty much dried out now."

"I had a chocolate ice-cream soda, mom," she lied. "I'm not hungry." And went into the house.

Alone in her room she had turned on the light and surveyed herself in the mirror. No wonder he had turned her down. She looked ugly, badly dressed, crude. And that girl out there, with a lady's maid—Nora was the first personal maid outside of the movies she had ever heard of—a lady's maid to work over her. No wonder Tom's head was turned. She had a vision of this girl she had never seen, lounging about on sofas in exotic negligees, bathing or being bathed—poor Nora!—in a perfumed bath, casting her siren's net over all and sundry, and especially over Tom McNair.

She had gone on as best she could.

"You're sure it's all wool?"

"You can ask Mr. Dicer. It's the very best grade. Mrs. Hutchinson just bought a skirt off that piece."

"Well, I don't know that that recommends it."

Measuring, cutting, wrapping up, and then long periods of idleness when the heat came in waves through the open door, and her mind wrestled with loneliness and despair. The Fair, with the Emporium closed in the afternoons and her heart stopping when the announcer bellowed through his megaphone:

"Tom McNair coming out on Stampede. McNair on Stampede."

The throwing open of the gates of the saddling chute, the hazers scattering, the judges watchful, the horse leaping, sun-fishing, rearing and bucking; and then the ride made, the pistol shot, the hazers closing in. She could breathe again.

She had only one comfort. Inspect the grand-stand as she might, she did not see the Dowling girl.

In the evenings she had waited alone on the porch of the bungalow, but Tom had not appeared. And now he had been drinking, and maybe old Dowling would fire him. Then he would go away and she would never see him again.

She leaned over the counter.

"Where'd you see him, Sarah?"

"Going into the Martin House."

At five-thirty Mr. Dicer in the rear of the store glanced up from an order blank at the clock, and then rising took his straw hat from its hook. And at this signal the girls, already poised for flight, with a simultaneous movement dipped under their counters, brought forth their absurd small hats, jerked them on their heads and moved to the door. Mr. Dicer, following them, locked it behind them.

"Good night, Mr. Dicer."

"Good night."

Under pretense of an errand Clare crossed to the drug store and entered. But when they had gone out of sight she emerged again and made her way into Martin House. Ed Clark, the clerk and general factotum, was cleaning his nails with a pen-knife behind the glass cigar counter which served as a desk.

"Hello, Ed. Is Tom McNair here?"

"He's got a room here. I can't say if he's in it."

She was certain however that Tom was upstairs, and after a moment's thought she wrote him a note.

"I'll be at the corner by the Court House, Tom. And I'll wait there until you come if it takes all night. Clare."

"Wake him up and give him that, Ed," she said. "See that he reads it, won't you? There's going to be trouble if he doesn't go home tonight."

"Right-o," said Ed. "I get you."

But after she left it she wondered. If she sent him back to the ranch she would be sending him to Kay again! She shrugged her shoulders and went on.

To Kay herself those two days of Tom's unexplained absence were sheer torture. Always she was on the watch for him, from early in the morning when the wranglers came in at six for breakfast to late afternoon, with Charlie the dairy-maid driving in the milk herd, great slow-moving beasts with full udders which swung as they walked. Once she went to the corral; but Tom's big gray was not there, nor was Tom's saddle on its peg in the saddle house. She could not ask for him, and now she felt that they would be gone before he came back. Her father was up and moving about, and they were to leave on Wednesday. Already Nora was packing the trunks.

"I'd better keep out your heavy coat, Miss Kay."

"Yes, please, Nora."

If they went before Tom came back what could she do? Could she leave a note for him? But what would she say if she did? "Dear Tom: I am so sorry we have to go without seeing you. I do hope—" Never! Better no word at all than that.

In spite of what Jake had told her she had no real suspicion of the truth. Monday passed like Sunday. Herbert was cheerful, almost blithe.

"Well, the old Mariposa won't look so bad to me."

"No?"

"Nor to you either, once you're headed East. You'll—forget all this."

But she ignored that.

To do Herbert justice he believed she would forget, and perhaps it was to make that forgetting easier that he followed her to the verandah that night. She could not stay inside the house. He sat down near her and began his usual preliminary tappings before he lighted his cigarette. When he spoke it was carefully, as if considering what he had to say.

"Kay dear."

"Yes."

"Aren't you taking this thing too hard?"

"What thing?"

"McNair's spree. Bat. Whatever you like to call it."

"You wouldn't dare to say that, if he were here to defend himself!"

"It's the truth. Everybody knows it. Ask Jake! Ask any of the boys! They may lie to you, but it's the truth. He got drunk and half killed an Indian in town the other night."

"I don't believe it."

"An Indian named Little Dog. He and the big Swede here, Gus, had a fight with him over a decision at the Fair, and Tom knocked him cold. They'd both been drinking."

She sat very still. She knew now that it was true. She even

felt that she had known it all along.

"Now listen, Kay. I don't bring charges like that unless I can prove them. If they hurt you I'm sorry. I'm more than that, as you know very well. But they're true. McNair's half a savage. Even the other men here have to handle him with gloves. He's violent; he fights and drinks. He doesn't just drink; he gets down into the gutter. And he's a bad man with women. Oh, I know he can ride; I know he's the type to appeal to a girl. But—for God's sake don't get interested in him, Kay. Either he would shame you to death, or he'd crush you and throw you away."

Kay did not move. She felt nothing save a curious numbness, and much of Herbert's last speech she hardly heard at all. It was enough, at last. She was through. While she sat and waited for him he was in the gutter. It had killed her madness; she was cured.

"I see," she said, very quietly. "Only don't be unduly agitated." She smiled at him. "He is nothing in the world to me. Let him go and wallow if he likes."

"Good girl," said Herbert, relieved beyond measure. He was happier than he had been for days. He knew Kay, knew every tone and inflection of her voice, knew her honesty of speech and action.

Suddenly she got up.

"Let's take a walk. I've been sitting around all day."

They wandered down the road together, amiably and cheerfully. Now and then Kay hummed a snatch of song, and although her hands were icy cold she felt quite wonderful. Except once when she saw a white flower gleaming in the dusk and stooped to gather it; then she felt slightly dizzy.

"I've been rather hateful lately, Herbert. I'm sorry."

A truce and a new peace. How faint the stars were in the evening sky, and how still the mountains! Still and peaceful, as if they were asleep. Or dead. Perhaps they were dead. It was only in the storms of winter that they lived. Then they shot down their avalanches, froze, crushed, killed.

Curious, the very world seemed dead. No color, no movement. She and Herbert were two spirits walking in eternal shade. She felt nothing, because she was a spirit—or no; her body was walking there right enough. It was her spirit which was dead.

Herbert reached out and took her cold hand.

"Lord, it's a relief to be friends again," he said huskily.

She let him hold it, and hand in hand like two children wandering in the dark they moved on under the trees.

There was a light behind them, and Jake's car came along the road. They stepped aside to let it pass, and Jake's voice called "Good evening." It was moving on; it was going. Suddenly Kay fiercely released her hand and ran after it.

"Mr. Mallory!" she called. "Jake! *Jake!*"

He heard her and stopped the car, and she caught up with it, breathless.

"Are you going to town?"

"That's what I reckoned to do."

"I'm going with you."

She jerked at the door and Jake opened it, too astonished for speech. She crawled in and slammed it shut. "All right. Go on."

"What about Mr. Forrest?"

"He's not coming. Go on, *please.*"

With a deliberation that drove her frantic Jake let in the clutch and the car moved on. None too soon. She could hear Herbert close behind it as it got under way.

She chattered feverishly at first as they went along, but Jake, uneasy and suspicious of he knew not what, had relapsed into taciturnity.

"I don't know what your folks'll say about this, Miss Kay," he said once.

"Herbert will tell them. It's all right."

And again: "You'd ought to have brought a coat or something. This night air gets mighty chilly."

"I'm not cold at all."

They went on in silence. Once they passed a round-up outfit camped beside the road. It was on its way to the Reservation, and in the moonlight she could see the horses of the remuda peacefully grazing behind wire. The cook tent was lighted, and from inside she could hear men's voices and laughter.

"Potter's," Jake said briefly. "They're shipping eight thousand head this fall."

If there was any bitterness in his tone she did not notice. Potter was going to buy the ranch. He was still holding out, but Jake knew it would come. He would buy the ranch and turn in black-faced sheep on the upper pastures and plant wheat lower down; and Hank Tulloss in town would finance the deal, or maybe take a part of it himself. He knew what the L. D. could be, did Tulloss. He never put a dollar into anything unless he saw two coming out.

He was very taciturn after that. Suddenly they rose to the top of a hill, and the town lay before them. A locomotive whistled down at the track, a disreputable white poodle dog dashed across the road in front of them.

"Old Dunham'd better keep that pup of his at home!"

Paved streets, neat houses under trees with bits of lawn in front, the high school, the Court House. And by the Court House under a lamp post a tall familiar figure with a girl. The girl had her hand on the man's arm, was looking up, talking urgently. Jake brought the car to a grating stop.

"That you, Tom?"

"Yeah. Who is it?"

"Mallory. You coming out tonight?"

"I'm starting soon as I get my horse."

Tom was peering into the darkness. Kay shrank back.

"That Nellie you've got there?"

"Yes," said Jake, and got under way again.

Jake only spoke once on the way to the side-track and the car.

"You all right still?"

"I'm cold," she said. "I guess you were right after all. Everybody was right!" But that was silly; she was talking nonsense. "I'll get a wrap from the car," she said.

Her teeth were chattering again.

Once in the Mariposa she pulled herself together. William, cheerful and garrulous after his long vigil on the side-track, the lights, her grandfather's stateroom, now her own, all of them helped to restore her to a semblance of normality. That strange madness of hers, which had grown through the day to that crazy impulse to run after the car, was gone.

She moved about, fingering this and that, while the cook made her coffee and Jake saw the station agent with his orders.

By half past nine Jake was back again, and with a wrap about her they started back. A half mile or so outside the town they overtook a horse and rider moving slowly, the man with bent head and drooping shoulders. Jake peered out, seemed satisfied and went on. Perhaps to the relief of both, when they swung into the lane from the state road the ranch buildings were dark. When Jake had stopped the engine and helped her out he held to her arm and detained her.

"You'll have to square me with your father for this, Miss Kay."

"Of course. But he mayn't know anything about it. Good night, Jake."

He watched her out of sight before he closed the doors of the old wagon shed which was now the garage. He was puzzled and uneasy; maybe it was a good thing after all; at least she knew now about Clare Hamel. But if she was as crazy about him as all that—

He grunted and made his way past the dairy to his own cottage. The milk cows were resting in their yard outside, and a calf, escaped from the enclosure, ran toward him, hesitated and then loped away. Tired as he was he opened the gate and drove the awkward thing back to its mother. "Go on in there, little feller." The calf shot by him, tail high in the air. He opened the door of his cottage—no doors were ever locked on the ranch—and found his wife still awake, in the double white iron bed with its sagging springs.

"What about Tom, Jake? Did you see him?"

"Yeah. He's on his way out now."

"Are you taking him back?"

"I'll make a few conditions," he told her grimly, and began removing his clothes. "He was with that Hamel girl."

"She'd better let him alone." She lowered her voice. "I kinda wish you'd let him go, Jake." She made a cautious gesture toward the next room, where Nellie lay asleep. "I don't know why girls are so crazy about him. He'd make any girl he married miserable."

Jake glanced uneasily toward the room she had indicated. "What's wrong now?" he said, cautiously.

"I don't know. She's been crying today. Says it's a toothache, but I don't believe it."

Sitting up in her bed, her muslin nightgown buttoned to the throat, she gazed at him anxiously.

"He's a good hand," Jake said, after a pause.

And she's a good girl," she flashed back at him. Then she lay down again and turned on her side. Jake, blowing out the lamp and crawling in beside her, felt that she was crying and put his arm over her.

Chapter Seven

Kay closed her door, and standing in the darkness of her room the iron repression of the evening, before William in the Mariposa, before Jake, suddenly gave way. She was suffering. She was suffering horribly. Tom could tell her what he had told her, imply what he had implied, and then go off and hunt out some girl of the town, some—

Her cheeks burned with the cheapness of it. He had cheapened her. He had turned the situation between them into a tawdry thing. Maybe he had laughed about her with that girl.

"I've got a girl out at the ranch. Some girl, too. You'd better watch your step."

But by the time she had taken off her light frock and put on her night dress and a dressing gown, she was already making excuses for him. They had hurt him unbearably, and he had drifted back to an old weakness to forget it. They were to blame, largely. And how did they know he had been drinking? Just because he had done it before they were ready to think it of him now. He had not looked as though he had been drinking. And he had never had a chance, with that father who was always ready to move somewhere, provided it was West.

"Used to move so much, every time the chickens saw the

team put in the wagon, they'd lie down on their backs and hold their legs up to be tied!"

It wasn't true. Even now he was plodding back through the night to the same thing again, if not here somewhere else. Hard work and small pay, hardships and dangers; for interest the care of another man's great herds of cows and horses, for relaxation the rough play of the bunk house, an occasional crap game, and for pleasure, what? The town and what little it could offer.

Who could blame him, if after weeks, maybe months of all this, he broke over? How many men she knew did not drink, even on occasion drink too much? She thought back resentfully to her life at home. There was the night of her coming-out ball, when Hilary Randall had drunk too much champagne punch and had had to be put to bed in the house.

Nobody had made a fuss about that. She had been supposed not to know, but she had known. And Hilary himself had seemed later to think it rather a joke.

After a long time she lighted a match and looked at the small diamond studded watch on her dresser. It was two o'clock. He must be very close. And soon after that she heard him coming in. She had made no plan, got nowhere, but the thought that the slow beat of the Miller's hoofs might be taking him out of her life was too much for her. Clad as she was she went down the stairs, opened the front door and ran toward the barn. She could hear him working there, unsaddling, turning the tired horse out into the night corral. As she got closer she could see him, saddle and bridle in his arms, staring in her direction.

"Tom!"

"Yes?" He dropped the saddle and came toward her. "What are you doing out here at this time of night?"

"I heard your horse, and I—"

"What's that got to do with it? Look here, girl, you go back to bed and quit worrying about me. I'm not worth it."

"I have worried, awfully."

"I'm not worth it. I'm telling you."

"But if I don't think that, Tom?"

He hesitated, glancing toward the house. "Maybe we'd better talk this out," he said. "But not here. Too many open windows, and I don't want to make any more trouble for you. I guess I've done my bit!"

Even then, however, he hesitated as he looked about him. If he soiled everything he touched, as they seemed to think out here, he was not going to soil this girl. There was to be no chance of any misconception of this meeting, if it chanced to be seen in the starlight.

"You might as well beat a drum as wear that white thing," he said uneasily. "But we'll stay in sight, anyhow. Over there by the fence, how's that?"

She agreed quietly. After the storm of the last few days, to have him near her, sober and quiet, was utter peace. And as he led the way, carrying the saddle for her to sit on, she felt that there was power and strength in him. Not only physical strength; a sort of courage. Like her grandfather; perhaps like all strong men, he had the courage of his sins. And his first words bore this out.

"You'd better get the straight of this, Kay. I've been drinking, and that's putting it mild. I expect you know it. Percy would sure have the little rope all ready, the minute I stumbled."

"I do know it, Tom."

"Then what are you out here for? That ought to be enough to spoil any—friendly feeling you had for me."

"I don't like it. But I've thought maybe we were to blame. I was to blame."

"Forget that! I've done it before. And the way things are I reckon I'm likely to do it again."

"What do you mean by the way things are, Tom?"

He looked away from her. He was trying to play the game, but she was making it hard for him.

"Between you and me." And after a pause, when she said

nothing: "Where are we going from here, you and me? Well, I'll tell you. You're going back East, home, and in about a month or two you'll be saying: 'Oh yes, that cow-puncher out at the ranch! What was his name now? Let's see—McNair. That was it. Tom McNair.'"

"You don't really think that, do you?" she said, her throat tight. "You know better than that, Tom."

"Maybe not in a month. I'll give you two, or three." And then in a burst of passion: "For God's sake, girl, let me alone! I'm trying to play this game square. I've done some thinking tonight on the way out, and that's the only way I can play it. You go away and forget me. That's the best advice I can give you."

"And you? What advice are you giving yourself?"

"The best thing that can happen to me is to break my neck and be done with it."

"It would break my heart, too."

She was mad surely. She was telling him she loved him, in so many words. She got up dizzily and put out both hands to hold him off.

"I shouldn't have said that. I'm going back now. Please stay here. Oh, please don't touch me. I must be crazy."

But it was too late. His arms were around her.

"Then we're both crazy," he said. "Ever since I first saw you I've been fighting against it, Kay. I'm mad about you. There's never been anybody else, not like this."

But the next moment reason, lost to her, reasserted itself in him. Without kissing her he let her go, and stood back.

"Now you go back to the house," he told her. "I'm not trusting myself too far. Nor you either."

"If you care, that's all I want."

"Care! If you think about it, you'll know. And you'll know you're all I've got, in heaven and earth. And I won't have that very long. Now go back to the house."

"You can have me always, if you want me."

"You don't know what you're saying," he said, roughly.

"Go on back when I tell you. I'll wait until you're in the house."

There was nothing left for her to do. The finality of his tone forbade her reopening the question between them. She started across the lawn, and half way over she turned and looked back. He was where she had left him, rigid and watchful. She went drearily back to the house and crawled into her bed. Toward morning, her slim bare arms relaxed on the counterpane, she even slept a little, but when she wakened it was to find that Tom had gone into the mountains, and would not be back until the round-up was over.

She was completely crushed.

"Kay, do you remember where you left your rain coat?"

"At the barn, mother."

"Run and get it, so Nora can pack it."

George Potter and the banker came out at noon. They lunched and then retired to the office and closed the door. After a time Herbert came out and got Jake Mallory, and Jake went in and the door was closed again. When Jake came out his face looked tired and old; he stood on the verandah steps and looked all around, at the mountains and the yellowing cottonwoods, at the long row of shelter yards beyond the barn, and the creek which had "the best water in the state, sir."

Kay was there too, looking out, but he did not see her.

She met the next day with courage, carried off the goodbyes with an air, was neither more talkative nor less than usual on the way into town. But never once did she lift her eyes to the mountains. She sat as she had sat on that journey out weeks before, in the front seat of the car. But now there was no lighted window ahead, no feeling of coming home. Only the Mariposa on a sidetrack, and William in a fresh white coat and a broad cheerful grin.

"Shuah am glad to see you fohks again," he said. "The old Mariposa, she's got stiff from sittin' so long."

Then her little room again, with its broad bed, and Nora laying out the things from her dressing case, the little gold brushes, the jars, the mirror, the boxes for this and that.

"I'll leave your perfume in the bag, Miss Kay. It might spill if I put it out."

"Thanks, Nora."

All set now, her hat covered, her traveling coat protected with a sheet, the far-away whistle of twenty-two, which was to pick up the car; Jake on the platform, Stetson in hand, anxiously receiving some last instructions from her father; her mother's low-pitched voice, speaking to Joe, the cook.

A little crowd outside, staring at this magnificence.

"Do they eat in there too? Or do they use the diner?"

And on the fringe of the group, standing by herself, a girl in a small pull-on hat and a very short skirt, surveying the preparations for departure with a peculiar intensity. Kay knew her. It was the girl Tom had been with under the lamp post. That was the last thing she was to see as the car moved out, the picture she was to carry with her over all the long miles of that journey East. Clare, on the station platform, waiting for her to go.

Chapter Eight

Tom had ridden out ahead of the outfit at his own request. He had slept very little, and the call to roll out at dawn the next morning found him with his decision made. While the majority of the L. D. cattle grazed in summer around or near the salt licks in the mountains, a wild bunch of almost a hundred had drifted over toward Elk Butte, and Tom's proposition to Jake that early morning was that he go and get them.

"By yourself?"

"I figured on going alone."

"You won't get much sleep."

"I wasn't figuring to sleep," said Tom simply, and waited.

Jake agreed. He felt that it was to be his last round-up for the L. D., and he was late as it was. It would be two more days before the wagons and the outfit could start, and at any time now the weather would break again and the winter come to stay. Already the slopes of the foothills were painted with mahogany splotches where the choke-cherry bushes had turned, and the ducks were coming in from the North, looking for their old halting places of reservoir and pool. And although the sun was shining that morning, low-lying white clouds, like banks of thick fog, filled the mountain cañons and hid the summits of the peaks. The early autumn of the high country was close at hand.

"All right," he said. "I suppose you know the family's going?"

"I guess I can bear up under it."

The swagger in his walk as he left was for Jake's benefit, and so Jake understood it. So also was the noisy cheerfulness with which he roped out and packed a buckskin horse and saddled the Miller.

"What you takin' a gun for, Tom? Lookin' for Little Dog?"

"Got to be careful, Tom. That Indian'll get you yet, if you don't watch out."

"Give him time!" he said, tightening his ropes. "He's buying more arnica than ammunition right now. I saw some wolf tracks last time I was up."

But Jake, watching him as he rode out, saw the smile fade and felt vaguely anxious. He had his own troubles, however. He busied himself half-heartedly that morning, ate very little at noon, and by three o'clock knew that the ranch had definitely changed hands. He left the main house and went down by the creek for a time, that creek that he and old Lucius had always meant to dam back in the mountains and use for power as well as irrigation, and then he went to his cottage. His wife was baking bread, but she knew before he spoke.

"Well, it's gone," he told her heavily. "Lock, stock and barrel to the Potters. They'll be turning in their sheep in a week or so. Sheep!"

She went on with her bread-making, but after a time she looked up.

"We'll have to be taking Nellie out of school."

"We might keep her there this winter."

"And leave me alone in the cabin?" she said. "Without a house nearer than ten miles? I'd lose my mind."

"The cabin" was on Jake's homestead, in the land which Herbert considered God had forgot.

"I don't know what else to do, mother."

She put her bread in the oven, and after he had gone she moved slowly around the cottage which had been her home for twenty years. It was a good house, like everything old Lucius built. It was warm in winter and cool in summer. And she had lived like a lady here. The women from the church in town drove out and called on her; she had standing. When she knew they were coming she baked enormous cakes and froze ice-cream for them, and they sat around the front room with stiffly laundered napkins over their best dresses, and held plates from which they ate decorously.

"Do have some more, Mrs. Billings. We haven't made a dent in that freezer yet."

All over. All gone. Only that cabin down south of the river, with the water to be carried from the well behind the corral, and winter coming on and no wood laid in. It was hardly weather-proof, that cabin. She couldn't take Nellie there. She wouldn't. Nellie was young; she had a right to live, and to live like a lady.

Suddenly she smelled her bread burning. When she threw open the oven door she could hardly see it for tears.

It was a melancholy day. Tom, climbing through the cloud banks, which were cold and saturated with moisture, was filled with anger and savage resentment. Heretofore he had taken what he wanted from life and had been answerable to nobody. Girls had come and gone; he had made his violent brief love to them, had taken them when he could, and then promptly forgotten them. "God's gift to women," they called him at the ranch. He had eaten when he was hungry, drunk whisky when he could get it, and because he asked nothing more of life, except a good top horse to his string, he had been satisfied.

And now had come this girl. She had attracted him first because she was different and unattainable. He had liked her small white hands, the tilt of her head, even the way she rode. But at first he had been wary. She was a Dowling, and what were the Dowlings to him? Perhaps had it not been for Herbert he would have let her alone entirely. But there was Herbert, obviously infatuated and jealous. And so he had played the game like the fool he was, at first for the fun of it and now—

Perhaps it was defeat more than anything else which sent him scowling on his way that day. Defeat and resentment that he had let himself be caught, and that now he was suffering like a trapped animal.

He looked back only once. Just before he entered the cloud bank he reined in the Miller and throwing a leg over his neck, turned and looked back. Spread out beneath him was the ranch, its white buildings gleaming in the early morning sun. Tiny dot-like figures moved here and there, but too far away for identification.

He sat there for a long time, while the buckskin grazed along the side of the trail and the Miller drowsed on his feet.

Then he turned and went on. The trail wound along, steadily climbing. Now it lay through some upland valley; again it hugged the bare face of a cliff, and at such times the buckskin went warily, for fear the pack would strike the granite wall and overthrow it. He had taken a short cut, not the broader and easier cattle route, and by noon he was high in the range. For the lunch hour he unsaddled, hobbling the pack horse but turning the Miller loose, and himself lying flat on the earth, his face turned up to the sky.

What did life hold for him anyhow? He was twenty-eight, and he was still a cow-hand. That was all he knew.

A bit of schooling, riding or walking miles through the snow to a small frame school house; snowed in on the range, with the cattle drifting before blizzards and freezing to death overnight, a trip once to Omaha with a load of cattle; some exhibition riding and first or second money, with luck—that had been his life so far.

And even that could not go on indefinitely. There was an age limit to his work. There came a time when a man could no longer ride in the teeth of the northwestern blizzards, his saddle blanket and latigo frozen stiff and icicles hanging from the horse's bridle. Or drift to some new "stamping ground" in Arizona or New Mexico, exchanging the icy North for the deserts and heat and cactus of the South.

Then what?

At one o'clock he grunted—he was still stiff from the riding at the Fair and the fight with Little Dog—and with a set face he started off again. He was putting as many miles as possible between Kay and himself.

But he was a cow-man as well as a lover. As he rode his quick eye automatically searched groves of evergreen trees. No coulée with brush, no grove offering shelter, or a hiding place, escaped attention. And he watched for signs of wolf and coyote as he moved along. Once he saw a herd of elk disappear over a rise, and made a mental note of the spot. There was to be a three-day open season on elk that fall.

He was rather more cheerful after that.

He missed nothing. The great blocks of salt, packed up so laboriously, had been licked almost to nothing. The streams were very low, pending another winter's snows, and where a pool still lay the mud showed innumerable hoof-prints. Once he saw the ominous dog-like tracks of a wolf.

After that he rode with his rifle across his knees, but he saw no wolf. Toward night the Miller began to show signs of fatigue; he moved along with the racking gait of a weary horse, and Tom had not the heart to spur him.

"Get along, horse," he said now and then. "Get along, can't you?"

At last he camped by a spring, set up a tarp as a protection against the cold night wind from the snow mountains just beyond, and having made a meal of sorts, crawled into his bed and slept. He had accomplished his purpose; no weakening on his part, no turning back, could get him to the ranch before Kay had gone.

He found his cattle late the next day, and began his round-up the following morning.

By noon he had them more or less in hand, and he commenced his single-handed drive. Once bunched they were tractable enough, but they moved with incredible slowness, and to his still sore and always impatient spirit the afternoon was endless. But now and then some recalcitrant would leave the herd, circle about and head for the back trail again; he would ride madly, head it off and return, to find that the herd had lost its compactness and must be once more assembled.

Then again the slow advance, calves wailing and mothers calling, young steers stopping now and then to lower their heads and confront each other, invitations to battles which never took place.

That night he held them in a box cañon, having first watered them at the stream below. The cattle were uneasy, suspicious of the towering cliffs above, and they were restless most of the night. He did not unsaddle, but stretched himself out near the mouth of the gorge, between two fires. He slept little, however.

At three o'clock in the morning he sat up suddenly, with an instinctive sense of something wrong. The herd had suddenly stopped grazing and was listening. The next moment he heard them stampede toward him, and he had no more than time to throw himself into the saddle when they were abreast of him.

Shouting and cursing, he tried to hold them in the bottle neck of the cañon, but they passed him, running like crazy things, into the open. Fortunately, once out in the broad valley, they quieted, stopped running and shortly fell to grazing again. But he could not trust them. He rode herd over them until daylight, alternately singing and whistling to quiet them, and without even the comfort of a cigarette, lest the lighted match start them off again. He did not relax his vigilance until at dawn they began quietly to graze. And at dawn he rode into the cañon to find what had caused the trouble.

He found the stripped carcass of a cow in the upper valley, and by the way the meat was cut from the bones he knew that Indians had been at work. Probably a hunting party which was looking for deer out of season, and failing had killed beef, after their easy fashion. Such thieving was common enough, and angry as he was he would probably have accepted the situation and gone on, had not a movement along the side of the cañon, a fluttering of the scrub which grew out of its steep sides, caught his eye.

Sitting on his horse, the cattle quietly grazing outside, he watched it. It was something in motion, something slowly climbing to the top. But it was so skillful, took such advantage of projecting rocks and scrub, that it was not until it reached the top and stood outlined against the sky that he knew it for what it was, the thief himself, carrying his booty in a sack.

In a frenzy of anger he reached down under his stirrup and jerked out his rifle, and hardly sighting the gun, fired it. It was an impulsive action, and ineffectual as well. The figure stood for a moment surveying him, then it made a gesture of derision and moved out of sight.

Two hours later he was ambushed.

He had been keeping to the center of the valley, but now it narrowed, and down timber from a forest fire made the going slow and extremely painful. And from somewhere on the rocky hillside above a rifle shot suddenly rang out. There was a second shot before he could lift his rifle, but both missed. He fired back as soon as he could, having taken what shelter he could find, but the attack was not repeated, and since to ride up the slope alone was suicidal, when nothing more happened he went on.

On Saturday he found the result of the first day's round-up bunched, as Jake had told him, on the hill above Timber Creek. He was dirty and unshaven, and his eyes were sunken with fatigue. He handed his cattle over to the men riding herd, rode to the camp and unsaddled the Miller, and then, whistling and slightly swaggering, wandered into the cook tent, where Slim was paring potatoes.

"Open a can of beans for me, Slim, will you?" he said. "Seems like I haven't had a meal for a week."

"You look it. What in hell made you tackle that job single-handed?"

"Maybe I wanted to show I could do it," he drawled lazily.

When Slim had filled a plate with hot beans and a tin cup with coffee, he found him sound asleep under a tree.

It was not until the round-up was on its fourth day that there came the repercussion from that unlucky shot of Tom's.

The men were working hard.

At three-thirty in the morning they rolled out and ate breakfast morosely, by the light of a lantern hung over the stove in the mess tent; at four or a little after they were in the saddle.

All morning until dinner at 10:30, and all the afternoon, they rode, throwing off the cattle, bunching them, and by mid-afternoon driving in these fresh accretions to the rapidly growing herd. When the day's work was done and the men lay in their beds, their faces to the sky, the night guards held the cattle through the long and nervous nights, making no unexpected movements, even riding far out to light their cigarettes. Each two hour period saw these guards changed. Quietly two fresh men rode out, exchanged a few words and took their places, and so until the day herders relieved them.

Tom was not popular with the outfit during those laborious days and nights. He worked like ten men, but he was brooding and morose. They watched him surreptitiously, handled him with more than their usual care.

"Just spoilin' for trouble, Tom is."

"Well, let them as wants it have it.

And, almost at the end of the round-up, trouble came.

Supper was over and the tired men lay about, rolling

cigarettes and talking. Tom as usual lately was off by himself, his hat pulled down over his eyes, his handsome hawk-like face brooding and unaimiable. Slim was washing dishes, when he looked up and said:

"Company coming, Jake."

Jake raised himself on his elbow, but he could see nothing.

"Who is it?"

"Looks like a couple o' Indians.

"Ridin' the grub line, likely," said Jake, and lay back again. But when the Indians rode into camp on their painted horses, it was evident that food was not their object. One was a Reservation policeman, in a dirty khaki uniform with a revolver in his belt; the other was a squaw. She rode cross-saddle, her calico skirts picked up, and her heavy figure sagging as she sat.

That there was trouble brewing was evident, and the men got up and waited. The policeman dismounted. The woman remained as she was. Jake went forward for the parley.

"You boss this outfit?"

"I am."

"This woman, she say one of your men he shoot her husband."

"That's nonsense. We haven't been near the Reservation. What do you mean, shoot her husband? Is he dead?"

"Not dead. Very sick man."

"Any of you fellows know what they're talking about?"

But apparently nobody did. The story was circumstantial enough. The wounded Indian claimed that he had been returning from across the range with a sack of potatoes which had been given him, and that his horse had got away from him; he had shouldered his sack and was on his way back when he had been shot.

"Sure there was potatoes in that sack?" Jake asked suspiciously.

The squaw, following a word from the policeman, nodded vigorously.

"Just where was all this?"

It was when he heard where it had happened that Jake turned and called to Tom McNair, haughtily aloof under his tree. And Tom sauntered over.

"Know anything about this, Tom?"

"About what?"

"An Indian shot over on the East fork."

"If it's the Indian who killed a cow up there maybe I do. He tried to kill me too."

Jake's frown deepened.

"You God damned fool!" he said. "You *got* the fellow."

"Then there's one bad Indian the less," he retorted. "He'd a sack of meat over his shoulder when I saw him."

"He claims it was potatoes."

"Then he's not dead! That's bad news."

He faced the stolid policeman and the almost equally stolid squaw.

"Now get this," he said. "Go back to the Agency and tell the Superintendent that I caught Weasel Tail killing beef and I fired and missed him. And tell him that later on he did his damnedest to kill me, and I fired back. If he got his he had it coming, and more too. And now get out. Vamoose. Good night."

But the policeman did not go at once. He took Tom's name, writing it slowly and carefully in a note book while the squaw watched phlegmatically, and then without further words mounted and rode away, letting the woman follow as she would.

The outfit watched them off. At the top of the rise, with the policeman out of sight, she stopped and looked back at them. Then she made an obscene gesture, grinned, and went on.

Late that night Tom saddled a fresh horse and rode to the cañon, but he found things as he had suspected. The carcass of the dead cow had disappeared; not as much as a horn remained to prove his story. He got back in time for the before-dawn breakfast, and worked all day as usual, having been in the saddle for thirty-six practically continuous hours.

It was on the next night that the outfit realized that the Indian woman's obscene gesture had had a special significance. They had moved to a new location and the herd, nervous on the strange bed ground anyhow, was stampeded just before dawn by a half dozen shouting demons on horseback who rushed at it in the darkness, yelling. The cattle scattered wildly in every direction, and dawn revealed the almost complete destruction of the results of their incessant care and labor.

When they were finally ready for the drive down to the railroad the weather had definitely changed; behind the slow-moving herd the men rode chilled to the bone. Now and then a wet snow would fall, and in the early mornings the socks they had taken off to dry would be frozen stiff. The very ropes on the saddles were too rigid for easy handling, and the horses were irritable when the icy saddle blankets were thrown over their backs. Now and then they bucked in the gray dawn, and cries of "Ride him, cowboy!" or "Stay a long time, Gus!" would ring out on the frosty air.

Physically comfortable and weary, and mentally despondent and discouraged, Tom carried on as best he could. This was his life; it always would be his life, until he was too old to live. Spooky horses and spookier cattle, the wagon boss grumbling; the wheels sinking into the mud to their hubs and having to be lifted out; cutting grounds, bed grounds, horns and swaying backs; heat of desert summers and blizzards of northern winters, his body either baked or frozen but never at ease for long—that was his existence.

But there were times too, as he drifted the cattle along—Jake was already at the railroad, and Tom was in charge of the beef herd—when he felt the born cow-man's pride in achievement. The big steers were coming through in good shape; they were losing no weight, even possibly were gaining. He drew himself up at those times; he was proud of the cattle, of the great back country which had reared them, even of his own strong and active body.

Then he would remember Kay, and his pride was gone. He would look at the other men, unshaven, dirty, cold and weary, and knew that he too looked like that.

"You can have me always, if you want me!"

That was a joke. A fellow ought to laugh at a joke like that.

He had erased the wounded Indian from his mind entirely.

Chapter Nine

Kay never remembered much of that journey East. One day she was leaving Tom behind forever, and some time after that, ages and ages, they were at home again. There were all the familiar incidents of such returns; the car meeting them in town and taking them out to the country. Hawkins touching his cap:

"Glad to see you back, sir."

"Very glad to be back, Hawkins."

Hawkins's hair newly cut, since Mrs. Dowling, having to look mostly at the back of his neck, was particular about this; Hawkins tucking in the rug.

"Directly home, sir?"

"Yes."

Moving along, the streets smooth, the engine gayly purring. Leaning back against soft upholstery, dropping Herbert at his apartment, Nora stiff and silent out in front beside Hawkins and discouraging conversation. It was not good form to have conversation on in the front seat. The country and the Club, set in its green links; still green, not burnt and parched like the plains. Big estates; gates of iron and smooth drives, and beyond them the houses, luxurious houses surrounded by trees and flowers. Turning in at their own gate, with its tidy lodge, and James at the door and

Rutherford in the doorway, very elegant, very English.

"Welcome home, sir. Welcome home, madam."

Inside the house now. The mingled odors of soap, furniture polish and fresh flowers. The parlor maid in the background, a study in black and white.

"Well, Hannah? Is everything all right?"

"Very nice, madam. Thank you."

Nora nervously counting the bags once more, and James and Hawkins carrying them up.

"Will you have tea now, madam, or later?"

"Now, I think, Rutherford."

Carrying accumulated mail and cards from the hall into the drawing room, with its tapestries and paintings, its old Italian chairs, and through it to the small tile-floored morning room beyond.

No use going up yet, until Nora gets the dressing cases unpacked. Mercy, I feel untidy!"

Tea, scalding hot, and her father's table laid out with whisky and soda.

"The Marshall Merediths are having a garden party."

"When mother?"

"On the nineteenth. Their dahlias ought to be very nice now."

James passing little cakes with cream inside, her favorite cakes, and Rutherford gravely watching. James really was funny in his livery, with the buttons down the long tails. Did he sit on them, ever? And how they must scratch the chairs! She must look at the chairs in the servants' dining room sometime.

"I don't see why people want to give dinner parties at this time of year."

"Gertrude Hazlett is having a dance at the country club tomorrow, mother."

Anything, everything. Only don't think.

Mr. Dowling had settled down in his deep chair, the tray with decanter and siphon at his elbow. He was glad to be at home again. He never entered either of his houses without a deep sense of satisfaction. After all, although his father had left him a great deal, he had not been content to live without effort. He had added to what he inherited. And this house was his, his and Katherine's. It represented their common tastes; together they had traveled and collected.

He could look around and remember where and how each piece was secured. The old glass decanter beside him, for instance—

Katherine was going upstairs. She gathered up her gloves, her bag and the litter of cards, notes and invitations from her lap and rose.

"Glad to be back, aren't you?" Henry asked.

She hesitated, glanced at Kay. The sense of home and of security, for her and hers, was suddenly strong in her. He had been a good husband, had Henry; safe and sound. Not a figure of romance, certainly, like that cowboy of the ranch, but he had never given her any trouble. She moved toward him, shyly, like a girl.

"Yes," she said, and would have stooped down and kissed him. But he reached for the siphon at that moment, and she turned and went out of the room.

After a minute or two Kay followed her and went up to her bedroom. It had been her bedroom in the summer ever since she could remember, and the day nursery was just beyond it. Now however the day nursery was her boudoir, a gay little room with a small balcony. There used to be an extra rail on the balcony, because Mademoiselle was afraid she would climb the railing and fall.

Now Nora and a housemaid were there, and Nora was in a sad way.

"They've broke your mirror, Miss Kay," she wailed. "I told them not to put that dressing case under anything."

"Don't mind about that. We can have a new glass put in."

"But it's seven years' bad luck!"

Seven years! But what did it matter? Who could think

ahead seven dreary empty years? They spread out before her, those years, filled with unimportant things. The telephone ringing, and some young voice at the other end:

"Hello, Kay! What's on for today?"

"Nothing much. I thought I'd ride this afternoon."

"How about some tennis? I'll get some extras in to tea."

"All right. Count me in."

Summer parties, centering around the club, winter parties, centering around the débutantes. Fluffy little girls, looking wide-eyed and more innocent than they were, standing before banks of flowers beside mothers elaborately coiffed and gowned.

"Well, well, Anne! And so you're out at last!" And Anne restraining an inclination to drop a curtsy, and offering instead a limp and a nervous hand.

She opened the door and stepping out onto her balcony, with its striped chairs and flower boxes, she faced the setting sun.

Somewhere out there the sun would be setting soon too. It would go down behind the mountains, leaving them first rose, then blue, and then gray. Like her life from now on.

But later on hope began to revive in her.

The dignified, almost ritualistic life of the household went on. In the morning her father's car came to the door, and he got in heavily and drove into the city. He kept almost as long hours as his clerks, but at four o'clock he went to his club, and there played bridge until six-thirty. Promptly at seven each day he came home, had a whisky and soda, and then went upstairs to dress for dinner. And at five minutes to eight he came heavily down the wide staircase, dinner suit, onyx studs and black tie carefully tied, and took the cocktail which James proffered him on an antique silver tray. Both tray and cocktail were, so to speak, hall-marked.

Sometimes they dined out. Then the only variation would be long tails instead of short, and pearl studs and white tie. And he would descend a few minutes earlier, and the car would be at the door. Or there was a dinner party. There would be a tray of tiny envelopes on the hall table, and after each gentleman had taken off his overcoat and top hat, he would take his envelope and look to see whom he was "taking in." And occasionally the information cheered him, but quite frequently it did not.

Sometimes some one fell out at the last moment, and Herbert filled in. Then he and Kay, as the only two young people, would be put together. They would make up talk.

"When are you going to open the town house?"

"Not while the weather is so good."

"You are looking very lovely tonight."

"Thanks. It's a new frock."

"I didn't mean the frock."

But that was as far as it went. She had a very definite idea that Herbert was marking time; that much as he worked out his days to a schedule, he was now patiently allotting time for her recovery. She even figured how he would do it. Two months to forget Tom McNair, two months for a restoration of his old relationship, and two months to courtship! That would take them—one, two, three, four, five, six—to the first of April.

"What on earth are you counting on your fingers?"

"I always count on my fingers. That's what they are for, isn't it?"

"They are for other things too," he said darkly, and glanced at her left hand. Maybe she had been wrong about the six months!

But she was marking time also. During those early days after her return she gained a little perspective on the situation, or thought she did. Thus she was convinced that Tom had been deliberately sent away, and that she would hear from him as soon as he could write. He could not ignore that last night together; he would not want to ignore it.

He loved her, and he knew she loved him; nothing but that mattered. Later on they could plan. Now all she wanted was to nurse the thought of his love and keep it warm, to lie awake in the darkness and recapture the ecstasy of that moment when he had held her in his arms. His strong arms. His brave, reckless arms.

She lived in a secret world of her own, and looked out from it at the environment she had never questioned before. Were they really satisfied, all these people who came and went, rustling in to tea and dinner, stepping out of their handsome motors, well dressed, well fed—too well fed—well mannered.

"I declare, Katherine, the ranch has made you over."

And her mother living her own secret life, as Kay had begun to suspect, smiling the correct smile, saying the correct thing.

"I'm so glad you could come. We have been away so long, and we have missed our friends."

"We, we." Kay had begun to notice that her mother seldom said "I."

It was such feeble living; men who had grown paunchy at desks and the tables of directors' meetings, women who welcomed even these familiar gatherings as breaks in the monotony of their luxurious days. Surely one *must* live, must do and be. No wonder old Lucius had revolted, had played as robustly as he had done everything else. And she remembered a story where a party of magnates, after a night of poker and certain accompaniments, had gone out to the swimming pool and jumped in, clothing and all. And one of them, who did not know how to swim, had forgotten he did not know and had almost drowned.

She was singularly detached those days. Never before had she questioned the life she lived, or Henry and Katherine's right to dictate to her. Now she did.

They still had, although she was of age, certain arbitrary powers over her which they would use unscrupulously; the power of affection, the power of money, the power of long habitual authority. And against them what had she? Aunt

Bessie, perhaps. She thought Bessie might understand, might even help her when the time came.

She was certain that some day, somehow, the time would come.

And then Bessie did come, and failed her absolutely.

She wandered in, said her maid was outside with her bags, that her house was too dirty to live in. She was staying until it was cleaned. Then she lighted a cigarette, sat down, and took off her hat.

"New hair cut!" she said. "Ears again. It's a frightful nuisance. One has to wash them and everything. Of course if they stick out it won't do." She eyed Kay with her head slightly on one side.

"What's the matter with you, child? You look washed-out. Didn't the ranch agree with you?"

"I'm all right. Maybe it's leaving the altitude. I don't sleep very well."

Bessie glanced at her, blew through her cigarette holder and getting up moved languidly toward the door.

"The usual place, I suppose, Katherine? I'm going to bathe and take a nap. Come in and see me after a while, Kay. I want to hear about things."

She wandered out, humming, and up the staircase, but in her own room, the door safely closed, she put down her cigarette holder and the hat she still carried, and stood thinking. Nothing had been lost on her downstairs, neither Kay's pallor nor the faint color which had followed her question. And the faint tightening of her sister-in-law's lips was a signal with which she was entirely familiar.

"They've been deviling her about something, or somebody," she considered. "The life's gone out of her. If it's that stick of a secretary—!" She considered that, discarded it. More likely it was somebody out West. "Somebody real and of course ineligible. They'd hate that like poison."

She slept until time to dress for dinner, and then swaggered downstairs in a dress with practically no back in it. But although she kept her eyes and her mind alert she got no clue that evening. Kay ate very little; Katherine talked politely, and Henry gave assiduous and critical attention to his food. She herself smoked after every course, and through the smoke haze that surrounded her watched them all in turn with bright and comprehending eyes.

Something was certainly wrong among them.

However, it was not until the third day of her stay that she learned anything, and then it required all of her philosophy to meet the situation.

In her casual way she drifted about the house. No door was safe against her unless it was locked; she had no reserves and very little sense of privacy. Indeed, once long ago her sister-in-law had been taken up to her dressing room, to find Bessie in a very sketchy négligée having her hair waved, and a young minor poet reading to her from a manuscript in his hand.

Mrs. Dowling had apologized and tried to back out again, but Bessie had seen her and called to her.

"Come in," she said. "Don't you want a wave while Pierre is here? He's about finished with me. Don't mind Jimmy here. Most of his poems are about ladies who don't wear anything at all."

Katherine had never told Henry that.

So now Bessie wandered about the house and grounds, talking to the servants, who adored her, singing her snatches of little French songs, smoking interminably, and even quietly interrogating Herbert when one evening he came to dine, and she got downstairs before the others.

"I don't think Kay is looking very well. Do you?"

"It's still warm."

"This isn't her first summer," she said, rather sharply. "She's thin, and I don't think she's very happy."

"I can't say as to that. She's rather quiet. But then she never is—boisterous."

"Now see here, Herbert," she said. "I've seen a lot of lives ruined by people keeping their mouths shut when they should have talked. I happen to be fond of Kay, and there's something wrong with her. She doesn't laugh and she doesn't eat. I don't think she's sleeping either. It isn't between you and her, is it?"

"Good Lord! No."

"Do you know what it is?"

And for a moment she thought he was going to tell her. Then he pulled himself up, all correct in his dinner jacket with his tie neatly tied, and remembered that there were some things one did not talk about.

"Really," he said, "I hardly feel that I can discuss Kay, even with you, Mrs. Osborne. Why don't you talk to her yourself?"

She turned away from him, exasperated.

Then, the next and last day of her visit, she walked into Kay's bedroom to find her face down on the bed, and a little, a very little snap-shot picture clutched in her hand. She had dropped asleep like that, and with no more compunction than she would have extracted a splinter, Bessie Osborne took the picture from her as she slept, and carried it to the window.

She was still gazing at it when Kay wakened and sat up. Bessie turned and looked at her.

"It won't do, darling," she said. "He's a handsome rascal, but it just won't do."

Kay slid off the bed and went over to her.

"Why won't it do? He's a man. A real man."

"He looks it, honey. But he won't do, just the same. What's his name?"

"McNair. Tom McNair."

"Very well, I'll take it for granted this Tom McNair is in love with you. I suppose he has told you so."

Kay nodded.

"And that this love is all you have in common. That's true, too, isn't it?"

"What have any other two people who love and marry?"

"Plenty," she said quickly. "Tastes. Habits. Ideas of life. You don't realize all that now, but you will later on. This—this early ecstasy we call love, it's only part of the whole business. And when it's gone—and it always goes, my dear—you have to have something else to fall back on. I suppose you met him out at the ranch?"

"Yes."

"What is he? Foreman? I thought Mallory—"

"He isn't anything. He just works there. I don't think he owns a thing in the world, unless it's his horse and saddle! Oh, don't tell me I'm crazy. I've gone through all that. And I've fought until I'm worn out. I can't fight it any more. It's just happened, that's all."

"Do they know, here?"

"More or less. They think I've given him up."

"But you haven't?"

"Not if he wants me. I ought to tell you this about him; I asked him to let me stay, and he sent me away."

If Bessie made any mental reservation about this heroic attitude of Tom's she concealed it.

"That was very noble of him," she said, and Kay accepted it literally.

But Bessie did not feel, as she went back to her room an hour or so later, that she had effected any real change in Kay's attitude. The mention of disinheritance she had put aside with a gesture. Talk of her father's and mother's sense of injury and deep resentment had brought tears to her eyes, but had not weakened her. Nor could she be induced to make a promise to do nothing rash without consulting Bessie herself.

"I might not keep it," she said honestly. "It's not stubbornness. I'm just afraid. I made a lot of promises to myself out there, but somehow—"

Late that night Henry Dowling, retired and reading the catalogue of a sale of old English furniture by way of soporific, was less surprised than he might have been when his sister came in and perched herself on the foot of the bed.

"What about the L. D., Henry?" she inquired, helping herself to one of his cigarettes. "Are we selling it, or giving it away?"

"There's no profit in the deal, if that's what you mean," he told her grimly.

"It's a relief, of course. Still, when you think of father, and all the lovely ladies—"

"Don't be vulgar, Bessie. And for God's sake don't be sentimental." He leaned back among his pillows and surveyed her critically. "What in the name of heaven made you do that to your hair?" he demanded.

"The search for youth. Lovely, romantic youth, Henry," she told him flippantly. "What you've forgotten you ever had, and never *will* understand."

She went to bed herself on that, leaving Henry to ponder over it. He knew she had meant something by it, possibly about Kay. Well, that was all over now. Well over.

He turned again to his book.

"Six Heppelwhite chairs in excellent condition. From the collection of—"

Chapter Ten

The shipping was going on.

The cars were on the sidetrack. In the caboose the conductor sat most of the day by the stove reading a newspaper and waiting for the coffee pot to boil. Slim had set up his tent a quarter of a mile up the line, and back behind the buttes the final cutting and working were taking place. The cattle huddled together, milled and roared, and into the mass of heaving backs and tossing horns the cow ponies made their way. Once they knew which animal was wanted nothing could stop them.

Off by themselves were the cuts, the two-year olds already sold and going to Omaha, the mature beef for Chicago, and the throw backs, that had drifted into the herd and had now to be separated again. The wind roared over the vast expanse of empty country, so suddenly awake and alive, cattle ran with horses and riders pursuing them, and down on the line the engine whistled shrilly.

Tom was in his element. Jake had gone in to Ursula, and he was again in charge. The infernal racket was music to his ears, the prosperous condition of the cattle soothed his sore spirit. After all, if this was his life, it was a good life. The weather, although still cold, was bright and clear; when he changed horses the Miller's great muscles under him responded with new vigor. Even the knowledge that it was his last round-up for the L. D. could not entirely depress him. He was young, young and strong and whole, and soon the cars would be loaded and he would be on his way to Chicago.

Chicago!

It was evening, and they were loading at the track, when Jake came back from Ursula and called him aside.

"I've got kinda bad news for you, Tom. Allison has a warrant out for you."

"What for?"

"That Indian business. Weasel Tail's still alive, but he's pretty bad."

"What the hell do they want *me* for?" Tom demanded, aggrieved. "The ornery devil tried to murder me!"

"I know that, but—"

"Besides which," said Tom, raising his voice, "he killed one good beef animal and got away with it. I went back and saw the carcass that morning. I'm telling you, Jake, if Allison thinks any jury in this country would convict me for what I did, he's welcome to try. But he's got to get me first."

He was furiously angry; his voice rose, his jaw was thrust forward. Jake took him by the arm and led him further from the pens.

"Look here, Tom," he said pacifically. "I'm kinda in a hole about this. If I let you out of the state now I'm in trouble. I was thinking—"

"Give me my ticket. The rest's up to me, isn't it?"

But Jake would not give him his ticket, and in a savage temper he turned and went back to the pens. That was the last Jake was to see of him for some time; the flickering flares, the timid milling of the cattle at the foot of the chute, the incredibly slow ascent, a pandemonium of noise and great terrified bodies, and Tom, sullen but efficient, prodding them and at intervals staring down the road.

When the Sheriff finally came he was not to be found.

Allison left his car in the road, and came heavily across to the pens. A big man, an ex-puncher of the old days who had come up from Texas with the early herds, Allison was popular with all the cowboys in his country. But he was not a soft man, and they knew it. They guessed his errand when they saw him, and after the manner of their kind, tacitly united against him. And because he knew them, he smiled grimly as he surveyed their expressionless faces.

"Tom McNair here?"

"No. What's Tom been doing?"

"I guess you know all right. Where is he, if he isn't here?"

"I ain't seen him since just about sundown," said Bill, glibly. "Any you fellows seen Tom?"

Nobody had. They stood around Allison, politely interested. Maybe he'd gone to town to see a girl.

"I thought he was in charge here?"

"Well, that wouldn't worry Tom none, if he wanted to see a girl."

Allison was suspicious, but he could do nothing. Tom knew every back trail of the neighborhood, every gate in the wire.

He refused Slim's offer of coffee and stood around for a few minutes with his coat collar turned up against the freezing night wind, then he turned and lunged back through the darkness to the road and his car, the warrant still in his pocket.

But as a matter of fact, he was very near success once on his way back to Ursula, had he only known it.

Tom had no idea of being cheated out of his trip. Long before the lights of Allison's car appeared down the road, he had made a plan and prepared for his escape. True, the horse he roped in the darkness turned out to be a green horse, but the Miller was weary and he needed speed. He managed to saddle it and tie it up, and to slip off into the night when Allison appeared was a simple matter.

But from that time on he was in difficulty. The horse was

kinky from the start; even holding him while opening gate in the wire was a test for Tom's long lean body, and every time he was mounted he threatened to break again. And seven miles out of Ursula Tom rode unseeing under a sagging telephone wire and was neatly pitched off backwards, with a cut across his forehead which blinded him with blood. When he picked himself up the animal was gone.

He swore furiously and tried to bind up his head. The blood froze almost as soon as it ran. But his anger only made him more determined, and in his high-heeled boots he set out to walk the seven miles remaining. That was when Allison almost had him. He passed within thirty feet of where Tom had dropped down into a swale when he saw the headlights.

But with the Sheriff out of the way, Tom's problem was only partially solved. Time was passing while he plodded through the mud, and he was exhausted not only from his fall, but from the hard work preceding it. His head needed attention, too.

He finally fixed on Clare. The Hamels had a car, and Clare could be trusted not to talk. He was more cheerful after he thought of that, even faintly amused. Clare would like it; she would like to think she was saving him. He grinned at the thought, and made better progress as he reached the better roads. Outside the Hamel house he reconnoitered. The houses all about were dark, and Clare's window was raised an inch or two. He put his face close to it and called her.

"Clare!"

He could hear her stirring.

"Clare. Come here. It's Tom."

She slid out of bed, trembling.

"What's the matter?"

"Get something on and come out to the shed. And don't wait to fix up. Be yourself!"

When she got out to the shed where the car was stabled, he had rolled a cigarette and was lighting it, and by the match flare she saw the blood on his face. He put a hand over her mouth before she could scream.

"Wire cut, that's all," he said. "You run in and get some warm water and adhesive, like a good girl, and then I'll talk to you."

But when, his wound cleaned and plastered, he told her what he wanted, he found her less amenable than he had expected.

"That's easy to say," she said. "What about me? They'll lock me up. And you know pop. He'd—"

"You can get back by daylight."

"With those roads? You know I can't. I'll be lucky to get back at all."

"What's all this fuss you've been making about me, if you won't take a chance?"

"Why should I take a chance? You threw me over for that Dowling girl. Do you know what they're saying here in town? They say you were crazy about her, and she just laughed at you."

"Oh, they do, do they?" He flung his cigarette away angrily. "Well, to hell with them. Will you do what I want, or won't you?"

"You couldn't take the car and leave it?"

"And have them telegraph ahead and grab me off the train?"

She was silent, and the next moment he picked up his hat and started out.

"Tom!"

"That's all right. I know when I'm up against it."

"Listen, Tom. You do like me a little, don't you?"

"That depends," he said guardedly.

"You know I care, Tom. I'm crazy about you."

"You act like it!"

"Listen, Tom. If I do it you'll owe me something. If I'm found out, the way this place talks—"

"Well?"

"I'm going to say we're engaged."

"So that's the little game, is it?"

"It isn't a game. You'd want to act square, wouldn't you? And that Dowling girl's gone; you'll never see her again." And when he still hesitated her voice rose shrewishly. "I'll be taking a chance, even at that. I'm not fooled about you. Not for a minute. You won't make any girl happy. You're too hard."

"Is that so!" he said. "Then what's all the fuss about?"

"You're the sort who will take all they can get, without paying for it," she told him bitterly. "I've heard that before about you, but I never believed it."

"I haven't run up any bill yet," he said stiffly. But nevertheless the drift of her argument was telling on him. After all, what difference did it make? Kay was gone; he would never see her again. What had he to look ahead to? Three or four more years of riding, and he would be through. A man couldn't ride forever; his joints got stiff. There came a day, if he kept on too long, when he couldn't get out of the way and the horse came down on him, and it was only the horse that got up again.

He was very weary, very cold. His head ached, the blood drummed in his ears.

"All right," he said. "Have it your own way. Now let's get out of here."

It was only later on in the little car, sliding along the greasy roads, that his conscience began to bother him. He took one hand from the wheel and put his arm around her, and she moved closer to him, relaxed and happy.

"I'm crazy about you, Tom."

And when she held up her face to be kissed, he stopped the car and took her into his arms with a gesture of pure passion.

Back at the siding the loading had ceased for the night. The new empties had not come up, and the men had laid their beds in the warm cook tent and were snoring heavily. From the loaded cars came occasional wails and the heavy ammoniacal odor of great bodies closely confined; and in the caboose the train crew slept on their leather couches, in the glow from a red-hot stove.

It was afternoon the next day before the last of the weary cattle had filed wearily into the cinder-bedded cars, lifting heavy heads now and then to cry out against this new and dreadful procedure, and against their masters, the sweating weary men who drove, cursed and cajoled.

But although two deputy sheriffs watched the train and the pens, and made a final careful inspection of it before it pulled out, Tom McNair had not appeared.

The locomotive took up the slack carefully, the cattle braced themselves against the strange and disquieting motion, and in the caboose Bill and Gus, the Swede who was traveling on Tom's contract ticket, settled their gear and proceeded to catch up on long arrears of sleep.

It was about midnight that night that the cattle train, having puffed and snorted up the long divide, stopped by a water tank to shift off the extra locomotive, and Bill, wakening, looked up into a face which was faintly familiar under a bandage. And the face was grinning cheerfully and pointing at Gus.

"What'll we do with that?" it said. "Throw it off?"

"By God! Tom!"

"You bet you."

He turned to Gus's coat, hanging from a hook, and calmly took the contract ticket from a pocket.

"Do you suppose he'd listen to reason?"

"Depends on what you mean by reason."

"Two reasons, then; you and me!"

"We can try, but he's sure aimin' to get to the big city."

Voices outside warned them that they had not much time. They had wakened the Swede, too, and he sat up and yawned.

"I yust got asleep," he complained.

"Shall we fling him off, or give him a chance to go peaceable, Bill?"

"Yust try it," said the Swede, wide awake now and getting up. But there was no time for parley; already the long train was giving premonitory symptoms of departure, and at any time the rear brakeman would swing up onto the step of the caboose. Before Gus had time to square off for a fight he was caught by the elbows and hustled off the train, and Bill was throwing after him the black valise which contained his change of clothing.

Tom had only time to call out a word of warning.

"You lay low until I get to Chicago," he said. "If you don't something's going to happen to you that'll surprise you. After that you can blow the top off to hell and spit in the hole."

When the brakeman came running up with his lantern he saw a stupefied figure picking up a black valise from beside the track. But he had no time to ask questions. When he got into the caboose he found the two men he had left still apparently sleeping.

If he sensed some small drama, if he realized that a change had taken place in the personnel of the two contract men, he said nothing about it to them. And the conductor, when spoken to, only chuckled dryly. He knew Tom. If Tom was smart enough to outwit Allison, that was his business. His ticket was all right.

The long journey continued, broken only by the stops every twenty-eight hours, when the cattle were taken out of the cars and at the pens beside the track were watered and given hay. Meal time was a casual matter of way stations and the end of the division.

There the crews changed, and the cabooses and engines. But the interminable game of stud poker with a pack of swollen filthy cards went on. Sometimes the conductor took a hand, again the brakeman would descend his ladder from the cupola above, or the forward brakeman would wander back over the tops of the swaying cars and sit in for a while.

Tom was happy, after a fashion. He was physically

comfortable, rested, and warm. In the morning he bathed with water from the open butt marked "Wash water" and he had managed to buy some underclothes and socks. His injury was healing, too. He looked neither ahead nor behind. Clare was as though she had never existed. He meant to come back from Chicago, of course; where else could he go? But he anticipated no serious trouble from Allison, or did not care to think about it if he did.

Now and then he thought of Kay, but there was heartache there, and he tried to forget her.

Occasionally he would look up from the game to glance out the window. As the bare treeless plains began to rise into the wooded hills of Iowa and Wisconsin he was conscious of beauty he was unable to express.

"That's sure pretty," he would say.

"Prettiest country in America," the brakeman might observe. "Look at them hills. Trees right to the top."

"Hills? You call them hills? You come out our way and let me show you something!"

But the towns began to daunt him, as they grew in size; the lines of automobiles drawn up, the well-dressed swift-moving people; and cowboy fashion both he and Bill expressed their discomfiture in jeers. "Look at him, Tom! I'll bet they'd pay a bounty on him back home."

"No! Not enough hair on his hide."

They became gradually conscious of their clothing and their big hats. And undeniably—oh, very undeniably—there clung to them both the odor of the cattle cars. Once a pretty girl at their table in a restaurant sniffed and then moved away, and Tom was indignant.

"What's the matter with us?" he asked, aggrieved. "The way she acted, we might be a pair of skunks."

"Well, we aren't a couple of perfume bottles at that," said Bill philosophically, and went on with his meal.

There were others, of course, who stared at the big cowboy in his wide hat, with his swaggering walk, his broad shoulders and slim waist. Now and then a girl made some signal to them—or to Tom, rather—and they would fall into step beside her, one on each side.

"I didn't know the circus was in town. Where'd you fellows come from?"

"Out of the West, where the men are men," they would chant in unison.

But these little dalliances were necessarily brief. They would saunter back to the track, swing into the caboose, and go back to the poker game again; the floor was littered with the stumps of endless cigarettes. One brakeman produced a bottle of moonshine, but there was not enough liquor to cause any trouble, or to interfere with Tom's luck at the cards.

He was a hundred dollars to the good when they reached Chicago.

Chapter Eleven

Cowboys in the garb of their occupation are common enough in the fall in the stock-yards district. They excited no comment when, having turned over their cattle, they went to a small hotel nearby and engaged a modest room. There was no hurry; a week or even ten days in the big town was their privilege, and their contract tickets guaranteed their return trip.

Tom was in high spirits. He sang as he shaved, and as he carefully polished his boots on the under side of the mattress, and when later on they found themselves on Michigan Avenue he swaggered, rather, and eyed the girls as they stared at him.

"It's a hick town," he confided to Bill. "I'll bet there's not a fellow in it could snap a bronc."

But Bill was not happy. The size of the buildings, the noise and confusion of the traffic, daunted him. When they finally wandered to the lake front he settled himself there with his back to the town.

"Lemme be," he said. "I want an eyeful of this water while I got a chance. Looks like there's enough water there to irrigate the whole Northwest and have some left over."

A policeman sauntered over to them and inspected them.

"Rodeo coming to town?" he asked.

"Yeah," said Tom. "We're the advance agents. We're just settling to move some of those buildings back. This town hasn't got room enough for us."

That night, still seeking the gayety they had hoped for, they found a combination vaudeville and moving picture house and went in. But the picture purported to be a western one, and after watching it somberly for some time Tom said in a loud disgusted tone: "Oh, my God!" After that they were asked to leave. They went back to the hotel and sat drearily in their bedroom, hearing on the street and all about them a life with which they had no contact. They had not even found a bootlegger.

It was on the second day that Bill, turning on his bench at a figure which had suddenly loomed up beside him, sprang to his feet and let out a whoop.

"Ride 'em cowboy!" he shouted, and then fell into rapt and admiring silence. From head to foot Tom had lost his identity. He wore a violently blue ready-to-wear suit, a trifle short in the waist and tight across the back, tan shoes and colored socks, and to top it all a soft hat which sat rather high on his head.

"Some outfit, eh?"

"You tell 'em," said Bill. "You go back in those clothes and stand trial, and the jury won't only acquit you. It'll kiss you."

They were a queerer combination than ever after that, Bill in his old clothes which he obstinately refused to change, his battered Stetson, his stocky figure, his bowed legs—the short man's penalty for years in the saddle. And Tom in his outrageously bad clothes and his tight yellow shoes which hurt his feet. But still gayety escaped them. They tried for it. They went back to the same theater the next night and found the stage entrance. But it was cold and dark, and Tom's feet burned like fire, and after all the girls who came out were not the creatures of enchantment they had seemed, but tired looking young women who might have been Clare Hamel, or any of the town girls who walked the streets of Ursula at twilight.

Partly out of bravado, partly out of sheer loneliness, Tom spoke to one of them, but after a quick look up at him she shook her head.

"On your way, little boy," she said, not unamiably. "And don't let the door-man see you. He'll whistle for a cop."

On the third day Bill announced his intention of going back home, and Tom hesitated. So far it had been dull enough, but the thought of going back, to Clare, to that fool Indian business, was worse. Much worse.

"I'm staying," he said at last. "There must be some way in this man's town for a fellow to forget his troubles, and I'm looking for it."

"Looking for trouble's what you mean," Bill said pessimistically. "And if you're looking for it you'll sure find it."

Bill left that night in a day coach for the West, and Tom was left alone. He wandered about, limping slightly, but neither trouble nor pleasure offered itself. Once he found a shooting gallery, somewhere near East Madison Street, and spent some time popping away with a small .22 rifle at rows of white clay pipes. A small admiring group of men formed around him; and because he was lonely and because applause was meat to him; he swaggered a bit and kept on.

"Sure can shoot!"

"Huh, you call this shooting? Come out to my country where bears are ripe and I'll show you something!"

But even admiration palled on him. He went back to the hotel, and with the tan shoes still on his feet, patiently soaked them in hot water and went to bed in them. He slept little, but they had stretched somewhat by morning.

It was in the intervals of waking that he began once more to think of Kay. So far he had fought her back with fair success. The round-up and the drive had left him little time, and on the train the incessant poker game, broken only by stops for food and sleep or to look after the cattle, had been a consistent distraction. But that night, lying diagonally on a bed which was too short for him, she came to him again in all her youth, her charm and her love for him. A hundred pictures of her began to torture him; he saw her gallantly riding, the wind blowing back her short hair, he saw her attentively watching him while he made coffee, up on the North fork.

"Why, it's quite easy, isn't it!"

"Mean to say you've never made coffee? You'll be a fine wife for some fellow!"

And most of all he saw her that last night.

"The best thing that can happen to me is to break my neck and be done with it."

"It would break my heart, too."

He gave up the effort to sleep, and began to pace the floor. Suppose he didn't go back West at all? Suppose he stayed in the East and tried to make something of himself? Cut the whole outfit, Clare and Bob Allison and all, and got a job here?

But what could he do? Go into a store and sell neckties, like that little shrimp he had bought his from a couple of days ago?

"If you like a bit of dash, here's one. Lots of class to that tie. They're using more color this year."

God Almighty, that was a man's job!

After half an hour of pacing, the loose boards of the floor creaking under him, he was brought up by a light tapping at the door, and opening it an inch or so saw a girl outside in a pink kimono over her nightdress.

"Are you sick or anything?" she asked. "I can hear you walking. I'm in the next room."

"Sorry I waked you up. I'm breaking in a pair of shoes."

"You're—what?" she asked. And then burst into uncontrollable merriment. He grinned sheepishly. But she did not move. She stood gazing up at him with bright interested eyes.

"You're a queer one," she said. "Don't you think you owe me a cigarette for disturbing me?"

"I'll have to roll one."

She laughed again at that, and while he closed the door and got into his trousers she stood, smiling and amused, outside. When he opened the door again she stepped in and closed it behind her, watching him interestedly while he made her cigarette.

"Cowboy, aren't you?"

"Yeah. What do you want to smoke and spoil a good set of teeth for, anyhow?"

"It hasn't hurt yours any!"

She was young, pretty and quite composed. When he turned from finding a match for her, she had seated herself on a chair and drawn her bare feet up under her. He was surprised and slightly shocked.

He lighted her cigarette and then indicated the door.

"All right," he said. "And now run along to your little bed, sister. I'm busy."

"Busy! What about?"

"I've got behind in my sleeping tonight. I'll have to try and catch up."

She eyed him shrewdly. Whatever her idea had been in coming in, she probably abandoned it then, but she made no move to go.

"Let me finish this, anyhow."

He smiled at that, rolled himself a cigarette and sat down on the bed.

"That's right. Now—what else, besides the shoes?"

"I've told you. You soak 'em and—"

Suddenly she laughed.

"You're a funny boy," she said. "You could do that in bed, if that's the idea. Come on, tell me. Is it a girl?"

He stiffened.

It is, isn't it?"

"You finish and vamoose, before we both get thrown out

of this hotel."

"Oh, that's all right," she said easily. "They know me. Doesn't she like you?"

"That's not the trouble."

"Is she married?"

"No."

"Or you?"

"No."

She got up, flicking the cigarette into his wash basin, and drawing her kimono around her.

"Then what's the matter with you?" she said. "Go and get her. With your looks you should worry."

The next moment she was gone. He stood staring at the door after she had closed it behind her. Go and get her. Go and get her. Well, go and see her anyhow. See how things stood between them. He reached into his trousers pocket and began to count his money.

With daylight he was somewhat less assured, and his feet hurt him damnably. But when he went downstairs there was the girl again, on her way out and looking quite neat and bright, and not at all the sort she had seemed in the night. And she came up to him and said:

"Remember what I told you. That's the stuff!"

He never saw her again; she played her small part in his life and disappeared. Later on he was to know others like her, girls pouring out their youth like wine to satisfy the thirsts of men, but he never saw her again.

At noon that day he sat in the day coach of a through train, on his way East.

No poker now to distract his mind, no girls to wave gayly at the caboose windows. No one even to talk to, save a woman with two children on her way to hunt up a husband who had deserted them.

"I should think you'd let him go, if that's the way he's acted.

"Let him go! And me with these kids to bring up! He's got

to see to them. He brought them into this world."

Tom considered this last statement with a certain humor.

"Must be a queer sort of fellow!"

"He's all that and then some."

But she got off toward night of the first day. He missed the children. He had not known many children, and the feeling of their little bodies crawling over him was new and warming. Even when he found that his new blue clothes were undeniably spotted from these contacts, he smiled at the thought of them.

"Funny little fellers," he muttered. He was saying "feller" again.

He slept in his seat that night, and emerged at noon the next day from the train considerably disreputable as to clothing and unhappy in his mind. Suppose he did see Kay? What could he say to her?

"Here I am! The Sheriff's after me, back home, and I'm engaged to a girl there. Also what I have in my pocket is all I have in the world. But aside from that I'm all right, so if you'll just step around to the preacher's with me—!"

He stopped in the middle of a street when that struck him, and narrowly escaped being run over by a taxicab.

"Not city-broke yet," he told himself ruefully, and went on.

And then he found that the Dowlings were in the country. He was suddenly very tired and depressed. His big shoulders sagged under the tight blue coat, the hat which was too small sat at a less rakish angle. But he had come too far to go back now, and the excitement of being near to Kay upheld him. He set his teeth, went back again to the railroad station, spent more of his small hoard for a ticket and got on another train. This was different, however. All around him were prosperous men reading newspapers, casually getting up at their stops and later climbing into cars with cap-touching chauffeurs; well-dressed women and girls, mincing along the aisles in high-heeled slippers; glimpses here and there of big houses, with carefully shaved lawns under trees beginning to turn with the early frosts.

And he had planned no campaign. The chances were, if he went to the house, that they would not let him see Kay. They might not even admit him.

"Not if they see me first!" he told himself grimly. "I'd be as welcome as a rattler in a prairie dog hole."

He decided to telephone and ask her to meet him some place. So careful had he become of money—he who had never considered money in his life before—that he reluctantly paid for a call, but the information he received was by way of being a relief.

She was not at home. She was at the country club.

When he found that a station hack would cost him a dollar he decided to walk, and weary and lame as he was, the four miles seemed endless. But a sense of exaltation carried him on. It was journey's end. He forgot the big houses, forgot weariness and the loneliness, and the homesickness for the back country where he belonged.

There beyond those gates was Kay, and journey's end.

Chapter Twelve

More than three weeks had passed, and Kay had had no letter from Tom. Twice a day she waited for the mail bag to be brought up from the village, twice a day she ran through its contents feverishly, and twice a day, fairly shaken with disappointment, she began again her tense watching of the clock until the next mail was due to arrive.

The strain began to tell on her.

She wakened one morning to see from her balcony the dahlia heads in the fall garden drooping on their stems, and the ground frozen hard. An icy wind from the Northwest was blowing before it leaves that sailed like birds and then settled to the ground. It seemed to her that a cold hand had come out of the West and caught her heart.

"Good gracious, Miss Kay, do come in! You'll catch your death of cold."

"I'm all right, Nora."

But she was not all right. The girls and men she knew were noticing it.

"What's the matter with Kay, anyhow? She has positively no pep any more."

"Maybe Herbert's been naughty!"

"Herbert's idea of being naughty is to forget to go to Sunday school. Try again."

She tried arguing with herself. It was not over, this affai of Tom's and hers. Things did not end like that. Two peopl who loved each other did not simply separate, without word, without a farewell. Life might separate them, but no their own voluntary act.

In an increasing agony of mind she reviewed their las meeting, trying to find in it some explanation of his silence She discarded all her old standards, the ones she would hav used in judging Herbert, for instance, and tried to see th affair from Tom's viewpoint. Had he, thinking things over i solitude in the mountains, decided like Aunt Bessie, tha there could be no happiness for them together?

Or—she knew by that time the curious pinnacle on whic the cowboy places womanhood—had he found somethin shameless and bold in the way she had met him, in he surrender? It was she who had forced the issue between then that night, and in the end it had been Tom who had sent he back, loved but repudiated.

And then, into her despair, came a day or two when hop bloomed again. Tom had not written because he had no dared. He was in trouble. And while she suffered for him was indeed frightfully anxious, she was still happier than sh had been for weeks.

She had dressed for a dinner dance at the country club and came downstairs to find Henry in the hall. She had a odd feeling that he had been waiting for her. She came down a slim little figure in a gay dress of silver cloth, and h watched her almost furtively.

"Off again!" he said. "Gay life you are leading, Kay."

"Frightfully gay."

"By the way,"—how transparent he was!—"by the way, have a letter here from Jake. You might like to see it. It' about that fellow who used to take you riding out there What's his name—McNair?"

But there was a certain delicacy in Henry; he did not loo at her. He pretended to search his pockets for it, and tha gave her a little time. Then, when he had found it, he gave it to her and turned away.

"Better not stay too late tonight," he mumbled. "You've all winter to dance."

She took the letter and went out to the waiting car. She felt quite calm as she switched on the light, although her hands felt rather numb; and she had to ask Hawkins, when they reached the main road, to stop the car. She was not seeing very clearly.

She ran hastily over the earlier portions, which in Jake's labored script referred to the shipping. Then she found it:

"We have had a little trouble out here. Tom McNair found an Indian killing beef, and being hasty fired a shot at him and hurt him pretty bad. At least that's the Indians' story, although Tom says different. Anyhow Tom has got away, as there is a warrant out for him.

"If it comes to a showdown I think we ought to defend him, as it was our beef, but that's up to you. The best man in Ursula according to my thinking for that kind of case—"

Of course they would have to defend him. And she must try to get some word to him, some reassurance. She ordered Hawkins to drive through the village to the telegraph station, and there she sent a wire to Tom in care of Jake.

> "Have just heard. Sure everything will be all right. Please write details."

She was so kind to Herbert that night that he was almost delirious with happiness, but although he tried to get her off by herself, she managed to elude him.

"Don't you want to sit this out, Kay? There's a moon outside."

"Well, it usually *is* outside, isn't it? No, I think I'll dance."

In agony of spirit Herbert compared that failure of his with Tom McNair's probable method under the same circumstances.

"This is my dance? All right, we're not dancing it."

"But I want to dance."

"You've got plenty of time to dance. You've only got a chance to sit out with me now and then. And this is one of them!"

And girls and women fell for that sort of thing! Well, if they liked it he would try it too.

"I'm going back with you, Kay. I don't like you riding alone so late."

"Don't be silly. Hawkins is driving. I'm not alone."

"I'm going just the same."

"And make Hawkins bring you all the way back here? Don't be foolish."

He tried to say: "To hell with Hawkins. That's what he's for." But the words stuck in his throat.

"I suppose that's so," he said, and smiled painfully. He had failed; he had known he would fail. Damn being a gentleman anyhow. It had never got him anywhere. That roughneck out in the West had it all over him; knew what he wanted and went after it. The thousand and one repressions of his code Tom McNair had never heard of. Damn McNair, too.

He tucked Kay in her car and then sadly got his own little bus and drove back to town. Not recklessly, but with due caution; even the memory of that early reckless drive to the ranch, that dare-devil sardonic figure at the wheel, could not force his law-abiding instinct to violate the speed limit.

It was the next day that Kay took her courage in her hands and went to Henry.

"Are you going to defend Tom McNair, father?"

He eyed her, his chin sunk on his breast, his mouth pursed.

"If the fellow had stayed and taken his medicine, I might have considered it. Now—"

"I don't see what that has to do with it. It was our beef."

"That's no excuse for shooting a man. He got himself into this scrape; let him get himself out."

He ran his hands over some papers on his desk—he was entrenched behind it, an old trick of his—and she knew he had said the last word. But Henry after his usual fashion with his family had blundered; Bessie could have told him that. It was Bessie who, when Katherine had wanted a crest and motto for her note paper, had flippantly suggested, "Get, beget and forget," as the Dowling motto for their womenkind.

To the truths and half-truths from which Kay had built up a superman in Tom were now added a yearning pity and a hot-eyed championship. She saw him making his escape with every man's hand against him. She saw him riding hell-for-leather along dangerous trails, skirting precipices, sitting on his tired horse, a dramatic and wonderful figure outlined against the setting sun, and gazing from under his broad hat down the mountain slopes for a revengeful sheriff and a posse.

When the following Sunday the family motored in to church—it was the opening of the church season, so to speak; during the warm weather Henry played golf—she prayed for his escape and his safety. It seemed strange and incongruous that she should be kneeling there, in that decorous opulent silence, praying for a cowboy who had shot a man. She was almost self-conscious when she sat back and looked around. But her mother was opening her prayer book at Morning Prayer and Henry, leaning back for easier access to his pocket, was feeling for the twenty dollar bill with which he always decorated the top of the plate. Henry had been a vestryman for many years.

That was the day before Tom's arrival; it was a Monday afternoon when she saw him.

She had been playing tennis. Now she sat on the terrace of the country club drinking tea. Around the wicker table were half a dozen girls and a man or two, all indolent from exercise and the sun. They talked desultory personalities, yawned, sipped their tea or highballs and drew on cigarettes, in the effortless ease of people who knew each other intimately.

"Where's Hugh?"

"Gone home. He was pretty well teed up last night."

"Anybody coming over tonight? You coming, Kay?"

"I don't know. I'm tired of dancing."

"Seems to me our Kay's kind of sore on the world lately." One of the men said this. "What's the matter, Kay? Not troubled in your little mind, are you?"

The group glanced at her, smiling.

"Maybe Herbert's been acting the cave-man again!" some one suggested. And with this picture of Herbert there came light-hearted delighted laughter.

"But I always say this," a girl drawled, "when Herbert does settle down, he will be all right. Don't you let them discourage you, Kay."

Kay was hardly listening. She was used to their humor, their little jokes among themselves. But she roused enough to answer them.

"What I was thinking was whether to listen to any more drivel here, or go home and read a book and learn something."

"Quick! I can't bear suspense. What did you decide?"

"I'm going home," she told them, and got up.

It was then that she saw Tom. He was standing at the foot of the steps, his hat in his hand, gazing up at her, and at first she did not know him. So faint was the resemblance of this rather haggard and certainly untidy youth in his absurd clothes to the heroic figure of her dreams that she hesitated. Then he smiled, and with that half-humorous, half-reckless smile she got up.

The group around the table was absorbed in itself once more. They had seen nothing, and deliberately, so as not to catch their attention, Kay moved to the steps. Her knees were shaking, her lips felt stiff and dry. And Tom never took his eyes from her.

"Tom!" she said. "Why, Tom!"

"It's me, all right."

He had whipped off the disfiguring hat, and he looked more himself. But she was aware, too, of a silence behind her, broken by a voice carefully non-committal.

"Cool in summer, you know, but with enough thatch on top to keep out the rain."

She flushed; the reference she knew was to Tom's hair, which had been carefully clipped to the skull except for the top, which was much as Nature had intended it. But Tom had not heard it.

"Listen," he said. "Can't we get away from that bunch of mavericks over there and talk somewhere? I've sure got a lot to say, and just about between now and the next train back to say it."

There came another voice, this time feminine.

"But who? And what? And why? I ask you!"

She did the only thing she could think of, took him up on the terrace, passed the group with her head high, and ordered tea.

"I wired you the other day, Tom, but I suppose you never got it. I didn't know you'd been in trouble."

"Trouble?" He was genuinely surprised. "What sort of trouble?"

"Why, you shot an Indian, didn't you?"

"Oh, that!" He threw back his head and laughed. "Shooting Indians doesn't count. Don't you worry about that."

But he had raised his voice, and at the nearby table the Greek chorus took it up.

"It appears that another Redskin has bit the dust. Reloading his trusty revolver, our hero—"

Tom heard it. Kay went a little cold as he turned quietly in his chair and surveyed the intent group behind him.

"Did any one over there refer to me?" he said, with deadly calmness.

Out of the general stupefaction only one individual

retained his self-possession; he jumped to his feet and came over, smiling.

"I apologize," he said. "My fault entirely. It isn't often we dubs can sit here and get a thrill like the one you have just given us."

Tom eyed his outstretched hand suspiciously. It was a white, well-cared-for hand. Suddenly he grinned.

"No," he said. "I couldn't fight that. It would be murder. All right, partner. We'll forget it."

He shook hands.

Never afterwards could Kay remember that nightmarish afternoon in any detail. She saw Tom swallowed up by a crowd of thrilled and amused young people, to which gradually gravitated a half dozen or so of older men. She saw girls flattering him, drawing him out, and turning aside to mutter: "Isn't it precious!" She saw bottles brought out from lockers, with tall glasses and soda, and Tom in the center of the hubbub, bland and cool but growing increasingly expansive.

"No, sister. I haven't got my gun with me. I'm a little hasty-like at times, and so I take it off when I'm going to be in a crowd like this."

"Can I ride? Well, say, that's what I don't do anything else but."

His drawl and good looks fascinated them. They drew him out; when they wanted to know how he had come East, and he told them in the caboose of a cattle train, they would have been less thrilled if he had said he had made a pair of wings and flown. But all the time Kay felt that they were somehow cheapening him, taking advantage of him for a half hour's amusement. And later on they would talk and take him off. She knew them. "As Kay's cowboy would say—"

She did not know how little he had eaten that day, but she did know they were giving him too much to drink. And to add to her confusion and growing distress was the certainty that the episode could not be kept from her people. It was madness; they were all mad, and she was the maddest of the lot.

They were certainly drinking too much. One youth was raising a highball glass to Tom.

"Are we all friends?" he inquired solemnly.

"We are all friends," said Tom with equal solemnity, and emptied his glass. The crowd had grown in size and noise. Her head ached and her heart was heavy. When at six o'clock the man who had precipitated the situation at the start appeared with a necktie tied around his head and a feather stuck in it, wearing a striped blanket around his shoulders and solemnly beating a tom-tom consisting of a wooden chopping bowl from the club kitchen, she had reached the limit of her endurance.

She worked her way through the crowd.

"I'm sorry, Tom," she said, "but I must be getting home. When are you going back?"

He was exhilarated, but more with excitement than with liquor. He had been sitting negligently on a table, and now he got up.

"Going home? But I haven't talked to you yet."

"You've been too popular. I'll have to see you another time."

He looked at her oddly, then he drew himself to his full height and glanced on the crowd around him with a certain arrogant good-humor.

"Now," he drawled, "you children run along and amuse yourselves somewhere else. I've got some business to attend to."

They took their dismissal with laughter, scattering about the terrace. The short October twilight had ended, and out of the darkness cars began to drive up, golf clubs were collected, there was stir and movement. But Kay was aware even then of polite but acutely interested espionage; she could not think, she could not talk.

"Now we've got rid of that bunch of loafers—"

"I *must* go, Tom. I must."

"And is this going to be all of it? How-d'ye-do, goodbye?"

"Be careful, please. They're watching."

"What do I care? What do you care?" He moved impatiently. "All right, I'll go back tonight. That's all I wanted to know."

"I'll come over this evening, Tom. I may be late, but I'll come. You can get your dinner here; I'll arrange about it."

"One of these play-boys has asked me to eat with him. You'll come, will you?"

"Of course."

He was still suspicious. In a way, the sight of Kay in this new environment had not had the effect on him that it had had on Kay to see him transplanted. He had expected something of the sort. But each scene and group at the club had been unconsciously emphasizing the difference between her familiar world and his. Here was not only luxury, but the involved machinery of play, and to utilize it people to whom play was a part of their daily lives, like food or beds to sleep in.

It made him feel inferior, and fiercely resent that inferiority. His pride was in arms, and to do him justice he had seen at once through the curiosity of the crowd.

But after one look at her face his voice softened.

"God knows I don't want to make you any trouble, girl," he said. "I've come a long ways just to look at you."

"Is that why you came, Tom?"

His charm for her was reasserting itself; she felt breathless.

"What else?" He glanced around, but no one at the moment was observing them. "Look here, you may hear things about me as time goes on. You will, maybe; I'm human. But this goes, now and for keeps. There's only you for me. I've been trying to think different, but it isn't any use."

Then the lights were switched on and he drew back.

She looked back at him from the top of the steps. He was

standing alone gazing after her with a sort of smouldering intensity, a queer, incongruous and lonely figure. She felt a choking pity for him, so out of place, his big muscles bursting through his horrible coat, the fatigue of his long journey and even the dust of it plainly in evidence. But with that pity there was pride, too. He was a man; beside those easy, well-dressed popinjays who had been amusing themselves with him, he loomed head and shoulders. He was a man.

Chapter Thirteen

Of the debacle that followed that night, Kay was never able to think except with a sense of shuddering horror. She dressed feverishly, intent only on getting back quickly to the club, and at seven-thirty she heard the telephone ring, and Rutherford coming heavily up the stairs and tapping at her mother's door.

"It is Mr. Trowbridge, madam. Mrs. Trowbridge has an attack of neuralgia, and will be unable to come."

Then shortly after that Katherine along the hall, her dressing gown around her shoulders.

"What are you doing tonight, Kay? Anything important?"

"There's a dance at the club."

"Oh, if that's all—Mrs. Trowbridge has a headache, and he is coming without her. I'm afraid you'll have to make a fourth at bridge."

"But mother—"

"It's only a dance, isn't it? You can go over later if you like."

"I've promised," she said desperately. "Can't you get somebody else?"

"I have tried. So many people have gone back to town, and the rest—I do think, Kay," she added with a faint asperity, "that when you think how little we really ask of you you might do this pleasantly."

She had to agree finally. There was nothing else to do. But Katherine did not go at once. She moved around the room.

"We will have to replace these taffeta curtains next spring. They have faded outrageously."

But Kay had an idea that she was not thinking of the curtains. When at last she went to the door she stood there, hesitating.

"You're feeling all right, aren't you, Kay? I've thought lately—maybe that dress makes you look pale."

"I'm all right, mother."

Later on they went down the stairs together, and some impulse made her put her arm around Katherine's shoulders. Perhaps she felt that she was somehow being treacherous to this Katherine, who had left her dreams all behind her, and who now said "we" instead of "I."

Mr. Trowbridge, being relieved of his hat, overcoat, gloves and stick in the hall, looked up at them with approval.

"Ought to be painted like that," he said. "Poor Sargent should have done it. Mother and daughter. Question: which is the mother?"

He was a large gentleman of an elephantine wit, and just now in excellent humor. He had walked over in the crisp air, he knew he would have a good dinner, and he was ready for it.

"Some day soon, Henry," he said as he followed them into the drawing room, "some nice young chap will be stealing this girl of yours. Make quite a hole in the establishment, eh?"

"Not necessarily, if she picks the right one."

Cocktails and fresh caviare. Very good cocktails, very good caviare. Mr. Trowbridge lingered over both. Rutherford was waiting in the doorway to catch her mother's eye, but she was not looking.

"There's Rutherford, mother."

"Have another cocktail, George? You've had a good walk."

"Why, I don't mind, Henry. Where did you find this caviare? The last lot we got—"

The old glutton, always thinking of his stomach! It was a quarter after eight already. She caught him by the elbow.

"Dinner's served," she said lightly. "And I'm hungry, if you're not."

They wandered out somehow. There was a new painting in the hall, and he must stop and look at it. Her feet and hands were like ice, and her head was hot. Dinner came on, course after course, her mother eating delicately, her father appreciatively and Mr. Trowbridge slowly and with unction. Oysters, soup, fish, roast; sherry and sauterne. "Very good wine that. Still some of the old stock? Yes, I think I will."

Salad and sweet. And then Mr. Trowbridge taking fruit, cutting it meticulously with the gold fruit knife, eating and savoring it deliberately. Wouldn't they ever get through? They had been years at the table. The candles were melting, splashing little drops of blue wax onto the lace cloth; the room was broiling hot. Mr. Trowbridge's jaws moved steadily, appreciatively.

"I think I'll have a few more of those hot house grapes, Katherine. They are really excellent."

Over at last. Pushing back the chairs and James opening the door. Into the hall and then to the library. Coffee. Coffee quickly and get it over. Where's the bridge table? Where are the cards?

"Do stop fidgeting, Kay. James will get the tables. Will you have more coffee, George?"

"You tempt me, Katherine. Even if I don't sleep to-night—"

Her eyes were burning. Her mother was pouring the coffee

with delicate deliberation; the gleam and glitter of the massive tray, with its tiny cups, its elaborate panoply of wealth, made her dizzy. And what nonsense it all was, James moving like an acolyte across the room with that ridiculous cup balanced on a tray, and Rutherford like some high priest, reverently bearing in the liqueurs. How much simpler and easier life had been at the ranch, with the cook in the kitchen doorway:

"I hope you folks'll like that coffee. It's strong enough to bear an egg."

The ranch. The ranch.

At half past nine she managed to slip away to call Tom from the telephone in her bedroom, but both Nora and a housemaid were in her room, Nora to lay out her sheer nightgown, the maid turning down the bed.

"Put a wrap down in the hall for me," she told Nora. "I'm going out later."

The game dragged on. Mr. Trowbridge played as he ate, slowly and with unction.

"Now, if Providence is with me, Henry, this will go. If not—but let me see. Four and three and three make ten. Hah, you rascal, you have another trump, haven't you? Holding out on me, eh? Well, let's have it."

A sort of madness began to possess her. Eleven, eleven-fifteen, and still they went on. She pleaded a headache, but they only offered her perfunctory sympathy and continued playing. Hawkins had been dozing in the car outside for an hour before Mr. Trowbridge reluctantly laid down the cards and plunged a hand into his pocket.

"Well," he said, "fourteen dollars is a small price for an evening like this."

She left them with hardly a good night, picked up her wrap and went out. Hawkins stirred, roused and started the car. She called to him to hurry, but the distance seemed to be interminable. However, the sight of the club house cheered her. The dance was still going on, and one or two cars were arriving. What had seemed the middle of the night over home seemed the beginning of the evening here.

All her vague forebodings vanished. She ran up the steps and inside, to find Herbert inside the door. He had evidently been waiting for her, and there was a look of pity on his face.

Chapter Fourteen

Tom watched the car down the drive; he had had a drink or two, but they had only served to stimulate him, to overcome his shyness in these strange surroundings, and to make him feel the equal if not the superior to the men he saw around him.

He was extraordinarily happy. He took a deep breath, and the top button of his coat flew off and hit a pillar with a whack like a pistol shot; but he only muttered "hell" and fell back into ecstasy again. In the darkness the links stretched away to unseen boundaries, beyond which here and there were the lights of houses. And in that cool darkness his girl, his wonderful girl, was moving toward one of them.

After a time he turned and looked into the club house behind him. He could see the man he was dining with, in consultation with two or three others, in a room furnished with a luxury he had never dreamed of. He was not thinking, certainly he had no plan. He was vaguely relieved that he had not seen Herbert Forrest, but that was about all.

The dinner was announced.

But he found that certain ceremonies preceded the meal. Back in the grill room bottles were produced from lockers, ice ordered, and cocktails mixed. The group toasted the West, and in another round of drinks he had to reply for the

East. His head was buzzing, but he managed something.

"To the East," he said, rather grimly, smiling. "It's crowded and dirty and ornery, but it eats our beef and drinks good drinks. God bless it."

It was after eight when they sat down to dinner, and all his resolves faded before their well enough meant hospitality. They ate in the grill, and by the time the dinner parties preceding the dance had been seated in the dining room he had taught them a song and they were lustily singing it. Scraps of sound penetrated beyond the closed doors: Tom's clear if slightly inarticulate tenor:

> "I ain't got no father,
> I ain't got no father,
> I ain't got no father,
>   To buy the clothes I wear."

And then a chorus, rather more noisy than musical:

> "I'm a poor lonesome cowboy,
> I'm a poor lonesome cowboy,
> I'm a poor lonesome cowboy,
>   And a long ways from home."

The song was interminable. It appeared that Tom not only lacked a father, but divers other members of a family. The wailing chorus rose over the clatter of dishes in the dining room, and over the hum of conversation. People began to listen and comment, and one of the governors of the club, a gentleman of great dignity in impeccable evening clothes, came in and made a protest.

"Not quite so much noise here, gentlemen," he said. "If you feel you must sing, there is plenty of room outside."

Nine o'clock came, and nine-thirty, and Kay had not come. And always they were pressing drinks on him. Out of the generosity of cocktails and highballs they expanded to champagne.

"The way you find liquor, you'd sure make a good bird dog!" was Tom's comment to the man who brought it.

By ten o'clock, although he was still perfectly steady, he was concealing his resentment at Kay's defection under a swaggering boastfulness.

"Sure I shot him. He owed me a bill for that cow, and I collected it. You don't think we fellows ride the range for our health, do you? Why, say, the Sheriff's got a warrant for me for everything from arson to murder, right now."

He puzzled them, at that. One of the men told an incident out of his extremely private life, and the others greeted it with roars and applause. But Tom flushed and turned on him.

"Out our way," he said deliberately, "when a fellow tells a story like that on a woman, we shoot him first and then hang him to make sure."

They laughed it off, but he sat for some time, plainly ugly and dangerous.

It was Tom, to do them justice, who suggested shooting crap. His swagger had returned, but his luck was bad. Not one of them suspected that he was broke when he quit. They had to drink to better luck next time, and then the group began to break up. But a few still remained, and some resourceful genius brought in a rope and asked him if he could use it. He was bored and increasingly tired, and the clock showed half after ten, but he owed a them a dinner and more other hospitality than he should have accepted, and so he took it. After that, poor as the rope was, there was no question of their admiration for him. Big loop and small loop, he did all he knew for them, and they were insatiable. They plied him with liquor and kept him at it, and finally some enterprising youth had a bright thought and the crowd took it up eagerly.

The plan was to go down the drive, and have Tom rope the driver of the next open car which came in. To be fair to him he protested, but the crowd was excited and hilarious. It had begun to put money up, too, and confused as he was by that time and increasingly reckless, he finally agreed.

And the driver of the car turned out to be Herbert! He did not lose control, either of the car or of himself. He brought it to a stop, loosened the noose from around his neck, and quietly got out into the roadway.

"Who among this crowd of drunks threw that rope?" he demanded.

"Don't get sore, Herb. We've got a wild man from the West here, and he's just practicing a bit."

"Then you'd better send him back where he came from."

But Tom had recognized the voice by that time, and it had partially sobered him. He shoved the crowd aside and stepped out into the road.

"Do you want to repeat that suggestion to me?" he demanded.

Herbert was bewildered. He stood there, trying to penetrate the darkness.

"Is that McNair?"

"It is, and I've just asked you a question."

"I don't quarrel with a drunken man," Herbert said contemptuously. "If you fellows have any respect for yourselves or this club you'll stop this kind of thing and clear out." He got back into the car. "As for you, McNair, better get to bed somewhere and sleep it off."

Before Tom could make a move toward him he had gone on.

The men he had left laughed, but they were vaguely uncomfortable. One of them picked up Herbert's hat, lying in the road, and they kicked it back to the club house. But Tom moved along morosely. There was bitterness and despair in his heart; the unexpected meeting with Herbert in the cool night air had effectually sobered him. And Herbert's contemptuous attitude rankled in his mind. He had stood in the light of the car lamps, immaculate in evening dress, and politely refused to soil his hands with him. Well, he could make him do that, if he wanted. He could walk into the club house and smack that tidy face of his. Or he—

At the foot of the steps lay Herbert's soft hat, battered and dusty. As the men went on he hung behind them, and when his chance came he picked it up.

He waited until they were on the terrace above him. He had no feeling of resentment toward them. They were good fellows, and he had eaten their bread and drunk their liquor. It was not their fault that Kay had abandoned him to them; had gone away and not come back.

"Well, so long, everybody," he said. "I reckon I'll be moving on."

They protested, vigorously and sincerely, but he only smiled up at them and shook his head.

"If I go in again I'll have to kill your little Herbert," he told them. "And I'd hate to mess up your place for you."

He drew on Herbert's battered hat with a flourish, turned, and went down the drive.

As a matter of fact, Kay passed him in the car on her way to the club. But she was engrossed and anxious. She never saw the tall, weary and disheartened figure, limping slightly in its tight tan shoes.

When he reached the railroad station Tom simply took to the tracks and turned west. It would be incorrect to say that he walked and starved to Chicago, but it would be fairly close to the truth. Now and then a motor or a truck picked him up, and he shared the driver's food. Or he lay overnight in a barn and the farmer's wife gave him a breakfast. In Chicago he was able to sell the blue suit, however, and so secured money for his meals on the train back. He could not sell the shoes; they were worn paper thin.

But in one way, the constant effort to move west and to subsist while doing so had been good for him. He had been cold and hungry; there had been times when the mere effort of putting one foot before the other had required all the will power he could summon. But there was little time in his general misery to think back. Such faculties as he had were directed only to getting back home again.

So it was that the Ursula paper one day announced his return.

"Tom McNair has returned from riding the big circle in the East. Tom looks a bit leg weary, but reports a good time was had by all."

At Omaha he had wired the Sheriff, but when one evening he descended from the day coach Allison was not in sight. The platform was dark and deserted save for the station agent, peering at him.

"That you, Tom? Well, say, I thought you'd lit out for good!"

God, it was good to be back; to feel the brisk night air, to see the loom of the mountains again, to find silence once more and familiar voices and faces. He stared at the lights of the town; he knew every one of them. This was home this little corner of the earth, and beyond the lights there was the great back country. His country. Let those who wanted to live the other life; for him the long trail or the open plain, and a good horse under him.

He drew a long breath.

"Allison around?"

"Why, no. He left a message for you to go around and see him in the morning."

He went up the street to the Martin House. Ed was behind the cigar-stand desk, cleaning his finger nails with a pen-knife.

"Hello, Tom. When'd you drift in?"

"Just now, on twenty-one. Anything new?"

"I guess your coming back is the latest! Some of the fellows are upstairs."

But Tom shook his head. He had no money for poker and

no inclination for a party.

"What I want's a good bed. I may be sleeping on a plank in the pen before long!"

But he discovered the next morning no immediate intention on Allison's part to curtail his liberty. He found the Sheriff in his office, a bare place with an oak desk for business and a cuspidor on a square of oilcloth for pleasure, and Allison received him without animus.

"Figured you'd be getting in about now, Tom," he said. "Have a good time?"

"Not so bad. You going to lock me up?"

"Well, I guess that's hardly necessary. We'll fix up some bail for you and let you go home. But don't take another notion to go traveling; it won't be healthy. Your man's still alive, but they throw out the doctor's stuff, and the medicine man's doing all he can to kill him. I suppose Dowling will go on your bail?"

And he was surprised to have Tom say:

"If that's the way I'm to get out you can lock me up until I rot."

"It was his beef, or so you claim."

"It was his beef all right, but I'm not taking anything from him in the way of help. You folks needn't be afraid I'll beat it. I'm seeing it through all right."

And, after complying with certain formalities, Allison let him go.

He knew Tom's popularity in the country; he was its best bronc rider and trick roper. And he knew too that the region as a whole supported his action in shooting Weasel Tail. He himself, an old cow-man, had a sneaking sympathy for him. Allison was coming up for reelection soon. It was no time to stress the law too hard.

By noon, to all intents and purposes, Tom was free. Old Tulloss, the banker, had to Tom's surprise gone on his bond. It was only when he was leaving that the Sheriff uttered a final word of caution.

"Better keep away from the Reservation, Tom," he said. "I understand your friend Little Dog's been stirring them up considerable, and they've got some bad actors up there."

"I'm aiming to get out of this trouble before I look for any more."

"That's the talk."

But Tom had one errand to be discharged before he left town for the ranch. There was no particular virtue in his attitude. The whole town was ringing with his return, and knew Clare must have heard of it. So to the bungalow, at Clare's lunch hour, he reluctantly repaired.

She was not at home yet, and her mother admitted him without cordiality.

"You can come in and wait if you want. She'll be here soon."

She started out, paused in the doorway with her lips tight, went on again.

He was uneasy; he rolled and lit a cigarette. After a wait he heard Clare coming in. She came slowly across the porch, and he heard her in the narrow hall.

"All right, mom."

Her voice was dispirited.

"You got company in the parlor," Mrs. Hamel called from the kitchen.

She opened the door, and the next moment flung herself at Tom with a little cry.

"I thought you'd gone," she said. "I thought you'd gone out to the ranch."

He released her as soon as he could, awkwardly.

"Couldn't very well do that, could I? After the little sport you'd been?"

His rebuff frightened her, but she kept her voice steady.

"Listen, Tom. They know." She jerked her head toward the kitchen. "I was late getting back, and they're raising hell."

"Well, what about it? They can't do anything."

"You promised, Tom!"

"There hasn't been any talk outside, has there?"

"I don't know. Maybe. Mom talks a lot. But you promised me, Tom."

"Now see here," he said desperately, "you've been fine to me, Clare, helping me the way you did. But I'm not a marrying man. You know that. What have I got to marry on? Besides, if this Indian dies—"

"I don't care what you've got."

"I wish to God you'd put me out of your head."

"I wish to God I could," she said shrilly. "Don't you suppose I know I'm a damned fool? I just can't help it. That's all."

And that was the way things stood when he left her. He was resentful and surly as he started for the ranch. After all he had not harmed her. She had been willing enough; she had the shrewdness of the small-town girl the world over, the knowledge of her physical power over a man once she had yielded. But some instinct of caution had saved him.

He shrugged his shoulders as he walked down the street.

"Then what's all the shootin' for?" he asked himself impatiently.

But on the way out the sheer joy of home-coming wiped her out of his mind. Even the knowledge that this home-coming of his was but a temporary thing, that before long, with luck as to Weasel Tail, he would be drifting again, all his worldly gear behind him on the saddle, had not the power to take away the sense of peace at last. The road left the town, rose over a hill and dropped again. And the hill wiped out the town as though it had never been.

The weather had moderated, and in the fields on either side of the road ploughing was going on. The sharp blades of the sulky-plough bit through the surface and laid the dark earth over in long ribbons; the four great horses abreast strained, the ploughman lurched in his small seat. Here and there a man was drilling in his winter wheat. Three horses instead of four then, and behind in the tiny furrow a delicate scattering of seed; the machine moved on, the wheat was covered. Soon, please God, it would come up, lie warm under the winter snows, and in the spring wax strong under the early sun.

His contempt for the men who were turning the old range into farms began to die in him. They were his friends, his own people. He waved his hand to them, and they nodded and bumped and lurched along.

Chapter Fifteen

Bessie Osborne was the first of the family, characteristically to hear the story. She heard it in town early the next morning, or rather as early as she could get on the telephone. And it was characteristic of her, too, that she lost no time over it. She sat up in bed—she was having a massage at the time. It was her substitute for exercise—and called Herbert at once.

"Come around and lunch with me," she said. "I want to talk to you."

"I'm pretty busy today."

"Well, come anyhow," she said and hung up the receiver.

She was a wise woman where young men were concerned, so she gave him an excellent cocktail and plunged into the matter while it was still, as she would have put it, getting in its work.

"Now," she said, "tell me the whole thing. And don't save me anything. I can get the surface story anywhere."

But Herbert knew disappointingly little. Tom had come, had got drunk, acted like a rowdy and disappeared.

"Where to?" said Bessie practically. "Those fellows got him tight. Why didn't they look after him?"

"I don't think they knew he was going. As a matter of fact, I believe he took my hat."

"Your hat!" said Bessie, astounded.

"His own was inside. He didn't go back, you see."

Bessie controlled her face. So there was something underneath, after all. Probably he and Herbert had had a set-to of some sort, and Herbert was not proud of it. She sat and inspected her carefully manicured nails thoughtfully.

"But it's tragic. It's terrible," she said unexpectedly. "Did he have any money?"

"I don't know. And I don't know that I care. He was tight when I saw him, tight as a drum."

"Well, he wasn't alone in that. And he knew enough to get out."

Herbert turned a trifle sulky, but she had not finished with him. She understood that this McNair had shot an Indian out there, an Indian who had been stealing their cattle. Was that true? And if it was, wasn't it up to them to defend him?

"I don't see that," he told her stiffly.

"Why not?" she demanded. "I daresay you'd just as soon see McNair jailed as not," she said shrewdly, "but I don't feel that way. I'm no keener on his marrying Kay than you are"—Herbert winced—"but I do believe in justice."

However, whatever she believed in, she found herself up against a stone wall of opposition in her brother. There was no proof that the Indian had been stealing their beef. McNair had acted on his own responsibility. Besides, the ranch was sold; he would send her an accounting soon. He personally washed his hands of the whole matter. He might have done something, but the impudence of the fellow in coming East and starting a scandal had decided him. He could take his medicine.

She never told Kay that she knew of Tom's visit. Indeed at that time she only mentioned him once, and was fairly shocked at the result. Kay turned a dead white and put out a hand to a chair to steady herself.

"Have you heard from your—western friend lately?" was what she asked.

And then Kay had turned the queer color.

"No," she said. "And I never will, now." She looked at her with painful directness. "You were quite right, Aunt Bessie. I know now. I think I always did know."

That was all. Bessie was not deceived, but she was somewhat relieved. She had her own philosophy. Time would cure Kay; she would marry Herbert or somebody else, and the handsome cowboy would be forgotten. Some day she would look back and smile at all this. She herself occasionally looked back and smiled. There had been an actor once, and she had been quite mad about him. What was his name? Anyhow, he had had a black mustache, and she had gone to all the matinées, and felt faint with jealousy when he kissed the leading woman.

On the first of November the Dowlings closed their country house and went back into town. The station wagon took the servants, happy at the end of their summer exile, and now once more to be within reach of the movies and the shops. The upholsterer's men had taken down the hangings and covered the furniture, men were stringing the doors and windows with fine wire, any tampering with which would warn a watchful individual at a switchboard in the city that something was wrong, and Henry's depleted summer store of liquors and wines had made a perilous but safe journey back to the great vault in the cellar of the town house.

Kay moved through all these activities quite normally. She talked and even laughed; if she ate rather less than ever, and if in the mornings sometimes her eyes looked a bit sunken, nobody mentioned it.

"Best thing that could have happened to her," was Henry's comment. "She's had her lesson, if she ever needed it. The fellow's a bad actor, from start to finish."

Katherine was not so certain, but whatever she suspected she kept to herself. And there had been no scandal, thank Heaven. A little talk, of course; that couldn't be helped. But the roping down the road had not come out, and mercifully the fellow had disappeared just after it. If there was any change in Kay, it was only that she seemed subdued. She was almost too acquiescent.

"I think the pink is better after all. It gives you a little color. What do you think?"

And Kay would turn herself, not before the mirror, but before Katherine instead.

"If you think so, mother."

It was during the packing that Katherine happened on the book of poetry she had brought home from the ranch, and reread the lines again:

> "The wide seas and the mountains called to him.
> And gray dawn saw his camp fires in the rain."

She put the book down thoughtfully. Had old Lucius ever read them? Probably not. Curious how they made her think of him; she must take some flowers to the cemetery. Bessie never remembered to do it.

Strangely enough, since that visit to the ranch she had seemed to understand the old man better. Perhaps people who had fought a hostile land and conquered it had a different sense of values; had even a right to have them. Then, wasn't it possible that they were wrong about Kay and this cowboy? Why should they assume that their way was the best? Who was to know or judge? One accepted certain standards without question because it was easy. Certain things were done, certain things were not. But old Lucius had said "I do certain things," and had let it go at that.

She never spoke those thoughts of hers. She went about her small efficient arrangements for closing the house; "Don't forget to cover the drawing room chandelier, James"; watched Kay furtively and with a growing anxiety, and later on went dutifully to the cemetery and placed a dozen roses in the jar before the ugly shaft.

It was as though she propitiated some old and possibly

angry God.

Perhaps even Henry was not so unobservant as he seemed. He bought some new pearls and had them added to his mother's string for Kay, and he even put them on her neck himself, with a sort of heavy jocularity. But if he noticed then how thin she was he said nothing.

The season in town had opened early. On the breakfast tray as it was brought into Kay's room would be numbers of heavy white envelopes, each containing an invitation to something or other. "Mr. and Mrs. Aurelius Fetterman request the pleasure of the company of Miss Katherine Dowling at a small dance," at dinner, at luncheon, at breakfast.

Varying these would be the times when the Dowlings entertained. When the social secretary, Miss Fane, would go about with lists in her hand and a hunted look in her eyes; when the florist's men would come in and standing in doorways with their heads on one side, surveying their work, critically, and Rutherford would be counting glasses and plates in the pantry.

"I beg your pardon, madam. Two of the sherry glasses have been broken."

"Well, don't bother me about it, Rutherford. Send down and replace them."

Then the hour arriving, and people with it, the first comers apologetic for being early, the tardy ones for being late. Bessie, bored but complaisant, wandering in late with a man or two in her train, and making up for the shortness of her skirts by the length of her onyx and diamond cigarette holder; and seeing a great deal while apparently looking at nothing at all.

She had heard the sequel of Tom's evening at the country club, and she had formed a new and higher opinion of Kay; Kay arriving at the dance, and being immediately surrounded:

"Say, Kay, the boy friend certainly got stewed!"

"Ask Herbert where his hat is!"

"Why didn't you fight him, Herb?"

And some one answering for Herbert, solemnly:

"Because he ain't got no father, he ain't got no father, he ain't got no father, to buy the clothes he wears."

And Kay in the center of the group, her head high, with a fixed smile on her face and dawning comprehension in her eyes, saying quietly:

"You seem to have had rather a thrilling time! But if you've used up father's best cow-hand he isn't going to like it."

But even Bessie knew no more than that. She did not know, for instance, that Kay had come quietly home after that, gone quietly upstairs, undressed and got into bed, or that she could not grieve, because Tom had left her nothing to grieve about. If he had died he would have left her some illusions, but he had only got drunk and disgraced her. She hadn't even the pitiful comfort of a secret sorrow. She had nothing; she was stripped bare.

The winter went on. Débutantes came out, flashed like meteors across the social sky and then settled quietly into the "among those present" lists in the society columns. New men came to town, were eligible or not eligible, the former greatly in demand, the second filling in at dinners and augmenting stag lines at balls. Some of them made their tentative overtures to Kay, sending in their small neatly engraved cards.

"Mr. Henderson calling, Miss Kay."

She would go down, talk and even laugh. She smoked a good bit, too—more than was good for her. Then, feeling that it made no difference to her if she ever saw them again, they made their polite bows, were let out of the house and went away, vaguely uncomfortable and relieved. And Kay would go upstairs again and sit in the dark until a housemaid came in to turn on the lights.

She did very little thinking, except sometimes about

Herbert. There was something to be said for Herbert; he was always the same, upright and dependable. A girl would be safe with him. She would always know what he was going to do next. He would never humiliate or shame her. If he lacked imagination and humor—perhaps because he lacked them—he was as fixed as the stars.

But she was very clear about Herbert at that. He was rather like her father. He would have the same heavy figure some day. Even now he loathed exercise. She knew what life with Herbert would be; giving correct dinners and going to them; Herbert sleeping through problem plays at the theater, and keeping unemotionally but interestedly awake at musical ones; his room adjoining hers, and his coming decorously to her with his occasional well-ordered demands; and then even that tie gradually relaxing, and the establishment of a formula between them.

"Good night, Kay."

"Good night, Herbert. Be sure to open your window."

When she reached that point she would shiver.

Chapter Sixteen

Once more the nights were very cold, and darkness fell early. The wranglers headed homeward blowing on their stiffened fingers, and guided by the oil lamps in the bunk house. The mountains were powdered softly white, and the leaves of the aspens and the cottonwoods were giving up their last feeble clutch at life and drifting helplessly, tiny gold and brown corpses, before the cold winds that whistled down their slopes.

In the mornings the pools along the creek were covered with a delicate coating of ice, and at dawn the deer, coming down from their frozen pastures to the still green grass below, broke through with dainty feet to drink.

Mrs. Mallory had already moved into Ursula, taking a small house and hoping to rent a room or two. Nellie had gone with her, and Jake was sleeping in the bunk house. It was understood that the sale was practically consummated, but while Jake was despondent and silent those days, nothing could daunt the spirit of the men. Soon they would be on their way before the winter storms, some heading South to the cow country in Arizona or New Mexico, others merely drifting. It was all in the game. Their hard lives had taught them philosophy.

"Bad luck's followed me so close," said Bill, "that if ever

I'd turned round I'd a bumped into it."

They sorted out their gear, ready for their war bags, and the stove gave out queer odors sometimes. And up in the barn there was many a feed of surreptitious oats to the horses which had carried them long and well.

Gus the Swede was staying. He had filed on a homestead near the Reservation, and Bill had a chance as freight brakeman on the railroad. One or two of the others were joining up with other outfits, to ride out in the winter snows from line camps; raw-hiding, with an iron ring on their saddles with which to etch on the brand, or looking out for sick and unthrifty cattle. But most of them were following the sun.

In the endless discussions around the long oilcloth covered table Tom took little part. Not only was his future vague in the extreme, but the joy of life, after that first home-coming, had gone out of him. His pride was hurt, his heart sore. He was less truculent than he had ever been.

Only once did his quick temper show itself. He was getting ready to turn in one night when some one of the crowd playing blackjack in the next room began to sing. "I ain't got no father. I ain't got no—"

He jerked the door open savagely.

"Stop that racket," he said, "and let a fellow get to sleep."

"Why, you ain't turned in yet."

"I'm telling you," he said shortly, and closed the door. It was Bill who broke the silence that followed.

"I feel kinda better about Tom now," he said. "He was so gentle before I thought maybe he was fixing to get sick."

The news from the Reservation was not good.

With the arrival of winter the Indians were moving from their tepees into their bleak untidy houses, where the younger generation had set up hideous sagging white iron beds, with an occasional rocking chair or cheap oak bureau, ordered by catalogue through the post trader; but where the old fullbloods still slept on their buffalo robes on the floor.

The squaws were taking off the hide or canvas coverings of their summer houses and folding them away, and the lodge poles stood like gaunt skeletons; the ashes and stones of their dead fires exposed little hearths now desecrated and abandoned.

Only the medicine man, Howling Wolf, still remained in his tepee, carefully tended by his wives, a trade blanket over his knees as he sat on his skin couch, his medicine pipe tied to a pole over his head.

The Reservation doctor, making his daily visits to Weasel Tail, found him one day in his house on the floor, lying among skins so old and filthy that he made a protest to one of his wives.

"Get him onto a bed," he said in Indian. "And get some clean blankets for him, or he will die."

"He will die anyhow," she told him.

He had a talk with Howling Wolf that day, but it did no good. The visit was very formal. In the center of the tepee was burning a small fire, and the doctor knew better than to pass between it and the medicine man. They smoked together in silence at first, and the women brought in food which he dutifully ate.

But the conference ended nowhere. Weasel Tail would die, and the white man who had shot him would die also. That was Howling Wolf's medicine. Old Man had sent him a dream, and this was how it was to be.

The doctor, in conference later with the Superintendent, reported all this.

"I don't like the looks of things," he said. "Weasel Tail could have recovered under ordinary conditons, but he hasn't a chance. And a lot of young bucks are making it a personal matter. Ever since McNair beat up Little Dog at the Fair there's been trouble."

But Weasel Tail was still alive when, around the middle of November, the Potter company took over the ranch.

By Jake's arrangement with the Dowlings he had kept

some stock of his own at the ranch, a hundred odd head of cattle and a dozen horses. Under ordinary circumstances he might have arranged with the Potter outfit for winter feed for them, but the circumstances were not ordinary. Not only was the company carrying all the stock it could manage, so that it needed every ton of hay, but there was an old grudge between Jake and the heads of the concern, and he was asking no favors of them.

On a raw day then, a week or so later, Tom and Jake started to drive the stock to Jake's homestead in the bad lands. Both men were bundled to the eyes, but the wind pierced their plaid Oregon coats, their mufflers and gloves. Jake was not well at the start; he rode huddled in his saddle, staring ahead, brooding. He had no hay at the homestead, nothing. The stock would have to winter in the breaks as best they could. On the first night out they slept in a barn, having put the cattle and horses into a pasture, but he shivered all night and slept very little.

Tom was worried, but Jake seemed better the next day, except for a small hacking cough. He was not cold any longer, and he talked more than usual. Tom, trying to forget the Dowlings, found himself willy-nilly involved in long discussions of them. It was a painful business all round, and it was not improved by Jake's revelation that Henry Dowling had refused to finance the defence in the forthcoming trial.

"What pains me," he said, "is that I sure thought he'd do it," Jake finished. "But it seems like something made him change his mind. You didn't write a letter to the girl, Tom, did you?"

"No," Tom said shortly.

When, after five days on the way they reached the homestead, Jake was a very sick man. Tom turned out the stock and came back to find Jake in one of the built-in bunks in the cabin, just as he had left the saddle. He built a roaring fire and Jake roused and looked around.

"I can't bring her here, Tom. Never."

"It looks bad now, but it won't take much to make it weather tight."

But Jake only groaned.

By morning Tom knew Jake had pneumonia, and that unless he had help he would die. He saddled the Miller, piled wood by the fire, put water by Jake's bunk and started off. It took him half a day to make the ride, going at his horse's best speed, and when he finally got to Ursula Doctor Dunham was out in the back country somewhere on a case. It was almost evening when they started back, this time in the doctor's car. There were no roads; only a track which led down into ravines, turned precariously on itself, led up again. Tom drove, the little old medical man sat huddled in the seat beside him. Only once, after the car had lurched and almost gone over a bank, did he protest.

"Hell's bells, Tom!" he said. "If you've got another attack of that recurrent homicidal mania of yours, better wait until we're on the way back."

Jake was practically unconscious when they arrived. The fire had gone out and the room was very cold. The sound of his breathing filled it. Tom, building up the fire while the doctor examined him, could think of nothing but that struggle for breath going on behind him. And soon the doctor would have to go away, and he would be left alone with it.

"How about sending for his wife?" he asked.

"Where is she?"

"In town."

"I'll get word to her, but I doubt if she'll be in time."

"It's as bad as that, is it?"

"It's about as bad as it can be."

He left some medicines and some whisky and went away again. He had secured Mrs. Mallory's address and promised to bring her with him the next day, and Tom held a lantern for him while he started the car. But the last words he heard over the engine sent him back into the cabin savage with anger.

"Remember, Tom, that whisky's for Jake."

He sat up all that night. He piled wood on the fire until the floor boards smoked in front of it, but back by the bunk where Jake lay it was still cold. And all night long that struggle for breath went on, all night and into the dawn. Then it quieted somewhat, and Tom fell into an exhausted sleep.

When he wakened the sun was up, and Jake was dead.

It was noon and snowing when the doctor arrived. Mrs. Mallory was with him. She looked old and gray, and Tom, meeting them outside, stumbled over what he had to tell her. She crawled out of the car and stood swaying, with her face working, and he put his arm around her and helped her inside.

He had been at work since dawn. The cabin was clean and a good fire going. Jake lay in the lower bunk, his hands folded over his breast. He looked very placid and faintly smiling; and the blankets were neatly folded over him. Mrs. Mallory got down on her knees heavily and gazed at him.

"Jake!" she said. "My Jake! How am I going to live without you?"

After a while she got up. Tom had made coffee but she would not touch it. She went to the window and stood staring out at the falling snow.

"I can't leave him here," she said, without turning. "We've got to get him back somehow."

They knew what she meant. If the snow kept on soon the roads would be closed entirely, and they would have to bury him there. And every hour counted. There might not be time even to send for the body; they would have to take it along.

Tom went with them, supporting Jake in the rear of the car. Mrs. Mallory sat in front, and not once did she turn around. She sat staring ahead of her, thinking of God knows what; remembering, no doubt, after the fashion of women at such times, the small contentions, the missed affections of all those years; blaming herself; looking back. Looking back.

When the funeral was over Tom went back to the cabin. There was nothing else to do. The stock required some sort of supervision. He carried back with him tar-paper to line the shack, groceries, what not. But his heart was heavy. One thing he did at once on his return. He took the half emptied pint of whisky the doctor had left, and put it out of sight on a rafter.

"Now," he said grimly to himself, "we'll see how much of a man you are, Tom McNair."

He never touched it. There were times later on when he came in, frozen to the bone, and looked up at the rafter with eyes almost swollen shut with snow blindness and the hard cold winds; once he even drew a chair under it. But he flung the chair away violently, and made himself some hot coffee instead.

The days were not so bad. He rode out, examining the fences, cutting water holes in the creek with an ax. Before his death Jake had leased some additional land, and the cattle fed along the bare ridges where the wind had blown the snow away. But the nights were terrible.

There were times, sitting by his fire, when he seemed to hear once more that struggle for breath behind him, and he would look fearfully over his shoulder.

Now and then he had a letter from Clare, fervid, immature notes to which, sitting at his table in the long evenings, he wrote occasional perfunctory replies.

Dear Clare:

Things are going along here all right. I keep busy and I guess that's the answer to a lot of things. Don't you worry about the Indian matter. I'm not pulling leather any yet. You might go around and see the Mallorys sometimes. I guess they are pretty lonesome.

Yours,

TOM

Sometimes he talked to himself aloud, as lonely men often do. Perhaps there were even times when he was not quite balanced; there was that obsession about Jake's bunk, for instance. And because he refused to admit Kay to his waking thoughts, she began to trouble him in his sleep. He wakened one night to see her standing by the fire in her riding clothes. He had to sit up in the bunk to convince himself she was not there.

Then, shortly after Christmas Weasel Tail finally died, and a Deputy Sheriff took advantage of a chinook and a spell of warm weather to ride out and tell him. The trial was set for February.

He was scarcely interested. He did not much care, these days, how the affair turned out. He was gaunt and unshaven most of the time. His small supply of clothing had practically given out, and he had refused money except for necessary food from Mrs. Mallory. His hands were broken and blistered under his ragged gloves, his eyelids swollen, his lips cracked.

"I'll be there. You tell 'em," he said to the Deputy.

And before the Deputy left he gave him the bottle from the rafter.

"You'd better keep it, Tom. You look as if you needed it."

There was a trace of his old swagger in his reply.

"Who? Me? Never felt better in my life. I'm as tough as a boiled owl."

But the story that went back did no harm to his case when it finally went to trial. The fact that he had taken hold of the Mallory situation and was staying alone to save Mrs. Mallory's stock was operating in his favor. Men who had only known the reckless side of him were more favorably impressed. When it was learned that he was taking no money from the widow, this feeling grew, and it was not decreased by the general opinion that Henry Dowling had shirked a responsibility that was his by right; that he had not only done this, but that by selling the ranch at an unseasonable time and turning Jake off, he had contributed to his death.

Chapter Seventeen

In February Tom was tried and triumphantly acquitted. There was almost a public demonstration of approval. Only the Indians were sullen and vindictive in manner. They left the Court House, got into their buckboards or onto their ponies and rode back to to the Reservation, talking in low voices among themselves. To their long tale of injury by the whites they now added this one more.

Allison, standing by Tom's elbow at the window of his office, looked out on the public square and analyzed the situation in a few pregnant words.

"They'll try to get you, Tom," he said. "This place is plumb unhealthy for you."

Tom only laughed.

Clare had been at the trial. She had dramatized herself and the situation by bringing her mother, and sitting in the front row holding her calloused hand all through the proceedings. Such demonstrations had been unknown between them, and the older woman was self-conscious and embarrassed. She would free herself now and then, to feel for her handkerchief, to straighten her hat, only a moment later to be caught again and to feel vaguely ridiculous.

Now Tom could see Clare, waiting patiently outside on the steps. He did not want to see her. He wanted to meet some of the fellows at the Martin House and satisfy his starved gregarious instinct, talk man-talk once again. But he knew there was no hope. He went down the stairs and out, shaking hands right and left, and with a fixed smile on his face confronted Clare.

If she had been effusive before the crowd he might have hardened himself to her, but she was not. Moreover, to his surprise, he saw she had been crying; her eyes were red, her handkerchief crumpled in her hand. And if there was method in her tears at least the noisy hearty group waiting for him outside respected them. They shook his hand, slapped him with mighty blows on the back, and then drifted cheerfully and delicately away.

"Drop in at the hotel if you can, Tom. Ray Masterson's got a room there."

"Maybe, later on."

He fairly ached to go, to meet the boys again, to sit in Ray Masterson's room on the bed, the floor, anywhere, and hear noisy commonplace talking going on around him. To talk himself; shop talk, of cattle and horses and riders; of how the Potters were making out with their new property; of the new oil field just opening up south near Easton. But there was Clare, making her silent demand on him; a proper demand too, he realized.

"Mom's expecting you to supper, Tom."

"I'll have to see Mrs. Mallory first."

"She might have come today, after all you've done for her."

"She's not well. Nellie was there. I saw her."

Clare sniffed.

"I'll tell the world she was!" she said. "If the whole court room doesn't know she's crazy about you it's not her fault."

"That's silly. She's only a kid."

He was irritable when she insisted on going with him to the Mallory house, a small two-story frame affair on a back street, and even on following him upstairs to where Mrs.

Mallory, still broken by Jake's death, lay in bed propped up with pillows. But in spite of Clare's frozen silence and her downright rudeness to Nellie, he relaxed under their gratitude and their relief at his acquittal.

"God keeps some sort of a balance sheet, Tom. And the way you've acted this winter sure paid off a lot of scores."

"I only did what any white man would have done," he said awkwardly.

But she had some news for him, too. Her nephew from Colorado was coming up. He had been a cow-hand, and he had agreed to work through the spring and summer, and up to shipping time in the fall. Then she could ship and have a little capital.

Clare listened intently, while she watched Nellie at the same time. Then she sprung her little trap. She got up and began to button her coat.

"Then I guess we can be married, soon as you get a job, Tom."

He could have killed her where she stood. He never saw that Nellie went pale, but he did see Mrs. Mallory's eyes narrow as she looked at Clare.

"If Tom takes my advice," she said coldly, "he won't marry for a considerable time. You hear that, Tom?"

"I don't know that we're asking any advice," Clare retorted, her voice sharpening. "That's our business."

"I haven't heard Tom say anything. And I'll thank you to go down those stairs and let me say a few words in private with him. I've got some business with him."

Clare had to go, and Nellie slipped out after her and closed the door.

"Is that little slut telling the truth?" Mrs. Mallory demanded.

"Well, yes and no. I'm under kind of an obligation to her, but she knows I'm not the marrying kind."

"What kind of an obligation?"

"Not what you think. It's just—"

"Never mind what it is. You let her go; do you hear me, Tom? She's no good. She's lazy and vain and selfish. If she's got you in a corner be a man and get out." Then she altered her tone. "I've got something here to show you. Maybe when you see it—"

She drew a letter from under her pillow and held it out to him. When he opened it a slip of paper fell to the floor. Mrs. Mallory was watching him from the bed.

"That's the check," she said. "Read the letter, Tom. It's from Kay Dowling."

He read it, his big hands shaking so that the paper rattled. Kay was sending on money, she said, because she felt it was not fair to Tom McNair to ask him to work all winter without pay. Indeed, she recognized fully her own responsibility in the whole matter. She would prefer not to be known as the sender, and she was apologetic for the small amount. She always had everything but money. The check was for two hundred and fifty dollars.

He put both letter and check carefully back on the bed.

"How did she know about me?"

"I wrote her, Tom. I wrote her about Jake, and I told her what you were doing. But that's all. I didn't ask for a cent."

"And I'm not taking a cent," he said roughly. "I aim to manage without the Dowling money, and you can tell her so for me."

In the small hall below Clare was waiting for him, tapping her absurd heels, and Nellie was not in sight. But either she had listened or Nellie had told her, for she asked at once to see the check.

"I didn't take it."

She stared at him, with two angry spots of color in her cheeks.

"Then you're a fool. Why shouldn't you have it? They'd have let you hang today if they could."

"That's my business, my girl," he told her, and stalked out.

Supper at the Hamels was a painful affair that night. Tom

was still furiously angry over Kay's tender of money, and resentful at being where he was. Mrs. Hamel passed the food, making frequent trips to the kitchen; Mr. Hamel ate enormously and noisily, and under the impression that shootings would interest a man just acquitted of one, harked back into long reminiscences of the bad old days when he ran the Last Chance saloon.

"Yes, sir," he would say. "He shot from the doorway and got all three of them in a row as they stood there. Just like stringing fish, it was."

"Pop, for heaven's sake! Let's be cheerful."

It was Tom's first meal with Clare's family, and as it went on he realized that to all of them it had a particular significance. It amounted to what in more sophisticated circles would have been a formal recognition of the relationship between Clare and himself.

"When you two get married," Mrs. Hamel said once, "pa and I were thinking maybe you could use the parlor until you get on your feet. We don't need it much, and it's bigger than Clare's room."

"I haven't even got a job yet," he parried.

"Well, you're young and able-bodied. You'll get something."

The trap was closing. He glanced at Clare, but she gazed fixedly at her plate. Afterwards, in the parlor with the door closed and the newly painted stove sending a thick odor of burning blacking into the room, Clare put her face up to be kissed and he held her off, his hands on her shoulders.

"Kind of pushing things a bit, aren't you, Clare?"

"What else did you expect? I told them right off. Pop'd have killed me if I hadn't."

"A girl's a fool to marry a man when he—when he doesn't want to get married. It's all wrong, Clare. You've got a right to somebody who's ready to settle down. You've got a right to be happy."

"I'm taking that chance," she told him. And because there

was something pathetic about her determination he kissed her. She clung to him feverishly, instinctively holding to him as if by sheer contact to inflame him into desire for her. But a thousand other things were milling in his mind. Resentment at the loss of his freedom; the depth to which Kay must think he had sunk to take money from her; and mixed in with that his desire to escape from the house, to see the boys at the Martin House, even after his long abstinence to get a drink of hot burning liquor, and wash away memory and the damned stench of that stove and Clare's cheap perfume.

He loosened her hold on him.

"We'll have to open a door or something, Clare. I can't breathe."

She opened the door without a word and went across to her room. He thought at first that she had left him, and was divided between relief and a sense of guilt, but she came back with an armful of linen and finery and demanded his attention. He tried his best to play up.

"What's that for?"

"It's for the dining room table."

"Better get one first. All I've got's a horse. Might look well on him."

But it was when she began on her personal wardrobe that he realized how firmly the trap had set. She held up little new undergarments of so private a nature that they made him uncomfortable and self-conscious. He passed them off with a joke.

"You mean to say you can get into anything that size?"

"I'm not very big, Tom."

And something in her tone, in the array of fragile feminine garments all around, in the fact that she herself was fragile, feminine and greatly in love with him, touched him profoundly. He put his arms around her.

"I'm not much," he said, "but if we do get married I'll try to be good to you. You know that, don't you?"

It was after eleven when he reached the Martin House. Ed

told him that the crowd was in thirty-four and that they were expecting him, but with his hand on the door knob he turned away. If he was going to bury Kay Dowling forever, as now he must, he was going to do it decently, not with liquor.

The hired car dropped him at an outlying ranch, where he had left his horse, and without rousing the family he got the Miller and rode off. He found himself looking forward to the shack as a sort of sanctuary. He was done for, in spite of his acquittal that day. He would marry Clare; that was all he could do. But in the back of his mind he knew that Mrs. Mallory had been right. Clare was all that she had said; and more. She could be shrewish, too. He would find himself with a scolding nagging wife, and there would be no love on his side to help him to tolerance. He knew his own temper; he turned half sick with fear.

It was very dark as he rode along. The Miller picked his steps carefully, finding the track where Tom could see nothing. Once or twice, a mile or so from the ranch house, he half stopped and snorted, but Tom quieted him with a hand on his neck. Tom himself was on the alert now, and the Sheriff's warning recurred to him. But for another half mile nothing happened. Then a shot came from somewhere to the left, and was repeated.

He felt the big horse jump and quiver and knew that he was hit, but he lunged ahead in a sort of broken gallop. Tom slid out of the saddle on the right side and hung there, but the Miller was still running, and the shots were not repeated. But at the end of a mile the animal came down heavily. Tom, dropping behind him for safety, hatred and savage anger in his heart, felt him struggle once and lie still.

He remained where he was until dawn, crouched behind the dead animal, waiting and listening, but nothing more happened. At times he talked to the big horse. With the first daylight he walked back to the scene of the tragedy, morose and blindly revengeful, but although he searched the creek foot by foot he found no trace of the killer. He went on foot back to the ranch, borrowed a horse and got a spade. Then he went back. But he could not bury the Miller. The ground was frozen hard.

He roped the body and dragged it away from the road, and then piled snow and rocks over it. But he knew it was no use. By nightfall the coyotes would have scented it, and be making their wary circles about it; then they would close in.

Chapter Eighteen

It was in February that Kay finally accepted Herbert.

She was honest with him.

"You know," she said, "that I cared for Tom McNair. I think it is all over, and anyhow I always knew it couldn't be. I would have been unhappy with him, and he would have made me wretched."

"I won't force myself on you, Kay. If ever you feel—"

"I know that. I shall feel safe with you, Herbert."

She told her father and mother that night, in her mother's bedroom. Katherine was lying back on her *chaise longue*—she seemed to lie down a great deal those days—and Kay felt slightly comforted by the relief in Henry's face.

"Herbert will talk to you tomorrow," she told him. "But I wanted to tell you myself, so you will know—"

To his credit he understood.

But when she looked at Katherine she saw, to her amazement, that there were tears in her eyes.

"I thought it would please you, mother dear."

"Is that why you did it, Kay?"

It was the nearest to an attempt at her confidence that Katherine had ever come, and Kay looked down at her ring.

"No," she said slowly. "I'm fond of Herbert, mother. I'll do my best to make him happy. I—we, that is—" She stopped suddenly; already she was saying "we!" "We have no plans yet," she went on painfully. "We are not in a hurry. But I wanted you to know as soon as possible."

After that she went into her own room, and closed and locked the door. And late that night she opened the wall safe where she kept her grandmother's pearls, and took out the snap-shot of Tom McNair. But she did not look at it. She took a match and set fire to a corner, and then held it while it burned. When the flame got too close to her fingers she dropped it into a cigarette tray—she was still smoking more than was good for her—and watched it until it was a heap of fine ash.

But for some curious reason she did not say her prayers that night. She had always done it, even at boarding school, kneeling on the bare cold floor.

"Sh! Kay's at her ablutions!" the girls would say.

Perhaps she felt that night that having taken her life into her own hands, there was not much use appealing to God. Perhaps it was because she had prayed for certain things recently, and they had not been granted. There was no particular revolt in her, if there was no particular hope. And another curious thing; she slept better that night than for months. It rather puzzled her the next morning. It did not occur to her that sleep as well as fainting may be an escape from the unbearable.

The engagement was announced as soon as Herbert had seen her father. She was entirely acquiescent. But she had a new Herbert to deal with after that, a debonair, self-assured Herbert, filled with plans. Henry was giving him a partnership in one of his subsidiary companies, and was setting aside a definite sum for Kay, the income to be paid annually. Herbert took to wearing a gardenia in his buttonhole, and was looking at houses.

"What we need," he said oracularly, "is a good dining room, Kay. We'll be giving dinners, and if we can seat eighteen or twenty it makes it easier."

He found one to his liking one day, and came to take her to see it. But she was not at home. As a matter of fact, it was the anniversary of old Lucius's death, and she had asked to take the flowers. She stayed there for quite a long time, staring at the shaft where Katherine had wanted to put "He has followed the trail into the sunset" and had been voted down. But she was very apologetic when she got home, and quite gay at dinner that night.

On the surface, then, she fooled everybody. But she wakened sometimes to find that she had been crying in the night; that some forgotten dream had dampened her pillow and swollen her eyes. She would get up and bathe them in cold water before she rang her bell, and then the day would begin and she could forget. Boxes would arrive, people would be coming and going. There were notes to write and clothes to be fitted.

Even Bessie was deceived for a time. Then one morning when Kay had been out late the night before, she arrived before she had wakened. She fidgeted about for a while and then walked into Kay's room. She was still asleep, but her pillow was wet with tears.

Bessie stood looking down at her, her long cigarette holder in her hand, and Kay stirred and roused. She felt the damp pillow and tried to turn it, but it was too late.

"Kay darling," Bessie said, "maybe I ought to keep my mouth shut, but—do you think you'd better go through with this?"

"I'm all right in the daytime, Aunt Bessie. It's only at night—"

"At night! Good heavens, Kay, you'll have to sleep with the man you marry! If you're going to cry about somebody else in your sleep it isn't fair to Herbert. It's—it's not decent."

"But I don't know who or what it's about. Honestly. I never remember."

Bessie sniffed and went out. The child never remembered! Then it must be a regular thing. She was breaking her heart about something, and she—Bessie—knew well enough what it was.

Henry had started making invitation lists. He would pore over the Social Register, and he took to making small memoranda of his own in the car, using the backs of old envelopes for the purpose and then mislaying them.

"Now where the mischief did I put that? I thought of two or three people today that I don't want to forget."

In time the wedding clothes began to come in; boxes from French shops containing sets of chemise, abbreviated little bloomers and nightdress to match, in palest shades of chiffon; tea gowns and négligées over which Nora folded her hands and turned up her eyes in ecstasy; evening wraps, sport frocks, dinner gowns, ball dresses.

"How soon?" Herbert had asked.

"Whenever you like."

The date was finally set for May, and after some argument, a country wedding was decided on. Now it was the country house which engrossed Henry and Katherine's interest. All through March and into April they made small chilly pilgrimages out to the country. Each opening bud had significance. As early as the ground could be worked men were digging and sowing. Borders were planted and replanted. And if Katherine now and then looked at Kay with furtively anxious eyes, the excitement seemed to be doing her good.

There ought to be new hangings in the long drawing room, and perhaps in the hall. And there were some old French chairs at Morley's still in the original brocade. However, since most of the furniture would be moved out anyhow, perhaps not the chairs. But the curtains. Yes. Certainly the curtains.

Kay seemed hardly to have finished writing the notes for her engagement presents when the wedding gifts started to come in. Herbert was frightfully excited about them, although he strove to conceal it. He would call up from town—they had moved out again to the country—and ask her about them.

"What's come in this morning?"

"I really don't know. A lot of boxes; they haven't been opened yet.

That was always a small grievance to him.

"But great scott, darling! There are about fifteen men around the place. Can't some of them get to work?"

In the evenings he spent most of his time in the three upper rooms where, on long tables and minus their cards, of course, the gifts lay in glittering rows; and one evening he brought out a book, a sort of ledger, and began to enter them for insurance.

"But we have a book already," she said, somewhat exasperated. "Everything is in it; who sent them, the shop they came from—"

"This is a different matter," he told her, in a voice so exactly like Henry's that she started. "There is a very large sum of money invested here, and it requires protection."

Even at that, she liked him better with a book in his hands than with herself in his arms. There must have been times when Herbert felt her recoil, and knew, for a moment anyhow, that what she wanted from him was not love at all, but relief from pain and security against some weakness in herself. If he did, he undoubtedly comforted himself with the fallacy of most males, that when he owned her he could win her. Indeed, he said as much to Bessie Osborne one day. There was little or no beating about the bush with Bessie.

"Kay's looking thin, don't you think?"

"She's doing too much. All these parties before a wedding are ridiculous."

"You think that's it?"

"Don't you?"

"I'm wondering. Does she ever speak of that cowboy of hers?"

He flushed with annoyance.

"I do Kay the common justice of believing," he said stiffly, "that if that were not over she would not be marrying me."

"I'm sure that's very fine of you," said Bessie cryptically.

"As for the inference you have drawn, it is unfair to Kay and unfair to me. Even if it were true, once we are married all that nonsense will be cured."

Bessie yawned slightly.

"I daresay," she agreed. "There is certainly no nonsense about you, Herbert."

The presents continued to pour in. The station wagon met every train, and came back loaded; the delivery truck from the express office made three trips daily. Silver. Glass. Paintings. Antiques. Mirrors. Kay writing notes: "My dear Mrs. Smith: I want to thank you, for Herbert and myself, for the exquisite old Chelsea tea set. It was dear of you to remember us so beautifully, and we—"

The wedding was still two weeks off, but already her wedding gown of rose point over white satin lay on a bed in an empty room, covered with a sheet, her veil of old lace beside it. Now and then the bridesmaids wandered in and lifting a corner of the sheet burst into little ohs and ahs of admiration. The gown was more than a gown to them. It was a symbol. They had an eager half-neurotic curiosity about Kay and Herbert. It was impossible to believe that these two self-contained people were soon to be one flesh, to share the same room, to enter into each other's most private lives.

Once, to please them, Kay put on her veil, with its bandeau of seed pearls, and Nora coming in whipped it off quickly.

"That's bad luck, Miss Kay! And you know it."

"What bad luck can touch her?" one of the girls drawled. "She's got everything, including—Herbert."

If there was malice in that Kay ignored it.

She meant to make Herbert a good wife. She did not believe in dutiful wives; she knew there must be more than that, so she meant to make him a loving wife. In a way she did care for Herbert; if she had not known the other thing she might even have called it love. He was consistently kind, and he took care not to ask of her more than she could give. And perhaps like Herbert she too believed in marriage as a sort of cure-all.

She was already saying "we" as well as writing it in her notes of thanks. And one night, when Herbert had kissed her and was about to go, she almost said a dreadful thing. He had got as far as the door.

"Well, good night, Kay."

"Good night, Herbert. Be sure—" She caught herself then, but Herbert had turned.

"Be sure what, darling?"

"I've forgotten now. It wasn't important."

But it gave him an excuse to come back and kiss her again. After that she was more careful.

Chapter Nineteen

Tom had a second and very narrow escape from death that spring, before the nephew from Colorado rode to the shack with a letter from Nellie Mallory in his pocket.

He had missed the Miller badly, and one early morning he roped a green bronc and started out on his rounds. But something stampeded the horse just outside the corral, and he ran. Things would have been all right, but the animal slipped and almost fell, and when he had recovered Tom was hanging head down across the saddle; with the horn caught in the leather belt of his chaps. After that the horse went crazy, and Tom stared death in the face; he could neither free himself nor right himself. At any moment he knew that the frantic animal might drop into a break or plunge over the steep side of a butte.

If he prayed for anything it was probably for death outright, and not to be left with a broken back in that solitary land. But his mind was working clearly, and just in time he began to work at the cinch buckle. When he had loosened it and the saddle fell, he picked himself up and looked about, but there was no horse in sight.

He found it with a broken neck at the foot of a gulch a few yards ahead, and it is typical that his main grievance about the whole matter was that he had to carry his saddle back!

Although it was the middle of March, the late spring of the Northwest was still far away; the earth was like granite, the trees so brittle that they broke at a touch. In his bunk at night he piled on all his blankets and yet shivered, and the heat from his fire melted the snow on the leaking roof, so that during the night small icicles formed, to drip drearily throughout the day.

The long winter had told on him. Outside of his daily routine he was listless and apathetic. He had no books, even had he cared to read them, but now and then a paper drifted his way. In one of them he read the announcement of his engagement to Clare: "Mr. and Mrs. Gustavus Hamel"—in the language of the society editor—"announce the engagement of their daughter, Miss Clare Hamel, to Mr. Thomas McNair." He read it, grunted and threw the paper in the fire.

And then came the Colorado nephew, and Nellie's letter.

"Dear Tom: I've had a postcard from Ray. He stopped over in Oklahoma at the Ninety Nine Ranch, and he says they can use some riders. Why don't you go, Tom? You sure can ride, and if I were you I'd get away from this town. Did you see what she had the nerve to put in the paper?"

There was more of the letter; Nellie had more or less poured out her heart, but Tom's eyes were glued to that first paragraph. After all, why not? And Bill was with the railroad now, running freight. He'd take care of him for part of the way anyhow.

But what about Clare? He had told her he was in no position to marry. She knew it, anyhow, and into the bargain he had a shrewd idea that whatever had come out about her part in his escape she had told herself.

"Wasn't taking any chances," he reflected miserably.

She had had time, plenty of time, to get back from that way station before daylight.

"Understand you're thinking of getting married," said the Colorado boy that night, conversationally. He was deeply thrilled at being there with Tom, who had killed a man and had his horse shot under him, and was a famous rider into the bargain.

"So I hear!"

"Take it from me," said the Colorado boy, "once a fellow in our line gets married, he's through. I've seen it tried out, but I've never seen it work yet."

Lying awake in the bunk that night Tom thought over that. It wouldn't work. In a month he and Clare would be at each other's throats. If she would not save herself, he would save her.

He got up and sitting at the table in the cold, wrote her a letter. He'd been thinking matters over. Of course she could hold him to his promise if she wanted to, but—

He ended by telling her that he was going away to look for work, but he was careful not to tell her where, and when he crawled into his blankets again, shaking with the cold, it was to sleep more quietly than he had for many nights.

The next day he inducted the Colorado boy into the new job, got him to ride that night with him to the water tank at Prairie Dog—coal tipple, tank and one house—in order to take his horse back, and with a war bag for his gear, and empty pockets, climbed Bill's train and found himself in the old familiar environment of water butts, lanterns, coal bin, bed-rolls, green order slips and dented coffee pot on a red hot stove. No one asked him any questions. Bill was glad to see him, the rest of the crew accepted him. And by the freemasonry of their order they passed him on; he moved from caboose to caboose, but always South. The weather moderated; he had left winter and was finding spring, and the young life in him, which had apparently been frozen, began to revive.

"Old Man's sure been good to these folks," he said to the last conductor, when they were rolling across the plains of Oklahoma.

"Sure has. Twelve feet of good earth on top and oil underneath."

He understood that later on when he got off at the town near the ranch and saw the great oil refinery and the miles of storage tanks. To and from the refinery engines were moving long lines of tank cars. They crept along endlessly, and as a result ships ploughed their way under forced draft to strange parts of the world, locomotives moved, houses were heated, automobiles sped along.

For the first time in all his hard-driven young life Tom saw the spectacle of easy money. Up to that time he had seen the earth as something from which one wrung a difficult livelihood, and Nature as a stepmother, alternating between moods of tolerance and cruelty. This then was how the Dowlings and their kind were made. They found where Nature was generous, and exploited her. It was not that they were smarter than other people; they just knew more. They borrowed money and built railroads, or they drilled holes and found silver or gold, or oil, and suddenly they were rich. When they had money they could travel and learn more; learn how to make more money and how to spend it. And by this erect barriers between themselves and the rest of the world.

He brooded. The rain penetrated his clothing and dripped off the wide brim of his hat. Cars passed him, but no one stopped and picked him up. They were all on their way somewhere. It was like Chicago.

But a mile or so from the ranch he suddenly stopped. Buffalo! Surely those were buffalo! He leaned on the fence and gazed across at them. They were in a field of young alfalfa, and they looked fat and contented. Once they had ranged the plains, following the grass; the bulls had fought in the spring, and the cows had been the prize of the victor. Now they were fed and cared for, inside the wire.

Wasn't that life all over? If you were footloose you were poor, but if you were rich you were always behind wire.

He thought of Kay. The wire was around her, and she couldn't get out. And when he tried to get through it to her it had thrown and torn him. Well, he was through with that. He was free. He trudged along.

Later on he found the chief cowboy in an office. He was bedraggled and weary, and Arizona, who was the chief, was busy. But when he told him his name he looked up.

"McNair? You the fellow Ray Masterson was speaking about?"

"Depends on what Ray said!"

"He said you were a rider."

"Well," Tom drawled, "I reckon to sit on as long as most, and then some."

Arizona grinned.

"We'll try you out and see," he said. "You'll have some competition."

"That's my middle name," Tom told him.

The Ninety Nine Ranch was the home of the Ninety Nine Traveling Rodeo and Wild West Show. During the season, from the first of May until bad weather in the autumn, its long train of yellow cars moved from city to city, preceded by advance men and bill posters. Its flaming twenty-four sheets had, at one time or another, adorned the boardings, empty barns and fences of most of the country. It was a complete unit in itself, from the cowboy band in their checked flannel shirts to the candy butchers; it had its sideshows like any circus, its "spectacular," popularly known as the Spec; it had its freaks, its Arabs, its ballet. It even carried with it a few camels and a half dozen elephants, in addition to its buffaloes, steers and its innumerable horses.

But it was, first, last and always, an attempt to show the Old West. It had its stage-coach holdup, its prairie schooner attacked by Indians, and mostly it had its cowboys.

They came in the spring from all over the cattle country, the southern ones sitting their bucking horses tight and using their long spurs only moderately, the northern ones looser in the saddle but apt to scratch "wider and higher." They wandered in, after the long lonely winter on the range somewhere, found good food and good housing, and between trials in the arena were content to sit on their heels in the Oklahoma sun and talk, or to buy pop and feed it to the bear in his cage beside the ranch store.

Tom was contented; his gregarious instinct was satisfied, the interest of the new life bid fair to put Kay out of his mind. He drew some money in advance and bought clothing at the store, a green silk shirt and yellow handkerchief, and a new enormous cream-colored Stetson. The girls—cowgirls and high-school riders—began to look at him and talk about him; when he was riding in the arena there would be a small gallery, ardent and applauding. He never looked their way, but he was intensely conscious of them. And one day he took a rope into the field and standing on his head neatly threw his loop over a running horse. He had to wash the dirt out of his hair later on, but the girls were thrilled.

He had misadventures, naturally. One day, carelessly standing too close to the pen of Tony, the bear, he felt a sudden clutch from the rear and left the seat of a new pair of trousers in the cage. Even the Indians standing about laughed at that.

"If you wanted these pants why didn't you ask for them like a gentleman?" he reproached the bear as he tied his coat around his waist.

He painted a sign that day and hung it on the cage: "T. Bear, gent's tailor. Apply at rear." His boyishness had come back.

He began to improve in physical condition, also. The food was excellent, and he put on a little weight. His waist remained as slim as ever, but his face was fuller and his good looks had come back. He even struck a friendship with a little Cossack, member of a troupe just brought from Europe. He made fun of his long coat, with the row of cartridge pockets across the chest, of his soft-soled boots and cocky high astrakhan hat. And the Cossack in turn would point to Tom's absurd Stetson, his high-heeled boots and leather chaps, and grin. They talked to each other with signs and smiles, and in their leisure time wandered about together. At first the Cossack could not believe that Tom spoke only his mother tongue; he tried him in German, in exquisite French, even in Italian.

"No savvy," Tom would say, cheerfully. "Now see here, Murphy—" he had christened him Murphy, "that's a cow. Say 'cow'!"

And Murphy would obediently say "cow."

Tom never knew that the little Cossack had been a great aristocrat in old Russia; that he had lived in a palace, and that serfs had bowed down to him as he passed along the road. In the evenings they would sit companionably in the door of one of the wooden huts where the show people were housed and smoke their cigarettes together.

"Friends, Murphy, you and me," Tom would point to the Cossack and then to himself. "Say 'friends.'"

Sometimes arm in arm they wandered about together, and because one was tall and the other short they were called Mutt and Jeff. They would climb amiably to where the dancing master worked in a great loft above the paint shop, and stand watching him. He was having a hard time. The dancing girls wore boots, short bloomers of blue checked calico, and anything above them. "One-two-three-four," chanted the teacher. Then he would hum a tune and himself dance the strenuous steps. The girls would watch Tom, pull their short hair over their cheeks, chew gum and idly follow the commands.

As soon as the little German saw the two of them he would order them out.

It was a new world, a world of strange sights and sounds.

One morning Tom saw one of a Zouave troupe come out of his shack, face to the East, and bow his head three times to the ground. He was stupefied with amazement.

"You can't beat that. What's he doing anyhow?"

"He's praying."

"Say, it's the hell of a big world, isn't it?" . . .

It was almost time to go. Schedules were posted for the use of the arena; the Colonel was reviewing the acts; Indians began to arrive in numbers, in flivvers or in wagons piled high with tepees and other gear, leading the pinto ponies they affected. They brought their women along, the local ones tattooed with blue ink on the forehead. Tiny papooses, strapped to boards and set upright, surveyed this strange new world out of wide black shoe-button eyes. The Navajos set up crude frames and began their rug weaving for the side show, or laid out the turquoises which were later to be made into silver jewelry.

One day the ranch peacock was found ashamed and humiliated hiding under a hedge, his insignia of masculinity gone, his great tail removed. The Navajos were suspected but it could not be proved.

In the sunny mornings the great red and gold wagons, the six-horse hitches, the eight-ups and ten-ups, were driven slowly up and down the road for exercise. Enormous beautiful animals, their coats glistening, they moved proudly and with dignity. Later on the elephants would lumber out of their barn and cross to their enclosure.

"Get on there, Babe! What's the matter with you, Louie?"

Their wise little eyes were filled with mischief. Standing demurely, they would back slowly against the fence, and try to throw it down, and Tom, fascinated like a small boy by them, would watch and say nothing.

Discipline was excellent. The company allowed no drinking. Otherwise it was extremely indulgent. It fed its people well, gave them certain hours of work and then let them alone. Order began to assert itself; the horses, fed oats daily and worked regularly, began to sweat off their winter coats. The Cossacks, riding them like demons for two or three hours, cared for them carefully afterwards, rubbed them down, watched them for saddle and cinch sores.

Emulation too began to put them on their toes. When the Cossacks rode standing on their saddles, their toes in their soft-soled boots caught in the tops of their saddle pockets, there was a raid on rubber-soled tennis shoes in town, and the cowboys tried it without pockets.

And then one day a switch engine backed onto the siding nearby, with forty yellow circus cars in its wake. Tom sat that evening as usual in the doorway with the little Cossack who had been a prince, but he taught him no English that night. He was oddly depressed and quiet.

"You are sad tonight, my friend," said the Cossack, in Russian.

Tom did not understand, of course, but perhaps the tone meant something to him. He stirred and pointed to the cars on the siding in the moonlight.

"Tea party's about over, Murphy! I wonder how you'll like it when it rains, and we're working in mud to our knees."

"Once, at home," said the little Cossack thoughtfully, still in Russian, "I fell in love with a lady of the circus. She was very beautiful. But my people—Ah!"

They smoked in silence. Each was thinking of a lost lady, but the little Cossack's eyes were tender, and Tom's were hard.

It was the next day that Little Dog joined the show. Tom, wandering into the store to buy a bottle of pop for Tony the bear, saw him and standing still, watched him warily. The store was crowded. At the rear squaws in black shawls over bright calico dresses were buying meat, stabbing at it with dirty forefingers and haggling over the price. Dignified old bucks in store clothes, with red or yellow flannel worked into their braided hair, leaned against the counters. The store was their club house, but since it provided no chairs they stood, stoical and observant. Mixing among them, intent on tobacco or soda-water or tentatively inspecting a new shipment of hats from Texas, were the cowboys. A pretty half-breed girl with plucked eyebrows and bobbed hair was buying bread.

Little Dog was standing alone, surveying the crowd. He was a full-blood, heavy and muscular of figure and broad and swarthy of face. He had cut his braids, and save that he wore no necktie he was dressed in town clothing. The half-breed girl seemed impressed by him, and he gazed back at her with close-set, rather arrogant eyes.

It was only when she moved on that he saw Tom.

For a few seconds they stared each at the other, the Indian defiant, with a challenge, Tom merely watchful. It was the Indian who looked away first, but as he did so he smiled, a jeering smile that sent Tom's blood surging to his head. He knew then, as well as if it had been put into words, that Little Dog had killed the Miller, and that the shot had been meant for him. He even surmised that the tribe had sent him here after him.

He knew the Indians. Behind Little Dog, now buying cigarettes at the counter, he could see that conclave around the medicine man's fire.

"Ai! Ai! Weasel Tail, our brother, has been done to death, and the white man's law has let the killer go free, and now our old men are too old to fight, and our young men have no blood in their veins, but only their mother's milk."

The small black pipe with its long stem passing from hand to hand, the lodge dimly lighted by its center fire, and perhaps the medicine man blowing smoke to the four directions of the world and seeking a sign. All the young bloods waiting and nervous, even Little Dog, for all his cut hair and store clothes; the air thick, the medicine pipe wrapped in skins hanging overhead and perhaps a young coyote crying outside at the end of a tether.

But although he watched Little Dog after that carefully, he began to think he had been mistaken. Even Arizona, when he knew the situation and was also on the alert, relaxed after a few days. Little Dog did his work, and in the leisure time swaggered about the Indian village flirting with the girls. Now and then after dark at their encampment the tom-toms would be held to a fire to tighten the skins, and then the sound of their monotonous beating would announce a dance.

Tom, sauntering there one night, saw Little Dog dancing for the benefit of the southern Indians. He was nude save for a breech clout, and he had painted his body red with stripes of white. He had borrowed a coup stick from one of the old men; the ancient scalps hung to it shook and trembled, and as he danced the Indians squatting about swayed their bodies and chanted some ancient apparently wordless air. . . .

On the night the show loaded Tom had his first real attack of nostalgia.

The wagons, carefully covered with canvas, were placed on the open cars. Up sturdy gangways went the horses, the camels and the elephants, the buffaloes and steers. The old stage coach was carefully loaded, and the covered Conestoga wagon. Cowboys, Indians, girl riders, Arabs, Zouaves, Cossacks and freaks stood by the track, suitcases about them, and waited to be assigned to their traveling quarters for the next eight months. At the "privilege" counter at the end of a car coffee and sandwiches were being served.

He put his suitcase into his berth and then went outside. The lights from the train shone out on the motley gathering, the babel of strange tongues. In their car the elephants were trumpeting uneasily. He moved away from the track and into a field of young wheat.

Suddenly he was homesick; for the faint aromatic odor of the sage brush at dawn, for the mountains in the sunset, for the long trail once more, and the Miller between his knees. Just to go back, a year, two years! To ride in on the Miller once more, and see the lights in the bunk house beckoning him home. To see the fellows again intent on their eternal poker game.

"You calling me? Watch your step, boy, watch your step. I got a pat hand."

"Lemme see them two pairs you're holdin'. I know you."

Just to go back.

Chapter Twenty

Whatever his purpose in joining the show, Little Dog gave him no bother, and except when he happened to see him Tom almost forgot him.

The wandering care-free life suited him. In a drawer under his berth in the train he kept his everyday apparel, and the professional trunk he had bought was carried in the baggage car, and at each stop taken to the lot. He had no material worries. In the morning he got coffee and whatever else he chose at the "privilege" counter on the train, and at ten or so he sauntered to the grounds.

There he was at liberty to sit on his heels in the sun and shoot craps, or exchange reminiscences with the other cowboys. The show ground would be humming with activity. Water wagons were moving about, and pails of water carried hither and thither; sprinkling carts were settling the dust in the arena if it was dry, and men with spades and rakes were leveling it. In the great tents where the horses were kept a thick bedding of straw had been thrown down; from the elephants came the usual howls, squeals and trumpetings; in the cook tent already the great copper cauldrons were boiling, and the steam tables were connected, and set up.

At half after eleven, or at twelve on parade days, he sat

down at a long table covered with a blue barred cloth, in company with dozens of other such tables similarly covered, and ate a substantial hot meal. When the meal was over he would take a toothpick from the glass holder in the center of the table, and with it jauntily stuck in his mouth would wander out. Later on he would wander into the dressing tent, past a row of laundresses asking for washing to do, and maybe he would gather up his soiled socks and shirts and body linen and pass them out. Then he would strip and bathe.

All about him would be men similarly occupied. The flat-topped trunks sat in rows, and beside each trunk was a folding chair and two pails of cold water. As the lids of the trunks were raised they showed a make-up box and a mirror, and into the lids were fastened divers toilet articles, and sometimes a photograph or two.

Tom's, however, merely contained a sign he had picked up somewhere. "Keep Out. This means you."

The tent would be full of nude men, bathing. The odor of smoke, soap and moist earth would fill it. Tom, scrubbing vigorously, would take a new pride in his big clean body, so lithe, so answerable to every call he made upon it.

He had almost forgotten Kay; he never thought of Clare at all. The show was a world of its own. It drew into a city, unloaded, played a day or two, and moved on.

"Where are we now, anyhow? Ithaca?"

"Syracuse, isn't it? Hey, boy, what town's this?"

He was handsomer than ever. His lean face tanned, his jaw clean cut and determined. He moved with lithe easy motions; he had worked hard at his roping, and now when seven horses abreast came thundering past him and the big loop lay ready, he would shove back his big hat and almost casually throw his rope. Bull-dogging or roping, or on some leaping, twisting demon twice a day risking his neck to make holiday for the crowd, he was a fine figure of a man. And he knew it.

The show was essentially moral. The family tradition held; troupes of riders were family groups, father, mother, sons and daughters. In the married cars women sat in the mornings doing their mending, sewing on buttons, even washing and ironing. Almost always, in the train or outside the women's dressing tent, little lines were stretched and women in slop shoes and wrapped in kimonos would duck out from underneath the tent and pin up in the sun the family washing, socks and stockings side by side, and even small undergarments which at first reminded him uncomfortably of those Clare had showed him.

He was not without sentimental episodes, however. If the married women let him severely alone, the girls found him rather a thrilling figure. They watched him and waylaid him.

"Let's see the new hat, Tom. Where'd you get it?"

"Sent to Texas for it. It's sure a good hat."

"Sit down, can't you? You're always going somewhere."

"I'm a busy man," he would say. "This show would be nowhere, if I didn't run around and tell 'em how to do things."

Perhaps he would sit down, and for a half hour or so there would be dalliances of a half-jocular type.

"Let's see that ring. Who gave you that?"

"I bought it. What d'you think? Some fellow gave it to me?"

He would hold her hand, under the pretext of examining the ring.

"Nice little hand. Doesn't seem right it should be doing work, somehow. You ought to get a husband and let him work for you."

"If you get a husband in this business you've gotta work too. They aren't carrying any dead wood."

But before long he would tire of her and move on, his hunger for feminine society temporarily appeased. He was no saint; he let women alone because they no longer interested him, but he still swore and sometimes swaggered, and he was still a fighting wildcat on occasion.

Once, indeed, he lost a portion of a front tooth in an encounter. He spent a hundred dollars to have it filled out with gold, and was excessively proud of it.

"If I die and don't leave any money," he told the little Cossack, "you pull this—see?—and bury me with it."

"Very nice," said the Cossack, not understanding. Tom threw back his head and roared with laughter.

"You're a cold-blooded little devil, aren't you? For all your circus lady!"

Again, coming on Little Dog one day just afterwards, he stopped the Indian.

"You try any tricks on me now, and see what happens!"

"What happen?" said Little Dog, glowering.

"I'll bite you with this." Tom told him, grinning cheerfully. "It's better than you deserve, but it's a magic tooth. Your medicine man's no good then. You'll turn into a dentist and go around in a white coat."

Just how much Little Dog understood is problematical.

But Tom was very popular with the show people, and later on with the Colonel himself. That was after the day when Rosie, one of the elephants, was frightened during the parade and started to run. She was under a railroad bridge at the time, and a deadly monster of steel and iron came roaring over her head. She bellowed hysterically, lifted her great trunk, stuck out her absurd little tail, hurled her huge bulk out of line and started.

Tom, taller than the rest, saw her, and putting spurs to his horse, raced the flying gray behemoth down the crowded street. But an elephant on the run can move very fast. When his rope settled and drew taut it was Rosie's tail that was in the noose. It brought her up short, and as the noose tightened she sat down suddenly, loudly wailing.

The Colonel was very pleased over that.

"Uses his head," he said. "Got a head and uses it. He's a good boy."

He sent for Tom that day and handed him fifty dollars.

That was his life, until one day he wakened to find himself in the city where he had come to find Kay. He scowled when he heard it. The place held nothing but bitterness for him. The thought that he was there to amuse it, to make holiday for it, was gall and wormwood to him. His head was very high when he rode out with the parade, his eyes hard under the brim of his hat.

"Say, mister, are you a real cowboy?"

"Sure am, son."

But there was no smile, no flash of teeth—one of them partly gold!—from his tanned young face.

Kay, fitting her wedding slippers in town, heard the approaching parade and stepped out to the pavement. She had no suspicion that Tom was in town. Or that already, riding up the street, he was on his way to her, more picturesque than ever, more romantic; that he was coming heralded by a steam calliope, excruciatingly shrill and off tone, and by a brass band on a great gold and red wagon; and led by great heavy-stepping elephants, splay-footed camels, and Indians in war bonnets, buckskin clothes and beaded moccasins.

Other traffic had stopped. The pavements were crowded, and there was desultory cheering up and down the street. She was still unsuspicious. The parade moved on, brilliant and exotic; Arabs, Indians, a colored minstrel troupe, a group of Cossacks, in astrakhan hats and queer long blouses, tightly belted at the waist. One of the Cossacks, small and young, seemed to pick her out of the crowd and saluted her with his whip.

But she hardly saw him; her eyes were strained back to where the cowboys, the aristocrats of the performance, were riding along, relaxed in their saddles. On they came, the sun shining on their bright shirts and colored neckerchiefs, on their spurs and chaps and coiled ropes. Under the broad high-crowned hats their faces were thin, young, and brown.

They swayed to the motion of their horses, the reins in one gloved hand, the other resting negligently on hip or thigh. And as they passed, like the little Cossack they picked out pretty girls and smiled at them.

One, in the lead, was on a tall bay horse. Every now and again he tightened his rein and lightly spurred the animal, and it reared above the crowd. The man on its back sat at his ease, smiling half scornfully at the crowd. He seemed to say: "Tie that, you bunch of pikers!"

Suddenly she heard herself calling:

"Tom! Tom McNair!"

He heard her. She knew that. She could see his eyes searching the crowd. But she could not call again. Too many eyes were on her, interested and curious. And after that first start of his he did not look around. Instead, with a half-mocking smile on his face, he dug his spurs into his horse, and the animal reared again.

It was like a gesture of defiance.

She went back into the shop and asked for a drink of water, and when they had brought it to her they stood around her. They seemed to think she looked ill. Maybe she was. She felt very queer. But she was thinking quite clearly, at that.

But she was determined to see him. She had no intention of communicating with him. What was the use? She would see him once more, and then she would go away and live her life as it was pre-determined. Perhaps he had forgotten her anyhow. All those pretty girls, riding high-school thoroughbreds in the parade—perhaps he was in love with one of them. He was vain as well as proud. The very way he had made his horse rear in the street, that was vanity.

But she would see him once more.

She called up the house and made some excuse or other, and later she took a taxicab and went out to the show grounds. Her head was throbbing and her hands icy cold. By the time the performance began the grand-stand was crowded, but she saw nothing of the crowd, and but little of what went on in the arena. All she saw was Tom McNair, winning the plaudits of the vast audience by his recklessness and accepting them with a mocking smile. If he suspected her presence there he gave no indication of it; he swept the reserved seats with a casual glance now and then, but that was all.

He had come into his own. In that dusty enclosure he was a king, and these people assembled to do him homage.

She had no idea that he was being unusually reckless that afternoon, or that Arizona was bursting with rage under his gaudy shirt.

"Look at that crazy fool! He'll break his neck or the horse's, and I don't give a damn which."

She saw him only as the apotheosis of all that she had remembered, the sublimation of her dreams—

She slipped out before the end of the performance, and drearily went home, to find Mr. Trowbridge in the lower hall, heavily and beamingly jovial. She forced a smile for him and he caught her by the shoulders and turned her to the light.

"Ah!" he cried. "Now that is what I call a happy bride's face! Look at that color! Look at those eyes!"

She went obediently upstairs with him to look at the gifts: more silver, some carved jade, a Heppelwhite sofa, a dower chest, very old. When it was opened it still smelled faintly of open wood fires and lavender. And Herbert was there, with an anxious pucker on his forehead and the notebook in his hand.

"Hello, darling." He kissed her abstractedly. "Look here, you know more about these things than I do. What's that tea service worth? Approximately, of course."

"It seems so calculating, Herbert."

"Not at all. There's a lot of value here and it needs protection."

Mr. Trowbridge was roaming about, his hands behind his

back, his head on one side.

"Now that's a pretty thing. What's it for?"

She stood beside him. Herbert had moved on. "Enamel and gold clock, $200. Antique Sheffield table urn, $100. Chest flat silver, $3000."

"Help an old man, Kay. What shall we send you?"

"Please, why send anything? We have more now than we can ever use."

He must not send anything. Nobody must send anything more. She wasn't going through with it. It would be a sin. A sin against Herbert and a sin against herself. To live with one man and love another was immoral.

"But of course I'll send you something. Don't you suppose I want to put at least a feather in the love nest?"

Love nest! Oh, God, if he would only go away; if they would only all go and give her time to think.

"What do you think these consoles are worth, Kay? Are they genuine or reproductions?"

"Father says they are genuine. Why don't you ask him?"

She got to her room at last and out onto the little balcony. But there were men just underneath, putting up a marquee on the lawn. Although it was late they were still working. They were putting down the floor, carefully pushing the boards home and then nailing them. It was like her father to want a floor in a marquee. In a day or two people would be sitting there, eating and drinking champagne. Her health and Herbert's. "A very long life together, and a happy one." A long life!

Suddenly she knew what she was going to do. She was going to Tom McNair, if he wanted her. She turned back into her room and closed and locked the door.

Chapter Twenty-one

That night, although he had been sleeping extremely well, Tom slept very little. The car was closed, filled with the sour odor of old shoes, well-worn clothing and perspiring human bodies. The men slept heavily and noisily, and a track engine panted back and forth. Once he fell asleep, and dreamed that he was pointing cattle to the pens, and a switch engine had come along and scattered them. He wakened with the feel of the Miller still between his knees.

In the morning he made his way morosely to the lot. Yesterday's anger was gone, and he felt only a deep dejection. What had he expected anyhow? She had shown him that she did not care for him, abandoned him to that bunch at the club and never come back. That call of hers from the street, that had been before she had time to think. She wouldn't follow it up.

He wandered to the dressing tent, promised his laundry to a waiting negress and went inside. When he had rolled it up he drew back the tent flap and handed it to the waiting figure.

"Here you are," he said gruffly. "And get it back tonight sure. We're leaving."

But the figure did not move to take it, and he stepped outside.

It was Kay.

He was too stunned for speech, and she too seemed to have nothing to say. She looked thinner than he remembered her, and her face was set and drawn. He stood there, staring at her.

"Well, here I am," she said finally, as if that explained everything.

And for all his later failures, that time at least he understood. He could not know what the step had cost her, or the finality of it. Perhaps he never did realize what that last twenty-four hours had been. But he looked from her to the dressing case at her feet, and he saw what she meant. She was there, to take or leave as he saw fit. He put out both hands.

"I've been waiting for you," he said, not to steadily. "Ever since—" maybe he meant to say "since yesterday," but he changed it. "Ever since God knows when."

It was a curious wooing. Later on Kay was to question whether it was a wooing at all, on either side. It was more like a simple obedience to some natural law they neither of them understood.

They picked up a taxicab at the entrance to the lot, and started off. There was a license to secure, and the time was short. Tom put his hand in his pocket and counted his money. He had twenty-one dollars.

"I suppose that's enough?"

"I should think so."

All very matter of fact. Something inevitable to be done, so get it done. Not all the powers of earth could part them now. Time to think later; just now there was a schedule to be watched, a routine to be followed.

They had gone perhaps three blocks before Tom whipped off his big hat and turned to look at her.

"My God! You and me, Kay!"

There was very little passion in that first kiss between them. The situation was still too strange. They themselves were like strangers; during their long separation each of them had built up out of their memories a dream figure, and was now attempting to recognize it in this flesh and blood reality.

Now and then in the intervals Kay would find his eyes on her, almost furtively studying her, and Tom would find her looking at him with strange half-frightened eyes.

"Name, please?"

"Katherine Dowling."

"Your age?"

What was she doing? Giving herself to this strange man, deliberately binding herself to him. It was madness; it was incredible. But she looked composed enough. The clerk, filling in the blanks, looked curiously at Tom's big hat and colored shirt, and at her own small and elegant figure.

"Show people?" he inquired genially when he passed over the paper.

Tom stiffened slightly.

"I am. The young lady is not."

Show people! That was where she belonged now. She had cast aside her old world of luxury and dignity, and now she would belong to that strange traveling fraternity which lived in back lots under canvas and traveled in circus cars about the country. But one didn't do that. One went there for a lark, and ate peanuts and threw the shells on the ground and even drank pop out of a bottle, tepid sweetish stuff which made one thirstier afterwards.

She had her one panicky moment then, and as if he felt that recoil in her, Tom put out his hand and took hers as they went down the stairs to the street. The strength of his strong lean hand was what she needed. After all, that was life, not the other; a hand to hold to, a warm hand, a tender and loving hand.

"Not getting scared, are you, girl?"

"Just for a minute. You do love me, don't you?"

"Before God I do."

They were married by a clergyman, selected at random from the telephone book in a drug store, and they ate their wedding breakfast back on the lot. There was a new lift to Tom's shoulders, a pride in her that he made no attempt to conceal. At the door to the dining tent they were halted.

"Lady with you, Tom?"

"I'll tell the world she is."

Afterwards he placed a box for her in a sheltered place and hurried to dress. A goat, chained to a tent peg, came to sniff at her and remained to have his head scratched, the cowboy band, eying her with interest, lined up outside the double opening by the bandstand, and all around in the spring sunshine people in costume were emerging from their tents, mounting elephants or camels or horses, and falling into line for the "spectacular."

She waited, her hands folded in her lap. The sun shone on her narrow gold wedding ring, where Herbert's square cut emerald had formerly rested. She had left that at home. She had left practically everything at home, except the money in her purse and her grandmother's pearls. Those were hers; they could not say she had taken anything that was not hers.

She was aware that she was exciting interest, and she got her handkerchief and wiped the dust from her smart shoes. She felt untidy and the sun was hot. Her head was beginning to ache, too. She moved the box further into the shade, and heard Tom's voice just beyond the canvas.

"Just get this. Either she goes with me tonight, or I stay here."

"You know darned well she can't go with you. We can get her on the train, perhaps, but the married cars are full up."

"Then I'll go by another train."

"You'll get a day coach to that burg, and sit up all night. Now look here, Tom, you're up against it unless you do what I say. If you'll—"

She moved the box back again. Her cheeks were flaming, and her head ached sharply. The thought that providing for her on her wedding night was a matter for an outsider shocked her, and it was her first lesson in her new life to force a smile when he came back to her, leading his horse.

"All right, girl?"

"Fine."

"And happy?"

"Terribly happy."

He put a foot into the stirrup, mounted, turned and looked down at her. And suddenly nothing else mattered but the two of them, there in the dust and the glare, loving each other, belonging to each other.

In the intervals of the performance when he could slip out and be with Kay he did so, sitting on his heels at her feet and turning the wedding ring on her finger while he held her hand.

"Sure funny to think of a little thing like that meaning all it does mean!"

"You're not sorry? You're sure you wanted me?"

"Wanting you's what I've been doing nothing else but, my girl."

But she had been doing some thinking, too.

"Will you want to stay with the—with the show?"

"I can't leave them in the middle of the season, Kay."

"Then I'd better learn to do something." She smiled at him. "I can't sit around on a soap box all day."

His quick pride was touched.

"If you're worrying about my being able to keep you, girl, forget it. I'm earning good money. Plenty. I can keep my wife without her having to lift her hand." His voice hardened. "I don't want any Dowling money either, girl. You know that, don't you? They're not going to come between us. You and I, we're going to steer our own boat from now on."

It was the first mention of her family between them, and her first real knowledge of his continuing resentment.

"They can't come between us now. It's too late, Tom."

And that restored him to good-humor. He looked about,

saw that they were unobserved, and quickly stooped and kissed her.

"You bet they can't. They can all go to—New Mexico!" he told her. But he smiled down at her boyishly. "You're going to like these people, you know. They're a fine lot. The world's best."

He swung easily into his saddle and rode off.

Later on he brought his particular cronies to meet her, cowboys like himself, gaily dressed, tanned, sheepish.

"Arizona, meet Mrs. McNair."

They came up, took her small hand in their great paws, dropped it and retreated. Only the little Cossack bowed from the waist, with his heels together, and then wandered off to survey the scene from a distance. It was a strange land, this America, where young ladies with real pearls—he knew real pearls—and plain very fine clothes from Paris, married cowboys. Truly, such was democracy; the rest of the world talked of it, but never would understand it.

Only one unpleasant incident occurred, and she did not recognize it as such at the time. An Indian in cowboy costume walked past her twice, surveying her with the impassive curiosity of his race, and the second time he spoke to her.

"You marry Tom McNair?"

"I am Mrs. McNair. Yes."

He smiled a little and Tom, coming out at that moment, swung toward him and confronted him.

"You keep away from that lady," he said menacingly, "and put all the distance you can between me and you, or—"

The Indian moved away.

In the intervals Kay's thoughts wandered back to her people. What were they thinking? Or doing? She could not let them know yet; there would be scenes, trouble of all sorts. Already she knew that Tom would resent any attempt at interference, might even be violent with them. That night, just before the train left, she would send a telegram, but until then she dared not risk it.

The afternoon passed somehow. She had checked a suitcase at the railway station, and she sent a messenger for it. She was afraid to go herself. And later on it was taken to the train. At six o'clock she ate her supper in the tent. She was accustomed to her paper napkin by that time, to the narrowness of the board seat she sat on, to having her food set before her in small dishes, heavy and unbreakable. The news of Tom's marriage had spread about, and after the meal people gathered about them. Only the girls remained aloof, watching and discussing her. The older women were maternal and solicitous; they asked no questions, and she soon realized that her identity was a matter of no interest to them. They were prepared to accept her, a newcomer from an outer world infinitely remote.

"You mustn't wear pretty shoes like that around. You'll soon spoil them, my dear."

If, by her manner and the quiet expensiveness of her clothing they realized that the world she had left was even more remote than appeared, that too they kept to themselves. But they accepted her. They even asked her into the dressing tent that night, and she sat on a folding chair, uncomfortable and embarrassed, while they unself-consciously bathed and dressed before her.

They watched her surreptitiously. The strong odor of scented talcum powder, cheap perfume and burning alcohol from the lamps on which they heated their curling irons, mixed with the scents from the animal tents and the stables nearby, had turned her faintly sick, but she smiled at them.

But there was one breath-taking moment that night after all. With the performance over, and only the working lights left on the lot, the cowboys rode their horses to the railroad siding. And once again she heard the slow tired movement of horses' feet in darkness, the rustle of chaps on leather, the faint jingle of bridles and buckles.

The circus world faded away. Just so had she seen the men

come in from the pastures on the range, sitting their saddles easily, swaying to the motion of their horses. They would go back, she and Tom, and pick up their lives where they had left them. This was an interlude; it was not life.

She plodded along behind them. Now and then she stumbled on the uneven ground; the high heels of her slippers turned. Once she stepped into a coil of wire and almost fell. Tom had arranged an escort for her, but she had wanted to be alone.

It did not occur to her that there was anything symbolical in that stumbling progress of hers, that blind following.

The men ahead began to sing softly. The day's work was over. Soon the horses would be in the cars. A voice would call out.

"Jerry next."

"Jerry coming."

A shadowy horse would sniff at the runway, eye the oil flare with suspicion, and then with a thunder of hoofs dash up and into the car. The loading would go on, and when it had been finished there was the privilege car, and craps, or a poker game.

So they sang and Kay could hear Tom's voice above the rest, happy and exultant.

> "I'm a poor lonesome cowboy,
> I'm a poor lonesome cowboy,
> I'm a poor lonesome cowboy,
> And a long ways from home."

Chapter Twenty-two

It was not until Tom joined her outside the cars that she realized that her wedding night was to be as strange as the day. When Tom came to speak to her he was awkward and self-conscious.

"There's a little complication about tonight, girl," he said, looking away from her. "The—married cars are kind of full up. They'll take care of you, you understand, but—"

"I'm sure I'll manage very well." She heard her own voice, apparently composed.

But whatever Tom felt, she was secretly relieved. The terrible pitiless publicity of the show life had been gradually getting on her nerves all day, and now in the semi-darkness Tom himself seemed a stranger, a stranger who had the right to put his arms around her, and did so. He felt her recoil.

"Don't you want me to do that?"

"It's so public."

"Well, I'm not ashamed of loving you, if you are."

Sitting on the side of her berth later on, Tom told her his immediate plans. When the train pulled in in the morning he would take her to a hotel, and they would have two days' honeymoon. After that it would be time to think of the future.

But she was very tired. The closeness of the car made her

dizzy; the narrow berth, a built-in box which held a hard mattress, was airless and uncomfortable. Girls in faded kimonos were sitting up, each in her tiny cubicle, sorting clothes, mending by the indifferent light, using cold cream, or putting their hair in order. Men wandered through, indifferent to the others but eying Tom and herself with humorous interest. Everything in her was crying out for privacy, for decent reserves, for quiet; even Tom's jubilant vitality seemed out of place.

"I've got it all fixed," he told her. "We're going to the Pelham. Nothing's too good for us the next few days." And when she only smiled. "Pretty tired, aren't you?"

"I feel a little crowded."

"You'll get over that. They're a fine lot; the best ever. And these girls are on the square, too," he added. "Don't you get any wrong ideas about them."

"You would like to stay on, wouldn't you?"

"It's the way I'm making a living. We've got to eat, you know."

She winced, but he did not notice it.

And she felt, when he finally went away, that she had been ridiculously cold to him. For him, the people around did not exist; for her, they formed a barrier she could not pass. If they could only have been alone together somewhere, anywhere, she felt that the barrier would have been swept away. But not alone in his sense of the word, in a hotel bedroom somewhere. Everything that was fastidious in her revolted at what seemed to her to amount to an assignation. But to be together, quite privately, in some quiet distant place, and there to make their readjustments, she craved that passionately that night.

The long train of yellow cars, with the flats carrying the great wagons protected by canvas, the animal cars, the crowded, cluttered sleeping coaches, got slowly under way. She lay back on her hard pillow, and after a while she reached into her dressing bag and found a cigarette. She thought it might quiet her. But the girl across, a kimono thrown casually over her shoulders while she mended a stocking, looked over quickly and then looked away again, with a shocked expression on her face.

It was indeed a new world.

Tom, too, was late in getting to sleep. He lay, his long body diagonally in the berth, his arms under his head, and tried to think out his new problem. He loved Kay; he felt now that he had always loved her. Mixed with that, however, was a sense of triumph over Herbert, over the Dowlings, over that mysterious life of hers which she had abandoned for him. He had no subtleties. He was physically rugged and mentally direct; his roots were deep in the soil. Vaguely he felt that Kay had been superficially rooted in something quite different. He called it society, but what he meant was something for which he had no words; cultures, conventions, traditions. And whatever they were he resented them.

"She's my wife now," he reflected. "She's got to forget the old stuff and begin all over."

So neither of them slept much. The train rocked along; the big wagons swayed in the cars, the tired show people snored and grunted in their narrow quarters.

But when Tom wakened Kay in the morning she gave him back smile for smile. He brightened perceptibly; ever after she was to realize, through all the difficulties to come, her power to depress or cheer him. Other power she certainly lacked. She could not force him to her way against his will, but she could make him happy or wretched as she chose. Later on she was to analyze that still further; when she met him on his own ground, conformed, agreed, he was happy. When she did not, when she opposed or disapproved, he was like a willful child, obstinate but wretched.

"Time to leave the bed grounds!" he told her, and then was queerly silent. There was something so virginal about her as she lay there, so almost childish in spite of her twenty-three years, that his heart swelled within him. He loved her, he adored her. He would always be good to her, always kind. With the curious eyes of the girl across on him, he bent down and kissed her awkwardly.

She dressed as best she could. The washroom was a litter of paper towels and the lock was broken; never before in her life had she put on in the morning clothing she had worn the day before, but now she did. She had hung up her dark suit the night before, and its fine white cuffs and collar were still fresh. But the matter of adequate clothing began to bother her. She must get some things somewhere, but she had only fifty dollars in her purse.

When she got out of the car she saw the Indian of the day before. He was lounging on the platform, and he leered at her, then turned and wandered off. But she was late, and there was a parade that morning. It added to the strangeness of everything that she had to go alone to the Pelham and there engage a room and bath. And when she was inside it, the door locked, to the sensation of strangeness was added one of dismay. The bleakness of the room, the two beds side by side, the frankness of the bathroom opening off it, shocked and revolted her. She was a wife, she told herself fiercely, not a mistress, but the sensation remained. The very bareness of the place, its reduction of life to its physical necessities added to it.

Never before had she occupied a hotel room in all its starkness. A trunkful of silk pillows, a bright slumber robe on a couch, little vases for flowers and family pictures in silver frames had always before created a temporary atmosphere of home. She could see Nora now, moving about, deftly pulling the chairs and putting out the luxurious trifles with which they had always traveled.

She could not bear it. After all, the room was a shrine; it must be, or she was all wrong. Everything was wrong. She set feverishly to work, placing the gold fittings from her bag on the dressing table, ordering flowers from the florist shop below, even finally going down herself and, fearful of being recognized, buying an armful of magazines from the newsstand. And as she worked, she lost that early panic. She had achieved, not a shrine perhaps, but a bit of home.

Actually she was working against time to think. It must come, she knew. She could not fight down forever the recognition of what she had done; the scandal and talk, the stricken household, Herbert. That must come, but not now. Not yet. She lived feverishly in the present; she could look neither back nor ahead.

At something before noon she heard the sirens of fire engines, and went to her window to look out. But she could not see them. She had, standing there in that room that was to be a shrine, no idea that that sound was to alter the whole course of her life and Tom McNair's. She listened to them and then went back to her roses, ignorant that they had set in motion a small chain of events that was to lead to catastrophe.

It was not a great matter at the beginning. The leaders of one of the big six-horse hitches, driven by Overland Jim, had frightened and started to run, and in the resulting mixup Overland was thrown and sprained his wrist. But Overland during the performance drove the prairie schooner during the Indian attack, and that day Tom McNair volunteered to take his place.

If he thought of Little Dog he put him out of his head. In all the weeks on the road the Indian had kept out of his way, had made no overt or covert move against him. And Tom believed in his star that day. He was recklessly happy, even boastful.

"Can I drive a six-horse hitch?" he said to the Ring Stock Boss. "Man, where I come from it takes six horses to the family buggy to get to church!"

There was no time to see Kay before the performance; he had hopes she would come to the lot, and he kept a pair of keen eyes on the alert for her. He was disappointed and somewhat hurt when he did not see her, and he went into the arena with his heart only half in his work. And then it happened. The wagon circled the arena in a cloud of dust, followed by the yelling Indians on their ponies, firing their blank cartridges with deadly effect. When it finally came to a stop and the dust subsided, Tom was lying face down on the ground, not moving.

The grand-stand applauded cheerfully, and went on eating its peanuts and drinking its pop. It was the little Cossack who was the first to recognize a tragedy. He ran out into the arena and held up both hands.

Chapter Twenty-three

On the day after Tom was shot, Herbert was waiting in the reception room of the hospital. His hat, stick and gloves lay on the table, and all about him was the odor of all hospitals, of disinfectants and drugs and floor wax, and above all the faint and penetrating sweetness of ether.

Save that he was very pale, he looked much as usual. His tie was carefully tied, his spats and shoes immaculate. Now and then he heard a light footfall in the hall outside and he glanced up. But mostly he just sat, his hands between his knees, and stared at the floor.

When the footsteps passed by he sank back again into a coma of misery. He was too tired to think or to plan any campaign. And after all, what was there to plan? The thing was done.

He had not slept at all. None of them had slept for that matter. At two o'clock in the morning he had drafted that brief announcement to the newspapers:

"Mr. and Mrs. Henry Dowling announce the indefinite postponement of the marriage of their daughter, Miss Katherine Dowling, to Mr. Herbert Forrest."

Henry had taken the memorandum upstairs for approval, and had come down heavily after a half hour or so.

"It's all right," he said, and with it in his hand had crossed to the window and stood looking out into the night. "Her mother's taking it badly," he said without turning. "She is in a strange frame of mind. Seems to blame herself for it, although God knows—"

Herbert pulled himself together.

"If any one is to blame, I am. I knew she cared for him."

"Cared for him! Cared for a fellow who can hardly write his own name?"

Herbert said nothing. The charge was absurd and they both knew it, but it did in a way set forth the hopelessness of the situation as they saw it.

It was after that that Henry announced his future course. So long as Kay remained married to the scoundrel she could not enter his house. He had done his best. He had nothing to reproach himself with. She'd soon get her fill of romance and come crawling home.

"Thank God there will be ways to get rid of the fellow," he said. "But if he thinks he has married into a soft thing he can think again."

But there was something pathetic about Henry, too. Bessie, sitting watching on a sofa, was rather sorry for him. He had been so sure of himself, of his well-organized life, his standing in the community. He had said "thumbs up" or "thumbs down," and all the thumbs in his vicinity had obeyed.

"It's a little soon to think of that," she said, lighting a fresh cigarette. She had smoked steadily all evening. "And it might be worse, you know. They're married, anyhow. What are you really thinking about? What people will say? Well, let them talk, and be damned to them. This is a fifty-fifty proposition. Either Kay will be happy, and I imagine that's what we all want, or she won't, and in that case she can go to Paris and get rid of him. For my part—" she hesitated.

"Well, get on with it," said Henry impatiently.

"For my part, I think she would rather be miserable with him than to—well, to be happy with anybody else."

She had meant to say, "to vegetate," but a glance at Herbert had deterred her. She found herself rather admiring Herbert that night. Thank God for good breeding. It was at least a crutch to fall back on, when everything else failed.

"You talk like a fool," said Henry. "Nobody chooses to be miserable."

But she only eyed him. How little he knew about life, really, and especially women. Nobody in love was ever happy. Love was a pain. When it ceased to be a pain it was not love. Contentment, resignation, call it what you liked, but not love. But she took refuge in flippancy.

"It's like the war," she told them. "Why worry? If you're dead, you're dead and won't know about it. If you're not dead—or however the thing goes. We ought to send her some clothes," she added practically.

Some time after midnight Henry went up to bed. Bessie could follow his thoughts as he went, his heavy shoulders bent, the yellow corner of Kay's telegram sticking out of the pocket of his dinner jacket. He had been a good husband and father; he had been upright in business according to his lights, and he had asked very little of life in his declining years; peace and a few friends, the love of his family and the respect of his community. Now they were all gone. Wiped out. She heard him stop at the room where the wedding gifts like small glittering corpses of dead hopes were laid out on their biers, close the door and go on.

Something of all this was running through Herbert's mind as he waited in the anteroom of the hospital, but only as a background to other and bitterer thoughts. If they centered on himself rather than on Kay, perhaps it was only natural. He had loved her sincerely. There had never been anyone else. He had built all his future about her. He had not even played around like other fellows; not since college anyhow. Now she had destroyed everything. Not everything exactly; he was precise even with himself. Henry had said that the business proposition still stood. But she had hurt him and made him a laughing-stock; she had jilted him at the last moment, an injury and an insult whose stigma would follow him always. He ought to hate her. But he could not hate her. If he did, why was he here? If he could hate her it would be easier.

His thoughts wandered on, to the receipt of Kay's second telegram that morning, that Tom McNair had been shot; to the long journey, sitting in a chair in a parlor car and watching a landscape fly by which had made no impression on his mental retina. Only one thing had registered, and that with a shock he could still feel and suffer from. By a sidetrack just outside of town his train had slowed up, and there beside him, close to him, was the long line of yellow show cars.

In one of those cars, their small windows partly occluded with clothing, their sills littered with jars and bottles, Kay must have spent her wedding night. To his sense of injury was added this insult to his fastidiousness. When she finally came in he was almost startled to find her unchanged, save for her pallor and the deep circles under her eyes.

Neither of them spoke at once, but Herbert was quick to realize that what was a critical meeting for him was to her merely an unimportant incident in a tragic day. There was a curious blankness in her eyes; it struck him later that she had looked at him much as he had looked at the flying landscape that day. And because that first silence and absorption of hers was too painful, he hurried to speak.

"How is he now?"

"Better, they think. But he is suffering; they say—" She put her handkerchief to her lips to steady them. "They say he will live, but he won't be able to ride again. His leg is badly broken. He doesn't know that, of course."

"Still, if he is going to live—"

"Yes, of course." She came further into the room, and seemed really to see him for the first time.

"I'm sorry, Herbert. Sorry I've hurt you all. I suppose you don't believe that."

"I believe it," he said carefully, "but that doesn't matter now, does it? The point is, are you sorry for yourself, Kay?"

She shook her head.

"It was not just an impulse, then?"

"Yes, at the last. But it had to be, Herbert. It was stronger than I was. I even think—"

"Yes?"

"I don't want to hurt you again."

"I haven't many rights, but I have a right to the truth about this."

"I even think that if we had been married, you and I, and Tom had asked me to go with him, I would have gone just the same."

That shocked him profoundly. It stripped the situation of all the careful disguises he had erected, and reduced it to primitive facts. And this ruthless destruction of his last illusion left him angry and humiliated.

"You don't know what you are saying."

"I didn't want to say it, but it's true."

"Then I wish you would tell me something," he said. "It doesn't pay, where a girl's concerned, to be decent and honest, does it? A man can go along doing his best, and then some handsome good-for-nothing can come along and steal all he has worked to earn; can rob his house and wreck his life! What's the use of it?"

"I don't know," she said helplessly. "I suppose the world couldn't go on without men like you—and father. I've tried to think it out. I don't know, but—of course it pays to be decent."

"It hasn't paid me."

She did not answer that. She made a quick impatient movement.

"Why, when a man comes along who is different, should you immediately say that he is an outsider and must be yellow? Tom's ways may not be your ways, but he *is* a man, no matter what you may think. Oh, I know what you think," as he made a gesture. "I know, because you and I have been trained in the same school. How a thing is done is more important than the thing itself. I daresay I shall have to fight that all my life. But I am going to fight it. Don't make any mistake about that."

But there was a vein of obstinacy in Herbert.

"The way a thing is done counts too; the small amenities of life are what makes it possible, for our kind anyhow," he said doggedly. "Don't sneer at them, Kay. You're in love now; maybe you think you won't miss all that, but you will. And when that time comes—"

"I can come back, I suppose, and be forgiven!"

"You can come back to me," he told her, going pale.

"Good God, Kay," he added. "You have dragged me in the dirt, and still I can say that to you! Some day you will know how much that means. I have my pride, although you may not think so, but I suppose there is such a thing as caring too much to remember pride."

That almost broke down her composure. Since Tom's injury she had neither slept nor eaten, she had hardly dared to think. Her lips trembled.

"I appreciate that more than you can know," she told him. "But I am not a child. I have done this with my eyes open, and I must work it out for myself."

The interview was less painful after that. Her family had taken it badly, and it would be better not to try to see them for a time; her father was bitterly disappointed just now. She only nodded to that. She had no hope of forgiveness, but she said nothing. It was only when Herbert went into his wallet, where his bills were always neatly disposed after the manner of a man who values money, that she flushed and made a gesture of refusal.

"It is not from me," he said. "Mrs. Osborne gave me a check for you, for a thousand dollars. I think she will be hurt if you refuse it."

And after a time she took it, this new Kay who hereafter

must think about money, even value it, like Herbert. She stood folding and refolding it in her hands. Tom would not like it, she knew, but then she need not tell Tom. And later on she could draw on it, to ease their way somewhat, to give him time to readjust.

Perhaps if Herbert had gone then, having made his magnanimous gesture, things would have been better between them. But her very acceptance of the check, the thought that she might even then be in need of money, roused his slumbering anger. He picked up his hat and gloves, and stood looking down at her.

"I passed that circus train as I came into town. You can guess how I felt; you among all that rabble, the subject of God knows what cheap talk, spending your wedding night among them! You!"

She flushed painfully.

"I suppose you are entitled to say that, Herbert. But it is not true. I came in the train, but by myself."

"Do you mean that your marriage has not been consummated?" he asked brutally. "Are you trying to tell me that you—"

"Exactly that," she said coldly. "And now perhaps you will go away. I am grateful to you. I know what it cost you to come. I am sorry I have hurt you so. But what I have told you does not change things; nothing you can say will change anything."

But he made a desperate effort nevertheless. There could be a divorce, or the marriage could be annulled; that was done all the time. How was McNair to support her, if he could no longer ride? Take a cowboy off a horse and what was he? A field hand! She had married him out of some sort of romantic idea of him, but where was the romance now? And leave that out, if she liked. How would it work out, with her eternally trying to make him like the men she knew, and Tom dragging her down to the level of his own small-town girls.

"Like that Clare whatever her name was," he said contemptuously. "That's the sort he cares about and understands. Either he'll make you like her, or he'll go back to his own kind. Don't forget that. He's had a bad name about women, and that sticks to a man. You'll hold him for a while and then—"

"That will be my affair, and his," she said, stony-faced. And turned and went out of the room.

Chapter Twenty-four

The show had gone on. It had its schedules to meet, its competitions to face. It put up its paper, and other rival organizations came along and tore it down. Now and then there was even a battle.

It was like an army, it cared as best it could for its casualties and then moved on, unloading, parading, playing and reloading.

"Gangway for the elephants! Get in there, Babe! Damn your thick hide, get in."

But for a day or two at least there was no singing as the cowboys rode their horses through the darkness to the siding, swaying easily in their saddles to the rustle of leather on leather, the click of buckles and spurs. Tom had been popular with them. He had been a fine rider, and he had been square. "A square shooter," they said among themselves. And there was a mystery about his injury. The property man had loaded the guns himself with blanks.

The Colonel himself had gone to the hospital to see Tom and get at the truth, but Tom had been curiously non-committal.

"Maybe some Indian had a grudge against me. You never can tell."

"You don't know?"

"No, and couldn't prove it if I did."

The Colonel had done his best, arranged for Tom's hospital bills, and for his salary to go on for three months, and then had gone away, not quite easy in his kindly mind. He thought Tom knew more than he would say.

Then, for a few days, Tom fought a good fight. He suffered intensely, but when Kay was around he kept it to himself. He seemed content to have her beside him, to hold her hand, even as he improved—to let her read to him. The reading rather bored him, but he submitted amiably enough.

"All right," he would say resignedly. "Let's hear what the poor simp did, after he let his wife up and leave him."

But he would drop off to sleep very soon. He had lived in a hard school, and the fetich of the printed word was not for him. However, if he roused and she was not in sight he was restless until she returned.

"Seems to me you're eating right hearty these days!"

"I have to walk two blocks to eat at all."

But over his injury and its cause he preserved a silence even to her. Sometimes she would look up from her book to see him staring at the ceiling, with a strange concentration that almost frightened her, and with his fists clenched.

It was a queer life for Kay. Her romance had got about, and well-intentioned nurses invented errands to get a look at her. And one day a very curious thing happened. A man down the hall said he knew her, and would be grateful if she would stop in and see him. It was Ronald Osborne. She hardly knew him at first, the dapper little man who used to pose for the benefit of the servants, and even now was smoothing his hair with one thin hand.

"Hello, Kay."

"Hello, Uncle Ronald. I didn't—have you been very ill?"

"Not very," he said. "Not very. So you've decided to live your own life after all, Kay! You got away from them, eh?"

"I'm afraid I've hurt them all pretty badly."

"Not you," he said. "They're thick-skinned. Look at your

Aunt Bessie!" He laughed a little, horribly. "Your mother's different, but she hadn't your courage. She never did get away."

She went back again a day or two later, forcing herself rather because she had never liked him. But the bed was neatly made and empty, and she learned that Uncle Ronald had himself "got away" the night before, quite comfortably and without pain.

It was indeed a queer life, and not the least queer thing about it was her relationship to Tom, and his to her. This long youth alternately lying back on his pillows and refined by pain into gentleness, or cursing the surgeon half humorously and half in earnest when he dressed his leg, was a stranger to her. Sometimes he caught her staring at him, and a gulf of self-consciousness opened between them. He would try to bridge it.

"Come on over here, girl. What're you thinking about?"

"Nothing. It seems so queer, doesn't it?"

"It seems pretty fine to me; the finest thing that ever happened."

"Getting hurt?"

"Now that's not like you, girl. Loving you and getting you. You're mine. Don't forget that."

She had managed to keep the papers from him, and he knew nothing of Herbert, or of the scandal. But once he startled her by asking about Herbert. His hands, calloused and hard, had begun to peel, and he eyed them ruefully.

"Nice hands for a real he-man!" he said scornfully. "They'll soon be as soft and white as Percy's!" He looked up at her. "What's became of lil' old Percy anyhow? He'd have made a fine girl, he would!"

"I suppose he's all right."

"It wouldn't surprise me to learn that he chewed a finger nail plumb off when he heard the news," he drawled.

It had never occurred to him that his injury was a permanent one. As he improved he began to make plans. He had saved some money, enough to get them back home, and he wasn't afraid after that. He could always take care of her; not the way she'd been used to, but he was strong and he wasn't afraid to work.

"You stick to me, girl, and I'll amount to something yet."

"I'll always stick, Tom."

She could not tell him. She would listen to his plans with a sort of terror for the time when he would have to know, and her hands would grow cold in his, and sometimes the nurse, overhearing, would look at her and shake her head. . . .

One evening she went back to that lonely hotel room of hers, to open the door and find Bessie settled in a chair by the window, and the room full of cigarette smoke. But Bessie, who was wise with the wisdom of the serpent, avoided any emotion by receiving her very casually.

"Hello, Kay. Had your dinner yet?"

"I was going to order something up here."

"Then order for two," said Bessie. "I'm over on some business about poor Ronald. I didn't even know he was sick. Well, how's your husband coming on?"

Bessie's matter-of-fact manner did her good. She missed nothing, did Bessie, from the handkerchiefs pasted to dry on the mirror to the strain on the girl's face. The hotel bedroom was "awful." But she brought Kay the news from home that she had been hungering for. Henry had locked up her clothes; she had tried to bring her some, but she could not. But her mother was less unhappy than Kay probably imagined. She was not as well as she might be. She had gone over to the cemetery and taken cold. Kay ought to write to her.

It was only when she learned that Tom's injury was a permanent one that she became grave.

"Then—what will you do?"

"I don't know. They haven't told him yet."

"What your father ought to do is to give him an allowance. I'll see what I can do, Kay."

"It wouldn't be any good. Tom wouldn't touch it, or allow me to."

Later on, after her own worldly fashion, Bessie tried to be helpful.

"You see, Kay, you have a lot to learn. This thing about love, now—you think everything's over, I daresay. You've got him and he's got you! But it isn't, you know. The greatest love stories come after marriage. If I hadn't married poor Ronald—" She checked herself.

And again, over the meal served in that dingy room:

"You can divide any woman's life into three parts: up to twenty, anticipation; from twenty to forty, fulfillment—if she's lucky. Usually it is compromise and resignation. Some, of course—!" She smiled. "Compromise or be compromised!" she ended, lightly.

It was only before she left that she mentioned Tom again. Out of deference to the object of her journey she wore very smart black, and she surveyed herself carefully in the mirror and then added an extra touch of rouge.

"Not that it fools anybody, except myself! Kay, don't try to make your cowboy over. Give him a long rope. If I know the type he'll need it. But he'll come back and be glad to, if you're clever with him. They all do, you know."

But Bessie felt, when she got on the train, that she had been trying to teach a child higher mathematics. That was one of the tragedies of experience; it could never help any one else.

Kay wrote a long letter to her mother before she went to bed that night. It was a tragic letter between the lines; her divided allegiance, her love for them all, her regret at having had to hurt them. She never received any reply, for Katherine never got the letter, but she was having her own troubles those days. She hardly noticed the lack of response.

One trouble was a small one, comparatively. She came back from her luncheon to find that Tom had had a letter, and that he had not wanted her to see it. The nurse was carrying it out, torn into minute pink scraps, when she went in. He did not mention it to her, but he was very gentle, very conciliatory, all the rest of the day.

The other was a big one.

The day came when Tom had to learn the truth, that his ankle would always be stiff. Kay never forgot the look in his eyes.

"Stiff?" he said. "Then what did you save me for? I'm through!"

"Lots of men go through life with one leg," said the surgeon. "You've got two. If one's not as good as the other—"

Tom laughed. It was not pleasant to hear, and his face was ghastly.

"So that's it!" he said. "Me kidding myself along, and all the rest of you kidding too, and I'm a cripple for life! It's a good joke, isn't it? Why don't you all laugh? Go on out, girl, and order me a pair of crutches. Good ones. They'll have to last a long time."

Then he groaned and rolled over on his face.

He did not move for two hours. Once or twice Kay ventured to touch him, but he drew away as if she had burned him. At the end of that time, however, he reached out gropingly, and she took his hand and held it.

"I've just about wrecked you, girl," he said, his voice smothered in the pillow.

"Do you think it makes any difference to me, Tom? I've known all along.

When twilight came, as if he had not wanted her to see his face before, he turned over in the bed and drawing her down to him, held her close.

"I've given you a pretty raw deal," he said, "but if you'll only stick, girl, I'll pull out of this somehow."

"Just keep on loving me, Tom. I can bear anything else."

"We'll beat the game yet."

"Of course we will."

"Just you and me, against the lot of them, eh?"

"Just you and me, dear."

He slept little that night, and the next day his temperature was up. Kay came in to find him sitting up in the bed and staring morosely before him. He let her kiss him without response, and as soon as the nurse had gone out he turned to her somberly.

"I've been doing some thinking," he said. "The best thing you can do is to go back to your folks."

"Do you want me to go?"

"I can't support you. What's the use of fooling ourselves? They'll take you back. And you can tell them you are purer than the lily, that—"

"Tom!"

"Well, it's God's truth," he said sullenly. "You go back where you can be comfortable; where you'll have enough to eat, anyhow." He avoided her eyes. "I'll have trouble enough keeping myself."

"Look at me. I'll go, if you say you have stopped caring and don't want me."

"It isn't a question of caring. You married a man, not a cripple, and I'm giving you your chance to get out from under. You'd better take it before I yell my fool head off."

The mixed emotions of the next few days almost exhausted her. He rose to heights of the tenderest love, only the next moment to thrust her from him and sink into depths of sullen despair. Once, determined to move the stiffened ankle, he got out of bed and tried to walk on it, and the nurse found him flat on the floor, in a faint. Again he insisted on proof that the company was paying his hospital bills, and not her family.

"Remember this," he told her darkly. "If you stick to me, you get no help from them. I'm no kept man, and I don't want their dirty money."

There was a terrible scene when they brought in his crutches. He sat in his wheeled chair—he was up by that time—and taking them in his hands turned them over with a mocking smile.

"Pretty, aren't they?" he said. "All shiny and nice and—Where's the tin cup, Kay? There ought to be a tin cup to go with them."

Suddenly he flung them across the room.

He was never reconciled to them. Now and then she coaxed him to walk with her in the hospital corridor. He would swing along, his shoulders hunched, the bad foot hanging awkwardly, but if he saw any one but the nurses he would turn abruptly and start back. And what was worse for her, she felt that he was harboring a suspicion that, in maiming his fine body, he had somehow lost his claim on her. He was less arrogant in his demands on her love, more inclined to those long and bitter periods when he lay and stared at the ceiling with his hands clenched, darkly plotting some secret revenge of his own.

But along with this he was, she discovered, cherishing a hope too. When they showed him his X-ray plates he scoffed at them, and at the surgeons after they had gone.

"Just because a fellow wears a white coat doesn't mean he knows everything," he told her. "I'm waiting till old Dunham gives the word. That old boy knows bones. He was settin' legs out in the mountains with a gun-barrel for a splint before these lady-killers were foaled."

And then one day, when they were almost ready to go and she was packing his clothing, the gay shirts and neckerchiefs, the boots inlaid with colored leathers, the heavy chaps, the broad-brimmed hat, the nurse brought in some old newspapers for packing. And he learned about Herbert! He was in his wheeled chair at the time, and she looked up at the rustle of paper and his intent deadly silence. She went to look over his shoulder, but he held it up beyond her reach.

"I'm finishing this," he said coldly.

It was all there; the brilliant preparations for the wedding, the gifts, her flight, Tom himself on horseback, and it ended with a highly drawn account of the shooting. She was terrified, but he was quiet enough at first.

"Why didn't you tell me about him?"

"It wouldn't have changed things, would it?"

"It would and it wouldn't," he said slowly. "I'm no kidnapper, that's all. If I'd known all that—"

"Are you trying to say you wouldn't have married me?" There was a catch in her throat.

"I'm trying to say I'd have gone to him like a man, and not acted like a yellow dog."

Later on, however, his jealousy of Herbert began to manifest itself in the form of scorn.

"And so you were going to marry Percy! With all the he-men there are in the world, you had to pick on him! A fellow that, if he ever saw a hair on his chest, he'd shave it off! And you let him hang around you and make love to you! God Almighty, girl, when I think of him kissing you it makes me sick."

She said little or nothing. She never saw that behind his outrageous talk lay the tragedy of his own crippled condition, his poverty and his bitter jealousy. She was frightened and not entirely just. She told herself that he had unsuspected violences, even cruelties; that he was primitive, savage, ruthless, and that he meant to break her, as he would break a horse. But she would not be broken. She was not old Lucius's granddaughter for nothing. After an hour or so she suddenly stopped her packing and put on her hat.

"I am going to the hotel, Tom." she said. "If you want me to come back you can send for me."

But he did not send for her. He came to her instead. She opened her door that night, to find him, crutches and all, standing outside.

"Well, here I am!" he said, much as she had said it the day she had gone to him. "Do I come in, or am I on my way?"

The next moment she was in his arms.

Chapter Twenty-five

"Tom McNair has come back to God's country once more, this time bringing a wife with him, the late Miss Katherine Dowling. Tom has had a bit of hard luck in the East, but says he will be all right soon. Good luck to the newlyweds."

To Clare Hamel the news of Tom's marriage had come as a crushing blow. Even his accident paled into insignificance beside it. And she got small comfort at home.

"I never did think you'd land him," her mother said. "He's too slippery. But this girl won't hold him either, if that's any comfort to you."

It did comfort her, vaguely.

"Why won't she, mom?"

"She's a Dowling. She's cold," said Mrs. Hamel, turning a pork chop with her fork. "And she's hard; they all are. Not that Tom's any feather bed," she added.

Hope, which had been dead in Clare, lifted its head again. Her mother had a fund of good common sense. Tom would live with this girl for a while, tire of her, and then—

It was mid-June when Kay and Tom McNair came home, and the hot summer of the semi-arid country was well advanced.

Except on the high peaks where the snow lay the year

round, the white patches up above in the range which had persisted through May had already disappeared. But although the snow was gone the creeks were still full. They came roaring down from their mountains turbulent and free, only to be captured, turned into conduit, high-line ditch or low-lying trench and fed to the thirsty land. Then, their youth thus spent, their joyousness departed, depleted by their travail of grain and grass, they moved on sedately on their two-thousand mile journey to the sea, carrying thither their strange freight from the far-off back country, small drowned creatures, charred trees from some forgotten forest fire, perhaps an empty tin from a cattle camp.

Morning and evening in still pools the trout were beginning to ride, cutthroats with their red-gashed jaws, delicately tinted dolly-vardens, and rainbows. On the mountain slopes some of the evergreen trees showed red from winterkill, and lower down certain of the cottonwoods and elders had bent under the heavy snows and lived on, twisted and anemic, like creatures recovering from a long illness. The deer and elk had retreated into the depths of the range.

There was hope among the stockmen that early summer. The winter had been normal, and freight rates were coming down. Their cattle were fattening on the new grass. True, the good days were gone beyond recall; the public domain had been taken from them and given to homesteaders, who lived awhile, starved, sometimes died, and left their wives behind them when they went! But the plains and mountains of the back country showed more cattle than ever before. If only the summer was normal like the winter and spring, then, please God—

The wheat men, too, were cheerful. There was a tariff wall against Canadian wheat, and their own fields were promising. True, they could not farm like the Newcomb job, north on the Reservation. Newcomb had made wheat-growing an engineering matter, connected his farm machinery to great caterpillar engines, harrowed, drilled and sowed with a dozen clattering machines connected in sequence, thought in hundreds of thousands where they thought in fives and twos.

But their fields were green and promising. Now, if they had enought rain, and no grasshoppers or hail, then, please God—

If. If. The eternal "if" of the Northwest, placing its hopes in the Almighty and a government which seemed to have forgotten it, and its confidence in itself and its strong men.

Tom was restless on the train until the last day. Then Kay, waking early, found him bending over and staring out at the rolling treeless country outside, with a queer look in his eyes.

"We're getting there, Kay," he said. "It begins to look like home."

She was astonished to hear his voice tremble.

He had been very quiet after that, content apparently to sit, her hand in his, and gaze out the window. He was even, she thought, somewhat tense during the hours when the train curved and swayed through the bad lands. She had taken to watching him in a way; she had sacrificed so much for him, was so completely bound up in him, so cut off from everything else, that his slightest action had significance for her.

"Isn't that cabin of Jake's down here somewhere, Tom?"

"Over that way." He made a vague gesture. "Let's forget that, girl."

He had told her very little of that winter before, nothing at all about the Miller, except that he was dead. She had learned to accept his reserves; that he lived a strong tumultuous inner life under a surface of stoical calm; that even she would never entirely know the depths of his heart or of his thoughts. But now she tried again.

"Was it as bad as all that?"

"It was all right." He stirred uneasily. "Lonely, that's all."

But he was cheerful enough when they reached the Martin House that night, and he limped up the stairs to the small close bedroom which was to be her home for so many weary weeks.

"Little old town sure looks good to me, Ed."

"It's sure missed you, Tom. Evening, Mrs. McNair. If you want to go right up—"

Getting up the stairs was troublesome. He saw Ed watching from below, and that Tom was resenting that slow progress and Ed's intent gaze with equal bitterness. But once inside the room, he took off his hat and bending down, kissed her.

"Welcome home, girl," he said. "God knows what's going to happen to us now, but here we are!"

He was still cheerful the next morning. He had sent out for a walking stick, and sending for George, the colored bell-hop and general factotum, gravely presented the crutches to him. Kay protested, but he only grinned at her.

"Why, say," he drawled, "if I went down the street on crutches the boys would shoot me, out of pity!"

She watched him starting out with anxiety and apprehension, so gay a figure was he, so carefully dressed, so helpless. But she did not show it.

He had made an elaborate toilet for the occasion, wearing the best of his show outfit, and grinning as he put it on.

"Got to hit them in the eye the first thing," he told her. "If they've got any idea that I'm down and out, they can take an eyeful and forget it. In a couple of weeks I'll be riding a horse with the best of them."

"But you can't mount, can you?"

"Shucks!" he said, "until this old leg loosens up, if I can't find an Indian pony that can be mounted from the off side, I can get one and learn it in a week."

"Teach it, you mean, don't you?"

"You're having a great time making me over, aren't you?" he said, but without rancor. "'Please don't use a toothpick where folks can see you.' 'You don't need to fold your napkin; they won't use it again anyhow.' Now it's the way I talk! If I've got to think about the way I say things I'll have to stop talking."

He kissed her and went out. And, whatever was to come, that first morning of Tom's in his own land, among his own people, was one of almost complete happiness. Some instinct kept him away from Doctor Dunham at first. Instead, he found himself making a more or less triumphal procession through the town. His cane clicked half a dozen feet and stopped. Men emerged from stores and offices to greet him, or halted cars and called to him. Half a dozen small boys followed him at a respectful distance, and an old Indian woman, frankly curious, added herself to his train.

He glowed and expanded.

"Hey, you fellows! Come on out. Here's Tom McNair."

And they came out, leaving their small businesses, their desks and counters, and surrounded him. He had brought to their circumscribed lives a touch of romance and color; he had traveled, been applauded and had his picture in the papers day after day. Then he had been shot, and no sooner had the town had the thrill of that when it learned that he had married Kay Dowling! For forty years the Dowling name had been one to conjure with in that part of the state, and now Tom—their Tom—had married a Dowling!

"Say, lemme touch you for luck, boy."

"You bet. But you don't call this leg luck, do you?"

"Well, look who's here! Why, Tom, you old son of a gun, when did you get back?"

"Last night."

"Missis with you?"

"Yes. We're at the Martin House for a day or so. Come in and see us."

"Sure will."

He expanded, the sense of constriction around his heart left him.

He asked questions. The Mallorys were all right. The Potter Cattle Company had been putting in some scientific sheep pens and dipping vats. And Bill was still on the railroad and seemed to like it.

But he passed the Emporium without looking in.

Finally, however, he had left the business portion of the street behind him, and his exhilaration gradually left him. The end of his cane seemed to sink in the hot paving, and small beads of sweat broke out on his face. Once when he was a youngster, about to ease himself into the saddle in his first bucking contest, he had known the same feeling of now or never. Only then he had been alone. If he broke his back or his neck it was his business. Now—

The doctor was at home. His ancient Ford was at the curb, but the old man himself was inside the open door, carefully pouring something out of a bottle onto the back of a woebegone little French poodle.

"Beats me," he said, scarcely looking up, "where she gets the dratted things. Stand still, Lily May, stand still!"

Tom grinned. He knew the old doctor. The little dog squirmed, the liquid poured down onto the dusty carpet, a bird in a cage somewhere inside began to sing. Not until the bottle was empty and a released Lily May had shot down the steps and under the porch, did Dr. Dunham so much as glance at him again.

"One bad horse too many, eh, Tom?"

He forced a grin.

"You can call it that if you like, doc."

"And after you've allowed all that disinfected emasculated white-aproned crowd in the East to paw over you, you've come to me, eh?"

"They grabbed me when I couldn't fight back."

The doctor chuckled.

"Come in, Tom," he said. "Come on in and let's see what the sons of bitches have done to you."

He did not wash his hands, but, dirty as they were, they were both skillful and kind as he cut off the bandages and poked here and there.

"Had pictures, of course?"

"Pictures! Sure, got an album full. Going to hand it to my kids, to show their friends. 'That's father's left leg at the age of twenty-eight!'"

He laughed, his throat tight, and the examination went on.

"What did those fellows say?"

"Oh, they cheered me up all they could; said it would always be stiff. Said I'd better learn a new trade."

The doctor stood up and glanced out the window.

"Well, what could you do?" he inquired.

Tom stared at him. His color slowly faded.

"That's all, is it?" he said slowly. "There's nothing to do? I don't care how far you go, doc. Dig in if you like, cut it open, cut it off—if you can't fix it."

"I'm not God. I can't make a new joint. And that one's gone."

He began in his business-like fashion to rebandage the leg, but he did not look up. In silence he finished, in silence Tom drew on his sock and his slipper. When that was done the old man disappeared, returning with a glass to take down a bottle from his shelves.

"I've got a little prune juice and sugar here," he said. "It's what they sell me now for *spiritus frumenti*, but it's got a kick to it. Better have some."

But Tom declined, not because he did not want the liquor, but because he was afraid it would unman him. He had a sickening fear that he might break down, and that the unkempt wise old man across from him knew it, for he did not insist. He put the bottle away, and Tom rose and picked up his cane.

"Well, that's that!" he said. "I always did have the luck of a lousy calf. Live all winter and die in the spring."

"You've had some good luck too, according to the papers."

"That depends on how you look at it. If I can't keep her—"

Outside Lily May had abandoned her refuge under the porch, and was now rolling frenziedly in the grass. On Tom's reappearance, however, she once more sought sanctuary. Of the train which had followed him up the street only the Indian woman had persisted. She now stood on the opposite corner, and there was a certain satisfaction in her glance. Tom saw her, and in all his agony of mind recognized the heavy sagging figure, the broad impassive face.

Suddenly fury seized him by the throat. He limped across the street and confronted her.

"You tell Little Dog for me," he said, white-faced, "that if I ever lay eyes on him I'll kill him. You savvy?"

"Little Dog no here."

"I know damned well he isn't here. He'd better not be."

She gazed at him, her small deepset eyes unfathomable. Then suddenly she smiled, with a flash of white teeth, turned away from him, slapped her buttocks with a gesture of derision and moved on. Tom stood where she had left him, ashamed of the fury which still consumed him, and fairly frightened by it. His hands were trembling, his breathing audible. There was no trace now of the blithe and gallant figure which had left the Martin House that morning; the sweat on his face was cold, small black flecks danced before his eyes. In that mood he could have killed, or died. The thought of Main Street again with its friendly back-slapping, its outstretched hands, its easy optimism, was insupportable. Of Kay he dared not think at all.

What he craved, like a drunkard liquor, was the open country once more, and solitude. To be alone, and to look, off and off, to where behind some distant butte the sky kept rendezvous with the earth; or to follow some narrow twisting trail over the edge of the world and beyond. To feel once more the spring and warmth of a horse's body between his knees; to watch the sunrise on a frosty morning, and see the moisture rise like smoke from the backs of the warming herd; to ride in at night by starlight guided by some welcoming light, to the good company of strong men, and to be one of them.

And now, never more! All over. All done. All through.

After a time he moved on. The Indian woman had disappeared. The doctor had come out, got into his ancient car and rattled away. Lily May was dejectedly sitting on the porch. Tom pulled his hat down over his eyes and turned instinctively toward the back country and peace.

The move was purely instinctive. He was still weak; the sweat poured off his face, the hand which clutched the heavy stick was blistered; but by some volition, of the spinal cord rather than the brain perhaps, he kept on. His slow progress stirred up the thick dust, which settled on his haggard face and tortured young eyes. He was like some wounded animal, crawling off to die alone.

It must have been an hour before he realized that the draggled white poodle had followed him. He stopped and tried to send her back, but she only lay down and wriggled in the dust at his feet. He regarded her somberly.

"Come on, then," he said. "You're as much dog as I am man anyhow." . . .

He was very quiet when he got back to the hotel.

"Some of the boys are planning a celebration up in thirty-four tonight," Ed told him. "They want you there at eight o'clock."

"What are they celebrating? This leg of mine?"

But he knew he would have to go. They were his friends; the memory of their cordial greetings that morning was still fresh in his mind. He was tired; he had eaten nothing since morning. And upstairs in that bare room his girl-wife was sitting alone, waiting for him. What he needed was to be in the twilight with her, and there to pour out his profound discouragement and his fears. And to be comforted. Oh, certainly to be comforted.

Kay was waiting for him. She had done what she could to make the bare shabby room comfortable. The gold fittings of her dressing case lay on the bureau, the sagging double bed was neatly made. She asked him no questions, gave him a quick glance as he kissed her and then looked away.

"Well, don't you want to know what he said?"

"I didn't like to ask, Tom. Besides, I think I know."

He wandered to the bureau and absently picked up one of the gold trinkets there. Suddenly his bitterness welled up again.

"Why don't you go home? Back to this sort of thing? I've been telling you all along that I'm through, but you won't believe it."

"Certainly you're not through, Tom. And I'm strong, I can work."

"And keep me? I'll cut my throat first."

At eight o'clock he went to thirty-four. Kay, listening to the tap-tap of his stick, was too filled with love and pity to feel any resentment. Maybe these men could do for him what she could not, cheer him, encourage him. But as time went on the nature of that cheering was only too obvious; voices rose, Tom's among them. George, the shirt-sleeved colored boy, was carrying trays and glasses past her room, a traveling salesman stuck his head out and shouted for quiet.

Then—at eleven o'clock it was—the door to thirty-four opened, and the crowd emerged into the hall. She could hear loud talking.

"Aw, get back, Tom. Jush a little shong to make her welcome!"

"Come on now, fellows, all together!"

There was a shuffling, restrained laughter, and suddenly a thud and silence. Then pandemonium broke loose. She got out of bed and stood inside her door, trembling. There was a free for all fight going on, within fifteen feet of her. She shot the bolt desperately and stood leaning against it.

Then above the confusion she heard a knock at the door, and Tom's voice, thick but triumphant.

"Lemme in, girl."

She opened the door, and he stood there, swaying but smiling.

"Tha' bunch of roughnecks wanted to sherenade you," he said, "but I told them you hadn't any ear for mushic."

A minute later he was sound asleep on the bed, still fully dressed.

The noise in the passage had ceased. Kay drew a chair to the window and stared out, dry-eyed, at the twinkling lights of the street. The town was very quiet, and the night wind from the mountains brought to her the faintly aromatic odor of the sage in the back country.

She sat there until morning.

Chapter Twenty-six

Then began a strange period for Kay. The days were endless and the heat extreme. The wheat men were watching the sky and praying for rain. Tom, inured to weather of all kinds, came and went on mysterious errands of his own. He was, she gathered, looking for work. But he had cleaned and loaded his revolver, and whatever that meant it frightened her.

Of the incident of the party in thirty-four, she found that to Tom it was simply that and nothing more. He had wakened in the morning, puzzled to find himself fully clothed but otherwise unrepentant.

"They didn't mean anything, you know, girl. They were just feeling good, and when a lot of fellows feel like that they just naturally want to sing."

He never knew that she had not gone to bed.

Shut up in the hotel room Kay suffered intensely from the heat and loneliness. She had no friends, even no books. True, some of the important ranchers' wives called on her. They came, kindly enough, smiling, intensely curious, and because she had no sitting room she saw them in the lobby, with its worn leather chairs, its brass cuspidors, the drinking fountain where one leaned over and by turning a lever, was enabled to drink without a cup. But she was too constrained, too bewildered to make friends of them, and one or two of them showed a certain pity which she fiercely resented.

She had, however, two callers who came to her room without announcement.

One was Bob Allison. She opened the door and he stepped inside, a big man with a heavy jaw and a broad brown Stetson hat on the back of his head.

"You'll have to excuse me, Mrs. McNair. Where's that young scapegrace of a husband of yours?"

"He's out just now. If there's any message—"

"Well, there is, and there isn't." He pushed the hat further back, scratched his head, looked at her again.

"How is he? Feeling all right?"

"He doesn't say very much, you know. I think he has a good bit of pain sometimes. But I can't keep him quiet."

"No," he said. "No, Tom's always been restless. Tom ever say who he was holding responsible?"

"No. It was an accident."

He considered that. Every one in town but this girl apparently knew that Tom claimed to have been shot by Little Dog, and that he was only waiting for the Indian to come back to clear up his score against him. But after another look at Kay he put on his hat and turned to the door.

"There's no message, then?"

He hesitated. "Well, you might say this to Tom. Tell him I was here—my name's Allison—and that I'm planning to handle certain little problems without any help from him."

She was no less mystified by the message than by Tom's reception of it."

"He's got nerve!" he said angrily. "Coming here and handing you a thing like that! For two bits I'd knock his teeth down his throat."

But he did not explain, and she asked no questions.

Her other visitor was Mrs. Mallory. She made an uneasy call soon after their arrival, sitting on the edge of a chair in the bedroom and eying Kay with frank interest.

"You certainly have lost flesh, haven't you?" she said, her surprise breaking down her earlier formality. "Well, don't you let Tom McNair wear on you. I know Tom, and he's right uncertain at times. But he's every inch a man, and I've a right to know if any one has."

She grew more expansive after that. Nellie was in school and taking piano lessons. They were making out all right; she had a couple of roomers now. The stock was in good condition too, although her nephew was not a real cattleman, like Jake or Tom. She sighed over Jake's name, and smoothed her black dress with her work-hardened hands.

Before she left she had relaxed sufficiently to straighten her respectable hat before the mirror. She stood there for a moment, staring at her reflection in the glass.

"Ranching sure ages a woman," she said. "It's all right for the men; it keeps them young. But for a woman—"

The bureau stood between the two windows, and she glanced out casually. Then her eyes narrowed, and going to one of them she jerked down the green shade with what amounted to violence.

"Somebody over there on Dicer's second floor, rubber-necking," she said tartly. "You'd better watch your windows. There's a lot of curious people in the world."

Kay, at the window after she had gone, watched her sail across the street below and into the Emporium, later to emerge still angrily flushed, and stalk down the street.

Like Bob Allison's visit, that puzzled her.

The few callers were almost the only breaks in the monotony of those early days. Tom's absences continued. Alone she read the local paper over and over:

"For sale, one Poland China male hog. Nellie Smith."

"Notice: we will trade flour for wheat. Fort Lumber Company."

And when Tom came back at night, after what she guessed was a fruitless day, it would be to eat little in the hot dining room below and then go early to bed, lying she knew wide-eyed in the darkness beside her long after she had found refuge in sleep, withdrawn into some unhappy retreat of his own where he apparently neither needed nor wanted her.

Yet he loved her. She was sure of that. Not after her own fashion, which still made her breathless when she heard his halting step outside the door, but in a queer, alternately violent and humble, way of his own. He would quarrel with her, generally over some matter of his sensitive pride, and then make his peace with a passion that startled her. One such difference was typical. The suit she had worn away with her was threadbare and none too cool. One day she suggested writing to Nora for some clothes. He had drawn her down onto his knee, but now he pushed her away and stood up.

"What clothes?"

"My own. I have so many at home, and I need them, Tom."

"Part of your wedding clothes, you mean?"

"I can't see what difference that would make. After all, I'm married to you."

"That's just where you and I differ," he said, white to the lips. "You *are* married to me, and I dress my wife or she goes naked. I'm owing the Dowling family nothing."

He had never seen her cry, but she cried then, first quietly, then in long-drawn gasping sobs that he could do nothing to quiet. All her loneliness and terror, her actual fear of this undisciplined and relentless side of him, rose to add to her wretchedness. She flung herself on the bed in complete abandonment to it. When he came over and sat down beside her she drew away from him, and miserable as he was he had to wait until her sobs began to die away.

"Do you hate me like that, girl?"

"It's not hate. I think I'm afraid of you."

If she had struck him he could not have been more astounded.

"Afraid of me! My God!"

Had she been a little older, a little wiser, she would have met him halfway then, but although he humbled himself before her, confessed his weakness and his unhappiness, made his young and passionate love to her in his own inarticulate fashion, she remained aloof after that for a day or two. She never sent to Nora for the clothes.

Their small supply of money was dwindling, too. True, Kay still had Bessie's check, but after that quarrel she dared not mention it to Tom. And to the heat was added the discomfort of a continuing drought. Dust blew into her windows and covered the shabby furniture in the room; the pastures were baked hard in the sun, and sandy clouds rose from under the cattle's feet and hovered over them as they moved restlessly; the wheat burned in the fields, and the mountains day after day lifted their heads into a blue and cloudless sky. Anxiety began to be widespread. There was talk among the cattlemen of early shipping, to get out from under, for a summer drought followed by a long hard winter meant ruin.

Tom, limping about or making his long fruitless excursions to outlying ranches, heard one hard luck story after another. The thought of Little Dog began to take second place in his mind, and the problem of actual subsistence for Kay and himself began to obsess him. Never once had he confessed that he was lamed for life.

"How about the leg, Tom? Riding at the Fair, this fall?"

"You tell 'em!"

Old Doctor Dunham overheard that one day, and went on his way dryly chuckling.

But he would not take Kay away from the Martin House, although Mrs. Mallory offered them a room. There was, in the back of his stubborn head, some determination to keep her like a lady as long as he could.

The situation was bound to reach Kay in time, however, and did. He had begun to bring his friends to see her, cowboys in from the range or the ranch, spurred, sombreroed, inclined to long abashed silences; rangers in khaki, with their matter-of-fact talk of forest fires and fire stations, those small neat boxes scattered over the mountains, each with its spade, its pick and saw, its oil jug and its lantern; small cattlemen, in town to buy groceries, or to make their anxious visits to where in his brick bank Mr. Tulloss sat, like a God whose manna of extended credit could save them from bankruptcy.

The hidden far-reaching activities of the back country slowly spread out before her. Gray wolves attacked cows, one checking the flight from in front, the other hamstringing the wretched creatures from the rear; coyotes, crawling under the wire, devastated whole herds of sheep. Glanders, lumpy jaw, mavericks, yardage, shrinkage, feeding, freight—a new vocabulary sounded in her ears.

And there was humor, too.

"Well, we knew the old silvertip was up there somewhere, so when Bill was leanin' over the creek cleanin' the fish I just went behind him and grunted and then give him a good strong hug. Say! He just said 'Jesus!' and went right into the water."

Or again:

"It looked to me like he was going to buy the horse, so he'd stopped at the spring for a drink and I says: 'Well, how about it? Do you want to buy it?' And he says, with the cup in his hand: 'Well, Joe, I'll tell you what I'll do, I'll pay you forty dollars, delivered at my ranch.' 'That suits me,' I says, 'I'll ride him out tomorrow.' 'Ride him!' says he. 'You blamed fool, I'm talking about this spring.'"

She liked these men. She would hear Tom's halting step in the hall, and he would usher in some sun-burned and abashed individual who would more or less tiptoe into the room.

"Come on in, Hank, and meet the wife," he would say.

Then for a little while he would be his handsome debonair

old self. He would throw away his stick and roll a cigarette, and then standing there, tall and smiling, he would seem to fill the little room. Sometimes George brought ice water and Kay made lemonade. The visitor would drink it solemnly.

He was inordinately proud of her, she saw, and she on her part liked these men he brought in. They reeked of the outdoors, their eyes were clear; when they took off their great hats their foreheads were white above the tan and somehow pathetic to her. When they had ridden into town they always stopped outside and took off their spurs. But she was not stupid. She began to see that this new world of hers had no place in it for the weak or the maimed.

But something else had happened to her. Those casual soft-spoken sagas of the range to which Tom listened as one who hears news from home had rebuilt his background for her. Through such a life of grinding hard work, adventure and escape, had he come to her; against this backdrop he once more loomed young and strong and god-like.

She must get him back to it somehow. These weeks in the town were only marking time, as she had suspected Herbert of marking time so long ago. And after a small incident which brought Clare Hamel into the picture, she was more than ever determined.

For the first time in her life she was jealous, not with the light and selfish jealousy of the girl, but with the furious possessive jealousy of a wife.

Considering her day and generation, she was curiously unsophisticated. It was fundamental with her, the romantic tradition which assumed, not only that a beloved woman was the center of the universe to the man who cared for her, but that she was his sole universe. All about her she had seen proofs to the contrary; men who loved their wives and yet were unfaithful to them or neglected them for their business, but the tradition had persisted. Even Bessie's warning: "You think everything's over, I daresay. You've got him and he's got you! But it isn't,"—even that had not shaken her sublime confidence.

Then one day Nellie Mallory came to see her.

It was a strange visit. Nellie seemed to have little or nothing to say, but her small curious eyes took in every detail of Kay herself, of the room, of the expensive gold brushes, jars and scent bottles on the painted pine bureau. It was only when she got up to go that she wandered to the window and looked out.

"Mother says she saw Clare Hamel rubber-necking in here the other day."

And when Kay said nothing:

"She just about had a fit when she heard you'd got him. She thought she had Tom roped and tied for herself."

Then Kay found her voice.

"Does she—is she employed over there?"

"Yes, at the Emporium."

Kay could think of nothing to say. She saw Nellie out, and then went back to the room and to the window. So that was what Mrs. Mallory had meant the other day! A girl who had "had a fit" when she learned he was married. A girl then who cared for him, as—well, as Herbert had cared for her. She thought about it more than was good for her, during those days when Tom was away, and the heat rose from the pavements below and beat in at her windows in waves. She even began to question Tom's absences, but she never questioned Tom himself. It would have been better if she had; but it was not an issue that she dared to raise. She knew his quick anger.

"Sure I had a girl. So did you have Percy! When I think of that lily-handed—" And so on and on.

Then came the incident which decided her. She was starting down the stairs one day, those stairs which led directly into the lobby, when she saw a girl come in. She came in almost furtively, and that she did not see Kay at once was due to the semi-darkness inside and the blinding glare without. Kay knew her at once, and stopped, and so she saw her leave a letter with Ed and start out again. When at the door she turned again she saw Kay coming down, and she hesitated. Then she threw her head up and went on.

Kay did not go out, after all. She went upstairs and stationed herself at a window, and there followed one of those small secret duels between women which are at once tragic and ludicrous. At the noon hour Clare, convinced that she had been discovered, crossed the street to the hotel, to find Kay talking to Ed, and precipitately fled. Kay's hands were like ice, and her eyes were burning, but she was determined to know where she stood; if life had played its final trick on her. But she was quiet enough when Tom came in and found her in their room.

"Well, did you get your letter?"

He had sat down and was rubbing his swollen ankle, but now he stopped.

"What letter?"

"I thought Ed said there was a letter for you."

For an instant their glances clashed. Then he went back to his rubbing.

"No letter for me. If you don't believe it you can look in my pockets."

They had both lied! A sense of shame overcame her, as well as wild jealousy. He had had his letter, and he had not dared to bring it into the room. He had deliberately deceived her. He had stood downstairs in the lobby and destroyed it before he came to her.

Lying sleepless in the hot bed that night while Tom slept she faced the knowledge that she had given all she had and had not even bought security with it; that while women had certainly occupied only intervals in Tom's life, these intervals had been recurrent and probably violent, and, even granting his love for her, that they might occur again.

Chapter Twenty-seven

It is probable that Henry Dowling would have accepted Kay's death with submission and Christian fortitude, would have pictured her, or tried to do so, among the blessed company of the saints, and—having been thus assured of the impeccable nature of her surroundings—have settled down to tender memories and a cherished grief. But she had left no such solace. By sheer violence alternating with cold contempt he bore down Katherine's feeble arguments.

"All we have! Of course she's all we have! You don't think that helps matters, do you? She knew that, and yet she chose this circus clown, this farm yokel, this—"

Or again, in a more temperate mood:

"She'll come back; don't worry about that. I only hope to God she doesn't come back pregnant and expect us to raise the fellow's child. That's what usually happens."

He faced his world with suspicion and distrust. Not that he had ever been too sanguine about it; it had a way of enjoying the discomfiture of others. And who should know that better than Henry himself? But he carried it rather far, even for him, held his head very high and took to watching the faces of the men he met on the streets, in business, at his clubs. One or two of them, absently passing him by at that time, were bewildered to find that they had somehow incurred his enmity.

He had made a new will.

"Not a dollar of my money to my daughter's husband," he said, setting his jaw. "If she leaves him and divorces him all right; if not—"

The estate was to go in trust to his wife, and later to his old university.

"I know those fellows," he said grimly. "If she tries to break the will they'll fight her to kingdom come. Charities are different; they can't very well bid too hard, and anyhow they haven't the guts." He had got that word from Bessie.

Immediately Bessie Osborne made a will of her own, and having done so wandered into his office and told him about it. After which she proceeded to inspect herself in a small mirror, and waited for the storm to break with her usual placidity. It did break, and in the midst of it he looked up to find her making the most hideous grimaces at him. He was startled into silence.

"Sorry!" she said, smiling at him. "I'd forgotten my facial exercises for today. Toning the muscles, you know. Well, go on."

He never quite recovered his former speed after that. When she got up to go she might have been listening to a rather stupid lecture, for all the effect it had had on her. She drew her wrap about her and picked up her bag.

"How splendid it must be always to know you are right!" she said brightly. "You and God Almighty—like old what's his name, the Kaiser." She surveyed him. "It's rather a pity I got all father's humor and his wickedness, isn't it, and you only got his virtues. A little sin would have helped you, Henry."

Then she wandered out.

But if she had her father's humor and what she called his wickedness, she also had a bit of that clear hard brain of his which had mixed up men, their actions and reactions, to the making of his fortune. She knew that her check had not been cashed, and that Kay had been right about her cowboy. Then the fellow must have more than a handsome face. He certainly had the intestinal investiture Henry had referred to.

But Bessie's sympathies at that time were divided. Herbert had come out of the affair with a dignity she had hardly expected. He had neither withdrawn himself nor assumed an attitude of artificial indifference. Now and then she saw him on the golf links, apparently intent on his game, or even once in a while at a club dance. If he added little to the gayety at such times, he never had done so. He was as carefully dressed as ever, as temperate, as courteous. She knew her brother had carried out his promise and that he had been moved up in the business somewhere, and she sometimes wondered if Herbert was finding consolation in that.

Then one night she had a talk with him, and liked him better than she ever had, as a result. She found him alone on the terrace of the club lighting a cigarette, and promptly appropriated both it and him.

"I haven't seen you for ever so long. Why don't you stop in?"

He lighted another cigarette for himself before he answered.

"I couldn't come whining for sympathy, and I was afraid that's what I would do."

"Nonsense! It's better to talk these things out. That's good modern psychology."

But with the door opened in that fashion he seemed to have little to say.

"I haven't anything buried, I think. I've tried to believe that I want her to be happy, but I can't. I suppose what I really want is for the whole thing to go smash, so that she'll come back again. Then I wonder what my own reactions would be if she did come back. You can't tell, you know." His voice trailed off vaguely, as though he was reviewing some old and painful train of thought. "It isn't only because she's been married, or not entirely. It's because she stood us up, McNair and me, side by side, and—he was the better man. For her anyhow."

"It wasn't as deliberate as that, Herbert."

"Perhaps not, but that doesn't help, does it? He had some attraction for her that I didn't have. Not just looks, probably. She's too intelligent for that. Something fundamental, like—like a chemical affinity. That sounds queer, but you know what I mean."

Bessie nodded.

"Cause of all the trouble in the world," she said succinctly. "Cyrano, for instance!"

"Cyrano had a mind."

"Don't be too sure McNair hasn't. He's nobody's fool, I imagine."

"A man who spends his life among cattle!"

"Well, it takes brains to raise cattle," she said shrewdly. "My father did it, you know."

He had no answer to that, and she left him there lighting a fresh cigarette. The match flare showed him white and absorbed.

Perhaps had Katherine been in better health she would have asserted herself more, but she was overborne by her husband's anger and too weak to combat it. She was a sick woman, more ill than even Henry knew, or perhaps he would not have kept Kay's letter from her, or forbidden her to write. She had accepted this pronunciamento as she had accepted others during all her married life, but her obedience this time was helped by her ignorance. She did not know where Kay was; before Bessie's visit she had known none of the details of Tom's injury; and even Bessie could only say that they meant to go West, that they had apparently no plans. At night, sleepless in her bed, she composed touching little epistles full of the things she had always been too shy to say, but with the morning her courage and her strength departed, and there was Henry, grimly insistent on her silence and even watching her with furtive suspicious eyes.

There had been a terrible day when Nora, red-eyed and smelling of moth preventive, came into her bedroom and handed a bunch of keys to Henry.

"That's all, is it?" he inquired. "You haven't left anything out?"

"You can come and look," said Nora with a sort of suppressed savagery. "And here's the list."

That had been Kay's clothes. The presents had been sent back long ago.

Life went on for her. People came and went. Sometimes she went downstairs and served tea, and it was quite like old times—without Kay, of course. The Sargent painting of Kay in her presentation clothes still hung on the wall; Henry had thought it would be conspicuous to remove it, but when he was in the room Katherine did not look at it. Little things like that upset him those days.

Now and then she was ill. Terribly ill. A pain began in her chest and ran down her left arm, her heart beat like a fluttering bird, and a cold sweat broke out all over her. It terrified her. She could stand the pain better than the terror. Then it would pass, and there would be Henry, strangely gentle and very pale. That would have been the time to talk to him about Kay, but she was always too weak to speak. And when she tried to he would bend over her, still white and shaken, and say:

"Hush now. Don't talk. Just close your eyes and rest."

The terror was that she would die before she had said to Kay the things she had been too shy to say all those years.

Then one day Henry opened his copy of the Ursula paper—his subscription had not yet run out—and read that Tom McNair had come back bringing a wife with him, "the late Miss Katherine Dowling." He rang for Rutherford and ordered the paper taken out and destroyed, and that night in his library he wrote a letter by hand, and marked it personal and confidential.

My dear Tulloss: Probably long before this you have learned what has occurred in my family. I need not enlarge on it. You will know what a shock and disappointment we have had. Scandal, too, I regret to say, but that is comparatively unimportant.

Before I make the request which is the purpose of this letter, let me make my position clear. I do not regard my daughter's marriage to this cowboy as a permanent thing. I know her. It is the result of a brief infatuation, of romantic nonsense picked up by her God knows how last summer, and of her own imagination. I fancy, too, that the stimulation of the altitude—but that is not pertinent. As I say, I know her. She has always had everything, and more. She is both fastidious and luxurious. If this fellow has not already destroyed her illusions about him he soon will. Her pride will carry her on for a time after that, but not long.

It is with this conviction that I am writing you. I want you to be cruel to be kind. She may come to you, or he may, for help of some kind. I am asking you to refuse any such application if it is made. Believe me, I have given this careful thought. I am fully convinced that her entire future life will depend on the position we take now.

I understand that McNair had been injured and is not likely to be able to go back to his old employment. He may have had a little money when they started back to Ursula, but probably not much. When this is exhausted the real test will come, and it is of that time that I am writing you now. I beg you to stand by me.

My regards to Mrs. Tulloss. I am sorry to say that my wife is far from well. It looks like angina pectoris, and we are gravely concerned.

Sincerely yours,
HENRY DOWLING.

Chapter Twenty-eight

Little Dog had not yet come back to the Reservation, although shortly after he had shot Tom he had left the show. And little by little Tom's thoughts of revenge died before the situation in which he found himself. Once he came back with the news that he could get work at the new filling station near the railroad, but he found Kay opposed to it and oddly anxious to get out of town.

"You're a good cow-man, Tom. All these men say that. Then why—?"

"You can't run cattle unless you've got cattle to run, girl. I've tried every outfit in the country."

He went on doggedly, borrowed cars and made his long trips into the back country, over roads now deep in dust; coming back at night or the next day, disheartened and weary from a region drying up and desolate, and from ranchers as discouraged as himself. The streams were low and getting lower, the pastures were baked as hard as brick, and the grass—the life of the cow-country—had ceased to grow and lay brown and burnt in the fields.

He was bitter, sometimes. Bill, coming to call on them and relaxing after a time, told some railroad stories of old Lucius Dowling and the billion-dollar crowd he had brought with him one summer.

"Sure was a great old man, your grandfather," he said to Kay. "Why, say, it wasn't anything for those fellows to bet a thousand dollars on the turn of a card."

Tom had been lounging on the bed, a habit which set Kay's nerves on edge. Now he sat up suddenly.

"Huh!" he said. "And where'd they get it? *How'd* they get it? Where'd they get money to throw around like that?"

"Don't ask me!" said Bill, good-humoredly.

"Well, I'm telling you. You're a cow-man, Bill. What happens to cattle if before you sell them you feed them a lot of salt and then fill them up with water? That's what those fellows did, and still do. Watering stock's the name for it."

"If you're speaking of my grandfather, Tom—"

"You've named him," he said, and relapsed into sulky silence.

But if he sang and whistled less around the room, he still had his moments of boyish passionate love for Kay. He would come in, weary and lamer than usual, to draw her down into his arms and sit for long periods of quiet, content just to hold her and rest his head against her.

"You still loving me, Kay?"

"I'll never stop. I can't. You know that."

Her personal daintiness never ceased to surprise and delight him, her fragrant bath powder and soap, the care she gave to her short sleek hair, the ribbons in her undergarments, laboriously inserted after each laundering.

"Say, I believe you'd put ruffles on a bunk house towel!"

"*You* see them, don't you? And like them?"

"I like everything about you," he would tell her solemnly. "You're prouder'n a wildcat, and you can be right ornery at times too. But I'm for you."

But sometimes he picked up and looked at her delicate, fastidiously cared for hands.

"You brought them to the wrong market," he told her once. "I can just remember my old lady's hands; they sure felt like shoe leather." She suspected him of inarticulate depths of sentiment about his mother.

He tried to please her, too, those early days when each was painfully learning the other. Put on his coat to go down to meals, with only a protest now and then. "Making a regular dude out of me, aren't you?" Shaved carefully and often, even blacked his boots!

"What pains me," he told her once, surveying himself in the mirror, "I can't go out and hire a hall to show myself off in!"

Clare seldom entered his mind at all. So lightly had the engagement weighed on him that he was astounded when he found that she took his marriage as an injury. What had she lost? He had never pretended to care for her. It was she who had put that fool announcement in the paper. And perhaps, with that queer intuition of his where girls and women were concerned, he was not far wrong when he suspected her of secretly enjoying her grievance, of dramatizing herself, publicly and privately, and so indirectly injuring him.

But he underrated one thing. Dramatize herself she could and did, going about with a sad smile that made Sarah Cain long to slap her. He underestimated her passion for him. She had never given him up. What did that dead-alive girl over there in the window of the Martin House know about Tom McNair or his kind? When to relax control, and when to tighten it up? How to give and then withhold, so as to keep him guessing?

"I'll give her three months," she said, to Sarah Cain.

"Yes, and you'd give her poison if you had the chance!" said Sarah Cain.

And so things were with all of them when one hot day Tom, standing on a street corner, saw Little Dog passing by in a Ford car.

Carrying weapons was as much against the law in Ursula as in any other civilized town, and it was twenty years since the six-gun on the hip had been a part of the cowboy's outfit, like his chaps and spurs. So Tom's revolver was safely back at the hotel. That fact, and that only, saved him from committing murder that day.

But he did the next best thing, leaped onto the running board and jerked the Indian out, and was in process of choking him to death when the crowd intervened.

As it was, he went to jail for ten days—

Kay was bewildered and shocked, her severance from her old world of polite amenities and amiable hypocrisies practically complete. She had a letter from Bessie at that time—Bessie, who loathed writing letters—but she did not reply. What could she say? "We are both well, although Tom is not working yet. Just now he is in jail."

Never.

It was Mrs. Mallory who softened the blow for her.

"What he should have done was to kill that Indian," she said, bloodthirstily. "First he shot Tom's horse—and he set a lot of store by that horse—and then he shot Tom. Don't tell me different. I know."

Kay got permission to visit Tom in the jail. He looked wretched, and he had little to say about the trouble.

"He had it coming to him," he told her grimly.

After that she sat around and waited. There was nothing in particular to wait for, except Tom. They seemed to be in a hopeless eddy, each still clinging to the other but both slowly drowning. But she did some thinking too, with that brain that she had inherited from old Lucius.

She knew nothing of money. The unfitness of the feminine mind to comprehend even the ABC's of finance had been one of her father's basic principles, a part of the tradition of his type. Never in all his married life had he as much as told Katherine the amount of his income or the extent of his holdings. It was not so much that he distrusted her intelligence; it was, as with most men of his type and training, an obstinate holding to the string of domestic power and sovereignty. By that and that only was he overlord, and this dominion of his was even carefully planned by will to extend beyond the grave.

To Kay, then, banks hertofore had been places where the silver and jewels were deposited on emergency, and where, as to money, one first put it in and then drew it out again. But by this time she learned that they had another function; they loaned money. Sometimes on a ranch, sometimes on cattle, even more rarely, on a man's character.

Tom was still in jail when she visited Mr. Tulloss. Mostly he rolled and smoked cigarettes. He had no regrets, except that he had not killed Little Dog, but he had a great deal of time to think. Most of his thinking was extremely bitter: thus, he could not support Kay. Then she'd better go back to her people. If it was a question between his pride and her comfort, better swallow his pride. Anyhow, what reason for pride had he? He was crippled. He could still work, but nobody believed it. And how long would she keep on caring, the way things were? A corner loafer, a—

When that got too bitter for him, he had devised a series of tortures for his bad ankle, as if by main force to make a joint where no joint existed. And he would keep on until the bars of his cell retreated into a gray and misty distance, and faint with pain he would have to sit down.

It was when things had reached that point that Kay had set her mouth one day, placed Bessie's check in her purse, and went to the bank.

Chapter Twenty-nine

Mr. Tulloss was at his desk. He could see from where he sat out into the tile-floored, neat-caged banking room, where tidy clerks handled money like merchandise. His bank was the heart of the community. It pumped, and life-giving blood went out, circulated and came back again. But, of course, sometimes it did not come back. That was Mr. Tulloss's tragedy.

Even then, naturally, something came in its place; notes, mortgages, what not, and these paid interest. There were those who said that, asked suddenly to name a number between one and ten, Mr. Tulloss would say nine automatically, and ten if he had his wits about him.

He had seen his bank grow from a one-story wooden affair to its present size; he had lived through two holdups, and in one he had been shot—preferring death to losing money, his enemies insisted. There was a rumor that the bullet was still lodged in the flesh under his left shoulder blade, and that when he was tempted to lend money on adequate security he always leaned back in his chair, so he could feel it.

But if he was a hard man he was a just one. He had been a cattleman in the old easy days; he knew that curious triumph of hope over experience which is at once the cowman's glory and his destruction. He had warned his customers against over expansion during and following the war, and had lived to see their ranches go for less than the cost of the fencing and buildings on them. He could not carry them all. Some of them left him and went to little fly-by-night banks which had sprung up overnight during that period of inflation, and, doing business on a shoe string, had promptly collapsed when the hard times came, carrying their wreckage with them.

On this particular morning, however, he was not looking out. The vista of his neat mahogany counters and brass grills did not interest him. He was rereading, not for the first time, a letter he held in his hand. A hand-written letter, the envelope of which had been marked "Private and confidential."

He had had Henry's letter for some time, but this new scrape of Tom's had reminded him of it. He had never cared much for Henry Dowling; old Lucius, with his love for the West, his Rabelaisian jokes, his roistering friends and his disregard of anything under a twenty dollar note as a medium of circulation, had always appealed to him. There had been something rather splendid about him. But he was just, too. He and Henry might have been cut out of the same cloth. Just so, given the same situation, would he have acted. But the act did not alter his distaste for the letter and the writer.

And now the girl was sitting alone in that hotel, with the heat and the flies, and the stale odors of bad cooking, and Tom McNair was in jail. Perhaps he'd better ask Jennie to go in and see her. But no—better keep the women out of this.

He had an uneasy conviction that the whole matter was somehow not quite respectable.

Then he looked up and saw Kay in the doorway. The feeling could not live before that vision of her, young and steady-eyed and certainly not abased. Oh, certainly not abased. There was a look of her grandfather about her, too. Odd that he had never noticed the resemblance before.

Mr. Tulloss, who made the common masculine mistake of considering that clear eyes and youth were essentially virginal qualities, felt that there had been an essential indecency in his previous thoughts of her, and by way of apology made his greeting unexpectedly warm.

"Well, well!" he exclaimed. "Haven't you been a long time coming in to see me?"

"I didn't think you would care to see me," she said simply.

He passed over that, put her in a chair, drew the shade to keep the sun out of her eyes, and sitting down across from her put the tips of his fingers together.

"And so you are a married woman!"

"Yes."

"Rather sudden, wasn't it?"

"I think I did the right thing, Mr. Tulloss. To marry without love, that isn't even—moral is it?"

Mr. Tulloss, who had married Jennie because she had ten thousand dollars and he had needed ten thousand dollars at the time, blinked slightly.

"Then you are fond of Tom, I take it."

"I love him. That has to be the answer to everything. All the answer I have, anyhow."

"Still? After—let's see—two months of married life?" He was rather arch about this, but she looked at him gravely, fearlessly.

"After everything. And above everything."

Mr. Tulloss was slightly abashed. There was, for all her virginal appearance, something shameless about this girl. He caught himself remembering the year old Lucius had brought a woman out with him, and how in this very room, brand-new then, he had gravely remonstrated with him. Old Lucius had eyed him with the same bland directness.

"Now see here," he had said. "My business is between you and me, Hank, but my private affairs are between me and my God. I like this woman and she likes me, and I'm damned if I care what you think."

He stirred uneasily in his chair.

"Then you're not sorry, Kay?"

"For my people, yes; and of course it is not always easy," she confessed, still with that strange honesty of hers. "We have lived different lives, you know. The things I think important sometimes don't matter to him, and the other way round, too. Then of course his accident—"

"He thinks Little Dog shot him, I understand."

"He has never told me so, but I know that's what he believes. That's why, the other day—"

"I see. And this lameness of his? Is it permanent?"

"I'm afraid so. His ankle is stiff, but he is sure he can ride before long. And he knows cattle, Mr. Tulloss. All sorts of men come in to see him, and ask him things. But of course they want men with the outfits who aren't handicapped."

Mr. Tulloss abruptly ceased to be the old family friend, and became the banker.

"That's natural. A man handling cattle needs all his arms and legs and then some. Tom had better put cattle out of his mind and get something else to do."

"But he knows cattle; he doesn't know anything else."

"He can learn. I had to. So have a lot of others."

Kay sat forward desperately.

"I think he ought to get out of town, Mr. Tulloss."

"Has he been drinking again?" he asked, shrewdly if brutally. She flushed.

"Just the first night, a little. Not since. But—if you could only lend him money, to start in business for himself!"

"What kind of business?"

"He only knows one thing. But he does know that."

"And on what am I to lend this money? It isn't my money, you know. On what security?"

"On character. Character and experience. You do that, don't you?"

He laughed grimly.

"Once in a blue moon," he said. "What between the

inscrutable acts of Providence and the Federal Farm Loan,
man who lends on character these days is plumb out of luck
Then, just now Tom's character—"

Quite unexpectedly she reached up and fumbled at he
neck.

"Then, on these?" she said. "They were my grandmothers
She left them to me. I believe they are quite valuable."

She laid a string of pearls on the table. They were sti
warm from her neck when Mr. Tulloss, surprised int
silence, picked them up. As if that shocked him he put then
down again quickly.

"I could get some imitations," she told him breathlessly
"They make quite good ones. You see, I don't want Tom t
know. What I thought you could do would be to send fo
him and say that you believed in him, and were going to giv
him a start. You know what I mean."

"Just like a fairy-tale, eh?" he said wryly. "The fatherly ol
banker and—"

He checked himself when he saw her face. His eyes reste
on Henry's letter, still on the desk. "I beg you to stand b
me." But what did Dowling want? She was going to stick t
the fellow. Did he want her to starve?

"Perhaps I ought to tell you," she went on hurriedly. "
have a check for a thousand dollars, too. My aunt sent it t
me. But I have not told Tom about it. He doesn't—"

"He doesn't want them to keep you, so he'll let you d
without," he commented. "Well, that's the nature of a man
Kay."

Nevertheless his opinion of Tom McNair rose somewhat
and of Henry Dowling's perspicacity decreased. If this wa
the brief infatuation, the romantic nonsense he had
contemptuously dubbed it, then there was no such thing a
lasting love. And this girl across was no fool. Reading face
was a part of his business; he saw clearly in hers that any
illusions she might have cherished were gone, but that she
had replaced them with something else, perhaps even deepe

and more profound. He had been prepared to pity her. He found himself respecting her.

"Did he know you were coming here today?"

"No. I don't want him to know, Mr. Tulloss."

"I see! I'm to call him in and offer him—just what am I to offer him, anyhow?"

And then she said something that might have come from old Lucius himself.

"A chance," she told him. "When a man who's worth while is down and out, and he gets a chance, he makes good."

It touched him. And was it such a chance, after all? He knew McNair was a good cow-man, provided he kept sober and let women alone. He would have to make that a part of the agreement. That Hamel girl, for instance.

"I'll do this," he said, in his dry old voice. "I'll make it a point to see Tom anyhow, and maybe we can work out something." He shoved the pearls toward her. "You'd better put those on again."

"Aren't you going to keep them?"

"I don't run a pawnbroker's shop. But I'd be right careful of them around the hotel. That nigger there may be light-fingered."

After she had gone he leaned back in his chair, maybe to remind himself of the bullet under his shoulder blade. But if he did he dismissed it. He was going back, a very long time back, to the time when he had stood at the cross-roads of life. On the one hand had been the open range and the great herds—they had been great in those days. He had owned a horse and saddle then and not much else; where he had unrolled his bed had been home. When he wanted money in the winter he had gone wolfing; he had killed one big gray with his hands once, and got a hundred and fifty dollars for it from the stockmen around. And when he had time off he had ridden into town like the rest and got drunk at Hamel's Last Chance saloon, and ridden howling and shouting out of town, firing his revolver into the air.

Then one day they began to survey for the railroad. He had stopped his horse on a hill and watched the men at work, and he got off then and there, sat down and watched them. Ursula was going to be quite a town some day. Cass Woodson, the trader, wouldn't be able to supply it. The place was a shame anyhow, with its stinking sheepskins and cowhides piled up to be freighted out, its cheap canned goods and calicoes, its fraudulent scales and the odor of blood from the shed in the back where he killed his beef. No. Stores would come in, and money, and somebody would have to take care of that money.

The bank down at Easton had flourished. Cattlemen, pocketing their big checks in the fall from Chicago or Omaha were taking them there for deposit. It came in bulk, was parceled out in loans, and paid interest. High interest. But why should they go to Easton? There would have been no answer perhaps had he not met Jennie. But Jennie had ten thousand dollars, and here he was.

Sitting inside the window of the Prairie Rose Café later on, he realized that had Kay been an older woman or an ugly one the result of the interview might have been entirely different. Well, that too was the nature of a man.

Chapter Thirty

There had been rain at last. Too late to revive the drying pastures and the scorched wheat fields, but rain.

The road was deep with mud. Every now and then the rear end of the heavily loaded wagon slewed round and slid into the ditch. Sometimes the team could pull it out again, but once or twice Tom had to take the fence post he had picked up early in the day, and with all the strength of his shoulders and back, lift a wheel out of a slough. Then Kay would urge the horses ahead, and once more on the crown of the road the wagon would jolt along.

At noon a second storm came up. The sky was a sinister dark gray, against which the bare and yellow hills and buttes stood out, tawny figures painted on a monstrous canvas. Every so often this canvas split, and to the sound of its rending forked lightning came through, like the split tongue of a snake.

The cattle huddled under the shelter of the slopes, in ravines and swales; horses stood with heads drooping, facing away from the wind. Then the rain came, like a curtain suddenly lowered. It erased the world, and left the two in the wagon like shipwrecked mariners in a rocking boat on a beating turbulent sea. There was no shelter. Here and there, with miles of empty road intervening, they passed the deserted log cabin or tiny wooden house of some forgotten homesteader; a door and a window, sometimes two windows; a barn, a shelter shed, and lying out around, exposed to the weather, broken-down wagon and rusty abandoned farm machinery.

But their broken roofs offered no security; they only added to Kay's depression, a melancholy she concealed under a fixed smile.

Tom, on the other hand, was flamboyantly happy. The rain and mud were powerless to depress him; all his life he had found nature fundamentally hostile, something to be fought and conquered. Wet, his boots inches deep with gumbo, he was yet triumphant and cheerfully hopeful. With every slow mile his spirits rose; he was proud of his team, of his wagon, of his wife; of the household goods that, piled high behind him, swung and lurched over the ruts in the road. He whistled, even sang.

"I'm a poor lonesome cowboy,
I'm a poor lonesome cowboy,
I'm a poor lonesome cowboy,
And a long ways from home."

Now and then he would reach out and take Kay's hand, and she would smile up at him and return his warm pressure. Not if she died for it would she have dampened that enthusiasm of his. He was off on the great adventure.

"We've got to make good, girl. And by heck we will. We've got to show the old man."

The old man was Mr. Tulloss.

"Of course we will show him," she said valiantly.

There had been a profound change in Tom since that day when he had come into the bedroom at the Martin House, with a new soberness in his face and a new straightening of his shoulders. He had told her very quietly: Tulloss had sent for him and talked over the cattle business with him; the old man thought things were looking up. Not like the old days, of course, but still—

And then suddenly he had dropped down beside her and put his head in her lap. He was to have his chance; Tulloss was going to stake him. He could take care of her now. There had been awful times when he had thought he couldn't, but that was all over. He wasn't afraid; he'd make it go if he had to work all day and all night.

It was only after that emotional paroxysm had passed that he gave her the details. The banker was going on his note for the purchase of a small herd, three or four hundred; cattle were cheap now, because of the drought. And he was to look around for some "dead" Indian lands on the Reservation, preferably with a ranch house on them. If he could buy such a place at a decent figure—

"On the Reservation! Is that safe for you?"

"If I let them alone I guess they're not hunting any trouble."

But he did not tell her that a part of his agreement had been a promise, solemnly made, to keep his hands off Little Dog. It had not been easy; he had even hesitated. But he had made it.

"I owe him a skinful of lead."

"You're going to owe me something more important than lead. Good hard money."

"If he keeps out of my way—"

"Don't be a pig-headed young fool. Take it or leave it, Tom."

So he had agreed.

It was after he had told her that, moving excitedly, exultantly around the room, that a new thought occurred to him. Some pause or other—for breath perhaps—brought him up before the bureau, with its gold trinkets, and he stopped and stared at them.

"I guess maybe I've been thinking too much about myself," he said suddenly. "What about you, girl? You've got a right to have a say in this."

"It's just what we have both been wanting, Tom, isn't it?"

"You don't know anything about it," he said, almost roughly. "It'll be no picnic. If I take hold I'm going through with it. I'll be away part of the time, and winter's coming. What I could do," he added, "you could get a room somewhere here, and—"

"And let you fight it out alone?"

"I've bached it before this. And I'm not talking about a ranch house like the L. D. If we get three rooms we'll be lucky."

"If it's only one room I'm going with you, Tom."

Even then he was not quite satisfied. He stood looking at her moodily. She was so young, so ignorant of what she was committing herself to. He turned over a little gold brush with his finger.

"You won't need that sort of thing there."

"Would you like me to sell it?"

"God! No!" he said.

After that a new life had opened before him. He even seemed to limp less noticeably. He laughed and talked with Ed at the desk below; she could hear him through her closed door. He ate prodigiously and slept like a baby. There was even boisterousness in his love-making; he would pick her up and hold her to him, as if for sheer joy in his returning strength. And he was busy. He had found a herd, and he was to "throw in" with the Potter outfit on the Reservation, bearing his share of the cost. At night he would sit and figure laboriously. If it cost forty cents a head per month for grazing, then— He would survey his totals. "Looks like a lot of money to me," he would say ruefully. But he had his moments of triumph also; one was when he had registered the old L. D. brand as his own.

"That's something to write home about!" he told her boastfully. "I'll bet old Lucius is turning over in his grave."

She suspected a certain malicious pleasure in that,

directed not at her, but at her people. She knew he had never forgiven them, and after his stubborn fashion, that he never would. He wanted nothing from them, but their dogged refusal to so much as acknowledge her marriage was a gesture of contempt toward him, and he knew it.

But aside from that he never mentioned them. He had bought horses, a work team, one or two green broncs that he meant to break himself, and a big gelding which he could mount from the right side. "Not much of a string yet," he said, but he had enormous pride in them, in everything. For the first time in his life he had the sense of property.

If Kay had her own reservations, her panicky moments, he never knew them. She was at least getting him away from the town and from Clare; there would be no one to offer him liquor, or send him letters, and she was too ignorant of the feud between Little Dog and himself to worry about it. There were others who knew Tom and the nature of Indians who felt less hopeful.

It took the last of their money to buy their household goods. The room at the Martin House was crowded with her purchases; gleaming pots and pans sat in the pine drawer among her toilet things, and Tom would gaze at them with proprietary pride.

"Now what's that for?"

She did not always know, and then Tom would throw back his head and roar with laughter.

"It's a fine wife I've got! Good thing for you I'm some cook myself!"

But he would not have been Tom had he not had his depressed and even violent spells. One day he took her hands and examined them.

"They're going to have to work, those hands," he told her, almost roughly.

"That's what hands are for, or ought to be."

"Not if you'd married Percy!"

And that thought seemed to madden him. He worked

himself into a frenzy over it. Why was she sticking to him? He wasn't worth it and she knew it. If it was because she was sorry for him, damn being sorry for him. He didn't want pity. He was more of a man as he was than any one of that crowd of mavericks he had met back East. And that memory lashing him to a fresh grievance, his undisciplined temper carried him on and on. She listened, her hands cold, her heart beating fast, until he flung out of the room. Half an hour later he was back, offering to get down and let her trample some of the "orneriness" out of him.

She began to feel the strain of meeting his varying moods. One day he went around to the Mallorys' and returning with his saddle, dumped it onto the floor with a strange expression on his face.

"Got to learn some new tricks, this old saddle!"

She was afraid to let him see the tears in her eyes—

So she had learned a great deal, this Kay McNair, sitting on the rocking swaying wagon, with her dressing case beneath her feet, and behind her the Lares and Penates of their migration; the bed and chairs and table bought at second hand, the box of provisions, the two Indian rugs which had been her sole concession to luxury. She had already traveled a long road from her old protected life, and she was still on the way.

The storm had settled into a steady cold rain, the wagon rocked and slewed, steam rose from the broad backs of the horses, Tom's new work team. As slow mile on mile was covered the motion became, first tiring, then painful, and at last an unendurable agony. Tom had brought out his old slicker from the back of the wagon and insisted on her wearing it, but in spite of it rain dropped from the brim of her small hat and ran down her neck. The slicker smelled of oil and horses; it began to nauseate her. Wire fences, sage brush, vast empty stretches of sodden country, ditches filled with little green frogs, a gray haze to the left that must be the mountains, and always the road going on, and on, seeming to drift aimlessly, to get nowhere.

"Look! There's a chicken."

"I don't see any chicken."

"A prairie chicken! Right good eating in the spring; not now."

He saw everything; he knew the birds, the wild flowers. To him the journey was one through beloved country among dear familiar things. He had the sense of home; better than that, of home-coming. He sang and whistled and talked. Now and then he reached over and tucked the slicker in about her, but if he noticed the lethargy of misery about her he said nothing. Occasionally he turned an anxious possessive eye to the rear and the load. He had an enormous pride in that new "gear" of theirs; he had had so little for so long.

"Funny, when you think about it," he said, "this is the way the old boys came out—the pioneers, you know. Everything they had piled up behind them."

He talked about them. There over that rise had gone the earliest trail of the covered wagons, often with soldiers from the last for to escort them for part of the way; there or hereabouts the Indians had killed some of them. They had gone on, leaving their hastily dug graves, and later on they had come back, some of them, to search for them; but they never could find them.

On and on. Talk, talk. Sing, whistle. Creak, creak. Kay felt her nerves getting out of control.

"So this old fellow, I took him all over the place. He picked out the spring where his son was killed but—"

"Tom," she said suddenly, "if you say another word I am going to scream."

He was dumbfounded. His face fell.

"Why didn't you speak up before, girl? I've been talking to keep your mind off your troubles!"

He smiled down at her, but she was too weary, too heartsick to respond.

"Look here," he said. "You need something to eat. That's

what's the matter with you."

"I'm not hungry. I'm just wet and cold and tired."

"Well, that's enough," he observed dryly, and stopping the wagon, crawled out into the mud and rain. She could hear him rummaging in the provision box behind her, and finally he came to her triumphantly with a box of sardines and some crackers.

"Now," he said, "if I can work the combination of this little fish safe—"

Suddenly she laughed hysterically, and he looked up.

"What's the matter?" he demanded, suspiciously.

"Nothing. Only it's so different, so—"

She began to cry.

Chapter Thirty-one

Dear Dowling:

I have always done business with my cards on the table, or most of them anyhow. I understand your position and realize that you find the present situation fairly unpleasant. But I am on the ground as to it, and you are not.

In the first place, I have an old-fashioned idea that when two people are joined together they ought to have a chance to try it out anyhow. Maybe they can make it go, maybe not, but they are entitled to their chance.

You are not going to like this letter, but first I want to tell you one thing. Your girl is going to stick. I don't imagine it has been all honey and roses, but she cares for McNair and I believe he cares for her. He is a hot-tempered devil, but he is considerable of a man for all that. He may not know how to use his fork—I don't know—but he knows the cattle business, and at the present moment I am banking on him. Literally. I have loaned him money enough to make a small start, and the rest is up to him. They have a little place on the Reservation—the post office is Judson, if you care to know—and she has fixed it up in good shape. I am banking on her too; there is a good bit of old L. D. in her.

Yours sincerely,

H. S. TULLOSS.

Kay never forgot that home-coming of hers, the bleak dreariness of the deserted ranch house in the rain, the isolation, the dirt. Nothing had prepared her for it. But she never forgot, either, the care Tom took of her that first night. The wood he cut and the fire he built, the superhuman energy with which he moved about, lame as he was; bringing in and setting up the bed, carrying in food, chopping firewood, and now and then looking at her furtively with anxious harassed young eyes.

"Getting better every minute, isn't it?"

The house was damp and cold. He put her in a chair and wrapping a blanket around her, forbade her to move. "I'm doing this job. You can boss all you like." And underneath it all was his pathetic desire to make her comfortable, to see her smile, to have her share his own sense of what he had had only once before, of journey's end.

Long after that first meal of theirs had been eaten and she was in the white iron double bed, he was still at work. He had the team to see to, the wagon to cover from the rain, more wood to chop. She lay there, listening to him moving about, and to the rain on the roof just over her head, and after a while she got out of bed and dropped down on her knees. She was going to stick, no matter what; just give her strength to stick, and she asked nothing else.

But she had to get up once again that night, to help Tom to get his boot off his swollen and discolored foot.

"Been as busy as a dog licking a dish!" he told her cheerfully. "And don't you worry about this leg of mine. It's got to get limbered up, that's all."

He was up at dawn, and he had the fire going and water carried from the well before she stirred.

"You mustn't spoil me like that."

"I'm just breakin' you in kind of easy! No use putting the saddle on until you're halter broke, you know."

The house had three rooms, a large one, opening directly from a narrow porch, and two smaller rooms, one the kitchen. It sat out on the rolling plains, unshaded from the sun, and below it, lined with a few cottonwoods, a thin and now muddy stream wound its way beneath cut banks from the distant mountains. In summer it was hot, and the dust came in and covered floors and furniture with a fine gray grit; in winter the gales shook it, and only a small area around the stove was warm. Tom, spending those tragic months later on, was to learn that, and finally to move his bed into the kitchen.

There was no other house in sight. Judson, the nearest town, was a line of nondescript buildings along the railroad track, some miles away. The only moving thing within Kay's vision, that first morning of their arrival, was cattle thinly spread out over the empty country, and a lonely cowboy silhouetted on top of a butte. When she stood still the silence was unbroken; the time was to come when that silence was to beat on her ears like thunder, when she was to rattle dishes, move her bits of furniture, to escape from it.

But at first there was healing in it. Tom, moving in and out, still watchful and anxious, was surprised to find her cheerful in the litter of mud, boxes and general confusion.

"Bearing up, are you, girl?"

"I like it," she told him. "It's so peaceful."

"So's a marble orchard."

"A marble orchard?"

"A cemetery."

It never occurred to her that, after all she had hoped of life, now she was asking for peace. . . .

If the ranch house, rather like Tom, had little resemblance to her earlier romantic dreams, at least it responded quickly to care and affection—and was rather like Tom in that, too.

To Kay, certain unforgettable pictures of those first weeks on the Reservation remained always. There was the fixing up of the ranch house, its development from dirt and squalor into a place of order and cleanliness and even comfort. The big room, with its floor painted and Indian rugs on it; the day by day touches; the evening when Tom came home to find the white dotted curtains at the windows; the day she labored all day at the rusty stove, and when on starting the fire they were both driven outside by the smell of burning paint; Tom putting up hooks in the kitchen, and then proudly arranging their pots and pans on them; the uses to which wooden boxes and packing cases could be put; the discovery that an old creeper lying in the grass could be lifted and trained up over the porch; the morning Tom called her out to see a cow grazing on a hillside close by, and proudly pointed out the L. D. brand on its side.

Small matters at the time, only to assume true proportions when from a far distance she looked back on them; when the fatigue and discomfort had been forgotten, and all that stood out was that she and Tom had been together.

Discomfort there was. The rain was as though it had never been, and again the heat was intolerable. The ground outside cracked and fissured, and the air that came through the opened doors was hot and lifeless, and laden with gray-white dust. She would wipe it away, only to have it come back again. She was always thirsty, with a thirst that the flattish alkaline water from the well did not assuage. The very thought of handling food sickened her, the bacon limp and running with grease, the butter a formless oily mass. The meat Tom brought once or twice a week from Judson had to be cooked at once or it spoiled.

The very stove in that weather became her deadly enemy. It seemed to play tricks on her with malicious intent. One moment would be burning intensely, devastatingly; the next she would find it had died entirely. She took to watching it, standing by it with a fresh stove-length of wood in her hand, as if she meant to beat it into submission. Her hair was always damp, her face covered with little beads of moisture, her hands burned and roughened.

In between these times there were hours when she had nothing to do. She would bathe herself and then lie down, but the bed would be blistering hot. She took to lying on the floor instead for coolness, and Tom, coming in unexpectedly one day, found her there asleep. She was so pale, she lay so still, that he thought she had fainted.

"Kay!" he said. "Kay!"

When he found she had only been sleeping he was angry with relief.

"That's a fool thing to do, lying on the floor like that! Suppose—" he cast around for something that might have threatened her. "Suppose a rattler had crawled in?"

During this part, as she looked back later, Tom had always been working. He worked at white heat, frenziedly and yet with a cool purpose behind that frenzy. He had freighted lumber from the railroad and was preparing for the winter. Now and then a half-breed from Judson came over to help him. He had wasted little time on the barn, but before long he had built a calf yard, and shelter sheds, and a high log corral. There were many times now at night when his foot was so swollen that he could not get his boot off.

"Let me help you, won't you?"

"It went on; it's got to come off," he would say doggedly.

In the intervals he worked his mixed herd, drove in his unthrifty cattle for feeding, watched his calves, broke and rode his green horses. There were days when he was gone all day; when he rolled a bit of lunch inside a slicker and tied it to his saddle, and was off from dawn until nightfall. On those occasions he always left his revolver, loaded, where she could easily reach it.

"But I'm not afraid, Tom, really."

"Just don't let anybody inside the house. That's all I'm asking you."

But they were young and still passionately in love. The outside world hardly touched them; there were whole days when she never thought of Henry, or Katherine, or Bessie Osborne, or Herbert. They belonged to some queer half-forgotten life where people still rang bells and trays were brought, or tea, or whiskey and soda with tinkling ice in glasses.

There were evenings, then, when the sun had gone down behind the distant mountains in a glory of rose and purple and gold, and the night breeze came rolling over the plains cool and reviving, when they sat hand in hand on the step of the narrow porch, and sometimes talked and sometimes were silent.

"Not tired of me yet, girl?"

"Not unless you're tired of me."

"Never, so help me God."

But there was a new angle to their relationship. It was Tom now who was dependent on her, was sensitive to her slightest withdrawal, who watched for her approval or disapproval. And that his jealousy of Herbert was only slumbering she realized one night when they sat watching the northern lights spreading their long pale-green streams across the sky.

"The Indians call them the campfires of the dead," he told her.

"That's rather lovely, isn't it!"

He squared about and looked at her.

"If anything happened to me, Kay, what would you do?"

"I'm not going to think about it."

"But if it did? Suppose a horse comes down on me some day—you never can tell in this business—then what?"

"I suppose I'd go home. I don't know what else I could do. Please, Tom—!"

"And marry Percy? That would be it, I suppose."

"I'd never marry anybody. I couldn't."

"You'd marry him," he said somberly, and was silent for a long time.

Outside of that one reference to her old life, he never mentioned it.

Time went on. The drought continued. Already the leaves of the cottonwoods by the creek had turned yellow and were falling; they dropped into the stream and were caught underneath by the eddies, where they moved along like small golden fish. The stream was very low, and what had been mysterious shadows in its depths were now revealed in their stark nakedness under a rock, a floating end of it looking like a long dead arm.

The trout had left the riffles and taken refuge in the pools, and the little pond surrounded by rushes, which was the ancient overflow from some forgotten irrigation ditch, was almost dry. Now and then a flock of early ducks flew over it, heads thrust forward, circled it and then went on in search of something better. The cattle kept slowly on the move in search of grass; one morning Kay found them all around the pool, and saw that they had eaten the rushes down. She could have wept, and thereafter the pool, like the debris, in the creek, lay naked and ugly, save when at sunset it reflected the colors of the sky.

But as time went on and the heat and drought continued, anxiety began to tighten Tom's nerves. He came in one day to have his bad foot catch under the end of one of the Indian rugs and almost throw him.

"Hell of an idea, having loose carpets lying about, anyhow!" he said savagely, and kicked it into a heap.

And Kay, tired and hot, came to her kitchen door and ordered him to replace it!

"I will not. You can break a leg if you like, but I need mine."

"I seem to need mine too," she said wearily, and got down to straighten it. He lifted her to her feet savagely, and kicked the rug back into place. Then he stalked out through the kitchen, and she could hear him angrily rattling the wash basin. He was quiet enough when he came back, but—and later she was to mark that incident as significant—he did not apologize. There was no tender making-up. The incident came, passed, was apparently forgotten; but it marked a milestone in their relationship, nevertheless. . . .

His good looks had not altered. Chaps or overalls made no difference. Kay, on the other hand, was showing wear and strain. He did not notice it; for all his occasional outbursts, she was still Kay to him. Her beauty or her lack of it made no difference to him. She was Kay, his sweetheart and his wife. Perhaps, man-fashion, he was taking her too much for granted. But he had his own worries, and grave enough they were.

The creek was almost dry.

One day Kay heard him stirring very early, even for him, and found him later throwing a small dam across the stream. Like everything he undertook with his handicap, it was a long and arduous piece of work. He would shovel earth from the cut bank into a barrow, wheel it, dump it. He had made a ridge of rocks across, and was filling it.

She never knew whether he had the right to dam the creek or not. He was exhausted at night, his hands badly blistered, but he only laughed when she asked if she could help him.

"All right!" he said. "You bring down one of those little silver-plated spoons you set such store by!"

But he kissed her, was genuinely touched.

Yet that very evening they had what approached a scene. He came in, went into the living room and stayed there. She could hear him moving about, but he did not come back to the kitchen.

"I need some water, Tom."

"I'm busy. Pretty soon."

She was suddenly angry. She took the pail and went out to the well. When she started back she saw him at the kitchen door, but he made no move to help her. He stood aside and let her pass him, and she slammed it down on the table.

"Must have been in a hurry," he drawled, watching her.

"When you're too busy to carry water for me, I'll do it myself."

And then her nerves gave way. She did not cry. She stood, white and defiant, and reviewed her grievances, the isolation, the heat, that she was a prisoner. And she ended by showing him her hands, roughened, the nails broken.

"You used to like my hands! Look at them!"

"I'm sorry, girl. I tried to tell you what it would be like."

They sat down to the meal in silence. It was when he began to eat that she saw what he had been doing when she called him. The blisters on his own hands had broken, and he had been covering them with adhesive plaster.

She got up and put her arms around him.

"I must have been crazy, Tom."

He drew his first full breath since the outburst.

"You sure had me ready to whoop and holler!" he said. "Thought you were getting ready to hit the trail for somewhere else."

That night, by the lamp, he began his eternal figuring again, and he told her that with luck after the shipping next fall he could pay his interest and have six hundred dollars left over. It stunned her. All this labor, the long hours, the worry, and—six hundred dollars! She had paid more than that for an evening wrap.

When he saw her face he tried to explain to her the cattleman's grievances; the demand for young beef in Eastern markets, as against the fine mature cattle which were his pride and his profit; the necessary accepting at Chicago or Omaha of that day's prices, "figured by a lot of crooks who go up an alley and get their heads together." And the necessity of accepting that figure, iniquitous as it might be.

"But why do they let them have them?"

"What's a man going to do? Ship 'em back a thousand miles?"

Even that was with luck. Without it—!

They had not much time together, now. Tom came in for his food, ate it hurriedly and went out again. But sometimes glancing out she would hear him whistling and knew that, heat and exertion and worry notwithstanding, he was happier than she had ever known him. He was looking better too; his hospital pallor had gone. He was not drinking at all.

Standing in front of the defective mirror in the bedroom one day, she remembered what Mrs. Mallory had said: "Ranching sure ages a woman. It's all right for the men. It keeps them young."

She could not even ride with him. She had no riding clothes, no saddle. And Tom was still afraid to trust her on his green horse. He was breaking one for her, he told her, but it would take time. She wondered sometimes if he realized that she was as truly a prisoner as though she had been shut behind bars. But what could he change for her, even if he would? For the first time in her life she began to think of the pioneer women all over America who had done this very thing. Out there the back country was still full of them, women who had come there, young like herself, and now that comparative ease had been achieved were too old to use it; who could only sit, on their verandahs or in their cars, their worn hands folded, looking out on a land which they had hoped to conquer, but which had conquered them instead.

And then one day, as if in answer to that thought of hers, he went into Judson, and late that afternoon she heard a strange sound coming up the road, a rattling and bumping which sounded vaguely familiar. She looked out, and there was Tom, sitting grinning cheerfully in an ancient and disreputable Ford. How ancient and how disreputable were revealed by his first words.

"Bought it in town for fifty dollars!" he called. "Ain't but half broke at that; tried to buck me out more than once. But it sure can go."

He was enormously proud of it. That its cushions were broken, with gaping holes from which the hair filling protruded, and that its mudguards were bent and its radiator a shame that cried aloud, meant nothing to him. It was his, and it could go. He even made her get in beside him, and raced down the road.

"Little old engine's sure purring fine."

"Wonderful. And it doesn't matter how it looks, if it can travel."

His face fell.

"I suppose it looks pretty poor to you, after that garageful back East."

"I wan't thinking of that."

But she had been, for a moment.

Chapter Thirty-two

Life was easier after that, for a time.

One day he took her into Judson. She had never seen Judson before. She had thought that it would resemble Ursula, more or less. In the back of her mind had been the thought that if the loneliness became unbearable there would always be Judson!

But Judson was not like Ursula. It consisted of one unpaved street fronting on the railroad track, a small red grain elevator, a water tank, and a quarter of a mile past the tank along a sidetrack, some shipping pens in a bare and empty field. The general store was on the street, the blacksmith shop and beside it, quaintly enough, a gasoline filling station. Beyond that was a three-story building faced with ornamental sheet iron, with a sign, Dry Goods and Hotel.

Before the general store was a few square feet of cement pavement, and on it a hen or two. Down the track two ancient freight cars had been turned into houses for Mexican section hands, and a forlorn goat nearby was investigating papers thrown from the railroad trains. She sat stupefied in the shabby car.

"And this is Judson!"

"Sure is. What did you expect, girl? Chicago?"

She climbed down, a little stiffly, and went into the store. There was a little man in spectacles behind the counter. A brisk little man, and a friendly one. She was touched by his friendliness; he was even, in a way, excited. He went to a staircase behind the grocery shelves and called up:

"Hey, Sally! Come down and meet Tom McNair's wife."

And Sally was big and buxom and kindly.

"I was just saying to George the other day, we've got to go up and see that wife of Tom's. She'll think we're right unfriendly. And I'll bet it's lonely out there. Don't talk to me about that place you've got. It's a good ranch, but it's too shut off for a woman."

She felt warmed and cheered. They helped her with her ordering.

"Now say, here's a good coffee. Not so dear as that Tom's been buying. He always gets the best, Tom does."

"I'll say he does!" said Mrs. George, smiling at her.

Kay expanded under their friendliness. She even bought, while Tom was filling up with gasoline, a dreadful little necktie for him. It was a bow, already tied, and it had an elastic which went around the collar and hooked in the back. She had it carefully wrapped, and when they were on their way back she handed it to him.

"I brought you a little present," she said, her eyes demure.

"A present!"

He was as eager as a boy while she steadied the wheel and he unwrapped it.

"Well, look what's here!" he said. "Say, now, I sure call that pretty."

He never knew that it was a joke! Long afterwards she was to find the absurd thing among some odds and ends where she had hidden it for fear he would wear it, and to shed tears over it.

But, although she was no longer a prisoner, she was still very nervous. The drought was continuing, and the prospects for winter browse on the Reservation increasingly bad. Even the well was very low; she had to be saving with her wash water. Her skin was dry and cracking, her hands so rough that mending Tom's socks was a torture. She began to feel as though she had a tight band around her head. She was even fretful, and any little thing, in that surcharged atmosphere, sufficed to bring on a storm between them.

"Are you going to eat without your coat, Tom?"

"That's what I aim to do. I'm just a plain man, and I've never said howdy to the Queen of England."

The aggression was generally hers, but as time went on, and Tom found that the Indians intended to sell him no hay, his own nerves suffered.

"What's the use of clean table napkins every meal?"

"Because I like to think that I live like a lady."

"Well, the sooner we can this lady-business and get down to brass tacks, the better. It takes water to wash these things."

"It takes work, too, Tom."

"That's what I'm telling you."

He was sorry for that, however. He went into Judson, bought a great package of paper napkins, and brought them out. And because it was to save her, although she hated them, she used them thereafter.

The tragedy was that because they still cared passionately, each could hurt the other so easily. And their quarrelling came only at the end of the day, when they were tired. But as the hot weather kept on, without a cloud in the sky, they found the making-up a harder matter. There were times when they went to their common bed, each to lie as far from the other as possible, in silence, until the one who felt most guilty put out a tentative hand, possibly long hours afterwards, and there was a reconciliation, abject and loving.

Such a quarrel came one day when Kay found that he was carrying the revolver about with him.

"I thought you'd promised to let Little Dog alone, Tom?"

"Who said anything about Little Dog?"

How could he tell her that the Indians were nursing their injury to their breasts? That there had been threats against him, and that on the roads the old full-bloods of the Reservation passed him without speaking to him, sitting the seats of their wagons like ancient kings, their Oriental faces impassive, and sold their hay hither and yon, but not to him.

"If you made that promise you ought to keep it, Tom."

"If I get killed you could go back East, eh? Well, maybe that's the best thing that could happen to me. And you too."

It was childish. He knew it and so did she. When she tried to argue with him he enlarged on it, nursing his sense of injury, like the Indians. She could go back home and live like a lady again. "Clean napkins every meal and extra on Sundays." He knew she was getting tired of him. What was he, anyhow? He was a cripple; a child could knock him down and tramp on him. And she would starve anyhow, if she stayed; if he didn't get hay somewhere he was through. Done. Wiped out.

She had to soothe him like a child that night.

Perhaps their occasional quarrels might have been forgotten, but there was something else, more fundamental. There was a complete difference in their point of view. One night, her nerves on edge, she asked him to roll a cigarette for her.

"Not on your life," he told her grimly.

"But why not? I used to smoke cigarettes. You know that."

"My wife doesn't."

She was surprised and indignant.

"That's ridiculous," she told him. It's—medieval."

"Sounds bad!" he drawled imperturbably. "Maybe I'm kinda old-fashioned, girl, but the women out here don't smoke, and you don't want to get talked about."

"You may ask me not to smoke. You can't forbid it."

"Since when?"

She made a curious little gesture of helplessness.

She lay awake a long time that night, thinking. She had been bred in the new school; even, in their own way, her father and mother subscribed to it. This school taught that the wife was no longer subordinate to the husband; that marriage was a mutual contract, in which each bore his part. Obedience was even being left out of the marriage service. The old medieval idea of the wife being a chattel, a—

How strange that such an idea should still persist out here! Not in the towns perhaps, but in the back country. Mrs. Mallory, for instance. She would have held it, or at least never disputed it. But she had been happy with Jake, apparently. Perhaps the issue never came up; she had never wanted to do anything of which he disapproved.

But Tom stirred in his sleep and put his arm around her. She lay still. What did it matter after all? . . .

And still the country dried and dried. The pond had disappeared; the dam had held, and all day the cattle stood or lay there, afraid to go far from the muddy pool which was all they had. At night coyotes came slinking to drink, and then retreating sat dog-like fashion on hilltop or butte and raising their muzzles, barked at the relentless sky. Outside of his cows and calves, which he was holding close in, Tom's cattle ranged far, hunting for browse. He worked them as little as possible; when they showed poor condition he brought them in, slowly, to such water and hay as he could provide. And to his other anxieties was now added fear for his calf crop; cattle were never prolific under poor feeding. He had to distribute his bulls.

Along with the other outfits he tried to scatter the stock over the range, and by salting in certain places to hold them there. And one day in desperation he went into Judson and bought all the cottonseed cake he could find. It left him practically without money.

Even before the Fair other men had begun to ship to the feeders the cattle they could not carry. And Tom, going to the Fair—he had been appointed one of the judges—stopped in and had a frank talk with Mr. Tulloss.

"I want to do the right thing," he said, standing in front of the banker's desk. "There is still time for you to get out from under if you feel like it. There would be a loss, but not so much as it may be later."

"Then you're going to quit on me, Tom?"

"Quit! I'm ready to hold on till hell freezes over! It's you I'm thinking about."

Tulloss looked at him. The boy was certainly thin, standing there in his gala attire, the brilliant shirt, the neckerchief, the leather chaps. And he had a strained look about the eyes.

"Show clothes, Tom?"

"Some I had left, yes."

"Your wife coming in?"

"She's bringing the Ford. I rode over. Have to have my own horse, you know. I can't mount the way I used to."

"No," said Mr. Tulloss. "No. How's Kay standing it?"

"It's mighty lonely for her, but she's—" He flushed darkly. "She's a pretty fine little girl."

"No trouble then?"

"No trouble," said Tom valiantly.

When he left he knew the banker was still behind him, and he felt happier than for weeks. He strode out, made that awkward mount of his, and rode to the Fair grounds. After all, life was still good to him; he was not down and out, he had a herd of cattle and a ranch. And he had Kay. His heart swelled a little as he thought of her, dauntlessly driving the ramshackle Ford along the dusty roads, and there was a bit of swagger in the way he rode onto the field.

The grand-stand was full, and in front of it the local band was playing. Earlier in the day the crowds had thronged the buildings, and had viewed the exhibits proudly, and with reason. They themselves had made them possible, had fought their hard fight and were slowy winning out. The school display, the vegetables and fruits, the very pedigreed cattle and the great stallions with crimped manes and shining hoofs, they had made them possible. They had taken this forgotten corner of the world and made it bloom. It was theirs; God had given them the land, and they had nourished it and made it bloom.

And now they were ready to play.

"Look! There's Tom McNair. Surely to goodness he can't be going to ride!"

"Roping, maybe."

And a deep masculine voice:

"Bull-dogging, most likely. He's throwin' enough bull now to make him champion!"

But if they laughed there was affection in the laughter. His lameness, his marriage, his refusal to accept his handicap, even his attack on Little Dog, had added to his popularity.

"What pains me is, why he didn't kill that Indian when he had the chance."

"Well, he got ten days' free board for it."

There was a rattle of applause as he rode out into the field. He ignored it, but he heard it; he sat a little straighter, put his gloved hand more jauntily on his thigh, and hoped that Kay had arrived to hear it. He was more nearly his old reckless self than he had been for months.

But Kay had not heard it. She came in rather late, to find the crowd assembled, the band blaring, and the races filling in the time until the bucking began.

The dust was intense. Her feet sank into it as into a cushion. Just as she passed before the grand-stand she was suddenly self-conscious and uncomfortable. It seemed to her that all the eyes had left the track and were focused on her. She even heard a voice:

"There she is now. I knew she hadn't come yet."

And once seated she was aware still of intent concentrated inspection. The chatter around her had practically ceased. Not for a long time did she dare to take her eyes from the dusty track before her and to glance around; when she did, the gazes around her became instantly absorbed in the racing. She saw only immobile faces.

After a time she relaxed. The judges in the stand across became individuals in straw hats and an occasional Stetson, with Mr. Tulloss among them. The bandsmen below them had taken off their coats and were playing in their shirt-sleeves. Boys selling near-beer and pop were moving about. Tom, with a dozen or so of other mounted men, was waiting by the corral inside the track.

She felt happier when she had located him, and less alone. She watched him, apparently so unself-conscious of his audience, and after a time she decided that he was less so than he seemed. She even thought he was quietly touching his horse with his spurs. The horse would rear and show excitement, but Tom sat him straight and somehow splendid, but certainly posed. Oh, certainly posed. She was vaguely annoyed. She looked around the grand-stand, and she thought she saw there an understanding as quick as her own. Quicker.

"Tom's some rider still."

"Well, don't tell *him*. He knows it."

It grated on her horribly. She began to look any way but at Tom. Even the knowledge that he had earned the right to pose if he wanted, that there was admiration mixed with their scorn, did not help her. Nor that in the world she had left, while there was little posing, there were a thousand hypocrisies instead. She took to watching the crowd before her, and it was then that she saw Clare again.

She was wandering, apparently aimlessly, back and forward; a queer figure in a very short scant black-and-white checked skirt, and above it a sleeveless blouse. On her head she wore a curious contraption of black satin straps, from which in front protruded a visor like a beak, and at the rear of her skirt was a pocket in which, carefully arranged to show, was a green handkerchief. All in all, perched on her high heels, she looked like some queer and rather sullen bird.

Each time she passed she gave Kay a long look, half scornful and half challenging, and Kay became acutely self-conscious once more. Clare would move along, her eyes down, until she came to Kay, and then the performance would be repeated. She was not alone; there was a girl with her, and this girl was obviously arguing with her and not too comfortable.

"For goodness sake, let me alone, Sarah Cain."

"But everybody's looking."

"Let them look. Do you suppose I care?"

Kay was uncomfortable and uneasy. She even, after a while, decided that the girl was dramatizing herself, not only for her benefit, but for that of the crowd. Like Tom! She felt a little shudder of distaste. If only she could get out, get away—

The races went on and on. The audience, hot and perspiring, waited through them stoically for the things that were to come later, the calf-roping, the bucking. When Clare at last ceased her tragic parading Kay got up and left the stand. She had no thought but to get out and away. She had not even missed Tom from the crowd around the corral. And thus it was that, hidden among the parked deserted cars outside, she came across them with a shock that made her feel faint and ill.

Tom was standing still, his expression one of distress and discomfort. And leaning against him, crying hysterically into the green handkerchief, was Clare. She was utterly abandonded to her grief; her body in her absurd clothes shook with her sobs. And as she stared Tom put his arms around her. It was only a flash. Neither of them had seen her, and Kay turned and fled on trembling knees.

After a while she found herself in the Ford again, and sitting there she tried to reason the matter out. Tom still cared for her; it was only that the girl was still crazy about him, and had trapped him there. What if he had put his arms around her? He might be sorry for her. Suppose she had belonged in his past? What was his past to her, Kay? All men had pasts, probably; perhaps even Herbert, only Herbert's past would be neat and discreet. It would never come in a jockey cap and hip-pocket skirt, and hang around his neck.

But jealousy cannot be reasoned with.

How had she got word to him? She must have written a note and sent it by some grinning messenger. And Tom had come, had left the field and come. She had sat there in the grand-stand, and people—many people perhaps—had known why he had left. It was dreadful; it was cheap, and she was involved in all this sordid scheming and cheapness; this shopgirl intrigue.

After awhile she forced herself to go back to the gate again. Tom had returned, and the riders were drawing their horses, the names written on slips of paper in a hat. All at once she knew she could not face that curious crowd again. Nor Tom himself. She needed to think things out, to be alone. She could not even face Ed at the Martin House, where they had intended to stay for the three days of the Fair. She found some paper in her handbag, and wrote a brief note:

"I am not feeling very well. Please don't worry, but I am going home. I'll be all right after a day or two of rest. Kay."

When she gave it to the gatekeeper to be sent to Tom on the field, he smiled, and she knew instinctively that it was not the first note he had sent to Tom that day.

A mile or two along the road she began to weaken. What was she running from? Because a girl had been crying in Tom's arms. How silly! A thousand things, which had nothing to do with Tom and herself, might lie behind that scene. But she did not turn back; Tom would have the note by then, and would know she was not ill. She would have to tell him, and she did not know which she dreaded more, his righteous anger or feeble explanations from him which would not explain.

She was quieter when she got home. She made some tea

and drank it, and afterwards she sat on the porch and looked at the distant mountains. They gave her their own message, of the passing of time and the smallness of human affairs, and when she crawled into bed she had determined on her future course. She would never refer to Clare or to what she had seen, and Tom was to find no change in her.

But she had not counted on Tom himself. She had been asleep for an hour or so when she was roused by the rapid beat of a horse's hoofs, and a moment later she heard him at the door.

"Kay!"

"Yes. I'm coming."

He was dusty and wild-eyed, and almost reeling with weariness as he came in. Outside she could see his horse standing with heaving sides and drooping head, the reins hanging loose.

"God, Kay, you've scared me almost to death. Are you sick?"

"I'm better now. I felt queer for awhile. I never thought of your coming all this way."

"Of course I came," he said shortly. He surveyed her intently, and his anxiety suddenly gave way to suspicion. He caught her by the shoulders, not too gently. "Is that all? You felt queer, and so you came home? Why didn't you go to the Martin House?"

"I wanted to come home. Sit down. Have you had anything to eat?"

"No. I don't want anything. I want to know what brought you back here, forty miles. You knew darned well I'd follow you."

"I never thought you would, Tom," she said honestly. "When I left—"

"Well?"

"Couldn't you have borrowed a car?"

"And let every damn fool around know my wife had run off and left me! No. I'm going back, as soon as I find out

what the trouble is." He was working at his boot. "You're n
sick. You weren't sick when you left."

"No," she said quietly.

"Then what was it?" he demanded.

"I think you know."

He glanced at her and his eyes fell. He drew off his boo
and sat rubbing his swollen ankle. Her heart was beatin
wildly.

"If you mean Clare Hamel," he said roughly, "you ca
forget it. She's always crying on somebody's neck."

"It was yours today, as it happens. She sent for you, an
you slipped away and went to her."

"And you followed!"

"No," she said patiently. "I didn't follow you. I hadn't a
idea— Has this Clare any call on you, Tom?"

"What do you mean, call? I used to know her. That's a
And since you know so darned much about my meeting he
perhaps you saw that I wasn't making any great fuss ove
her. Not so you could notice it."

"Then she hasn't any claim on you?"

"No," he said sullenly. "I'm married. She knows it. An
that's all there is to it. Look here,"—he was suddenl
angry—"what about yourself? *You* were engaged to Perc
when we were married. Have I ever thrown that up to you?
have not."

But he saw that he trapped himself, and he changed colo

"Then you were engaged to her when I—?"

"Yes," he said sulkily. "And I treated her like a yellov
dog."

In the lamplight they stared at each other. His boot lay o
the floor, one of those gay boots which he had donned s
happily the day before. Above it was his tall weary figure, hi
face streaked with dust and sweat. He looked olde
unhappy, defiant. Across from him, her red dressing gow
held around her, a haunted look in her face, was Kay. Only
few feet separated them, but neither could cross it.

"Then," she asked, painfully quiet, "when I came to you she was expecting to marry you?"

"The same as your Herbert."

"But it isn't quite the same, is it? I came to you. You had to marry me, or send me back home."

"Oh, for God's sake, Kay! I wanted to marry you."

"I wonder if you did."

She turned and went wearily into the bedroom, and crawled into bed. He sat for a time as she had left him. After awhile she heard him strike a match, and the familiar odor of his cigarette came through the open door. When he moved finally she braced herself for a renewal of the scene between them, but he did not come in. Instead she heard him lighting the kitchen fire and putting the kettle on, and later she knew he was soaking his swollen ankle in hot water. Her thoughts milled about: Clare, Tom, herself, That day when she had gone to him, and they had been married. His easy casual ignoring of his engagement to Clare, his almost equally easy and casual marriage to her. Yet was she being fair to him? He had worked hard. He had been faithful to her, so far as she knew. He had even ridden forty miles that night, for fear she might be ill.

But had he? Might he not have suspected that she had seen him, and have come desperately to make his peace?

She waited and listened in the darkness. Surely the next move was up to him; in her morbid condition his very silence gave corroboration to her fear. But he did not come, and at last she fell into an exhausted sleep. When she awakened it was dawn, and he had gone again.

She did not see him for three days.

Chapter Thirty-three

During that three days Kay suffered more intensely than she had ever suffered before. She tried hard to reason with herself; after all, why not take him at his word? He had wanted to marry her. He need not have done it. A word to her that day and she would have gone back.

But now and then Herbert's words came back to her. "He's violent; he fights and he drinks—and he's a bad man with women."

A bad man with women! Then if that were so, perhaps this girl *had* a call on him. And he had said he had acted like a yellow dog to her. What did that imply? What was he doing in town all this time; this man who fought and drank, and perhaps debauched? This strange man who was her husband? A little more time, perhaps, and she would have been fairer, but in the early morning of the day after the Fair had closed, Kay who had been sleeping badly, heard his horse coming slowly up the lane, and sat up in her bed.

Tom did not come in at once. He went to the corral, grained the animals, waited until they had finished and then turned them out. Even then he seemed loath to come into the house. From the window as she was getting the breakfast she saw him rolling a cigarette by the corral. He looked very tired, and when he finally started for the house his limp was painfully apparent. He came slowly and evidently unwillingly, and as he neared her she saw a vivid bruise on his cheek.

She turned a little sick. Herbert was right after all! He was weak. He was one of the brotherhood who sought escape from reality in liquor. When he finally opened the kitchen door she was busy at the stove. She could not speak, and after eying her for a moment he threw up his head.

"I'll get you some water," he said without further greeting, and took the pail out to the pump. When he came back he had clearly made up his mind to a course of action.

"Breakfast's ready."

"I'm not eating. Not yet. You and I've got some things to clear up first."

"You'd better have some coffee," she said coldly. "You look as though you need it."

"About this girl," he began, ignoring her remark, "I just want to say this. She—"

"It isn't about the girl; not now. I daresay I was foolish. That's all over."

He stared at her.

"Then what?"

"I think," she said, her lips shaking, "that you've been drinking again."

"What makes you think that?"

"Drinking and fighting," she persisted. "Maybe you haven't seen the bruise on your face."

She could hear the shrewish overstrained note in her own voice, but she could not control it. Tom put his hand to his cheek, and then turning went into the bedroom and closed the door. When he came out again he had a blanket over his arm, and the old felt slipper in his hand.

"When you're in a reasonable mood we'll talk this thing over," he said. "Until you tell me you're ready I'm sleeping in the barn."

She had a wild hysterical fit of crying after he had gone,

lying face down on the bed; she was filled with self-pity. She had abandoned everything that made life worth while, recklessly staked all she had on one throw of the dice, and luck had been against her. But after a time the will power which was her inheritance from old Lucius Dowling asserted itself. She got up and set about the routine of the day, heated more water and washed the breakfast dishes from which nothing had been eaten, and swept and dusted the sitting room.

Tom did not come in again, and later on she saw him in the Ford, starting out. He never so much as glanced at the house as he went by. Suspicion was still doing strange things to her; was he going after more liquor? Some of the Mexicans at Judson were bootlegging. Or again, maybe he had brought some with him from town, and secreted it somewhere? In the barn, maybe.

White and wide-eyed, very near the point of a nervous collapse if she had known it, she waited until he had gone, and then went out, past the breaking corral to the barn. But she found no liquor. What she did find, hidden under his saddle, was Tom's boot, one of that handsome pair which he had put on so proudly. Rather than ask her, he had slit it with a knife. Rather than ask her.

He did not come back until late that night. Then he stalked into the house, the bruise on his cheek an even darker purple, laid the Ursula paper before her without a word and stalked out again. His supper was waiting, but he had not so much as glanced at the table.

She looked at the paper. He had marked a paragraph. It was entitled "Is riding dead in the West?" and ran as follows: "Anyone who believes that this country is not raising riders equal to any, should have watched Tom McNair yesterday in his battle with the Cheyenne horse, Satan, which came here with a record of never having been ridden before. The horse had thrown two good men on previous days, and only by clever work was Bert Ramson, on Thursday, saved from being trampled to death by the killer.

"Yesterday, McNair, who is still badly handicapped from a recent injury, fought the horse to a standstill—"

But she did not finish. She was on her way to the barn.

Tom was just outside, unloading some packages from the car. He did not stop when she reached him.

"I'm sorry," she panted. "I can't bear it, Tom."

"Well," he said, without any particular feeling in his voice, "those little mistakes will happen."

She put her hand on his arm, but he evaded her and carried his parcels inside. When he came out again he stopped a little distance from her, and began to roll a cigarette.

"But if I say I'm sorry—!"

He was silent. In that world she had left an apology was accepted, on the surface at least. Rancor and discord might remain, but they were glossed over. She felt helpless and defeated.

"What more can I say?" she asked desperately. "I can't go on fighting you, Tom. You're stronger than I am."

He gave a short bitter laugh.

"Me? Why, I'm a cripple! A child could knock me down and tramp on me!" Then, more gently, "You go back to the house, Kay. Don't worry about me. I'm doing fine."

After that for some days they lived a curious sort of life. He came in for food, short constrained meals quickly over; he carried the water, chopped the wood for the stove, but he continued to sleep in the barn. Once again it was childish, absurd. But Kay began to wonder if something else did not lie behind his sense of injury; if this girl, this Clare, had not said something that had devastated his fierce pride, if she had not sown some seed of suspicion or distrust over which he was brooding. And in this she was correct. Out of all the hysterical reproaches of that unlucky afternoon, Tom had retained only one speech of hers, but that had stayed in his mind.

"I've watched her, Tom darling. You go in now and look at her. She thinks she's too good for this earth. She won't even speak to the folks around her. She acts as if they'd poison her if they touched her. And if she's too good for them she's too good for you. She'll leave you. She's sorry now. I used to see her from Dicer's crying her eyes out."

She believed it. There was sincerity in her red-rimmed eyes, in her weak quivering chin. And because she voiced his own fears they became fact to him.

"I've got to get back," he said morosely.

Her face hardened, her eyes narrowed.

"And there's something else," she said, her voice shrill. "She saw you in the show, and it carried her away. But it's different now. You're lame. I'll bet she hates that. It makes a difference, and don't you forget it."

"It doesn't seem to have made any difference to you," he reminded her, and smiled. But his heart was sick within him.

In the end it required what was by nature of a small calamity to bring him back to Kay.

He heard her calling to him, and he ran to the house. She was standing just inside the bolted door, and when he tried it her voice was frightened.

"Who is it?"

"Did you call me?"

She threw open the door, and he had a wild desire to catch her to him, but the next moment his pride took control once more.

"There was somebody outside the window, Tom. Looking in."

"Sure you didn't dream it?"

"I haven't been asleep," she said simply.

He looked down at her. In her bare feet, without the heels which gave her height, in her sleeveless nightgown, she looked small and young and infinitely appealing. Frightened too. For fear he would take her in his arms he swung around and stepped outside. After the lamplight—she had lighted a lamp—he could see nothing. He went back, got his revolver and started out again. There was starlight but no moon.

He made a round of the house; somewhere she heard him lighting matches, but when he opened the door again his face was impassive.

"I'll look a bit further," he told her. "Put out that lamp and lock the door again. I haven't seen anything, but you'll feel better."

She sat in the darkness, crouched and listening. There was no sound outside. After a time she could see, as she had in the bedroom, the faint rectangles which were the windows; she watched them, terrified, but that queer immobile outline did not return. Later on she crawled into bed for warmth, and sometime later, an hour or so, she heard him coming back. She admitted him, shivering. In the darkness he was a stranger to her, a big looming figure that did not reach out to her, but stood carefully just inside the door.

"I didn't find anybody, but if you're scared I'll roll up on the floor here."

"Why?" she said, her throat tight. "Why shouldn't you come into your own bed?"

"And be as welcome as poison ivy?"

"That's not true."

She tried to say "Oh, Tom, come back to me. I'm sorry. I love you; I love you madly." But her lips were stiff, and as if he had been waiting for something of the sort, he drew a long breath and moved into the room.

"I'm not asking any favors."

"I'm afraid to be alone, Tom."

He said nothing; he went out once more and looked around, and she stayed inside the door, waiting and listening. If he did not come back, she told herself, she would go home. She had reached her limit. She would cash her Aunt Bessie's check and go away. But soon she heard him coming from the corral; she had only time to get into the bed before he was at the door. Her heart was beating fast, her feet and hands were like ice. She listened to him moving about, preparing for the night. Once he struck a chair and swore under his breath, but he did not speak to her. When he got into bed it was to lie as far from her as possible, but toward dawn she wakened to find him sound asleep, with his arm around her.

It was late in the morning when he discovered that some one had cut through his dam and let out his precious hoard of water.

Chapter Thirty-four

For a time the gulf between them was bridged.

Toward the end of September it rained again, but too late to save the range. One day the sun was warm and bright, the next small grayish clouds began to gather around the horizon to the Northwest, and slowly to coalesce. Fitful gusts of wind set the dried vegetation on the plains to rattling, and Tom, coming home that night, said:

"Looks like something doing around Medicine Hat!"

The next morning Kay rose to a world clothed in a gray veil. The clouds covered the mountains and hung so low that she felt she could almost touch them, and from this irregular roof came the rain, steady, penetrating and cold. The roads became impassable. Tom, freighting cottonseed cake from Judson, was marooned on the way, and leaving his wagon there, rode the team back.

All over the vast empty country the round-up outfits were at work. Cattlemen were frantically shipping all the cattle they could not hope to hold over the winter. The Potter company, out of twenty-two thousand head, was shipping ten thousand. Kay watched one evening while a dozen cowboys bedded down a herd on a hilltop not far from the house. Until late she could see the red glow from the stove in the cook tent, and at intervals during the night she heard the night guards moving about. When she wakened in the morning they were already on the move.

The days had begun to shorten. At five o'clock twilight fell, and by six she lighted the lamps. Perhaps she never knew just what the lighted windows of the ranch house meant to Tom; he had always been inarticulate in his love for her. But when, after the long day, he rode over some nearby hill and looked down, those warm yellow rectangles of light were his first welcome. His heart swelled, great thoughts surged in him; then he would scrape the mud off his feet outside and, limping in, could find no words for them. He would hang up his hat, kiss her, and then, indignant at his own stupidity, stand around awkwardly, watching her.

Only once did he refer to the matter of their quarrel over Clare. She was mending by the fire in the living room, and he had been apparently busy over some reports from the Department of Agriculture. But she knew he was not reading.

"D'you mind if I tell you about that girl, Kay?"

"What girl?"

"Now what's the use of that? You know and I know. I never wanted to marry her, and she knew it."

She bent lower over her mending.

"Do we have to talk about it?"

"I do."

"You were engaged to her, you said."

"That's what I want to tell you about."

And he did tell her, sitting there by the fire, his hands dropped between his knees. His threatened arrest, his determination to go East with the cattle, his appeal to Clare and the condition she had imposed. It was then that she looked up.

"And she was found out?"

"She says she was. I don't believe it myself. Either that, or she took mighty good care to be found out. She had plenty of time to get back."

But woman-like, she had seized on one part of the story and ignored the rest.

"And on this long ride with her, did you—make love to her, Tom?"

"Not what you think," he told her. "I've lived the way a man does live, I reckon, but Clare's got no call on me. I'll swear it, if you like."

Later on she was to wonder if there had been a motive behind that frankness of his, but she was warmed and comforted that night. When, after his old manner, he came over and sitting on the floor, put his hand against her knee, she had a new and different feeling for him. He was her husband, but he was also her lover and her child.

The days went on. The rain ended, and it turned bitterly cold. Tom rose in darkness in the mornings and came back to her after darkness had fallen again. He was working as a "rep" now with other outfits, but he was afraid to leave her alone at night. Not for him the long evenings in the warm cook tent, the poker games, the early turning in. He would come back in the car, turn in to sleep like a dead man, and be up and off after a minimum of rest.

He had left his revolver for her, against her protest.

"You're the one who may need it."

"I'm not worrying about myself."

But as a matter of fact, after that malicious breaking of his dam, nothing happened, nor was to happen for a long time yet. When the drives ended at the railroad, sometimes the outfits would work side by side with the Indians, and at such times Tom kept a wary eye open for Little Dog. But he never saw him, and later he heard that he was working on the other side of the range. After that he was easier.

He himself was doing no shipping that year, but his purchases of hay and cake had practically exhausted his money. When the last cattle car had been loaded at the railroad near Judson, he went in one day to see George Seabright at the store, and asked how good his credit was.

"Good as money in the bank, Tom."

"Well, I'm not asking for interest on it!" he drawled. "But I may have to stretch it some this winter."

"That's all right, Tom. Anything you say."

But George was practical too. The big Newcomb wheat job was still threshing, and it needed men. The paid good money.

"I'm no farmer," he objected. "And what's more, I'm not leaving my wife alone these days."

"Send her into town," George suggested. "Sally and I've been talking about that. She's young. Send her in and let her go to the movies and see some life. She's got a long winter ahead."

Tom considered that on the way back to the ranch. After all, why not? He needed to earn, needed it desperately. Kay needed clothes; she must be warm that winter. He could manage food, with George's assistance, but cash was different. Under ordinary circumstances he could have taken in horses to break at ten dollars a head, but that avenue was closed to him.

And Kay needed a change. He thought of her, alone all day in the house. She had grown thinner lately, and she was very quiet. Her hands, when she mended by the fire in the evenings, were like small white claws. Not so very white, either. Poor little hands!

By the time he got up and put the car away he had it all planned. There was a new lift to his shoulders when, having scraped his boots outside, he went in.

"How'd you like to go to town for awhile, and live like a lady?"

"And leave you, Tom? I wouldn't think of it."

"I've bached before this. Anyhow, I won't be here."

"Where would you go?"

"The Newcomb company needs me. Says it can't get along without me! That's the kind I am!"

She was relieved. For a moment she had thought he had meant to go to Ursula too, and a sickening fear of Clare had taken her breath away. But she did not easily fall in with his plan, even then. She liked Mrs. Mallory, but to take a room there—that was different. Here she had her work, but there!

What would she do with herself?

"You could go to the movies."

She laughed at that, but she had a small uneasy feeling of apprehension. Ursula meant nothing to her; she had been watched there, although she did not tell him so. But he was singularly determined to have her go. He picked up one of her hands and examined it. Then he kissed it.

"First thing you're going to do," he said, "is to get that healed up. Can't have them saying I work my wife to death!"

In the end she yielded.

He sat up late that night making his plans. He could come down over week-ends and see after his cows and calves. There was nothing to worry about, until when the cold weather came. And she was to get some warm clothing while she was in town. He'd been paid; he had plenty. There was something magnificent in the way he handed her fifty dollars.

"Warm!" he insisted. "All wool and a yard wide. There's the hell of a long winter coming."

She was strangely uneasy, although on the surface she was acquiescent enough. She moved around, doing her small packing the next day, making her arrangements.

"You know about the damper in the stove, Tom, don't you?"

"Me? I took a course in dampers before you knew there was such a thing."

His cheerfulness was forced, she thought, but his determination held. Only once he weakened, when she was packing the gold brushes and jars from the bureau. He had always had an odd sort of pride in them.

"Little old house is going to be mighty"—he hesitated—"mighty bare," he said.

He seemed to loathe to leave her, stood around awkwardly, got in her way, ate little. Once he said, apropos of nothing at all:

"How'd you like to stay in town all winter?"

"What have you got in your head now?" she asked. "If

you're trying to get rid of me—!"

"You've never spent a winter out here. You don't know what it means. That little old stove won't keep this place warm. What you ought to do's to dig in like a bear some place. Only you haven't got any fat on you."

But she knew he was only arguing to have her oppose him.

He was very talkative on the way to town, very cheerful when Mrs. Mallory had taken them up and showed them the plain little room.

"It isn't much. But it's warm," she said.

"Warm—that's the word. And it looks pretty fine to me."

Then suddenly he went away. He took his hat off, kissed Kay quickly, and disappeared. Mrs. Mallory listened to that one step at a time descent of his as he went down the narrow stairs.

"He never was one to show what he feels," she said to Kay, half apologetically. "Now I hope that bed's comfortable. If you want more blankets—"

It was their first real separation since their marriage. After the beginning Kay accepted it stoically, but she missed him. Now that he was gone, after the fashion of women the world over, she forgot his failures, his occasional moroseness, his quick angers, his moments of actual violence. And, also after the fashion of women, she began to rebuild her romance. Her letters to Bessie, with their enclosures to her mother—Bessie had suggested that finally—took on a new note.

"Dearest mother:

Aunt Bessie says you are feeling better, and I am so relieved. And I am not on the ranch just now. Tom has had to go north on business, and I have a room in town. I am more than comfortable, but of course I long for my own little house. I had no idea I would miss it so much. I am getting some warm clothes for the winter while I am here—" And so on and on.

Never a word about Nellie practicing on the old piano downstairs, hour after hour; or of the odors of cooking, or of the long periods when Mrs. Mallory sat creaking in her rocking chair and talked about the old times when Jake was still alive. Nor of Little Dog, nor Clare Hamel, nor of the "business" which had taken Tom north.

It was a business which threatened to keep Tom rather longer than he had thought.

He was working hard, new work which tired him more than he cared to admit. By dawn the engineer and crew were waiting by the big caterpillar. Then, when the time came, the engineer threw over his lever, the great belt began to move, and into the ever hungry jaws of the separator went the first waiting sheaves of wheat; the thresher roared and shook, the men in the growing light, forks in hand, bent, straightened, pitched; the belt writhed, the jaws crunched, the brown wheat kernels flowed from the side of the machine like blood. But it was not blood, it was bread. Bread for the world.

There was competition among the separators, scattered over fifty thousand acres of wheat, and so there were hours when life for Tom narrowed down to the slats that climbed endlessly in front of him, to the fork in his hand and the incessant bend, straighten, pitch of his job. When his boot bothered him he took it off, and the wheat stubble cut his foot and hurt him painfully.

But at night, unable to sleep for very weariness, he would lie awake and think about wheat. Maybe Jake had been right after all. Wheat was king now, not cattle. He and his kind were through, or nearly through. They would hold on for awhile, but the end was in sight.

He did not go home that first week-end, but on the second Saturday he filled up the Ford and started back. It was threatening rain, and he made all the haste possible. But it was after dark before he halted the car near the house and stared at it in amazement. There was a lamp lighted inside.

Never once did he doubt that it was Kay. He left the machine where it stood and fairly ran to the kitchen door. But when he flung it open, it was Clare Hamel who stood busy over the kitchen stove.

Chapter Thirty-five

It was on the Tuesday following that Mrs. Mallory gave her lunch party for Kay. All morning in her front room on the second floor Kay had heard the preparations going on for the meal; the squawking of chickens in the back yard, followed by a tragic silence, the arrival of the grocer's boy, Nellie turning the ice-cream freezer on the porch.

"You keep that lid down, or the salt will get in."

"I've got to look at it, haven't I? How do I know if it's freezing or not?"

Later the smell of cooking filled the house, and at half past twelve Mrs. Mallory came heavily up the stairs and tapped at the door.

"You'd better be getting ready," she said solemnly. "I just got to slip off this apron." She came into the room. "Would you mind if they came up here to take off their hats and coats? It's the best room. That George Smith's got his place so littered it's hardly decent."

George Smith was the railway freight brakeman who occupied at intervals the bedroom across.

"Of course not." She went over and put an arm around Mrs. Mallory's heavy shoulders. "You're sweet to go to all this trouble for me."

"I want you to know people. They're not the society folks,

you know, Kay. They're plain people."

"Well, so am I 'plain people.'"

"No, you're not. And it wouldn't hurt some folks I know of to come and see you. They came fast enough when you were out last year at the ranch."

It was an old grievance of hers. Kay had heard it more than once in the two weeks she had been there. She changed the subject.

"Anyhow the rain's over," she said, and Mrs. Mallory went out.

Left alone, Kay went to the window. For three days it had rained, turned the roads into slime and Mrs. Mallory's heart to despair, but today was cold and clear. She was glad of that. If Tom had gone to the ranch for the weekend he could get back, now the roads were drying. She wondered how he had managed over that week-end. Long ago she had learned that his idea of making a bed was to fling the coverings over it anyhow, and as he said: "Let nature take its course." She was smiling a little as she went down the stairs.

The guests were already arriving. They came in soberly, creaked up the stairs, took off their dark substantial wraps, their unfashionable hats, and creaked soberly down again. They were not, as Mrs. Mallory had said, society folks; some were the wives of small storekeepers in Ursula, others had come in from the back country, from small cattle ranches; still others had been forcibly detached from their isolated hard-working lives by the recent hard times and were trying to fill in the empty anxious days. One and all they were elderly women; their hands, as they offered them, felt rough in her clasp, their faces were dried and lined with years of sun and alkali dust.

She felt her heart warming toward them. They were genuine. There rose before her Aunt Bessie, her short hair, her carefully massaged face, her long fingers with the long pointed tinted nails. She was as old as they were, older maybe. Suddenly she resented what life had done to them, and behind her resentment there was a pang of dismay. This was her future; in time, she too would dry up and wrinkle. Her youth would pass, and there would be no one to note its passing.

They shook hands and sat down. Mrs. Mallory had brought in extra chairs and arranged them around the wall. They sat stiffly, their tired hands folded in their laps. A decorous buzz of talk arose. Kay, in a low rocker in the center, felt like a very young kitten encircled by motherly cats softly purring. From the dining room came the clattering of plates as Nellie put them down, the pungent odor of coffee drifted in, and then she became conscious of another conversation in low tones, carried on behind her. The voices were carefully subdued.

"I hear Dicer isn't going to take her back."

"Still, with the roads the way they have been, no car could—"

"Dicer says she didn't go to Easton at all. He thinks she went to the Res—"

"Sh!"

Mrs. Mallory opened the sliding doors. She was highly flushed from excitement and the stove.

"Come right in while everything's hot," she said. "And I guess some of you ladies will have to bring in your chairs."

There was a move toward the dining room, a little suppressed laughter, a small confusion. Kay found herself moving in, sitting down; later she found herself eating. Great platters of fried chicken passed around, light biscuits, vegetables, honey. She even talked.

"No, we didn't ship anything this year. Maybe next year, if we're lucky—"

"Well, I know that place. It's a good house, but it's lonely."

Food. More food. Wheat. Sugar beets. The five-and-ten, newly opened. The negro who had tried to kill a sheriff's deputy. Ice cream.

"Any of you ladies have some more ice-cream? We haven't

made a dent in the freezer yet."

The early self-consciousness was wearing off, the talk was louder, more cheerful. When they went back into the parlor Mrs. Mallory urged Nellie to play the piano for them, and Nellie simpered and complied. She had been taking lessons for a year. They sat politely silent while she hammered away, their tired hands folded again, their strong bodies relaxed. They were comforted with good food they had not cooked themselves, they need not even talk. With natural good manners they kept their eyes from Kay. She had brought a bit of romance into their busy lives, for a little time they had seen their beautiful arid land through her eyes; they were even consumed with curiosity about her. But they kept their eyes away.

After awhile Kay slipped off. She went up to her room, where on the bed lay their substantial wraps, their unfashionable hats. She went inside and bolted the door, and then stood staring ahead of her. It was Clare they had been talking about. Clare had gone to see Tom and had been storm-stayed there. How long had it rained? This was Tuesday. It had begun Saturday night. Then she had been there for two days, living in her house, perhaps even occupying her bed.

And Tom had been there. She knew that, beyond the question of a doubt.

From downstairs there came a clapping of hands, a murmur. Nellie began again, even more vigorously. The thin floor vibrated under Kay's feet. She sat down in a chair and put her hands to her burning face. She had no doubts whatever: she knew. She was fair, even then. She could see Tom's early annoyance, even his angry protests, but as the storm continued she could see Clare, moving about the little house and making it livable again; cooking meals, and then the two of them at the table across from each other. Or in the long evenings in the lamplight, Clare curled up in a chair, her pretty face transfigured with love, her short skirt outlining her young body, deliberately feminine and tempting. His anger would not outlive that. How could it?

She was still trembling when she went downstairs again. When at last the party was over, when the last heavy figure had descended the porch steps, she jerked on her small soft hat and the blue coat, and went out. She went deliberately into the Emporium, made a small purchase and saw that Clare was not there. Then, with fear and anger in her heart she started out along the street which led to the Reservation Road. She had thought it all out; if Clare had been with Tom she could hardly have left until noon, when the roads were dry enough to use. She would have to come slowly, too. She might even now be nearing Ursula.

It had turned bitterly cold after the rain. The wind whipped her face. Somewhere Dr. Dunham's draggled white poodle had picked her up and trotted sedately at her heels. Where the town abruptly ended she took to the road, a road which wound across the empty open country. It rose to a hill and was lost. So far as eye could judge it served no one, went nowhere. But she knew better. She knew that it led to the Reservation and to Tom McNair.

She sat down and waited, and the dog shivering with cold, crept into her lap! It smelled to heaven of flea-killer, but because it was cold she held it close. She had no feeling of shame at what she was doing. She was beyond shame. She neither hated nor loved. She waited.

And after an hour she had her answer. A small muddy car labored over the hill and began to descend. It followed a rut already made, advancing drunkenly and ribaldly, and as it came closer she saw Clare at the wheel. She was intent on driving. Not until she was almost abreast of her did she see Kay. She looked frightened, but the next minute she had stopped the car.

"Want a lift?" she said airily.

"Thanks. I'm out for a walk."

They stared at each other, Kay pale, Clare defiant. Then

Clare started the car again, with a faint smile.

"These roads are sure hell," she said, and went on. Not until she was almost into the town did she remember that she had one of Kay's plaid blankets across her knees. She was frightened then; she stopped the car and rolling it up, dropped it into an irrigation ditch beside the road. And Kay, suspecting some such action, saw it lying there on her way back.

What was she to do? She had already done her best. She had worked for him, loved him, been lonely for him, forgiven him over and over. But there was a limit to what one could forgive or endure. She had tried. She was fairer than that, they had both tried. But he had never really wanted to marry her. He had had this girl then. Perhaps he had never let go of her, for all his protestations. How had she known that he was going to be at the ranch that week-end, unless he had told her, or written her? That was it, of course. He had written. He had got rid of her, sent her into town, so that he—

Her world was profoundly shaken; what she wanted was sanctuary, security, the reserves of a society which, whatever its hypocrisies and weaknesses, covered them decently away. The ease and dignity of living; cars stopping at the door, and liveried chauffeurs with cards in their hands.

"Is Mrs. Dowling receiving?"

"Madam is not receiving today."

Or its amenities:

"I am so sorry that John had to fall out at the last moment," when every one knew that John was having one of his periodical "spells," and had not been home for three days.

But her despair was more profound than that. What common ground had she and Tom ever had, except their love for each other? When that was gone, what was to take its place? What was it Aunt Bessie had said? "Tastes. Habits. Ideas of life— When it"—love—"has gone, you have to have something else to fall back on."

What had they to fall back on now? Nothing; only their mutual poverty, their mutual anxieties, to hold them together.

She thought of her people. She was in the house now, in her room, and Nellie's voice was raised from below in angry expostulation.

"For gosh sake, ma! How can I answer the bell with my hands in dishwater?"

Time and distance had softened her memories of her people; she saw them loving and forgiving, kind and understanding. They had been right after all. Her marriage had been doomed to failure from the start. Herbert had been wrong that day at the hospital. He had said it didn't pay to be decent and honest, but surely it did.

Suppose she confessed her failure and went back? Wasn't that the answer? How could she face the long winter with Tom, knowing what she did? The long hours, without even books to read, except those eternal reports of the Department of Agriculture, with nothing to talk about but the cattle, or the small unimportant happenings of the day:

"Saw Red this morning. He says Bill's got a girl in Easton."

"Has he?"

And always that shadow between them, of a girl with a pert face and defiant eyes, passing with one of Kay's blankets over her knees.

She could not do it. Before Mrs. Mallory tapped at the door she knew she could not do it. And Mrs. Mallory held a special delivery letter in her hand.

It was from Nora.

Chapter Thirty-six

When Tom went in Clare was standing by the stove in her absurd skirt, busily frying potatoes. The table was set, after a fashion, for two. She glanced over her shoulder, smiling but wary.

"Hello!" she said. "I thought maybe a little food wouldn't go so bad."

He was speechless with disappointment and anger. He came inside and closed the door before he could trust his voice to speak to her.

"What brought you here?"

"You eat something and you'll feel better. Anyhow, you needn't worry. I'm going back tonight."

"I'll tell the world you are," he said grimly. He hung his hat on its nail, glanced into the bedroom and saw Clare's hat and coat there, and limping inside brought them out and closed the door.

"What's the big idea?" he asked disagreeably. "Trying to make trouble for me?"

"That's all the thanks I get for cooking you a decent meal, is it?"

He still held her hat and coat. She had a terrified moment when she thought he was going to force her to go at once, but now he put them down slowly.

"You're liable to get talked about, doing things like this," he said, less unpleasantly. "And the sooner you've eaten and run the better. It looks like rain outside."

She put the supper on the table while he watched her. He was still suspicious and angry, but after all his own conscience was not too clear concerning her. If this made her happy—

"I'm not joking. It's going to rain."

She was dishing up the supper, practical, competent. She moved back and forward, talking and laughing. She disarmed him by her matter-of-fact manner. And then suddenly, passing him, she stopped in front of him and held up her face.

"Just once, for luck," she said. "It won't hurt you!"

What could he do? He stooped and lightly kissed her, and the next moment her arms were around his neck. He was thoroughly uncomfortable, her small body brought no thrill to him, he even felt slightly ridiculous. But when he released himself it was gently.

"I'm all through with that, Clare."

She made no protest, sat down with him and ate her supper, talked, even laughed. She had no plan. She had simply followed a desperate urge to see him again. She was ready to stay an hour or a week, depending on his reception of her. If it was to be only an hour—

"Things taste all right?"

"Mighty fine. You sure can cook. How'd you know I was coming back?"

"A little bird told me."

She chattered on, playing for time. There was a new clerk at the National Drug Store. Some good-looker. He wanted her for steady company, but she didn't care about him. Sarah Cain was crazy about him. She made her lunch of ice-cream soda now, so she could look at him. And Ed at the Martin House had been caught bootlegging and was in for trouble.

Then suddenly the rain came down; it came without warning, like a cloudburst. It fell in sheets on the roof, on the ground, on the road. It rolled in yellow torrents down the trails and paths; it slid off the bare dry hillsides, carrying earth and gravel before it. The note of the creek rose higher, and in front of the porch when Tom was at last able to open the door there was a small lake, shining yellow in the lamplight. The first burst over, it continued to rain. The shingles of the roof, dried from the long drought, began to admit it. They ran around with pails and pans.

"It's dropping here. Tom! Quick!"

When that was over they sat down and looked at each other. There was anger and despair in Tom's face, and amusement in Clare's.

"You look as if I'd made it rain."

"You've got me into the hell of a fix, and you know it."

She moved over to him.

"Who's to know?" she said. "You can go out and sleep in the barn if you want, but who'd believe it?"

"That's where I'm sleeping, just the same."

"I'll bet it's wet out there," she said, and laughed again.

Her laughter angered him. He felt absurd enough as it was. But he was grimly determined to let her alone. He did not want her. He knew her psychology, the result of her careless rearing, her narrow life with its emphasis on sex. She had no passions; she and her kind preyed on passion, that was all.

By eleven o'clock the worst of the storm was over, but it was still raining. No car would have moved a hundred feet along the road. Even if it cleared now it would be a day, two days, before Clare could get back. She sat, relaxed and slightly sulky, in Kay's chair by the lamp, while Tom raged about the room. He hated her; the very sight of her in that chair made him murderous. At something after eleven he took his hat and a slicker and went out, and shortly after she heard the splosh of horses' feet in the water outside.

She got up, angry herself now, and confronted him when he came in.

"What are you going to do?"

"Put a slicker on you and take you to Sally Seabright, at Judson."

"If you think I'm going to ride all those miles tonight in this rain you can think again."

"You're going to do just that."

She fought savagely against Kay's slicker when he put it on her, but he was relentless. He even stuck her hat on her, and then opening the door when she refused to go through it, dragged her out forcibly. She tried to bite him in her helpless fury, but he only laughed, and lifting her up in his arms carried her to her horse. She did not speak to him during the long ride through the darkness and rain. At the store she slid out of the saddle herself, and stood waiting in savage silence while he hammered at the door.

Nobody answered. After a time he saw a card against the glass and lighted a match. "Away until Monday," it said.

Clare read it too, and shook with silent laughter.

He stood uncertain on the bit of pavement. Only one passenger train stopped at Judson, and that at noon. And even that did not run on Sundays. To take her to the hotel over the other store at this hour meant gossip, ugly talk. After a long bitter silence he said: "Well, we'd better go back."

They rode back. It was still raining with a threat of snow. Clare's teeth were chattering when he got her back; he built up the fire and then, taking a blanket as he had once long before, he went out to the barn and rolled up in the hay. He did not sleep at all. The mischief was done now. Whether she went back the next day or in a month would not matter.

The next day when the rain persisted, he hardly fought her dogged refusal to take that ride again. He carried out more bedding to the barn and nailed up newspapers to keep out the wind. When she called him he went in to eat, surly, unhappy and hopeless. Only once he brightened. She told him her family believed she had gone to Easton, and on that frail hope he built.

When on Tuesday she took her departure he felt conscience stricken. Her face rather alarmed him; it was set and unhappy. She let him put the blanket over her knees, which her absurd skirt left uncovered, without comment; she even recoiled a little from his touch. He was ashamed of his relief at her going. He tucked in the blanket and stood back.

"Well, so long, Clare."

"Good-bye," she said drearily. And started off.

Could he have gone at once to Kay things might have been different; but the storm had left him with work to do about the place; fence posts had washed out and let down the wire, a shelter shed roof had to be repaired. The threshing did not bother him; the rain would have stopped that for a while. But he worked in a frenzy of haste. Argue as he would, he knew that Clare's absence would have excited comment, even alarm, and that if the story reached Kay she would know.

He was not so much startled as appalled, then, when on the next day he entered Kay's room, to find Mrs. Mallory in tears and Kay resolutely packing her bag. On the bureau lay a small stack of bills, but he did not see the money at first. He was stricken by the disaster, at the preparations, at Kay's white face and set mouth. He stopped in the doorway; he was trembling, but he controlled his voice.

"Looks like somebody's going somewhere."

"I am, Tom. I'm sorry, but— My mother's very ill."

"That's it, is it?"

"That's enough, isn't it?"

"Not if you were going without letting me know."

"I was going to write."

"So I'd get it after you'd gone! I'm much obliged to you."

"I didn't see any use in worrying you about it. I'm going. I have to go."

Mrs. Mallory slipped away then, closing the door behind

her. Tom stopped to bolt it and then advanced into the room and took her by the shoulders. His face was very white.

"Now we'll get to the bottom of this," he said. "That about your mother, that's a lie, isn't it?"

"Let go of me, please. You can read the letter if you like. It's on the bureau."

He released her, puzzled.

"And that's all? You haven't any queer ideas in that head of yours?"

"I know you've had Clare Hamel with you for three days, if that's what you want to know."

"*Had* her with me! Good God!" He laughed bitterly. "She got storm-stayed, the damned little fool! And I treated her like a yellow dog."

"That seems to be a specialty of yours," she said cruelly. "Treating her like a yellow dog. But she appears to like it."

"I never touched her, Kay."

"I suppose you were shut up there together for three days, and you never even kissed her."

He hesitated, then came out with the truth.

"Once. She asked for it."

But he saw that the admission was fatal. She could not believe that he would do that and not go further. She resumed her packing, folding something carefully on the bed, smoothing and straightening it. He saw that her hands were shaking.

"I'll bring her here, Kay. She'll tell you."

"She would lie. Anyhow I never want to see her again."

"Or me either, I reckon."

"I didn't say that."

"But you don't believe me."

"I can't, Tom. I want to, but I just can't."

"You're going then?"

"I must," she said desperately. "I've told you the truth. Anyhow, I'll have to have time, Tom. I have to think, and somehow I can't think here."

"You know what it means, don't you? You'll never come back. Oh, I know; you think maybe you will, but you won't. They'll get their hooks into you somehow. They'll talk you over. They'll bribe you."

And as he thought of them his old anger rose. He saw them, fat and sleek and rich, grinning over their triumph, putting their heads together behind closed doors, whispering, conspiring. Conspiring against him.

He saw her back again on the country club porch, idle, surrounded by idlers, luxurious, filling time with play, with lovers, with Herbert. His gorge rose, his voice tightened.

"Oh, no," he said. "You'll never come back. You won't want to come back. They'll get you. And if you ask me, it isn't them you're going back to. It's that fellow. And who's he? They wouldn't pay a bounty on a dozen of his kind out here."

"I should think they would," she said evenly. "He's a gentleman. And they seem to be scarce."

She had not meant to bicker. When love dies it should die silently and decently, and be laid away with secret tears. But Tom recognized none of the amenities. He could not even let her go with dignity.

"Oh, please don't quarrel," she said wearily. "I haven't minded the hardships, but—maybe it was all wrong. I don't blame you only; I blame myself too. If I'd been right you would never have turned to her." He made an angry movement. "I'll have to get away and think things over."

"And if you decide in my favor you'll come back! Not on your life! If you go you go, Kay, and I'm telling you. I'll never ask you to come back, so help me God."

Mrs. Mallory tapped at the door; the taxi from the station was waiting, and Kay had only just time for her train. She closed her bag, pulled on her hat. All the time Tom stood staring at her, helpless, defeated. Only once did he speak at all, and that when she picked up the money from the bureau and thrust it into her purse.

"Where did you get that?"

"Aunt Bessie sent me a check for a thousand dollars. I've left the balance in your name, in the bank."

"Oh, you have, have you!" he exploded. "I'd burn in hell fire before I used it."

And that was their farewell. He did not even go down the stairs with her. He stood inside the door, his hands clenched, a cold sweat on his face, and heard the taxicab drive away. But he made no move to follow it. His mind—such of it as was functioning at all—was busy with this new aspect of the situation. She had sent East for money to go home with. Then she had planned ahead to leave him. It was not because of Clare. That had only been an excuse ready to her hand.

Chapter Thirty-seven

Kay had not telegraphed. She simply walked up the steps of the city house and rang the bell; the taxi driver had carried up her bag and left it beside her, and so she stood when James opened the door.

He stared at her, holding to the doorknob.

"Don't you know me, James?"

"Yes, Miss, I—"

Suddenly Rutherford pushed him aside and threw the door open.

"He's just surprised, Miss Kay," he said. "Come in. Get that bag, James."

She held out her hand, her eyes full of tears. "I've come home, Rutherford," she said pitifully.

He had been there as long as she could remember, tall, immaculate, impassive! "Yes, Miss Kay." "No, Miss Kay." But he was a human being. He was moved; he was glad to see her, and he was frightened for her. She held out her hand.

"Maybe they won't want me, Rutherford."

"It's your home, Miss Kay."

"I know, but—"

James had brought in her bag, shabby and worn. She caught a glimpse of herself in the old Italian mirror over the console beside her. She looked shabby and worn too, like the bag, out of place. No wonder James had hesitated.

She went into the drawing room, like any caller. Rutherford had suggested that. Her old rooms were closed and anyhow her mother was not to have any excitement. He would see the housekeeper. Yes, they had a housekeeper now; a Mrs. Manly, quite a capable person.

She stood by the fireplace, under the Sargent painting of her in her presentation dress. Nothing was changed, save for a hard formality in the arrangement of the room, as if it were not much used now. There was a sickening hush over everything. It was as silent as the little house on the ranch.

Rutherford brought in Mrs. Manly. She was a thin little woman, neat and capable, with small inquisitive black eyes. If Mrs. McNair would make herself comfortable for a few minutes she would have her rooms opened and made up. Perhaps she would like tea. Nora came, dour and repressed as ever, faintly embarrassed at Kay's shaking hands, but glad to see her nevertheless. Afterwards she was to remember that her only real welcome home was by the servants.

Mrs. Manly went out. Nora stood by the door.

"How is she?"

"Up and down. They have a nurse now."

"What do the doctors say?"

"You know your father, Miss Kay. We don't hear anything. But she wants you. I've seen it in her face over and over. That's why I wrote to you."

All at once Nora's face began to twist. She fumbled in the pocket of her black silk apron and found a handkerchief.

"I think she's dying, Miss Kay."

Kay felt faint and cold. The tea tray came in, Nora still standing there weeping. She looked up. Rutherford stood by the tray, James behind him with the curate stand, and Nora by the door. There they were, all four of them, grieving together, and yet with that terrible artificial barrier of class between them.

"Lemon or cream, madam?"

Oh, my God, and her mother dying upstairs alone, surrounded by this barrier, cut off by this gulf. Lonely. Horribly, terribly lonely.

"Lemon, please, Rutherford."

But she could not hold the cup. For the first time in her strong young life she fainted quietly away in her chair.

When she came to there was another person in the room, a white-clad young woman, cold, efficient, capable. Kay sat up in her chair and said, strangely, "That makes five." She felt very dizzy, but her mind was quite clear.

Later on they took her upstairs as quietly as possible, Mrs. Manly and the nurse, with Nora trailing behind. Her mother's door was closed. There was a new housemaid making up her bed, and the parlor maid was taking the covers off the furniture. They put her carefully on the *chaise longue* and went away. All but Nora. Nora was unpacking the shabby bag, with its shabbier contents. She laid out the things on the bed, the underwear Kay had made for herself, the cheap cotton dresses, the aprons, and as she worked she wept softly. Once she came and stood over Kay, her wet eyes burning.

"When your father comes I'll get out some clothes for you. Your mother and I wanted to send them to you, so he locked them up."

"I didn't need many clothes, Nora dear."

Nora glanced at the bed, and suddenly went out of the room.

Reluctantly Kay dragged her thoughts from her mother to her father. What if he would not let her stay? If he turned her out? She had never thought of that contingency; his anger and resentment she had prepared herself for. All that nightmare trip East she had known she would have to face them. But a hostility which would lock away her clothes and shut up her rooms might go further, might close his door to her. And there were other complications. Nora, calmer now, and coming back to draw her bath, asked her not to say that she had written the letter.

"He'd put me out, quick as not," she said. "And I want to stay, Miss Kay. I've been with her a long time. I'm not leaving her now."

She had to promise, but it left her own position anomalous. Was she to say she had left Tom? Would she have to say she had left him, in order to stay with her mother? But hadn't she left Tom? The battle which had raged within her on the train renewed itself now. She knew Tom himself thought so, had considered their parting final. Lying there, the water running into the tub in her bathroom, the scent of the bath salts rising with the steam, she saw him again as she had left him in that hideous room at the Mallorys', tall, anxious, grim.

"I'll never ask you to come back, so help me God."

When her bath was ready she undressed. No word had come from that quiet room along the hall. She dropped her clothing and stood in her single plain undergarment while Nora threw her worn dressing gown around her. Suddenly she felt Nora's cheek against hers.

"My poor lamb!" she said. "My poor thin little lamb."

She put her arms around Nora. For the first time since she entered the house she felt love and a welcome.

Later on she put on the same frock again—she had no other—and brushed her short hair. Her watch said five o'clock, and at any moment now her father would be coming in. She braced herself, for her hands were shaking. But when he finally arrived he did not come upstairs; she imagined that Rutherford had told him, and that in his library below he was considering the situation, turning it over, this way and that. The waiting was terrible. Nora had gone. She took to pacing the floor, to opening her door and listening, but there was nothing to break the dreadful hush of the house. It was not until she was ready to scream that James tapped and said her father wished to see her in the library. It was poor preparation for her; it placed her at a disadvantage. Perhaps he knew that; maybe that was why he had kept her waiting.

She had expected to find him hard and pompous. Always in her mind he had been unchangeable, florid, heavy, immaculately dressed, a little cold. Now she was shocked to find him perceptibly aged, his face no longer ruddy, his clothing hanging loose on him. He was an old man! But he had not softened with age; he was standing, erect and stern, behind the barrier of his great desk.

"Come in," he said. "And close the door."

She did so, turned and faced him again.

"First of all, I must ask the nature of this—visit. Am I to understand that it is temporary? Or permanent?"

She hesitated.

"I don't know, father."

"What do you mean by that?"

"It's a rather long story." She tried to smile. "I'm tired. Do you mind if I sit down?"

It was characteristic of him, of his type and his breeding, that he came around and drew up a chair for her! But he did not touch her. He was still coldly, acidly polite. He went back behind the desk again.

"Have you left this fellow McNair?"

"I haven't decided."

"Decided! Good God, you're old enough to know your own mind."

"It isn't as simple as that, father."

"Are you going to have a child?"

"No." She colored.

"Have you quarreled?"

She hesitated.

"No. Not exactly that. We differed about some things, but—" She looked up at him with the eyes that were like his father's—"I still care for him. I think you have a right to know that. Only—"

"You couldn't get along," he finished for her. "If you hadn't been a headstrong stubborn little fool you'd have realized that before you married him. A cowboy! A ranch hand! What in God's name got into you? And Tulloss! The man's senile; he's losing his mind."

But he controlled himself.

"Before we go any further," he went on coldly, "I'd better make my own position clear. Your mother is ill, critically ill." He stopped, cleared his throat, went on. "I do not believe she will be with us for very long. And I think she needs you. She has needed you badly for some months. At the same time I shall make no pretensions about myself. Your marriage hurt me; it was selfish, reckless and outrageous. For a piece of romantic nonsense you have spoiled Herbert Forrest's life and you have very nearly wrecked my own. You think you have a grievance now, because that marriage has gone wrong. You have no grievance. It was wrong from the start. Some day you will learn that you cannot build happiness on the misery of other people."

"If I had married Herbert—"

He raised his hand.

"Just a moment. Under the conditions I have named I have a right to make certain stipulations. You have come back. You came without request from me, but this is your home. I could not refuse you shelter if I wanted to, and I do not want to. At the same time, I shall require certain assurances from you. I shall ask you, if you stay at all, to stay until—until your mother no longer needs you. And I will not have McNair in the house."

She sat very still. After all he was right, in a way. And Tom had said— She moved a little, put her hands on the back of a chair to steady them.

"May I see mother before I decide?"

He was not brutal; her face, her thin figure, her shabby dress, all had shocked him profoundly. But they had angered him too. She was never to go back to that man; over his dead body would she go back.

"I have told you your mother's condition. If in the face of

that you insist on bargaining—!"

"The bargain was your suggestion, father."

He had unlocked a drawer of his desk and taken out a bunch of keys, but now he put them back again and closed the drawer.

"When you have made up your mind, I shall give Nora your keys."

And it was then that she said something that roused his pity for the first time. "Do you think she should see me, like this?"

He looked at her. She was thin, shabby, profoundly disillusioned. He got the keys again, and going around the desk, stooped and kissed her lightly on the cheek.

After she had gone he sat down heavily. Through the open door he could see the hall, and beyond it the drawing room. The lamps shone on his tapestries, his paintings, his fine old furniture, his rugs. More than fifty years of his life gone, and that was all he had! He was losing his wife, he had already lost his daughter. Soon he would be alone.

When Rutherford brought in the tray with his whisky and soda he found him still motionless at his desk, staring through the opened doors at what life had given him. Things.

Later on Kay saw her mother. She went in, with the nurse standing guard; fortunately she had been warned in advance, so she bore herself well, but even the rose lights in the room could not conceal the change in Katherine. Her small face had fallen in, there were deep livid circles under her eyes. Her white hair, however, was as carefully waved as ever, her hands, the left with its enormous square cut diamond, were as carefully manicured. She was wrapped in lace and soft silk.

She held out her arms and Kay went into them, determinedly smiling but sick at heart.

"My little girl!"

"Mother darling!"

And after a pause, each holding the other: "Did they send

for you?"

"No, indeed. I just came."

No, Henry wouldn't have sent for her; she ought to have known that. She stroked Kay's head.

"I was afraid—" she said, and stopped.

"Afraid of what?"

But she lied gently.

"Afraid you hadn't got your clothes. But I see you have. You look so pretty, Kay. I think I had forgotten how pretty you are!"

And then, before anything real had been said between them, the nurse signaled for Kay to go.

But Katherine knew; had known from the moment she had learned that Kay was in the house, was certain of it when she saw her. She had left her husband. Tragedy was written all over her, smile as she might.

She lay very still that night, for fear the nurse would report her sleeplessness to Henry, and Kay would get the blame. She seemed to be seeing very clearly a great many things; for instance, one could choose security, as she had, and be left always to wonder where the other path would have led. Or one could compromise, as had Bessie, for instance; holding to security but making her small tentative explorations into more or less shady by-paths. Or—again—like Kay, one could take the hard road to life and adventure, suffer, stumble, but somehow have lived. Like old Lucius, too.

Toward morning Henry tiptoed into the room. She closed her eyes immediately, but she was touched. Perhaps after all, security; a strong hand to hold to at the end. He looked at her, turned and crept out again.

Chapter Thirty-eight

Kay never told Katherine about Clare, but gradually, little by little, she learned some of the details of those missing months. She saw the little ranch house, the struggle to live, and between the lines the attempts at adjustment. She saw the town on the Reservation: the loneliness, the dust and heat of summer, the work; but in none of these things did she find the reason for the tragedy which was written on Kay's face. She lay still and thought: "There is something else, something else she won't tell me. There is something else."

But she learned that Kay was staying indefinitely. It comforted her, while at the same time it worried her. She liked to have her coming in, to listen for the click of her high heels outside, and then see her enter in one of the dinner frocks from her trousseau.

"That's really a sweet dress, Kay. Do you remember how Louise fought to put pink on it? It's much better as it is."

That the dress hung looser than it was meant to she never mentioned.

She even went downstairs more often, sitting behind her tea table with a delicate pink flush on her face. People came and went, sedate well-bred people who greeted Kay as though she had never been away, and waited until the door of their limousines were closed before conjecturing. Although it was already almost winter on the high plateau Kay had left, it was only autumn in the East. A few leaves still clung tenaciously to the trees, there were days almost as warm as summer. Socially the city was taking its fall respite, between summer resorts and the opening of the season the first of December. The houses of the neighborhood were being gradually opened. One day their wooden shutters would be up, and a card, "Deliver mail and parcels to the caretaker in the rear." The next the windows would be open, an advance guard of servants would take possession, and house cleaners, paper hangers, painters, upholsterers come and go.

Bessie was in New York. Kay never saw Herbert; once, passing the library door, she heard his voice beyond it, and saw his car at the door. She went upstairs as quietly as she could. She could not see Herbert; not yet anyhow.

But the news of her return gradually spread. The telephone would ring, and some excited high feminine voice would call her.

"Why, Kay, I've just heard you're here! I absolutely *must* see you."

They came in, in their short skirts, their thin legs in sheer stockings, their plain little hats which were somehow so costly. They opened gold or platinum vanity cases and worked over their smooth faces, or lit cigarettes stuck in jeweled holders; early as it was they were usually going somewhere. Sometimes they demanded a pick-up, and Kay rang and ordered cocktails for them. They put their arms around her so that the scent they used smothered her, after her months of the pure air of the back country. They admired her clothes, her hair, her hands. Her hands! And underneath it all they were avidly curious. If she turned suddenly she found their eyes on her.

"I do think that frock's too divine!"

But they were not thinking about her frock, but about her. She had been married. She was one of the initiate.

Moreover, she had married dramatically. "A cowboy! Imagine! I didn't see him, but they say he's the handsomest thing!" Had she really left him, or was she—they examined her figure furtively.

"Tell us about your ranch. You have a ranch, haven't you?"

"It's a little place. Very lonely. On an Indian Reservation." She would smile over the teacups, her lips a trifle stiff.

"And do you really raise cattle?"

"They raise themselves, rather. Of course they have to be worked."

"Worked? Do you hitch them to things?"

And when they departed they were still avidly curious, unsatisfied.

"It's my belief she's left him."

"Well, she'll never tell you!"

She seldom left the house. They came to her, these girls, and when they did not come she did not miss them. Their small affairs seemed trivial and frivolous to her, against the great adventure of living and dying as she began to see it. Sometimes when they came in to luncheon and sat around the table in their bright frocks, she saw instead of them Mrs. Mallory's party. The tired capable faces, the worn capable hands. And she felt nearer to those older women than she did to these young ones.

Her tumultuous inner life she buried always. For a time she had expected to hear from Tom; even on the train East the entrance of a boy with a telegram had set her heart beating fast. But as the days went on and no letter came she abandoned the hope. He had meant what he said; he would never ask her to go back.

At the end of three weeks she wrote him a letter. She wrote in a discouraged hour, and the letter was not particularly calculated to heal the breach between them:

"I have found my mother very ill. She may live a few months, but that is all. I am glad now that I came. It has made her happier, and of course I shall stay until the end.

"What else can I say? I know now that although I did my best, it was not enough. I could not even hold you for six months. There is no reproach in this. Maybe all men are unfaithful to their wives, or at least disloyal at times. I don't know; I find there is so much I don't know. Of course you know that if you send for me I shall come back, not now but when I can. But you must realize that you must want me and ask me first. I came to you once; I cannot do it again.

"I am not happy here; even without mother's illness I would not be happy. I am spoiled for this life. I miss—" she hesitated there—"the mountains and the open country. I feel shut in."

She found that she was crying, had to get up and find a handkerchief, moved about the room before she could compose herself to go on. She was homesick for the West, heartsick for Tom. She dabbed at her eyes angrily. How weak and childish she was still to care so much for a man who did not care for her! She was one of the hopelessly faithful. It was awful, it was degrading, but there it was. She went back to her small desk:

"And I did love you so dreadfully, Tom! I must have, to do what I did do. If I have been unfair I am sorry, and when you want me—and I can come—you know I will."

He never answered it.

One day without warning Bessie Osborne wandered in. She went upstairs, opened Katherine's door, sauntered past the scowling nurse, and kissed the invalid.

"You're looking better," she said, lying as unconcernedly as she did everything else. "I hear Kay's back."

"Yes. She came some time ago."

"Has she left him?"

Katherine cast an agonized glance toward the nurse.

"Nora wrote her I was not well, and you know the winters out there—why, Bessie, whatever have you done to your hair?"

Bessie had taken off her hat, and not only revealed an evident intention to remain, but a head of a hue closely resembling orange.

"New color," said Bessie calmly. "I've tried everything else; this was all they had left. Well, how *is* Kay?"

The nurse had recovered her voice.

"Excuse me," she said, "but the doctor's orders are against visitors."

"I'm not a visitor," said Bessie, glancing at her coldly, "and if there is anything you can do conveniently for the next ten or fifteen minutes, I should like to talk to my sister-in-law."

The nurse went out defeated, and Bessie moved her chair closer to the *chaise longue*.

"How is she? How does she look?"

"I think she is a little thin."

"I daresay!" said Bessie dryly. "Hasn't she told you anything? Was it a fight, or another woman?"

Katherine flushed.

"Really, Bessie!" she said. "I can't ask her, and she has told me nothing. They have had this small ranch, and—"

Bessie listened as she went on. She had never had any opinion of her sister-in-law's brains, and before her ten minutes were up she rose and picked up her hat.

"Where is she?"

"In her room, I imagine. She seems rather tired. She doesn't care to go out much."

In the hall Bessie stopped and made a few faces to relax the rigidity she felt about her mouth, and then she tapped at Kay's door. She had always been fond of Kay; there had been something of old Lucius in her. But if she had let this scatterbrained marriage of hers go on the rocks so soon, then perhaps there was something of her mother in her too. Some softening of fiber, some— It was probably another woman.

She opened her attack abruptly, almost the moment she entered the room.

"So it didn't go?" she said, standing inside the door.

"Not as well as it might."

"And whose fault was it?"

Kay shrugged her shoulders.

"I don't know. Both, I suppose."

Nevertheless, in the end she told her story fully. One could do that with Bessie. And Bessie sat with her long cigarette holder between her long fingers with their pointed nails, and listened uncompromisingly. She never spoke until the end.

"Then you simply walked out and left him to that girl!"

"If he wants her he can have her."

"Oh, don't be such a little fool! Men always want somebody else, at intervals. It's the woman's business to see they don't get her."

Kay looked at her.

"If they do it isn't love."

"Nonsense! They're a polygamous lot. They can't help it; God made them that way. It has nothing to do with love, really. It's—" she hesitated. Kay was married, but how could she discuss the occasional volcanic passions of men with her? "It's the nature of the beast," she finished lamely.

"Then you believe in infidelity?"

"You don't even know he was unfaithful. And of course I don't believe in infidelity; a clever woman keeps her husband faithful. That's all."

"I'm not clever, not that way."

"You're young," said Bessie. "You have a lot to learn."

She was puzzled, nevertheless. Where did happiness lie for this child-woman before her? To send her back to that dreadful little ranch house and poverty, was that the answer? If Henry only had an ounce of sense and would finance the man—but then Kay had said he would not accept help from them. That made it difficult, but also it showed that McNair had what Bessie had referred to before, namely, guts. Again, did the man want Kay back? His long silence, this cheap girl out there—

"Have you seen Herbert?"

"Not yet. I daresay I shall have to, some time."

"But you're through with that?"

"Yes. I've spoiled his life, among the rest, but I—"

"Spoiled his life!" said Bessie, getting up impatiently. "You have a lot to learn. Men can spoil women's lives; women enjoy unrequited affection. They hold on to it, dream about it. But men! Men don't remember anything unpleasant if they can help it. They wipe off the slate and start over again. It may please them for a while to think they are injured, but when that ceases to please them they stop."

"Then Herbert—?"

"It still pleases him, but he'll get over it."

She sauntered over to the dressing table, rouged her lips thoroughly, put on her hat. She could see Kay's face in the mirror.

"Don't let any one influence you," she told her. "It's your life. If you want to go back to your cowboy, go. If you want Herbert, stay and get busy. He's on the branch now, but he won't hang long."

And with that she went away.

Chapter Thirty-nine

Tom had taken up his life again as best he could. On the day Kay left him he had driven furiously out of town, but at the top of the hill he stopped the car and got out.

The train was already disappearing in the far distance. He stood gazing after it, his hands clenched, his eyes hard and hopeless.

She was gone.

It had grown very cold. The wind swept across the plains, rattled the top of the old Ford, penetrated his none too heavy clothing. His bad foot ached, the brim of his broad hat flapped in his hand. He had taken it off when the train went out of sight.

He was still stunned. He looked around him. This was the place he had come to last summer through the dust and heat, to mourn! To crave, like a drunkard liquor, for the open country; to be alone and to look, off and off, to where behind some distant butte the sky kept rendezvous with the earth. And now he had the answer to his prayer; he could watch the sunrise on a frosty morning, and see the moisture rise like smoke from the backs of his warming cattle; he could follow the narrow twisting trail, if he liked, over the edge of the world and beyond. He had had his answer, all right, and what was it worth to him?

She was gone.

He went back to the Reservation, lit the fire and the lamps, limped about automatically preparing his supper, but a curious thing had happened to him. He tried to see Kay in the little house, but he could only see Clare. She had spoiled the house, as she had spoiled his life. He tried to visualize Kay in her low chair by the lamp, and he saw Clare.

"You can go out and sleep in the barn if you want to. But who'd believe it?"

Not Kay. Kay was gone. She had left him. Never again would he come home to the lamps lighted and Kay— God! What had he done to deserve it?

He returned to the Newcomb job the next day. Bend, straighten, pitch. Bend, straighten, pitch. The machine roared and shook, the belt writhed, his foot swelled, his arms and back ached. But the labor was good for him; at least he could sleep.

He was silent and morose with the men. When the threshing was over he took his pay check and limped out, to get into the car without so much as a "So long." He went back to the ranch house, unlocked the door and went in, stared around him and went out again.

After that he entered the house as little as possible.

He settled down, in a way. Winter had come. There was no snow as yet, but it was already very cold. The enmity of the Indians and their refusal to sell him hay, the poor condition of the range and his responsibility to Tulloss, added to his real heartache as to Kay, sent him about in a state of savage loneliness.

He took to carrying a rifle with him, on the pretext to himself of killing coyotes and wolves. But it is as well that he did not meet Little Dog at that. In his brooding anger his hatred had settled on the Indian; by a sort of twisted reasoning he blamed Kay's defection on his lameness. "If he had been a whole man she would never have gone."

He was liable to violent and explosive angers, too. One

day, coming over the top of a rise, he saw a gray wolf running, and found a cow down and dying. He shot at the wolf and wounded it, and in a frenzy passion he finished the job with his bare hands. He was ashamed of it when he had ceased to see red, and he carried a badly mangled finger for a long time.

Later on, however, with every intention of a long winter to come, he buckled down to work. Day by day he picked up his "poor" stuff and brought it slowly in for feeding. Along with the other outfits he planned for the preservation of winter pastures, not to be grazed over until it was needed later on. Owing to the scarcity of grass the cattle ranged far; forty acres was hardly enough for a cow now, and later it might need more. He covered incalculable distances in the saddle, to go back at night to an untidy house which was cold beyond his power to warm it. The water would be frozen in the kitchen pail, the remnants of his last meal still on the table, his bed unmade. Finally he nailed heavy papers over the windows, and at least kept out the wind. It made it dark and gloomy, but as he seldom entered it in daylight it did not matter.

He hardly ever went to Judson. George and Sally had asked no questions after the first.

"Wife's gone East, I understand?"

Tom knew how news traveled up and down the railroad. He nodded.

"Her mother's sick."

"Well, I'm sorry to hear that. What you needin' today?"

Once he saw Bill. A freight had pulled in for water, and from the cupola of the caboose he saw Bill waving. He limped over and climbed in. It might have been the same car in which he and Bill had gone to Chicago; the same worn black leather berths, the same stove and tin coffee pot in the center; the same desk for the conductor with its oil lamp, its green order slips, its calendar, time-tables and box of pipe tobacco; the same fuses and torpedoes in their places on the wall. But Bill was constrained.

"Hear you've got quite a herd of your own now."

"You can call it that! Still like this job?"

"S'all right. I get to hankering now and then for a horse—you know how it is—but it's not so bad."

The engineer whistled to call in the other brakeman, the train jerked.

"Well, I'm off. So long, Bill."

"So long, Tom."

That was all. Tom turned and waited until the train pulled out. Bill was up in his chair in the cupola again, leaning out and grinning.

"Remember the night you threw the Swede off?"

"Sure do!"

The train moved on, and Tom was left on the platform, staring after it. Then he drew himself up. There had been pity in that last look of Bill's.

It was soon afterwards that Kay's letter arrived. He took it quietly, put it in his pocket and left town. Only when he was well out on the frozen road did he dare to open it and read it. It was like a blow between the eyes. She still believed he had been unfaithful to her, after all he had told her! "Maybe all men are unfaithful to their wives, or at least disloyal— And I did love you so dreadfully, Tom." Did. Did! Well, that was clear enough anyhow. She had cared for him, but now she was through.

He took to brooding over that phrase, in the saddle, in his untidy house. More than once he got out paper and ink and set himself to answer it. He would sit there, his elbows squared, the pen held in his cold and roughened hands, trying to think how to put all his seething thoughts into words. But he could not do it. What could he say that would bring her back? Why should she come back to this, anyhow? Or to him?

Once he roused in the icy dawn, to find that he had slept all night by the table, his head on the paper. He wakened stiff with the cold.

He worked on doggedly, but the heart had gone out of him. Fortunately he had little leisure in which to think; the struggle for existence for himself and his herd absorbed him utterly. He was never rested, he was always cold. Out on the range in the piercing wind it was nothing unusual to find his rope, his saddle blanket and his latigo frozen stiff. Luckily the snows were not heavy until the first of the year. His dry stock, wintering outside in "breaks" or broken places, followed the ridges blown bare of snow, and somehow managed to subsist. His "poor" cows and his calves he fed, going short on provisions for himself to buy oil-cake.

When, on the range, he met other cowboys muffled to the ears, he heard similar tales of woe, but with this difference: they could go back to the line camps and be fed. When they needed oil-cake they could get it, even if grudgingly, from the owners. But Tom had no such resource. He was determined not to go to Tulloss for money, and not to touch what Kay had left in the bank. He would make good or starve.

There came times when Kay almost faded from his mind. She became an intolerable memory, associated with days of warmth and sunshine and hope. He did not know it was Christmas eve until he met a lonely line rider on the range. The day was dark, with a fine hard snow driving in his face. He was almost on the other man before he saw him.

"Hell of a Christmas eve, isn't it?"

"Didn't know it was Christmas eve."

They passed and were lost in the storm. Tom rode on, his head bent, letting the horse choose the way. So this was Christmas eve! A long time ago, years and eons ago, he and Kay had sat on a little porch in the sunshine and had planned for Christmas.

"I'm going to get some turkeys, so we can have one on Christmas. Isn't Christmas without turkey."

"I'll have to look it up in the cook book!"

"Shucks! I'll show you how to fix it. You've married a

cook, Mrs. McNair, if I do say it."

He got home that night and took off his boots. He had made a bootjack now, so he could do it alone. Then, for some reason he could not explain, he hunted around and found a candle and put it in the window. He had seen a Mexican puncher do that once, a long time ago, on Christmas eve.

"What you doin' that for, Mex?"

"Maybe somebody outside and want to come in," said Mex, mysteriously.

So he lighted his candle and sat looking at it, and after a while he slept in his chair. . . .

So far there had been little snow. The temperature fell as low as twenty-six degrees below zero once or twice, and Tom carried an ice axe on his saddle to cut water holes in the frozen creeks; it required strength and skill, for to cut where the water would flow over the ice might mean a steer down with a broken leg. But soon after the first of the year the snow began to come down in earnest. Tom wakened one morning to find the mountains glittering white, like snowy giants over which had been carelessly flung a robe of gray. And this gray was the pine trees, now strangely the color of sage. The ranch buildings seemed flattened out, familiar rocks had lost their contours, and with every breath of the icy wind the cottonwoods by the creek sent down soft snowfalls of their own.

He rode into a line camp that day, to hear that Gus, the Swede from the L. D., was still on his homestead and likely to be snowed in. Tom had no particular liking for Gus, but the law of the frontier was still the law of the back country; no man to be passed by in trouble. The next day he packed some of his small supply of food on an extra horse and rode the eight miles to Gus's cabin, near the foot of the mountains.

The snow was still falling, the road no road but only a track, and that deeply covered. But by watching his landmarks he found the place, and was only just in time. As he opened the gate he saw that the snow around the cabin was not broken, except for a few dog tracks, and that no smoke was arising from the chimney. He concluded that Gus had gone, and might have turned back, had he not heard the dog barking inside. Then he opened the door.

There was some daylight outside, but the one room was dark. There was no fire, but a heavy sickening stench hung over everything. There was no sound when he first opened the door; then a small black and white shepherd dog came crawling to him, and Gus's deeply accented and familiar voice spoke from one of the built-in bunks.

"Come in, stranger," it said. "You're yust in time."

Piled in the bunk on top of him was a heterogeneous collection of wearing apparel, a saddle blanket, and a coyote skin, badly cured and odorous, and above these coverings his gaunt unshaven face was lifted.

"Sick, Gus?"

"I run an axe into my foot here sometime back, and the thing's festering."

"Festering" it certainly was. Tom, working about the cabin after examining it, wondered if he could get Gus out after all. The Swede was feverish; he had had little food for a week, and for the last day or two had been eating snow for water. He could not get to the creek. But that was not the worst of his grievance. His two horses had been stolen.

As he ate and drank the coffee Tom made he grew more garrulous. It was plain that his fever was rising. He began to ramble; Tom gathered that he knew who had taken his horses, and tried to find out, but Gus's eyes grew cunning.

"That's my business," he said shortly. "Yust keep out. I'll attend to it."

Later on he fell asleep; he tossed and muttered, but when he roused he was apparently rational enough. Tom was overwhelmingly weary. He piled wood on the fire and lay down in the bunk across, and was soon asleep.

He was roused by the creaking of boards and opened his eyes. A long knife in his hand, Gus was coming stealthily across the floor; his eyes were blazing, his face tense. Tom sat up.

"Here!" he said. "What're you doing?"

"Oh, for Christ's sake!" Gus bawled. "I'd have had him in a minute."

"Had who?"

"That pack rat. He was yust over your head. He's the one that's carried off most of my grub."

Grumbling, Gus went back to his bunk and to sleep, but Tom did not close his eyes again. He never knew the truth; whether there had been a pack rat above him that night or whether Gus, in a fit of delirium, and dreaming of some mysterious revenge, had meant to kill him.

The next day he got him out and sent him to the hospital at Ursula. Sometime later on Tom heard he had lost the foot; then he lost sight of him for months, until it was time for Gus to take his place in that small and unimportant drama of the back country which was Tom McNair's life.

But the snow continued to fall, and Tom's anxiety for his herd steadily increased—the drifts banked high against drift fences, it even covered the ridges, usually wind-swept and clear. On the railroad great snow-ploughs dug into the mass, flung it to right and left, and cleared the track only to have it buried again. By keeping on high ground Tom could get about, although slowly, to see his cattle snowed-in in the washes and coulées below. They had gnawed every twig and branch, had eaten the tops of the scant bushes, even the bitter sage where they could get at it. Some had made their way to the ranch, and stood outside his fences, snuffing hungrily at the hay spread in the feeding yard under the shelter sheds for his weaners, his cows and calves. They made an incessant mournful plea which almost drove him mad, but he was helpless. The snow fell, thawed, froze, fell again.

Ruin stared him in the face. Steers went down and did not

rise again. He made a circuit of the line camps, to find the hay shovelers working overtime, and no feed to spare at any price; and even if he could have bought it at the railroad he could not have freighted it in.

Then, one night, he hit on something.

He went home, cooked a bit of supper and then taking a lantern went out to the barn. The horses stirred uneasily when he entered. He limped through to the corral and found two strong logs and some lumber left from his repairing of the house; he dragged them inside, found his tools and set to work. In that terrible freezing silence the sound of his hammer was like pistol shots, but in a couple of hours he had made a crude snow-plough.

He went to bed then, without taking off his clothes, and in the early morning he began again. Harness, this time. He had only two horses broken to harness, but he had no time to worry about that. He took latigos, raw leather, anything he could find, and by noon he started out. The broken team led, and after a time the other horses fell to work. He could not touch the drifts, but on the ridges he cleared a track, doubled on it, widened it. The cattle were terrified; he had later to round them up and drive them to the exposed grass, scanty as it was. But they learned before long; they even followed the plough. For the time at least they were saved.

He was completely exhausted, almost snow-blind. The rims of his eyes were swollen and excruciatingly painful, he limped badly, he had not shaved for three weeks. He went back to the house, fell on his unmade bed, and slept twenty-four hours before he moved.

When he got about again he heard terrible tales of disaster. Only the disappearance of the snow would enable the cattlemen to total their losses, but compared with theirs his own were negligible.

He was not through, of course.

Early in February came a chinook. A warm wind began to blow, the snow melted rapidly, and the cattle, inured now to the cold, began to drop all over the pastures. They would get down and be too enervated to rise, and there they would lie until they died unless they were forced to their feet again. Once again he began his battle, this time to "tail them up." It took all his strength and more agility than his bad foot permitted him. More than once a "tailed" steer, on his feet and angry, tried to hook him. Once indeed he was knocked down, but the animal was too unsteady to pursue his advantage.

But at last, miraculously, the spring came. In the tracks made by his snow-plough, in the bare spaces on the ridges, the brown grass took on a greenish hue. The nights were still cold, but at midday the sun was warm. His eyes commenced to improve. His cows began to drop their calves, awkward little creatures, pop-eyed and dazed; they lay for a time, moved, got up, and stood gazing about on legs which still shook under them.

He felt no exultation; only a vague relief.

Chapter Forty

Katherine died in May. She lay in her Empire bed draped with primrose silk, with her hair carefully marceled and dressed as usual. And the mortician had put a little—just a very little—rouge on her dead cheeks, so that she looked quite well and as if she were sleeping.

Naturally Henry, being Henry, saw that her departure on her long journey was attended by adequate ceremonial. Exactly the right people came, much as they had come to tea in happier times, the men in morning coats and dark ties, taking their silk hats carefully in with them for fear of damage in the hall; the women in rich dark clothes. From upstairs in her bedroom Kay could hear the rustlings and whispering, followed by the silence which meant the Bishop had taken his place on the stairs, and then strong and full-voiced, reassuring, came his voice:

"I am the resurrection and the life, saith the Lord; he that believeth in me, though he were dead, yet shall he live."

She could not cry. An hour or so before the service her father had gone into Katherine's bedroom and closed the door. It was not, she thought, that he had deliberately shut her out, but that he had forgotten her. Somewhere across the hall were Aunt Bessie, other and more distant relatives, the close friends. She sat in a chair and looked at her hands. They were very white once more, against her black frock.

"First thing you've got to do is to get those hands healed up."

Well, they were healed up now. But she must not think of that; not now, when her mother was dead, and downstairs they were committing her soul to God and her body to the soil. The soil. She herself had fought the soil, and it had beaten her.

Later on they went, rather rapidly, to the cemetery. There was a sort of indecent haste about it; instead of the slow and mournful carriage procession of her childhood, moving with reluctance toward the outskirts of town, the long line of automobiles twisted and darted through the traffic. It was an incredibly short time until they were standing on heavy mats under a great marquee, with a rose-lined pit at their feet, and old Lucius's ugly shaft towering beside it. What was it her mother had wanted to put on the shaft? "He has followed the trail into the sunset." And they had not let her do it. Her poor mother. "Your mother's different, but she hadn't your courage. She never did get away." Well, she had got away now. Her poor mother.

"For as much as it hath pleased Almighty God—"

It had been raining. They made their way back to the limousine through a thin moist covering, into which Aunt Bessie's high heels sunk and left little pits behind her. She was very smart in her black clothes; she always looked her best in black. And the best people followed decorously, also making small pits in the ground, and got into their limousines and drove rapidly home for tea and a rest before dressing for dinner.

Kay was stunned. She had known that it would come, but the dreadful finality of it, the horror of leaving that delicate, carefully nurtured body out there alone in the cold earth was horrible to her. And with this there was remorse, that she had added to the distress of the last few months, that she might even have hastened the end.

In the car she reached out and took her father's hand, but although he pressed it he released it very soon. He sat staring ahead, his silk hat just grazing the top of the car, his heavy figure lurching with the movement of the car, dry-eyed, silent, solitary. She could not reach him. She never had reached him, really. After awhile Bessie opened her vanity case and powdered her reddened nose, and then they were at home again.

The sickly odor of flowers still hung over the house, the servants and the undertaker's men were folding up the camp chairs and carrying them out, and in the hall was Herbert, correctly dressed with exactly the proper dark tie, overseeing the straightening of the house.

She had hardly seen him all winter. He looked thin, but his hair was as sleek as ever. And if he paled somewhat when he saw her he did not lose his composure.

"I've ordered tea," he said. "It will be in at once."

She went into the drawing room, and rather to her surprise he followed her.

"I need not tell you how grieved I am, Kay."

"No. I know, Herbert. The only thing—"

"Yes?"

"I think I shortened her life."

"Not at all. I've been over that with the doctors. I was afraid you would think so. They say it was a purely physical condition, and—I think I ought to tell you this, Kay. I always knew that in her heart she felt you had done the right thing. At the beginning, after you had gone, I used to see her. She never actually said so, but—"

"And then she found it wasn't the right thing after all!"

He looked at her gravely.

"Was it as wrong as all that, Kay?"

"I was all wrong, I think. You are being very kind to me, Herbert. I thought you would hate me."

"Never. If I really loved you, I had to put your happiness first."

"Happiness!" she said. "What is happiness anyhow, Herbert? To want something and get it? But then the moment one got it one would have to go on wanting something else! There isn't such a thing, then, is there?"

"Not all the time," he said steadily. "You can't live on a mountaintop always. But there is contentment, and now and then the bigger thing comes."

Bessie joined them for tea, but Mr. Dowling remained in his library. Kay, looking across, could see him working at his desk, and knew that he was himself addressing the handsomely engraved cards which thanked their friends for their flowers and letters of sympathy. But there was no message of condolence which received no acknowledgment.

On the day after her mother's death she had sent a brief telegram to Tom: "Mother passed away quietly yesterday." His reply did not come for almost a week. That did not surprise her. She knew what the roads must be. But the message itself, with its bitterness, was like a blow in the face: "Sorry to hear of your trouble, but there are worse things than reaching the end of the trail after a hard day."

No suggestion that, now that her contract had expired, she could return to him. A perfunctory sympathy, an implied reproach, and that was all. She thought back over her letter to him last autumn; she had told him she would come back if he wanted her, but it had been a hard letter, in a way. If she were writing now it would be different. How could one be hard, when life was so insecure at the best, and so short? When every time the clock ticked there was just so much less time to live, to love and to be loved? When to quarrel was to lose precious time; time, which was all one had.

She found that her mother had made a will, leaving her all her small estate. It was not much, but she had taken great happiness in doing it. It had been Bessie Osborne's suggestion.

"You know Henry as well as I do," she had said, more gently than the words would indicate. "All the Dowling men have used money as a club over their women. And Kay has her own life to live. If she wants to go back West—"

"Do you think she does?"

"I don't know. But she ought to be able to if she should.

She'll get all I have, of course, but I—"

She had stopped abruptly. It would not do to say to this dying woman that she, Bessie Osborne, expected to live a long time yet, and to enjoy every minute of it.

"I think she ought to be free to make her own choice," she finished, rather lamely.

So Katherine, like old Lucius, had made her will, and after it was signed and witnessed, just before it was put into the heavy envelope and sealed, she added a line or two in pencil: "My darling girl: You must make your own choice, and maybe this will help. Do what you think is best. I only want you to be happy."

Kay almost broke her heart over that when she saw it.

Later on, able to think it over more calmly, she realized that one cannot devise happiness by will.

Henry had resumed his life decorously and regularly; save for the band of crêpe on his left arm he exhibited no signs of his loss. He was more detached, perhaps. He spent more hours in his library, looking ahead at nothing at all. But for any part Kay had in his life she might not have been in the house. His office, his club, his dinner, and then an early going to bed comprised his days. He went to church as usual, creaked decorously up the aisle for the plate, passed it, returned with it, stood until the offertory was finished and the morning collection elevated before the altar, returned to his seat. At the proper times he prayed.

But now and then he found his eyes on her, with a furtive sort of appeal in them. It never went further than that, and as the days went and he resumed his ordinary routine she wondered if she had been mistaken. Did he need her? Or did he care? They were not often alone; his friends dropped in, elderly men like himself, prosperous, slightly dull, their illusions lost, their enthusiasms long dead. She studied them sometimes.

Did men, like women and even life itself, reach a climacteric, and was everything sterile after that? Was the very essence of life creation; and when that power went did all zest go with it? These men seemed to ask so little of life; good food and comfortable shelter, a busy day at the office, a few old friends. Did they ever lie awake at night and listen to the clock ticking away the time? Time, which was all they had left, and which was rapidly decreasing.

She contrasted them with the men she knew in the West, men as old as themselves, but fighting to the end; wearing out, not rusting. Perhaps success was like happiness; there was no such thing. It was only the fight for it that mattered. When you need not fight any more—

It was not until three weeks after her mother's death that the question of her future course became imminent. Her father called her into the library, and as he had when she first came back, fortified himself by placing the desk between them.

"Have you decided what you intend to do now?"

"That depends on you, father. If you need me—"

He waved that aside with a gesture.

"Your mother," he said, and paused. "Your mother wished you to have full freedom of choice. You have followed your agreement with me, and—"

"I did not stay only for that reason."

"I understand that. But I must know your plans now; I must know where I am. I have had an offer for this house. Of course, if you stay I shall not sell."

"You don't really need me at all, do you, father?"

"You cannot take your mother's place, but of course I shall miss you."

And again she caught that half-stealthy appealing glance of his, of which he was ashamed.

"On the other hand, if you wish to go back to that fellow—have you heard from him?"

"I had a telegram when mother went away."

"You have been corresponding?"

"No. I wrote him I was staying on, but he—never answered."

That angered him. His florid color, which had been

subdued lately, rose high, he ran his finger inside his collar.

"And after an affront like that you are ready to go back to him! For God's sake, where is your pride? Are you going to tell me that a daughter of mine would force herself on a man who doesn't want her?"

The scene, for it amounted to that, went on. He was angry at Tom for not wanting her, but he would have been equally furious had he done so. She could not reason; after a time she could not even talk. It seemed to her that nobody really cared, except as a matter of pride, what she did. Except Herbert. She began to think of Herbert as at least representing peace, as against the truculence of her father and Tom's stormy nature. She was not startled therefore when he was brought into the conversation. A gentleman. A kindly gentleman who could and would care for her, according to her father. A man of her own breeding and stamp. Good blood, good looks, good family. But she said the first thing that came into her head, and was instantly sorry for it.

"That's the way they describe a pedigreed bull, out West!"

He got up, moved around the desk and opened the door for her.

"I see that I have been wasting my time," he said, and she went out.

Early in June they moved out to the country house, and one day she went out onto the terrace to see Herbert coming up the drive in his car.

"Won't you come and take a ride?" he asked. "I won't even talk, if you want to be quiet."

She went. Why not? They drove a couple of miles before she spoke.

"I'm glad you came, Herbert. I was feeling rather—lonely."

"I thought you might," he said quietly. "You see, I know what loneliness means."

She was warmed by that, somewhat comforted. After all, to be loved was something. It was easier than loving; it hurt less.

Chapter Forty-one

In May the various cattle outfits began their cow and calf round-ups. Here and there over the leased lands of the Reservation were small branding corrals; the herds were gathered near them and held, cows with calves were cut out and driven to the wide log jaws which led into it, the line of riders closed up solidly behind them, and to pitiful outcries and wailings the burning and ear-cropping went on. The calf was roped from its mother's side, thrown, branded and released; the acrid odor of burning hair and flesh filled the air, and then the bewildered animals were turned loose, to retreat once more to coulée or protected valley, there to ponder on the inscrutable ways of mankind.

The spring had been late, and the winter loss heavy. Potters' men, gathering together in the cook tent after dark for poker or conversation, were disgruntled. They had worked hard, but the calf crop was low. And their tallies showed other losses, not to be accounted for by the drought and the hard winter. Rumors of rustlers went around. The Bristols, to the north of them, claimed to have lost three thousand head out of their herd of forty thousand during the past year, but the old days of quick justice were over. The rustler moved his cattle by night and hid them during the daylight. When he got them far enough off he sweated on a new brand or reworked the old one, and if he was caught there were always shyster lawyers to get him off.

"Not enough neck-tie parties," they said among themselves. "Nowadays, unless a fellow follows a hide to Chicago or Omaha, he's got a poor chance to prove anything."

Sitting on their heels, smoking their eternal cigarettes, they threshed out the matter. And Gus would listen and grin to himself, a mysterious smile that nobody noticed. Gus was helping the cook. He had not been quite the same since he lost his foot; he talked to himself at times, and the men found it dangerous to tease him.

"You and your rustlers!" he would say. "Couldn't winter your herd, so you blame it on somebody else!"

He was reported to have a knife and a revolver hidden in his bed-roll.

Only for Tom did he show any affection. He would fill Tom's plate for him, his long body hanging between his crutches, his one trouser leg flapping loose at the bottom; fill it as full as he could.

"Come and get it, Tom, or I'll throw it away!"

He had an inordinate pride when Tom's tallies showed that he had a good calf crop.

"He's a cow-man, he is," he said. "While the rest of you buckaroos were sitting on your hind ends, he was working."

"Oh, go and hire a hall!"

"It's the truth."

"Yes, and the devil's a Sunday school teacher!"

Tom never heard any of these discussions.

He was gaunt and untidy those days; his clothing showed the wear and tear of the winter, his hair was long and unkempt. And he was taciturn in the extreme. He worked hard; his rope was always in his hand. He was the first out in the morning and the last in at night. He was a sort of trouble-shooter for the outfit, in spite of his lameness. His leg was bothering him again. But he was not popular with the men. His brooding silences, and perhaps the fact that his cattle had wintered better than the rest, set him apart from them.

Sometimes when he limped into the cook tent conversation would suddenly cease, and he knew they had been talking about him and his affairs. He would glance around at them with a mocking smile, get his plate and sit down, and after awhile they would find a safe topic and start again.

But he had had a good calf crop in spite of everything. Sixty-five calves now bore his brand, and were fattening and growing on the young spring grass. He had made good. If all went well he could pay Tulloss his interest that fall, maybe even reduce his loan somewhat. He played no poker during those days of the round-up. He had no money to lose, and no inclination anyhow.

He was still on round-up when Kay's telegram came.

"Mother passed away quietly yesterday. Kay."

He stood—it had been brought out with the mail for the outfit—and stared at it.

It was like a voice from beyond the grave; she had been dead to him for a long time, and now, for a moment, she lived again. She was real. She even remembered him.

That night, lying out in his bed with his face to the stars, he was sorely tempted. After all she was still his wife, and she had said she would come if he sent for her. Suppose he demanded that she come back? That would force *them* into the open, at least. Then, if they tried to keep her, or she wanted to stay—

But of course she wanted to stay. She had planned ahead to leave him, had written home and got money. It was not Clare who had parted them; she was through before that. Weeks maybe before that.

At the end of the round-up he sent his reply, went back home and cleaned up the ranch house as best he could, and then went to Ursula. He looked rather better, although the story of the winter was written on his face for all to see, and his leg was very bad. He had had to split the front of his old boot. But Tulloss had not seen him for months, and he was startled.

"Looking kind of moth-eaten, Tom."

"I'm all right. At least I've pulled through, and that's saying something."

"So it is, Tom. I guess you know your business."

"It's a damned poor business, but it's all I know. Maybe the wheat fellows are right. After a winter like this last one—"

"They've got their troubles too."

They worked over their accounts together, Tom with secret pride, the banker satisfied and rather thoughtful. It was not until they had finished that Mr. Tulloss leaned back in his chair, perhaps to feel the bullet reputed to be there—and stretched out his legs.

"Tom," he said, "I want to know something. If you answer that squarely— But first of all, where's Little Dog?"

"I haven't seen him. Maybe it's just as well. When things were bad last winter, if I'd happened on him I figured to put a bullet in him, agreement or no agreement."

"Why, if he hasn't given you any trouble?"

"He cut my dam last fall. All the water I had."

"When was that?"

"Before I sent—my wife into town here."

"I see. Tom, don't you owe me a little information on that matter?"

"I figure that's between me and her," he said stubbornly.

"Well, look at it this way. I loaned that money for two reasons: first, because I thought you would make good, and second, because I was fond of your wife. In my mind it was a partnership arrangement. If you have dissolved that partnership I have a right to know."

"I'm ready to liquidate, if you are."

"Oh, don't be such a God-damned fool, Tom. She has left you, has she?"

Tom nodded sullenly. He could not speak.

"Why?"

"She'd been planning to go for some time. Then something happened, and she took the first train East."

"The something was the Hamel girl, I suppose?"

There was little that Jennie Tulloss did not know.

Tom nodded and got up.

"There was nothing to it," he said somberly, "but she thought there was." He picked up his battered Stetson and rose. "I didn't come here to discuss my troubles," he said. "I'm not asking her back and she knows it. She wrote once, saying she would come if I did, but I hadn't done anything I was ashamed of. She was tired of me, that's all." He stood, fingering his hat. "I was just something for her to play around with for awhile. That's all."

"You're sure of that, are you?"

"She'd been planning to go anyhow. She'd written for money before that happened. With what she left here, and what she took with her, she must have had a thousand dollars or so."

"Is that so!" said Mr. Tulloss, suddenly cheerful. "Is that so, indeed! Well, my young buckaroo, you may be a good cowman, but you're a fool about women. That little girl of yours brought that check West with her when she came. Bessie Osborne gave it to her for emergencies. She brought it in here herself and offered it to me as security for your loan. And her grandmother's pearls too, by heck!"

Tom sat down. The self-righteousness which had upheld him all winter was suddenly knocked from under him, and his hands were trembling.

"You're sure of that, are you, Mr. Tulloss?"

"I'm telling you."

There was a silence, broken by Mr. Tulloss.

"You're in good shape now, Tom. We won't have another year like this last one for a long time. Why don't you go East and see her? Bring her back, Tom. She's lost her mother, and if I know Henry Dowling— You've been an obstinate young fool long enough. Put your pride in your pocket, man, and go and get her."

"How do I know she wants to see me?"

"Well, there's such a thing as finding out!" said the banker.

Tom sat very still. His leg was stretched out in front of him; it ached like a toothache, and it was badly swollen. It was a most disreputable leg indeed. He tried to smile.

"With that?" he said.

"If it was my wife," Mr. Tulloss said rather tartly, "I'd go if I had to sit down and slide on the seat of my pants."

It is hardly likely however, that he was thinking of Jennie. "Go and see Dunham," he added, more practically. "He'll fix you up. And if it's a question of money—"

"I can manage that," Tom got up. "I—you've been mighty good to me, Mr. Tulloss." He stood fingering his hat, after his old habit. "I'm not much good at talking, but—"

He stopped. He had a horrible lump in his throat. He blinked wildly, turned and limped out.

He had recovered himself when he got to the street. It was a day of brilliant sunshine, like the one when he and Kay had come back to Ursula; the same heat, the same procession of cars from the back country, the same friendly greetings.

"Tom, you old son of a gun, what you doin' in town?"

"I figured on getting a hair-cut."

"Well, it's sure time!"

He moved up the street. His foot was very bad, his grin a trifle fixed, but he was supremely happy. The Indians had taken advantage of the good roads to come to town for their buying; in brilliant shawls and high moccasins the squaws stared into the shop windows, sometimes with a bead-eyed baby looking over their shoulders. Tom thought he saw Weasel Tail's widow among them, but he was not sure. But what did it matter? Weasel Tail and Little Dog had faded to the background of his mind; the long hard winter was as though it had never been. Summer was here again; the trees were in full leaf, the little gardens in bloom, the creeks running bank full, the wide plains green and lush with grass.

And Kay—!

He passed the Emporium without a glance or a thought, but in front of the new haberdashery on a corner he stopped. There was a complete outfit in the window, a suit of a violent blue, a straw hat, a pair of yellow shoes. He would see Dunham, and on the way back he would stop in and buy it. Time enough later to figure how to pay for it. Kay mustn't be ashamed of him.

He limped on, up the street. . . .

Lily May was on the doctor's doorstep, and the old doctor was inside. It took both of them, with Lily May looking on, to get his boots off, and when the old doctor had examined the leg, he straightened and glared at him.

"What the hell have you been doing to it? Are you trying to lose your leg, like Gus?"

"I knocked it some, a while back. Horse threw me against a post."

The doctor looked at his watch.

"It's eleven o'clock," he said. "I'll operate at the hospital at one-thirty. You'll get no lunch today, my handsome lad."

Nor did he.

He made no protest; accepted the operation and the delay in his hopes with that new stoicism of his, fixed Kay firmly in his mind as he went under the ether, made frantic efforts to reach her as she began to slip away—

"Tom, you young idiot! Hold him, somebody!"

—And came out to find himself kissing the hand of a strange elderly nurse, to be saved from any embarrassment by being instantly deadly sick.

Recovery was harder for him. He was not ruined; save for a small amount of unthrifty stock his cattle were on the range growing fat, filling out their lean flanks, their hollow backs. But the days were endless, the nights interminable. Life had become one long waiting, for some fulfillment of which he hardly dared to think. He slept as much as he could, to pass the time away. And he had needed sleep.

Sometimes the nurses brought him books and he tried to read them. Kay liked books and books could learn—teach—a fellow a lot if he kept at them. But his eyes would close, the volume would drop on his chest. Occasionally, as he had in Jake's cabin, he dreamed that Kay herself was in the room, or beside him in the bed. Once indeed he flung out his arm, after his old fashion, and it touched something; but it was Clare, sitting beside him with a bunch of garden flowers in her hand.

He stared at her, still half asleep, and she bent over and kissed him.

"There!" she said. "I guess that didn't hurt you any!"

"Oh, for God's sake quit it, Clare!"

She only laughed, and hid her flowers on the bed.

"What's the use of acting like a spoiled child, Tom? You did me as much harm as I did you."

"I never did you any harm. You lied, that's all."

She only smiled. But she did not stay very long, and when she had gone he asked the nurse not to admit her again.

He had one or two visitors, Mr. Tulloss, Bill, Mrs. Mallory. Once even Gus came on his crutches and stood grinning his strange smile in the doorway. Gus was "sure touched in the head."

"Reckon them Indians put a curse on you, Tom!" he said, and disappeared chuckling, as mysteriously as he had come.

Even Nellie Mallory came. She was growing up now, was self-conscious and delicately made up. But although she simpered and posed somewhat for Tom's benefit, the old infatuation was apparently gone. She was "going with" the new clerk at the drug store.

"What's he like, Nellie? Nice fellow?"

"He's the best dancer in town."

"That's the h— that's a mighty poor recommendation for a husband, my child," he said paternally. "You better look him over before you close the deal."

But Nellie only smiled.

Mr. Tulloss's visit was only a trifle less mysterious than Gus's. He was, he said, going East. Jennie wanted some theaters and clothes, and he—well, he had a little business of his own to attend to.

"You hurry up and get well, Tom," he said. "Maybe I'll see you there. You never can tell." Then he went away.

And so matters stood when one day Doctor Dunham signed his card for him, and gave him a parting admonition before he left.

"You'll have considerable more use of that foot from now on, Tom, if you're careful. But if you abuse it, don't come whining back to me."

"I'm plumb grateful to you, doc. And if you'll let me know how much I owe you—"

"You don't owe me a red cent," said old Dunham testily. "It was worth the price of admission for me to get in there and see what those eastern fellows with their rubber gloves and folderol thought they were doing to you!"

Tom was very happy that day. He left the hospital, walking carefully, and going up the street he bought the very blue suit, the hat, the yellow shoes. He could only fit one shoe, but what did that matter? Soon he would be on his way; he thought of that earlier trip of his from Chicago, the sticky children with their warm small bodies, the day coach, even the contretemps at the club house later on. Like the shoe, what did that matter now? Things were different this time. Kay was his wife, his own wife. She had not planned to leave him, and when he told her how he loved her—if only he could find the words—she would come back.

He whistled as he got the old car from the garage, and let the clutch in. Careful? Of course he would be careful. He was taking mighty good care of that leg from now on; there was a reason, a darned good reason.

"Well, so long, Tom. She's got a gallon of gas and a pint

of water."

"What do you think I'm doing to her? Trying to wean her?"

He was off, on his way to the ranch. His bundles bounced in the rear, the loose mud-guards rattled, and once out of town, for the first time in months he began to sing under his breath:

"I'm a poor lonesome cowboy,
I'm a poor lonesome cowboy,
I'm a poor lonesome cowboy,
And a long ways from home."

Two days after he got back he knew that the rustlers had been at work again, and that he had lost practically his entire herd.

He was ruined.

Chapter Forty-two

Mr. Tulloss sat in the tile-floored morning room of Henry's country house, with a bottle of whisky and a siphon of soda at his elbow. His straw hat—he had abandoned his Stetson at Omaha, at Jennie's order—had been taken from him in the hall, and it had apparently required two men to bring in the refreshments. Two men. He must remember to tell Jennie.

He could look beyond into the drawing room. Not that he called it a drawing room. To him a drawing room was a place where one drew. It was a parlor, a very fine parlor. Even Kirkenbride, the Senator back home, had no such room as that.

For the first time, not so much the hopelessness of his errand as a doubt of its rightness, began to trouble him. So this was what the girl had given up, to go out with Tom McNair to that God-forsaken place on the Reservation! Perhaps Tom had been right after all. "She was tired of me, that's all. I was just something for her to play around with for awhile." And the incident of the Hamel girl had simply forced an issue that was bound to come.

He was very warm, and the whisky had made him warmer. He got out his handkerchief and mopped his face.

"It's the humidity," he said. "We get hot as blazes out

home, but it's a dry heat."

Henry nodded. He did not like Tulloss; not since he had ignored his request and written him that letter. "I have always done business with my cards on the table." Well, his cards—Henry's—had been on the table from the start. Let Tulloss turn his up now. He had come for something. Henry eyed him warily.

"I don't suppose you came to see me to talk about the climate, Tulloss."

"No, although climate has something to do with it. We've had a bad year. Maybe you know it, maybe you don't. But it's about wrecked the cattle business, for a while anyhow. It looks as though I'll have to take over Potters' end of the L. D. Either that, or—find somebody to buy it."

"If that means me, no," said Henry, unequivocally. "I'm through."

"It's a good ranch. With proper handling, and wheat to fall back on, it's a paying proposition."

"With the cattle failing on good wheat years, and *vice versa!*"

"I've found a man who doesn't know a bad year for cattle when he meets it."

"Who is it?"

"It happens," said the banker, clearing his throat, "to be your son-in-law, Tom McNair.

Suddenly Henry was very angry. His neck swelled, his face was deeply suffused.

"I regard that as a distinct impertinence, Tulloss. That name is not mentioned in this house. The fellow has wrecked my family; he virtually killed my—killed my wife. He has ruined my daughter's chances for any satisfactory marriage. And you can come here and ask me to discuss him!"

"You don't have to say a word," said Tulloss blandly. "Let me do the talking, Henry. In the first place, I don't put all the blame on Tom, but that's neither here nor there. I didn't come here to quarrel. And when your girl tells me she doesn't want to go back to Tom McNair, I'm ready to hunt up my hat and go away. But I have a sneaking idea, Henry, that the time comes when all a man can do for his children is to help them to be happy. And by the time he's able to do that, generally speaking, he's so old that he's forgotten how."

Henry stirred in his chair.

"I'll ask you this: is Kay happy?"

"Happy? She's just lost her mother."

"I'll change it, then, is she happier here than she would be out West?"

"At least she's fed and clothed! Do you know how she came back to me? In rags, and half starved! I was profoundly shocked. Even now, when I think of it, my blood boils."

"She'd be comfortable enough on the L. D. And fed, too—although I think you're wrong about that. They were poor, of course; they didn't have any flunkeys bowing and scraping around, but they did have enough to eat."

That last speech was hardly tactful, but it only hardened in Henry a resolve already made. He would never lift a finger to help Tom McNair. He said so in a variety of ways, some of them rather reminiscent of old Lucius in their luridness.

"And you can tell McNair that for me," he finished.

Mr. Tulloss got up. He was hotter than ever, and the flunkeys had taken his hat. Where the devil was his hat?

"All right, Henry. All right," he said. "No reason for getting excited about it. If Potter's in the shape I think he is I'll take over the L. D. myself. And—" his voice rose somewhat—"I'll put McNair on it too, by God. Then when your girl goes back to him, as she will, she'll have a home anyhow. And no thanks to you!"

He stalked out, located his hat, jerked it from James, jammed it on his head, and got into his taxicab.

When he looked at the meter it said four dollars and eighty-five cents, and he sat in silent fury all the way back. Nevertheless, he had not spent all of the four dollars and eighty-five cents in vain.

Some of Henry's complacency had been destroyed by that visit. At dinner that night—those long deadly dinners where Kay and her father sat across from each other at the massive table and made conversation for the benefit of the servants, and fell into silence the moment they were alone—he looked at her more carefully than he had for a long time. She looked badly. By gad, she looked sick! For the first time in many weeks he addressed a personal question to her.

"How do you feel, Kay? Are you all right?"

He was startled to see that the look she gave him was actually grateful.

"I'm all right, father."

"Do you—sleep?"

"Not always, but I read, you know. I don't mind it."

When the long ritual of the meal was over he went into his library, as was his custom now, and closed the door. There were some drawings on his desk; he had to select something for Katherine's grave. He picked one up and sat holding it. She had hated the shaft over his father's grave, but he had put it up, nevertheless. And what was that queer thing she had wanted to put on it? "He has followed the trail into the sunset." It was a silly, sentimental thing, and he had not let her do it. There were a great many other things he had not let her do. Maybe Tulloss was right, and he had been a hard man. Katherine. Katherine.

He made up his mind then that if Tulloss reopened the matter of the L. D. he would consider it. Then, if the fellow actually made good—

But he was the old Henry, nevertheless. He reflected rather grimly that perhaps a reconciliation would be better than a divorce. He had had enough publicity; all he could stand. And Tulloss was no fool. He had never spent a dollar unless there were two in sight.

Mr. Tulloss, however, did not reopen the matter. He went on to New York, miserably put on the suit he had bought for the Bankers' Convention years ago, tied his white tie, and wandered self-consciously through hotel and theater lobbies, never quite accustomed to clothing indecently short in front and awkwardly long behind.

And then one night, getting his key from his box, he found a telegram there waiting for him.

He read it twice, and then looked at his wife.

"I guess we'll be hitting the back trail, Jen," he said. "How soon can you be ready?"

Tom's entire herd had been stolen, and Tom himself was out gunning for Little Dog.

They went back, Mr. Tulloss and Jennie; Jennie unwilling but acquiescent, the banker watching schedules, uneasy, impatient. He puzzled his wife. He was not a soft man.

"What difference does it make to you whether Tom McNair kills an Indian or not?"

"He'll get life this time, or maybe worse. That's why."

It was not an answer, but she let it go at that. She thought that somehow there must be money at stake, and watched to see if he leaned back to rub that old bullet of his. She never thought it might be pity.

Tom was in the mountains when they reached Ursula. Allison told Tulloss that, and that Tom had taken a pack horse and "all the armament he owned."

"He's plumb crazy," said the Sheriff. "Not talkin' any, y'understand. Just ridin' and lookin' round."

"You get word to him I want to see him," said Mr. Tulloss grimly.

"I want to see him myself!" said the Sheriff. "But that's easier said than done."

Chapter Forty-three

There had never been a question in Tom's mind as to who and what lay behind his ruin.

He had known rustlers all his life; men who made their pick-ups of cattle, drove them off, hid them and later rebranded and sold them. His easy philosophy had accepted them with the same easy tolerance with which at one time he had accepted his own drinking; like himself, they were tempted and they fell.

But this had been an organized raid against him, personally. The thieves had cut out his stock, and outside of the hospital cattle at the ranch, had made a clean sweep. It differed from the occasional pilfering of the Indians, the small depredations of a meat-hungry people which the stockmen accepted because they must.

He saw in it the Oriental patience of all Indians, and of Little Dog in particular; and he saw too the fiendish ingenuity with which he had worked, waiting until he had saved them through that ghastly winter, until they had fattened all spring and summer, and then making off with them, to hide and rebrand them, and to ship from some distant point in safety.

He went to the Agency, tramping in, throwing aside any one who stood in his way, and confronted the Superintendent with his fists clenched. But the Agent could not help him. He was an able man, administering a difficult duty to the best of his ability. He only shook his head.

"I'm sorry, McNair. Of course we'll do what we can, but you know about these cases. You're only guessing as to Little Dog and his crowd. Personlly I don't think he's on the Reservation. I haven't seen him for months."

When the magnitude of Tom's loss dawned on him, however, he became more alert. Now and then he had cases of small pilfering brought before him; he had a sneaking sympathy for the Indian who was hungry and killed a steer for food. But this was different.

"Of course," he said. "I always felt it was a mistake for you to come on the Reservation at all. I told you so at the time. But I'll have Little Dog looked up, if he's here."

"If he's here, I'll kill him on sight," Tom said, white to the lips. "I'm warning you."

He went back to the ranch, got out his revolver, oiled and filled it. He was afraid to carry a rifle, for fear they would take it from him. For he was not alone in his search. The cattlemen were uniting now against the criminals as a matter of self-protection. Outfits were starting, small posses from different points, going in different directions. A telephone message to Ursula had started out the Sheriff, and shipping pens and way stations along the main line were being watched by deputies sworn in for the purpose.

But Tom hunted alone. He was quiet enough on the surface; but the men who met him knew and let him be. He had little or no hope of his cattle; even the Reservation, with its wild broken country, offered a thousand hiding places. But they would not be on the Reservation, he knew that. Like the Indian Medicine Man, blowing his smoke to the four corners of the world, he could take his choice of direction. Up and down the line, however, was already being watched; the range far across the valley meant long forced drives through open country. But the mountains close at hand offered, if harder territory, more chances of quick concealment.

He took to them, then, with death in his heart and within easy reach of his hand, and as has been said, he rode alone. As he rode he rebuilt the tragedy from start to finish; the conspiracy, its deft and sudden execution. The rustlers closing in, cutting, holding; then the first night out, the forced drive, the riders camping on the tails of the cattle, urging, cursing, pushing on; dawn, and a sheltered spot somewhere, with the thieves far enough from the herd for safety, looking down from rocks, sleeping while a sentry watched. And then another night drive, and another.

Two weeks, three weeks ago! Already the new brands would be healed or healing. They would pass inspection; be shipped and sold, and nothing would be left to him. Nothing, that is to say, but Little Dog.

He even resented the posses, the machinery of the law. Let them keep out; this was between him and the Indian. Each would kill the other on sight, and knew it. He was convinced that Little Dog was hiding in the mountains.

After a time he had stopped thinking, to all practical purposes. He had become a killing machine, moving rapidly but automatically; riding to the top of some steep slope, surveying the country, going on. When he climbed through a cañon his revolver was in his hand. At night he lay where he happened to be; sometimes he got himself a meal of sorts, but he had no hours for food, no hours for anything. The day was divided into two parts; darkness and light. He resented the darkness fiercely, because it stopped the search.

One day, finding that his foot was again too swollen for his boot, he took off the boot and threw it away. Then he went back and got it again, for fear it would put Little Dog on guard. Another time he came across an old mining camp back in the range. He circled it carefully, watching, and was astonished to see Gus, crutches and all, come out of a cabin and go to the creek for water. The thing puzzled him. He rode down and confronted Gus at the door of his shack. He was vaguely suspicious, but Gus met him with a cheerful smile.

"What are you doing here, Gus?"

"Me? I yust come to shoot deer. That's all I'm good for now. Shootin'."

"You're sure it's deer?"

And Gus chuckled.

"Don't you worry about me, Tom. I'll send you a haunch, when I get it."

The Swede wanted him to spend the night, but Tom remembered the night in the cabin and grimly refused. Not that he gave a damn for his life now, but he had work to do first. He mounted his horse again, and Gus stood by, still grinning.

"You'll never get him, Tom. He's a smart Indian."

"Maybe not, but I'll die trying."

The time came, however, when he had to start back. His provisions were gone, his horse exhausted. He started down for fresh animals and more food, and on his way down he came across his first and only clue to his herd.

The mountain pastures were already drying up, and the cattle which had summered on the range had begun to work down again. They filled the trails, or stood on steep hillsides eying him as he passed them. He worked through them, scrutinizing their brands and ear-marks, hoping against hope, and at last among the foothills, he saw an old bull which he recognized at sight. His heart leaped. He spurred his horse and rode slowly behind and to one side of the animal. There was no doubt about it, nor of the comparatively recent reworking of the brand. It had been skillful work. The L had been extended to the D, a line drawn across, and another D reversed added to the other end. A brand changed like that would pass inspection anywhere.

For the first time, however, he felt a faint hope; the instinct to kill died away. He rode to the ranch, got out the car, flew into Ursula. But the lead, although it established certain things, led nowhere in the end. The brand had been registered some months before as the crossed link brand. It was owned by a doubtful outfit across the range, and the Sheriff went over there. But there was nothing to be done.

"They're the fellows, all right," the Sheriff told him, "but what are you going to do? The brand's theirs, the cattle have been shipped and sold. The fact that you claim the bull is yours won't help much. You can claim him all you like, but he won't come when you call him! You can go to Chicago and try to locate the hides, but even if you can, how are you going to prove it isn't some of the old L. D. stock these fellows got somewhere?"

He was three days in town, savage, sullen, heart-sick. Limping badly, too. One day he met Doctor Dunham in the street, and the old doctor stopped him.

"I thought so!" he said. "What did I tell you? From what I hear—"

"I don't care what you hear, and I don't give a damn!"

The next moment he was sorry, but the doctor had gone on.

Then one day he found that he had lost even his chance to get back at Little Dog. He was stripped of everything, even of revenge.

Gus had come into Ursula, had gone to the Sheriff's office and given himself up.

"What for?" asked Allison, staring at him.

Gus smiled.

"I've yust killed a fellow," he said. "I told Tom he was too smart for him, but he wasn't too smart for me. He came into my cabin. 'Hello,' he said. 'So you come through winter all right, eh?' 'Sure I did,' says I, and holds up my leg. 'All but that,' I says. He looked and started out, but I was too quick for him."

When Tom heard the news he went to see Gus in the jail, but he had little to add to his previous story. Little Dog had run off his horses the winter before, and left him there to die, so Gus had killed him. He seemed quite cheerful, although it was clear that he was not entirely balanced. He shook hands with Tom pleasantly when he left.

"The way to catch wolves is to think like a wolf," he said and chuckled.

The next day Tom got a letter from Arizona. The show was going to England that fall, and needed an Assistant Boss Hostler.

"I understand you've had some hard luck," he wrote, "and I've recommended you for the job. It pays good money, and we are going to show the Johnnie Bulls something to make them drop their h's right down on the ground. You know the work. There's no grand-stand stuff about it, but it's a heap sight better than sitting on your thumbs all winter to keep them warm."

He decided to accept. He saw Tulloss and told him, and the banker did not demur. He had done his best, and it had got him nowhere. The Potter company was still holding on to the L. D., although the banker knew it could not be for long. And Tom's face was the strongest argument of all.

"Well, maybe you're right, Tom," he said heavily. "You'll get a change, and—maybe later on—"

"It's not a change I'm after. I've got the interest to pay on those notes, and this way I can earn it."

In the end it was so arranged. The remaining stock was to be sold, the ranch put on the market. Tulloss, worried at Tom's face, asked him to lunch with him at the Prairie Rose, but Tom refused.

"I'm not good company for man or beast these days," he said, and went out of the office as uncompromisingly as he had come in.

He went back, sold the stock, even straightened the ranch house. And on his last night there he lighted a lamp and began to pack, with a face set with misery, the small and unimportant things that Kay had left; her mending basket, her bits of clothing, even the little face pillow she had been so fond of.

"It's a pillow for a baby!"

"Well, maybe some day—"

God!

On the mantel still sat the remnant of that Christmas candle he had put in the window. "Maybe somebody outside and want to come in." But there had been nobody outside to come in, and now there never would be anybody.

He stood looking at it. Then, curiously enough, he took it down and put it into the box. She would wonder about that. It would puzzle her. She would wrinkle up her forehead, the way she used to, and hold it up and look at it. But she would never know.

After he had finished he nailed the lid on the box and carried it out to the rickety car. It was a small box to carry what it held: all the man's hopes, in this life or the life to come. He put it into the car gently, like some poor dead thing.

He started early the next day, but early as it was the cattle were already on the road. Once more shipping time was approaching. At the railroad locomotives pulled their great trains of empty cattle cars and left them, so many here, so many there, on the sidetracks by the shipping pens. And from all parts of the back country the herds were converging, driven by patient cowboys with their neckerchiefs over their mouths against the dust they raised.

"So long, Tom. Good luck."

Along with the cattle was moving the wheat. Trucks and wagons, their bodies built up with temporary boardings, rocked and careened along the roads toward the small red elevators along the track. They moved onto the scales, were weighed, dumped, weighed again. The men who drove them waved their hands and shouted:

"So long, Tom. Good luck."

And as the car bumped along the box in the back seemed to echo the words:

"So long, Tom. Good luck. So long, Tom. Good luck."

Chapter Forty-four

Bessie Osborne returned from Bar Harbor unexpectedly early that autumn. She had heard some disquieting rumors, and she came back in haste and what amounted to indignation.

Her own philosophy was a simple one, based on her conviction that one only lived once and must therefore make the best of it. She shed her yesterdays as a snake sheds its skin, and ignored the tomorrows unless they offered something pleasant. It was only today that counted, so she wakened happily to a hearty breakfast tray, read her letters, made grimaces into a hand-mirror for five minutes, took a bath with reducing salts in it—to offset the tray—and then dressed ritually, if it be dressing to don one thin underslip and a frock. And thereafter she faced each day with a determination to make the most of it.

But if, as old Lucius cruelly had asserted, Bessie was a retarded adolescent, she was also an incorrigible romanticist. She stalked into Henry's library one night, then, dressed in what Henry considered very "fast" black, and sitting down across from him, demanded to light her cigarette from his cigar.

"What for? There are plenty of matches."

Henry's cigar was a precious thing to him; he tasted its

quality by the length of the ash.

"I like the flavor. I'd smoke cigars, if they didn't twist my mouth. Well, I see you are still holding on to Kay."

"Holding on? What else am I to do?"

"Send her back to her husband. Have you happened to look at her lately?"

He moved uncomfortably.

"I've asked her. She says she's all right."

"And what is your plan?"

"Plan? I haven't any plan. I don't know what you're talking about."

"Oh, yes you do, Henry! You always know. You may be a pig-headed sort of brute, but you're not an idiot. Is she to divorce McNair and marry Herbert? I hear he's always hanging around."

"Really, Bessie, you are impossible," he said irritably. "If McNair wants her, why doesn't he say so? She doesn't even hear from him. And as to Herbert—he's not around as much as you say. He's here, of course."

"So I understand," she retorted. "Under foot, coming back to be slapped, like a pup. What do you do with a pup like that? You stop slapping and begin to pet him. I know; I've been there. Send her back, Henry. Let him beat her, if he wants to. It isn't such a bad life, you know. Mother stood it pretty well, and—look at us!"

But she was not so certain after she had talked to Kay.

"What are you going to do with Herbert? Marry him?"

"I am married," said Kay flushing, "Herbert understands all that."

"Well, you are getting talked about all the same," Bessie retorted. "If you must have somebody hanging around, why always Herbert? Why not somebody else? The woods are full of them."

But Kay had no answer for that.

Bessie stayed for a week, while her town house was being opened, and left at the end of that time as unenlightened as she came. Kay, she saw, was still wearing her wedding ring. She had developed a curious habit of turning it around her finger, especially when Herbert was there. And Herbert, Henry notwithstanding, was there a great deal.

Bessie thought he had changed his attitude since the spring. He was more assured, faintly possessive.

"It's cool out here. Where's that cape of yours, Kay? I'll get it."

And if Kay was rather like a wooden image when he put it around her, Bessie knew that it was not the first, or even the tenth time he had done so.

Nora was very outspoken. She waited one day until Celestine was at her early luncheon, and then slipped into Bessie's room.

"She's just drifting along, the poor lamb," she said. "I can't say a word against Mr. Forrest; he's always polite to me. But you mark my words, Mrs. Osborne, they'll be wishing a divorce on her before she knows it."

"You knew this—you knew Mr. McNair, Nora. Why do you think she never hears from him?"

And Nora, wise in the pride of the poor, was ready with an answer.

"What has he got to offer her, against what she's got here?" she asked shrewdly. "If she goes, that's one thing; but if he has to ask her, that's another. If you'd seen what she brought back with her—"

Her face winked, she fumbled in the pocket of her black silk apron. "Just rags," she said, "and poor little things she's tried to make herself. If you'd see the way she put in a sleeve—!"

"Is she grieving now?"

"I think she cries in her sleep, poor lamb. Her pillows are wet sometimes in the morning."

Bessie's thoughts went back swiftly, to that other morning long ago, when she had found Kay's pillow damp with tears.

"But I don't know who or what it's about. Honestly, I don't

remember." She could not say that now.

As it happened, Bessie was still there when Tom's box arrived. The top boards were taken off downstairs. And it was placed in Kay's boudoir for her to unpack. Kay was not there when all this happened, and even Bessie did not know it was there.

She was having her hair waved, and after her usual fashion her door stood open. The first she knew that anything was wrong was a sort of wail from Kay's room across. She listened, and then she saw Nora outside with her finger to her lips. Bessie acted immediately, jerked her hair free and ran across to find Kay sitting on the floor beside a queer-looking box, holding a dirty little pillow to her breast, and staring at nothing at all.

"Kay! Kay dear, what is it?"

Kay looked at her blankly.

"My things," she said slowly. "He's sent me my things. It's all over."

Later on they got her into her bedroom, Nora and Bessie, and into her bed. She was very cold, and Nora filled hotwater bags and put them around her, while Bessie noticed again how thin she was; that the coverings were hardly raised over her body. Still later on Bessie and Nora unpacked the box.

"Well, whatever would you make of that? It's a candle!"

"It must have got in by mistake."

But the tragic poverty-stricken contents of the box appalled Bessie. That, and Kay's reception of them.

She sat thinking after Nora had gone. What a tragedy it was that the only thing age could offer to youth was its own experience, and that the experiences of others were never profitable. Not that her own—! She brushed that aside.

The thing was to find out if McNair still cared. If Nora was right, probably he did. This other girl had been an episode. Men often were unfaithful to women they adored; a man's passion and his love could be two entirely different matters;

only women never believed that, because with them passion was only a further development of love.

Sitting there, the sunlight lighting up her short yellow hair—slightly darker at the roots—Bessie gave herself up to the unusual indulgence of thought. There had been Ronald; dying alone in a hospital. She had never cared for Ronald; he had been one of those who kept his passions and his love far apart. But she was sorry he had died alone.

She had made the best she could out of life, but lately it had grown a trifle stale and unprofitable. What was the use of pretending to youth, when it was gone. Gone forever. There was a little Russian now; he admired her, because he said she must have looked, in her youth, very like a lady he had once loved!

"A lady of the circus; she was very beautiful. But my people—"

After rather a long time she rose, looked at her reflection in the mirror, in the pitiless sunlight, sighed and going downstairs, wrote a telegram on Henry's desk; a telegram to Mr. Tulloss at Ursula.

"Please wire how a letter will reach Tom McNair." And she gave her city address. The local telegraph operator had a bad habit of telephoning her messages.

Late that night she went into Kay's room, but Kay had at last fallen asleep. Her reading lamp was going, and her hand still lay on an opened book. Bessie slid the book out carefully and looked at it. It was an oldish little volume of poetry, and there was a fine pencil mark around two lines:

"The wide seas and the mountains called to him,
And gray dawn saw his campfires in the rain."

Bessie left the next morning, and found her telegram waiting in town. Tom had had bad luck, and had gone back to the Ninety Nine Ranch show. He was on his way to England, if he had not already sailed.

There was apparently nothing to be done, and as the days went on Bessie decided that perhaps it had been as well. Kay never mentioned the box again; was even on the surface quite normal. She went out a little, played tennis—although she tired easily—smiled rather too often and too quickly, went about her duties efficiently.

"Can you get some fresh caviare at the club, father? Mr. Trowbridge is coming to dinner."

When Trowbridge came Herbert generally came also, to make a fourth for bridge. The game would drag along:

"Now let's see. Put your king on, Henry! I've got you coming or going. That's the boy! Now, Herbert—"

On and on; nine o'clock, ten o'clock, eleven; Herbert playing neatly and safely and generally winning. He took no chances, did Herbert. Mr. Trowbridge paying up reluctantly.

"Got any change, Herbert? I've nothing less than twenty."

And Herbert getting out his wallet, with the bills neatly laid inside, and carefully counting them out. "One, two, three, four, five—"

She had stopped watching for the mail carrier long ago. She had stopped hoping. Sometimes she thought she had stopped living. Nothing really mattered. Some day there would be a divorce, probably. Tom had a right to his freedom. Then, if he still wanted her, she would marry Herbert. Herbert had a right to something, too.

On Sundays she and Henry took flowers to the cemetery after church. Henry would get out carefully and stand by her mother's grave, holding his silk hat in his hand; Hawkins would take out the old flowers, and put fresh water in the container; and then she would arrange the new ones. Sometimes, when they reached the car again, Henry would turn around and look back.

She felt at those times that she owed him something, also.

Then, one day, something happened to shock her back into life again. She was in town for some shopping, and suddenly there was the screech of a calliope ahead, and people ran out of stores or stopped on the street to line up against the curbing. Hawkins drew in to one side and stopped the car.

"Circus coming, miss." She was still "miss" to the servants.

But it was not the circus.

She was suddenly very cold. Just so, a year and a half ago, had Tom come back to her like a young knight, haughty and arrogant and wonderful to see. She had called out to him, and he had dug his spurs into his horse until it reared. And the next day—

She sat twisting her ring while the procession passed; the cowboy band; the heavy-stepping elephants; the Indians in their war bonnets and buckskin clothes, their faces Oriental and inscrutable; the Cossacks, in their high astrakhan hats, their long tunics, their soft-soled boots.

There was no escape for her. She saw the cowboys coming, their bright neckerchiefs, their chaps and spurs, their coiled ropes. They sat easily, swaying to the motion of their horses, one gloved hand resting easily on hip or thigh, and as they passed they picked out pretty girls among the crowd and smiled at them.

"Are you a real cowboy, mister?"

"Sure am, son."

She searched their faces, lean and tanned under their big hats, but Tom was not among them. How could he be?

When the parade had passed she went about her shopping methodically, but there was a strange leaven working in her. For the first time she looked back and saw the girl she had been when she ran away to Tom. Saw herself carried by a romantic impulse, swayed by the beating of drums, emotional, unstable, immature. Why had she married him? Because she loved him? Or because he was like those boys she had just watched, picturesque, carefree and reckless? This last, perhaps, or so he must surely think, for when the lean days came, when he had been making his hard undramatic fight, she had abandoned him. What did it matter about Clare? What did it matter if he had kept his dogged silence all this time? She was the one who had failed, failed and run away, to live softly and at ease.

Then, if that were so—!

She never knew just when she made her decision to go back. She was moving as automatically as had Tom on his search for Little Dog. She went to the railway ticket office, to the bank. She had plenty of money now, plenty for both of them, if he would only take her back. And he could not object to it; it was hers. Her mother had left it to her.

She was half feverish with excitement, her hands cold, her head hot. Impatient too, while her ticket was stamped, her reservations made. She would not even telegraph. She would go to Ursula and get a car there, and then—

Suppose he did not want her? Suppose she got there to find that he had definitely put her out of his life? Suppose he opened the door of the house, and looked at her, as he *could* look, and she had to turn around and go away again?

Well, she could only try. It was her life, as well as his. She had taken her courage in her hands once before. She could do it again. And she would not even go home, for fear of Henry.

She went to Bessie's instead.

Chapter Forty-five

The show was working its way to New York, to embark for England. All day the wardrobe woman and her assistants worked over new costumes, to make the British drop their h's plumb onto the ground. And in the mess tent there was much joking about sea-sickness.

"Say, you better fill up while you can keep it!"

"Who, me? I'm going to swallow a handful of buck shot after every meal. That oughta hold it down."

Outside of these preparations, there was not much change. They drew into a town, unloaded, paraded, played a day or two and moved on. But there was more interest now in where they were.

"Where are we now anyhow? Ithaca?"

"Syracuse, ain't it? Hey, boy, what town's this?"

Tom himself took no particular notice. One town was the same as another to him. He did his work efficiently but grimly, loaded and unloaded his big teams, was largely his own veterinarian, worked hard all day and at night dropped into a berth that was too short for him, to sleep because he did not care to think.

Now and then he watched the performance, but not often. Arizona saw him one day, and looked after him when he turned on his heel and limped away. His shoulders were sagging, his head down. But there was nothing he could do. Tom fiercely repulsed any attempt at sympathy.

"They tell me you used to be some rider," a new cowboy said to him once, with a hint of patronage.

"Yes," Tom drawled. "They used to have some good riders in this show. Now they've got a lot of kindergarten kids that lose control of themselves the minute some poor old skate gives a crow-hop or two."

Only "lose control" was not what Tom said.

Now and then he was quarrelsome. The colored hostlers and grooms stood in deadly terror of him.

"Here, you Jefferson, what you doing with that team?"

"The feed pile man, he sade—"

"To hell with the feed pile man. Bring it here."

But he had no time for violence. He was the first man up in the morning, the last man to board the train at night. Under the lot superintendent, it was his men who moved the show to and from the track. The train pulled in, the great baggage teams were unloaded, the enormous red and gold wagons and trucks were rolled down from their cars; then rocking and swaying, carrying their heavy loads of poles, of canvas and of collapsible seats, they started for the lot. At night of the last day the process reversed.

Tom did not mind the work. In a way it suited him. He had little time to think, no time for vain regrets. He had no friends. Murphy had left the organization, and he no longer joined the crowd for craps or poker. His weekly salary he sent, with practically no deductions, to the bank at Ursula. He was very shabby; when his clothing got too bad he put on overalls, and let the Boss Hostler be the gentleman of the outfit and the Ringmaster its dandy.

But now and then, mostly during meal times, he would limp into the long tent where the saddle horses munched their hay, and walk the length of it. He cared well for his own big horses, but it was the saddle stock that he loved. Sometimes, but not often, he thought of the Miller.

When he found he was in Kay's city it scarcely roused him. With the canvas set, however, he wandered around to the men's dressing tent and stood staring at it somberly. That was where she was standing when he first saw her, and over there was the place where she had sat on a box, after they were married, and waited for him.

He went over. There was a box there now, an old box; it might have been the very one.

"All right, girl?"

"Fine."

"And happy?"

"Terribly happy."

During that afternoon he had a visitor, a well-dressed dapper little man whom he did not know at first. It was the little Cossack, Murphy.

"Ha! Tom! You remember me?"

"Murphy, you son of a gun! And all dressed up like a plush horse. Don't you kiss me, Murph!"

For the Russian, in his excitement, had almost done so.

Murphy, it appeared, had done well. He had found friends, was in the foreign department of a bank, was learning English rapidly. One lady had been very kind to him; she was not young, but she had a Russian soul. Tom listened, his eyes twinkling, his worries momentarily forgotten.

But there was a suppressed excitement about Murphy. He could not stand still. He darted about here and there, shook hands with his old friends, came back to Tom.

"You will be here tonight?" he asked, in his precise English.

"Sure will. Are you bringing the lady with the Russian disposition?"

"I bring a lady," said Murphy. "Not that one. Another. A very nice lady. I have but just met her, at luncheon today. We shall come tonight."

Tom looked after him as he went rapidly away. So

Murphy had forgotten his lady of the circus after all! That was the thing to do, forget them. They came along and played hell with a man's life, and his only course was to forget them.

Out of sheer perversity he kept on his overalls that night. Let the cowboys pull their stuff; him, he was a hostler, a sort of head groom. He was a stable-man. Let Murphy bring his girl, a dozen girls. Girls made no difference in his life. Let them see him as he was.

And it was literally as he was that Kay saw him that night, sitting on an overturned pail behind a tent and rolling a cigarette.

She stood still, looking at him. The little Russian had tactfully disappeared.

"Tom," she said quietly, "aren't you going to speak to me?"

He got up, peering into the semi-darkness.

"Who is it?"

"It's Kay, Tom."

He stood very still, still holding his cigarette.

"What is there to speak about?" he said, after a pause. "You and I—we got talked out a long time ago."

"Do you really feel that way, Tom? Because if you do—"

"It's not a question of how I feel, is it? You showed me plain enough when you left me."

"You're still angry, then?"

"Angry! God, no. Angry's not the word. What's there to be angry about? You got out in good time, that's all. I've had some bad luck, but that wouldn't interest you."

She had not known what she had expected, but not this. Certainly not this. She felt half sick, defeated. She tried again.

"In that letter, Tom, I told you I'd come back if you wanted me. When you didn't even answer it, what was I to think?"

"I swore I'd never send for you; you knew it when you

wrote that letter."

She could see him better now. He was standing with his arms folded. She could see his overalls, his unshaven chin, the set lines of his face. Her heart sank, but she felt a yearning pity for him, too. He looked like some trapped wild creature.

"Tom," she said desperately, "I came to you once before, right here. Why do you think I did that?"

He gave a short bitter laugh.

"Why?" he said. "Because you didn't know me then, that's why. You thought all a cowboy had to do was to ride around and look handsome. When you found out different, good night!"

"If I ever did think that—"

"You've had a chance to learn better! What's the use of talking, anyhow? I haven't got anything. I've lost my cattle. I've lost everything. Hi, Joe! Bring that lantern over here."

He took it from the negro boy, and held it up. "Look at me," he said. "Do I look like anything you want to waste your time on? I do not, and you know it."

"You look like my own dear Tom," she said, her voice breaking.

He put down the lantern, not too steadiliy.

"You run on home, girl, and be comfortable and happy. Don't be sorry for me. I'm getting on fine, and I'm paying my notes, too. If you ever hear different, it's a lie."

"You don't want me, do you?"

"I haven't said that." He moved, looked around. "Sorry," he said awkwardly. "I'll have to get busy. We're leaving tonight." He hesitated, took off his hat, and suddenly she saw that he was holding out his hand.

"Well, good-bye, girl," he said. "I'm sure glad I saw you again."

She did not take the hand.

"And that's all?"

"What else is there?" he asked, smiling down at her. "You've got your life to live, and I've got mine. You said that to me once, a good while ago."

He looked down at his rejected hand, dropped it, put on his hat.

"So long, girl. Good luck."

He was going. Incredibly, uncompromisingly, he was going. She had made her gesture and been rejected. He was the same Tom; nothing had changed him, nothing ever would change him. If she went back to him it would be on his terms, not hers. But she could not even go back to him. He would not have her. He needed her, but he would not have her.

"Tom!" she said desperately.

He stopped.

"I won't be sent away like this, Tom. I've come back to you, don't you understand? I was going West tonight. Look here," she fumbled feverishly in her purse, "here is my ticket. My bags are out there in the car. Read it, if you don't believe me. I can't go on without you, Tom. I think I'll die if I have to. Feel my wrist, how thin I am!"

She was shaking violently.

Inside the arena the cowboy band stopped playing. There was the sound of galloping horses, the shouts of Indians, the sharp fusillade of their blank cartridges as the prairie schooner was attacked. Only this time all the casualties got up cheerfully and walked off, and there was no little Cossack to run out and hold up his hands.

Suddenly Tom came back to her, stood over her.

"That's the truth, is it, girl?"

"You know it's the truth, Tom. It always has been, it always will be."

Then, and only then, did he take her into his arms.

"I've been through hell, girl."

"It's all over now. We won't think about it. If only you love me as I love you, Tom—"

"Love? What does a little thing like you know about love? I'm the fellow that can tell you. This li'l old heart of mine's been just about busted."

He was himself once more. The sag had gone out of his shoulders. There was a ring of pure happiness in his voice. When he released her he jerked on his hat at its old rakish angle, and looked down ruefully at his clothes. But he brightened when he remembered that over in the car, in the drawer under his berth, lay the bright blue suit, neatly folded, the straw hat, the yellow shoes.

"You mean it? You're coming right along?"

"Wherever you go, Tom."

Moved by an impulse, he left her for a moment. When he came back he had a weather-beaten old soap box in his hand. He stood eying it for a moment, then he placed it on the ground.

"You're sitting on that, Mrs. McNair, until I come back. I'm a working man, and I've got a job to do. But I'm not trusting my luck any. You stay right here."

She sat down. The elephants were plodding past, each clutching the absurd tail of the one ahead with his trunk, the trainers with their prod sticks running alongside. In the darkness their great gray bodies looked like houses walking. She looked at them. For a little time, this, perhaps. But soon, please God—

Like the stockmen and the wheat growers, sitting there in the dust she too made her small inarticulate prayer; for love and peace in the back country, for the sun, for the rain in season, for all the growing things; for the scent of the sage at dawn, and the mountains turning purple after sunset; for the women who sat with their hands folded, resting after the heat of the day; for the men who brought in their tired horses at night, led by the lights of home.

Suddenly Tom dropped down onto the ground beside her, and putting his arms around her, dropped his head onto her knees.

"Oh, girl, girl!" he said. "It's been hell all right. But here we are!"

she sat as he had left her. Time later, to make plans. They would go back again, but this time they would have a fairer chance. She would never change him; as he was he would always be. But it was as he was that she loved him. He was Tom, her lover, her sweetheart and her child.

When he came back to her the performance was over, and the cowboys were riding their horses to the cars. Once again she heard the slow tired movement of horses' feet in darkness, the rustle of chaps on leather, the faint jingle of bridles and buckles. The day's work was over. Soon the horses would be in the cars. A voice would call out:

"Jerry next."

"Jerry coming."

A shadowy horse would sniff at the runway, and then with a thunder of hoofs dash up and into the car. The loading would go on, and when it was finished there would be the "privilege" car, and then the night's rest.

So they moved on, and as they moved they sang. Tom's hand was on her shoulder; there was love and peace and understanding in the air.

> "I'm a poor lonesome cowboy,
> I'm a poor lonesome cowboy,
> I'm a poor lonesome cowboy,
> And a long ways from home."

He stooped and kissed her.